Hidden Beneath The Pines

All Families Have Secrets

Mike Walters

The hardest job in the world to do well?
Parenting.
Thank you, Mom & Dad, for
Always doing your absolute best!

"In Troubled Families, Abuse and Neglect are Permitted; It's the Talking About Them That is Forbidden."

Marcia Sirota

Prologue

The sound of the ice pick pressing inward, puncturing the soft vanilla-scented skin, repulsed him as it slid up the back of the neck and into the brain. Nearly retching, he realized it was the popping sound the pick made during penetration. If it weren't for his mind's fascination of the outcome in the victim's eyes, and the intense magnetic propulsion of his hand and arm, he would have emptied his stomach for sure. How in the world did the body not scream? Shock, fear, a combination of both, or human spite? Despite the realization of impending death, which kept the victim from any escalated sound beyond breathing, the breathing faded as silence held the dark-morning at bay.

Hopping out of the boat, he looked around the lakeshore figuring the sun would be up in another two hours or so. Unbuttoning his jeans, he relieved himself of his pre-sunrise coffee. Buttoning up, he hoped for once there would be no urine-dribbling leaving another damn wet spot. It sucked aging; and no the pumpkinseed oil he researched online didn't provide the necessary free-flow affect that evaded him. Unable to remember exactly when his post-pee dribble problem started, he looked downward waiting for a dark spot to appear in the crotch of his jeans. Staring away, waiting for the inevitable delayed color change in his pants, he looked down again to faded blue denim. Pleased no spot appeared, he found a moment of joy knowing he'd be able to row without any unpleasant discomfort.

Pushing the boat outward and into the lake he jumped in stepping on the body. His foot slipped as he prevented entry into the cold water by catching the edge of the wooden boat with his hand. The body gasped, causing him to jump inside his skin at the unexpected surprise of the body's unwillingness to let go of life. Looking around the bottom of the boat and seeing nothing, he pulled a rag he was saving for later out of his pocket and pushed it against the body's lips. The eyes refused to send the inevitable news to the victim's brain as the mouth made an efforted force to scream. The clear eyes now bulged in terror. He felt his adrenaline rush with unmistakable energy watching the eyes go from a deep clear bronze to a static milky stone color. Fascinated by the eyes ability, all on their own, to tell a story, he took the rag and stuffed it back in his jacket pocket. So far, each death had been different and each held its own unique reaction. This one, the eyes didn't want to let go and seemed as if they fought the outcome more than the others.

Grabbing an oar in each hand, satisfied another life was gone, he straightened the boat. Propelling the boat forward, he rowed on. Fifteen minutes later he reached his intended destination. The nearly full moon aided his goal as he lifted, and then eased, the body over the edge of the derelict wooden boat. He saw a leg kick, causing additional splashing.

"Are you kidding me?" The man said out loud. Too loud perhaps? Fearing discovery, he looked around, then returned his attention to the body gasping for air -- fighting for survival. He removed an oar from its oarlock and pushed the body down deeper into the water. Within seconds the resistance faded. He held it down a good minute longer in light of the damn things reluctance to let go.

Finally, watching the face-down body settle upward and start its slow drift toward the chosen bank, he hoped in the next couple of hours it would find its way to the intended target. At least close enough to raise suspicion. Anticipating the thick lake-grass would do its job and hold the body, he guessed the victim wouldn't move far if at all. No worries if it did as the intended culprit would certainly become an instant suspect.

Whistling a little ditty he remembered from high school, one of those annoying songs you hate but can't get out of your head, he pushed the oars hard toward the bank and his vehicle. Wondering what the Southern Oregon sunrise would look like this morning, probably magnificent again since there were clouds in the sky, he let go of an oar and felt the damp rag in his pocket. Hoping it dry enough to start a fire, he wondered how easily this shanty of a boat would burn to ashes.

A Sigh of Relief

The body of water, indifferent to its contents, supported the bobbing and gliding of a small gaggle of Canadian geese. Making their way to the lakeshore which held welcome to a black-tailed deer and two yearlings, the grey and black fowl glided around a cold cloth-covered slab of flesh paying little attention. Face down, the lifeless body moved with the lake's ebb and flow.

As Matt Walker stared out his kitchen window, watching the sun crest over the Siskiyou Mountains, another day of Southern Oregon beauty unraveled before his eyes. The rays of earth's life-force made the surface of the lake shimmer, a beauty Matt cherished. The sun, as she peaked over the mountains, never danced across the water the same way twice. The variation comforted Matt. A changing, unpredictable, singularity of purpose. He loved knowing that no one else saw a sunrise the way he did. His eyes delivered a unique perspective and performance every time.

Watching, as something unusual floating, maybe a log off the shoreline, Matt noticed ripples dancing across the lake as the sound of water slapped against the bank's smooth stones. The unknown object seemed to have a fluid motion to it, unlike a rigid log. His mind initially thought of a dead goose, but it looked too large. A human body perhaps? Chuckling at the absurdity, Matt debated whether he should go investigate the water's edge. He opted for no, not wanting to disturb the deer or geese.

Taking his last drink of black as Oregon soil morning coffee, he watched the fowl move forward on the water in their choreographed fashion. Reaching the shore, they left the water with awkward grace in route to their morning stroll in search of food on the banks of Emigrant Lake. The Pacific Northwest had been overdue for a long, intense winter, and the past year did not disappoint with record-breaking snowfall throughout the Cascade Range. Lakes, rivers, and streams were brimming throughout the summer with an above average amount of water still in the lake. And what had become the norm of August, forest fires lessened with the woods holding on to the moisture as long as possible.

Matt contemplated the lake's volume, a welcome sight, realizing it had stayed high throughout the summer for the first time in years. The melting snow in the high mountains coursed its way down feeding the creeks and streams and into the belly of the lake.

Popping his neck from side to side, Matt thought about the day ahead of him. Embracing the challenge of owning his own business and the unexpected issues thrown at him from every direction, he could count on them like the rising sun. The unknown, along with the adventure of each day, fueled him, spiking his adrenaline. He promised himself long ago that if he ever grew tired of going to work, he would make a change. Almost two decades later, he still anticipated the day ahead.

Honking geese brought a smile to Matt's face as he returned to the kitchen from the deck. Pouring more coffee for himself, he then grabbed one of his wife's favorite cups. A fragile piece of white ceramic covered in yellow and blue flowers. He filled it two-thirds full. Returning the coffee pot to its base, he opened the refrigerator and gathered the vanilla soy creamer, adding enough to turn the dark java a rich beige. Stirring the now lukewarm coffee he dropped the spoon in the sink.

Matt headed back to the bedroom to set his wife's coffee on her nightstand before sliding himself into the shower. Climbing the stairs, counting eleven steps, he straddled over the final step so as not to jinx himself. His wife's coffee started to spill, but his reflexes compensated, keeping the caffeine brew in the cup. Breathing a sigh of relief for no spillage, Matt smiled. He liked his odds today.

Number Two

"Jane, come on, you're killing me!"

"I told you I'd be right there. I am in the middle of something."

As if she were a baseball umpire calling strike three, Jane covered the mouthpiece on the phone.

"Look, I'm sorry Matt, but it's Kate again. She says it's urgent and needs to talk with you. Even if it makes you late for a meeting. Please pick up? I'm tired of putting her off."

Matt couldn't help but hear Jane. He shook his head and chuckled over how loud she spoke.

Jane was a great secretary. Hell, she was more than a secretary—she was a professional office administrator. Matt knew his business ran well, in large part due to her professional acumen. He paid her a high salary and treated her with tremendous respect.

With him twelve years now, give or take, Jane was a dear friend to Matt, and had introduced him to his recent wife, Kate, a couple of years ago. Frustrated over his choices of women, Jane encouraged the chance meeting of Kate and Matt when she found out they had an interest in each other. A trip to Britain popped into Matt's head, which he found odd, and it reminded him of the term aces. Matt liked to say, Kate is "Aces". He overheard a British man use the term at a pub in England while he and Kate were on their honeymoon. Great fish and chips in a small town outside of Leicester, called Oadby. He and Kate had a wonderful time and Kate giggled every time Matt used the "Aces" phrase, so it stuck.

"Dammit," Matt mumbled in frustration before yelling out the door toward Jane's desk.

"Okay, Jane, put her through and tell the staff I'll be a couple of minutes late. Have Jim get the projector fired up and his presentation queued, so we can start when I walk in, okay?"

"Sure, and thank you, Matt."

Jane's only fault was her loyalty towards Kate. It frustrated the hell out of Matt, but short of firing her or divorcing his wife, he knew he'd have to get used to their relationship. He wasn't going to fire Jane that much he knew. Divorcing Kate was the better choice, but the first year had been good. So, looking for wife number four was too early in the cards. And frankly, when was loyalty a fault?

Matt overheard Jane as he reached for the phone.

"Kate, I am putting you through now, okay?... Yes, I am up for dinner with you Saturday and looking forward to it. I got tickets to the new play at Angus Bowmer Theatre you suggested. You get the dinner and I got the play.... Uh-huh,... yep,... okay, got it. Here's Matt."

Matt's hand hovered over the handset in anticipation. He picked it up before the first ring finished.

"Hey, babe, what's up?... Okay, yes, I know.... Okay, I get it."

Matt never any good at hiding irritation, and today was no exception, tried to listen without a noticeable attitude.

"Look, like I already said this morning, if you want to get the dog, go for it. Remember, though, I don't want to be responsible for walking, feeding, clean-up, etc. I had my share of dogs as a kid, and as much as I love them, I don't want the responsibility of taking care of one."

Matt looked at the clock on his office wall, then at his wrist watch. It was only a couple of minutes past the meeting time, but he hated being late. He focused on the call and tried to ignore the clock.

"Of course, I will go on walks with you."

Matt paused, trying to keep his irritated tone at bay. He focused on his next words.

"Remember Kate, we agreed how critical honesty needed to be if the relationship was going to work. I won't want to go all the time, so when I say no, you can't get pissed. Okay?"

Listening while staring at the clock, he heard Kate's words of understanding on the other end of the line. He wondered if he should make a note in his planner about how she understood and agreed.

Matt hated being on the phone. He would get distracted, never able to give full attention to the person on the other end. Now, he was going to be later than he liked to his own meeting. He wanted to end this call without being rude. Kate's happiness mattered to him, but so did the meeting.

"Kate, you know how much I love dogs, so I say go for it. If having one is important for you, then do it. I need to go babe. I am late for my own meeting. You know how I hate being late."

Matt stood, tried not to roll his eyes, grabbed his stylus and started leaning over in anticipation of setting the phone down in the cradle. His chin got closer and closer to the desk before he could say his goodbye, hanging up the phone. He wondered if Kate said goodbye as well. He grabbed his tablet and headed for the conference room.

Jane, caught his eye before he cleared her line of sight.

"Matt, number two is on line one."

"Hah... funny, Jane."

"I'm serious, Matt."

Number two was Matt's second wife, Betheny. Matt had little to no contact with number two, so receiving a call from her was a surprise. Matt's mind raced as it flooded with memories of a relationship that started with a seemingly solid friendship, quickly entered the always exciting romance stage, took the next logical step to marriage, and then almost as abruptly ended in an odd and expensive divorce. Odd in the sense that it was amicable, but tense and surreal in that Betheny and he agreed on everything. And expensive, for him, not number two he always reminded people.

He wasn't sure what he did or why she wanted out of the marriage. Neither had cheated on the other, at least Matt thought she had been faithful. Perhaps he was a naïve fool, and she was looking for a wealthy caretaker and Matt had obliged. He wasn't sure he would ever find out. Anyhow, she struck gold as Matt liked to say. All he struck was another small dose of life's regrets and a second lost home.

"I don't have time, Jane. Put her through to voice mail and if she gets belligerent with you, hang up, okay?"

Jane knew all about Betheny and never approved of her. She called the failed marriage from the beginning, and Matt wished he had listened to her. His damn male libido did him in, yet again.

"Sure thing, Matt. I hope she gets belligerent."

Matt entered the conference room to head shakes and hellos as he mentally reminisced about Betheny. Closing the door behind him, he plopped in his chair wondering if his good day had just shifted.

No Pretention

Three marriages, two failed so far, and thirty-nine years later, Matt Walker figured the time had come to talk about childhood experiences which left him bitter and confused. His current wife, Kate, struggling with her own childhood family issues, had remained close-lipped. Matt seeing how it hindered growth, decided to clear the path of life and empty out the garage in his mind. He had no more room for extra boxes of regret.

Pleased with his counselor and progress, he recommended his therapist to Kate. She agreed, and after a few sessions said she gained clarity out of the visits but wasn't yet ready to share them with Matt. Thankful she went, and not wanting to risk pushing her away, Matt didn't pry. He wanted, and knew he needed, to listen and be supportive. She would talk when ready he reminded himself.

Matt had grown tired of the bitterness and anger dictating life decisions. So, as a start, years ago, Matt told wife number two, Betheny, what happened to him as a boy. As she listened, without judgement, Matt took a next step.

Over the next couple of years, once a week during fifty-minute sessions, he learned through regurgitation of vivid memories, his family, for whatever sad reason, felt a need to hide and hold on to their secrets. As if they were a precious, life-sustaining, commodity. Walker family secrets seemed horrid, but Matt realized they were no worse than most other families. In fact, he learned, they were mild compared to others. He now understood that abuse was only part of the fragility so common in the American family.

Until his counseling sessions started, number five if he remembered correctly, Matt naively thought his family was the only one holding secrets. Other families, he learned, will talk to cleanse and heal.

His family did not. Kate's family did not. Both families held on to shame as if they didn't they would whither like chaff and blow away.

Matt got it, he finally did. Few people admit their weaknesses and failures. Hell, he couldn't for the longest time. At some point—he couldn't remember the exact age—Matt didn't subscribe anymore to pretending shit didn't happen. He now understood each of us has, in our own minds, mountains to overcome. Combined peaks collectively making up the greater family.

He had an epiphany that stuck one day, "life is too short." A concise, direct phrase his second wife always espoused. The eloquent words, probably the product of someone other than his wife, were entrenched in Matt's conscience. He grew to under-stand the four-word phrase and focused on it; hell, obsessed over it, knowing every day could be his last.

His time to deal with the past had arrived, and Matt wanted to be the force moving the key piece of his own crumbling shale. It was time for him to exert control over his own little world. He scaled his mountain, focused on the journey, and would never again look back.

Matt liked who he was. Only took him about forty-five years to figure it out. Everything, good and bad that happened to him in his life-journey made him who he was. If he could, he'd change parts of his past. The abuse, without a doubt. But, as of yet, no one had this power. No time-travel. No magic alien arrows filled with juice that flowed through veins allowing people to time-jump. Just solid earth—the here and now.

So, as far as changing things, you bet he would. But again, he didn't dwell on them, because they did not complete him. Shape him, yes, but they did not define his entirety as a human being. Take the abuse at the hand of a family member for example, which was the worst of it growing up. Lots of other nasty moments were sprinkled around the incidents. Growing up in a low-income family, toward the bottom on the socio-economic scale, made for plenty of those moments.

His was a family like so many in America that lived to hide behind their Christianity. Which meant family stuff could be prayed away, forgiven, ask God to handle. They didn't need to face reality and confront problems when they had a God to hand it off to. Matt realized this in his early twenties after a short stint traveling abroad got him away and out from under the incestuous family umbrella.

One of Matt's other of life's regrets was having to be involved in the church as a kid. Not the pre-incident church though, just post. The pre-incident religion, fond and dear in his memories, was a picturesque small Episcopalian building with a steeple and a separate stone bell tower. The bell was not attached to the church, but planted smack dab in the front yard, encased in large stones and cement, as if the old church had burned down and the bell tower just settled where it landed. All the children would race to ring the massive bell when the service came to an end. Matt reached the tower first many times and glowed with righteous pride each time he got to pull the tattered, torn, and coarse rope attached to the bell.

One Sunday after listening to not a single word of what the old preacher said, but rather focusing on his bell-pulling strategy, Matt, successful again, beat his arch nemesis Deb Ward for the right to pull the heavy rope and ring the bell. While Matt glowed holding the rope, Deb had a dismayed look on her face. She asked him if he understood the importance of what he was doing; said he needed to take it more seriously. After all, he was signaling angels that church was over, and they could go back and tell God what the preacher taught on this day. Matt, with his eight-year-old wisdom and attitude, shrugged his shoulders, tilted his head sideways and said,

"I beat you and I am just ringing a bell."

Deb, a year older and much wiser, stormed off. She started trying to have Matt removed from any future bell-ringing responsibility. The petition to stop Matt failed, but darned if the snooty little Deb, with her piercing green eyes, didn't forever change Matt's bell-ringing competition.

Not long after his "just ringing a bell" comment and Deb's failed petition in its original form, the preacher decided there would be a drawing for the kids to ring the "angel's tool," as the preacher referred to the bell. Any child wishing to ring the angel's tool had to memorize a verse each week and whoever did, got to put their name in a hat and if drawn, the bell-ringing privilege was theirs.

Matt never rang the bell again. He still raced to the bell each Sunday after service to show the chosen little goodie two-shoes for the week that he really had won. He would tell the other kids he couldn't be bothered with memorizing a verse. Anyone could do that, he would say. But not everyone can beat me to the bell.

A memorable Sunday stuck in Matt's head. Easter Sunday, to be precise. Deb once again had memorized the verse, and on this glorious resurrection Sunday, the heavens rewarded her piousness and brazen good behavior with angelic control as the preacher drew her name out of his fedora.

Matt plotted, schemed, and strategized his perfect route. In his mind, he worked his way between the pews careful not to rub against them and catch a splinter on the old shredding oak. He darted and weaved between the overweight grandmas adorned in their dresses made from what looked to be curtains. He avoided eye contact with the sneering fathers who resented his speed and athleticism–something their kids apparently didn't have.

When the Preacher said, "Amen, go in peace children of God," Matt took off like a cheetah. Everything flowed as he envisioned. His speed and precise ability to maneuver made him smile. He made it to the bell before anyone else. It was too easy, he thought. It had to be record time. Standing in the tower, holding the rope attached to the Angel's Tool, Matt watched Deb as she walked toward him.

Smiling, and just before Deb could reach his Olympic Medal stand below the bell, Matt pulled the rope and said God told him to do it. At first, he thought it was funny, but when Deb, who he had a crush on, broke down and cried, he felt awful. It was the first time he could remember feeling bad about something he did to another person.

Matt's parents grounded him for a week and he had to mow the church grass for a month. He also had to sit in the front church pew every Sunday for the next month and wasn't allowed to stand until everyone had left. He didn't think the punishment was enough. Only eight, he thought he deserved a life sentence in the hardest prison known to man. Matt remembered the Sunday School teachers were sweet, mostly parents, and older folks as well who had no kids–at least not young enough to be in Sunday School.

The priest was a tall, distinguished man in his mid to late fifties with a great preacher's voice. Matt remembered little of what he said, but always felt comforted when he was speaking to all the sheep. All of them sinners in one form or another, according to the good book. That much he heard and remembered.

Matt had read plenty of the bible over the years and felt there were many other "good" books. The bible wasn't even in his top ten. Too disjointed, too many authors, and too many loose interpretations. How could anyone change God's word unless it wasn't God's word, but mans?

When Matt listened, he liked that the priest talked about neat things from the bible. Lions in a den, a guy with long hair who was super strong, and a little guy who beat a giant with a slingshot– a favorite of his. Matt never remembered feeling like God would get him and send him to hell for being bad as an Episcopalian.

The priest was a kind man who belonged in front of a crowd teaching the bible. No judgement, no glaring eyes looking deep into your sinner past, and no constant badgering of a person's duty to give ten percent. Matt loved dropping his quarter into the plate each Sunday, figuring the preacher knew exactly what to do with it.

Matt recalled that the Christmas pageant every year was exciting for him. All the boys wanted to be a wise man. The costumes were fantastic. A parent or two, who know how long ago, handmade the beautiful kings' robes that looked like garments royalty would wear. And the crowns, bravo! What little boy wouldn't want to wear a king's crown?

It was tough being the youngest of three boys though. Matt's brothers always got to do everything first. His oldest brother got to be Joseph first and then got to be a King first. Matt started out as a little shepherd boy. He even remembered being an animal one year, a sheep he thought, before he could rise to the proper age and don Joseph's burlap outfit. Then was the ascension to the Myrrh king, which was the ultimate for any of the St Barnabas boys.

Growing up in that church would have been good. Or would it? Who can say about fate? Perhaps something worse would have happened had his mother not up and left the family for a missionary trip to Africa. Dad had to raise the boys on his own, and it didn't go well. Years later, four to be exact, the mom returned, said she was sorry and moved back in as if only days had passed. Matt paused in contemplation wondering why the story popped into his head. Why now? He tilted his head sideways a touch and gazed over the heads creating noise in his meeting room thinking about his behavior as a little boy and how people change. He still felt guilty about how he treated her and...

"Matt, you agree with this approach?"

Matt cleared his mind of the memory and looked at Dave who had just given a sales presentation to the staff. He remembered almost none of the talking points but was confident they were spot on. Dave, always prepared, had no need for coaching or direction. Matt, so far down the fox hole with his memories, felt guilty for not paying attention. Thoughts of Betheny and his childhood had triggered unexpected thoughts in him. He wasn't sure what to do with them but he told himself he could think about it later.

"I think so, Dave. Let me go over it again this afternoon in my office, and if I have any concerns, I will let you know. Otherwise, same as usual, go sell the shit out of our software."

Dave smiled, and the rest of the staff laughed. There was trust amongst his team. Matt had a good sense of humor, his employees appreciated his self-effacing ability, and they all seemed to enjoy the freedom of laughter in the building.

Watching as the staff headed back to their offices, Matt stayed seated. Staring at the smooth wood finish of the oak table, he contemplated what would make Betheny call.

Regrets in Life

The rich suppleness of the therapist's leather couch felt comforting, but Matt fidgeted regardless. He wondered why he wasn't allowed to lie on the couch. He knew not lying down was a good thing though. With his affinity for falling asleep anywhere, at any time, he was certain of not getting his money's worth if he got on his back.

His therapist, Ms. Janice Farley, had to be nearing sixty. She tended to push things toward Jesus Christ and his loving attitude, except of course when he was allowing someone to enter hell for being human, but Matt always successfully steered her back away from the cross. She was respectful and always let up on the accelerator, accepting Matt's lack of belief. Matt gave her mental kudos for always trying to "save" his soul. He appreciated persistence, and counseling had been a life-salvage for him, so his therapist got a pass.

"What's the first thing you remember as a kid? An actual memory, not a photograph or a super eight film reel your parents shot."

Pausing in thought, Matt contemplated the question. Her mentioning super eight film reels shifted his focus to nothing else. They fascinated him as a child, and the thought of them took him right back to his childhood.

"Come on Matt. You know how this works."

"Well, you had to go and mention film reels. My parents shot a ton of them, so they are flashing through my mind. Give me a second, please."

Matt reached out to the coffee table and grabbed his glass of water. The glass, scarred and covered with the haze of hard water deposits, felt sturdy in Matt's hand. He wondered how the glasses were washed. Were they run under hot sink water and rinsed off in between sessions, or run through a dishwasher? He wanted to ask as the tepid water ran down the back of his throat.

"Okay, Matt, your dime. What do you have?"

Matt sat the dirty glass on the table. Thoughts of his grandfather came to him.

"My Grandpa loved basketball and the Boston Celtics. Growing up on the west coast, I always wondered why grandpa liked an East Coast team. I asked him one day, and I remember him oddly looking around the room. I wasn't sure why as a kid, but I understand now."

Matt paused in thought.

"Why is that, Matt?"

"He didn't want anyone else to hear what he was going to tell me."

"What was that, Matt?"

"Grandpa leaned forward in his recliner and said, 'I like them because they are mostly white'. I wasn't sure what he meant, and remembered feeling odd, but again, I didn't know why so I just said, 'Oh, okay grandpa'."

Matt paused.

"Looking back, as an integral part of your memory, what does it mean to you now?"

Matt, irritated by Farley's cut and dry lack of emotion and directness, focused on the fact she was just doing her job. He didn't need to get sidetracked over an issue of empathy, but at times he felt Farley lacked in that department. Perhaps she had to, so the sessions stayed on track.

Returning his thoughts to Dr. Farley, Matt had an idea as to her question, but wasn't sure he wanted to answer. He knew he could choose silence and not say a damn thing. One hundred and twenty-five dollars an hour was too much to keep his mouth shut though, so he spoke.

"Well, now I know enough to recognize that grandpa wasn't entirely confident in his response. Perhaps Jesus, or Grandma more likely, wouldn't like him saying how he felt. I liked the Celtics, like grandpa, for a while, until I realized the Portland Trail Blazers were a lot closer to where I lived. I remember not wanting to tell him for fear he might not be happy with me since they had a lot of guys on the team that weren't white. I liked their players, plus they had cool colors and a neat logo, not to mention the fact that they represented my favorite state in the U.S."

Matt smiled thinking about his loyalty to Oregon, wondering why he felt such an intense pull toward the state. He assumed most people loved their birth state, but he wasn't sure. Matt heard the therapist talking, and it snapped him away from dreaming about the Oregon beaches, mountains, lakes, and rivers he grew up on.

"Is that it, Matt?"

"How do you wash the drinking glasses?"

"Matt?"

"The glasses. How do you wash them after one of your patients uses them?"

"Matt, the glasses are clean. Focus please."

Matt, wanting a drink of water, started to reach for the glass, but stopped, able only to think of the dirty mouths that had been pressed against the glass. He watched Farley tap her pen against the pad of paper. He rolled his eyes before continuing.

"I think less of grandpa now, I suppose. And I adored him as a child. He had skeletons in his closet. Looking back, I am certain there were a few. I don't want to know. Best to keep the man I wanted him to be in my head. Despite any issues he may have had, I know he loved me. That counts in my book."

"Well, it..."

Matt, not listening, cut off Dr. Farley in mid-sentence.

"Do you think there are ethical problems or concerns when you buy honey, Doc?"

Matt stared at the ceiling, down at the floor, and then directly into the eyes of Dr. Farley. Silence held its sway over the room for a good thirty seconds.

"Excuse me, Matt?"

"Honey. When I stand in the aisle of Trader Joe's, I look at the honey. For a good five minutes or more. I find myself torn over what to buy. Think about it. Bees are so important to life on the planet. I can't reconcile what to buy. Organic, Natural, True Source Certified, and on and on. I stand there wanting to do the right thing. But then I wonder if it matters. I mean how in the hell can anyone say the bees are organic? What if a stray flies in, immigrates itself into the hive, and all of a sudden... Do you buy honey only in the U.S.? What about Brazil, or Europe? Are bees treated any better there? You know, fewer pesticides?"

Dr. Farley took a turn cutting Matt off. He couldn't help but notice the frustration in her voice.

"Look Matt, where are you going with this?"

Matt, fully absorbed in the thought of honey, switched back to thoughts of his grandfather.

"Well Grandpa had bees, and he loved them. I never saw him treat another human being bad, ever. I know he wasn't perfect, but a racist? So where do thoughts about white basketball players vs. black ones come from? Was he a racist?"

The termination ringer interrupted Matt's question, putting a stop to the cash meter.

"Well, Matt. You certainly took an unexpected direction, but one we certainly will explore next week."

Matt stood, debated bringing up the cleanliness of his water glass once more, but instead he nodded, spun around, and left the room. He noticed the little white machine, making a faint whirring noise, at the base of the door. It was supposed to keep those outside from hearing what was being said inside. As he contemplated whether the little hunk of plastic plugged into the wall worked, he closed the door behind him, wondering if he said bye.

Loud and Clear

Matt walked out of the therapist's office nodding to the front desk attendant. The afternoon air was cool as autumn began to display its full array of colors. Cars entered and left the parking lot in an orderly fashion. Matt looked around and counted the cars in spaces. Twenty-three total, leaving twenty-seven empty spaces. He couldn't remember if he had ever seen the lot full.

Grabbing the key fob out of his front pocket, Matt pressed a button and the door of his Tesla clicked, opening outward in a precise seven seconds. He slid into the driver's seat and the door automatically closed behind him in another seven seconds. He applied slight pressure on the break and the dashboard lit up before the luxury auto's voice started speaking. A nice feminine English sounding voice, which Matt enjoyed.

"Good afternoon, Matt. Shall I plot a course for home as usual?"

Matt rubbed the steering wheel with both hands, in a back-and-forth motion, several times. Eleven to be specific. He almost stopped on ten to be different today. Out of reflex, he reached up with his right hand and adjusted the rear-view mirror which was in perfect position. Tapping the top of the gearshift knob twice, he slid the lever into the R position while speaking a voice command to his car. Out of habit, Matt commanded the car to plot a course.

"Tesla. Navigate to 1321 Summers Lane, 97520."

"Navigate to 1321 Summers Lane, Ashland, 97520. Yes, or No?"

Matt tapped the brake two times and then applied pressure to the accelerator.

"Yes!"

"Course plotted. Proceed with caution."

He wondered why he always asked the car to plot a damn course since, being born and raised here, he knew his way around the valley. Instinct, or just an OCD creature of habit? He told himself it was all about getting alerts on where road construction and the cops were. Tomorrow, he decided he wouldn't ask for directions to get outside his habit zone. Shaking his head, knowing the thought bullshit, he'd ask as sure as the sun would rise, he eased the burnt orange Tesla over the speed bump and out of the parking lot. Turning right, he reached over and pressed the button for the radio and selected the Pandora app on the LCD screen. Moving through the stop sign while listening to the voice directions, he followed along as James Taylor sang "Up on the Roof," a favorite of his. He tapped the steering wheel with his left hand to the beat of the music and sang along. Not too loud and cover up James unmistakable sound.

Seventeen minutes later, Matt pulled onto Juniper drive where his old house, now the full legal and sole property of Number Two, was. He let off the accelerator and applied pressure to the brake as he noticed what looked to be half a dozen police cars and emergency vehicles with lights swirling and flashing.

A policewoman was standing in the middle of the road. She had Matt stop and signaled for him to roll down the window as she walked to the side of the car. Bending over with one hand on the door, and the other poised in a hovering position above the gun on her right side, she spoke loudly and with an unusual clarity, Matt thought.

"Good afternoon, sir. There has been an incident and we are only allowing residents to enter now. Do you live on this street?"

Matt's too-quick reflex got the best of him. Regret echoed in his brain as the impulsive words flowed out of his mouth and over lips he realized were dry. He thought of the dirty water glass one more time.

"Not anymore. I used to own a home on this street and was coming to visit a former."

Matt noticed the officer's eyes, a deep ocean blue, get brighter as her hand stopped hovering over her gun. She rested it on the handle. Matt thought, for a fraction of time, she was going to draw on him.

"You said 'former', sir? What does that mean?"

"Ex-wife. Ex sounds negative, so I call them formers."

The officer's bright eyes morphed into a dim, hazed looked as her facial expression changed to puzzled. Matt hated the term ex, and a dear cousin of his said, "*why not call them formers then, Matt?*" He liked it and tried to remember to use it whenever applicable.

"Which house, sir?"

Matt couldn't remember the question. "What?"

"Which house did you used to live in?"

"1321. Why?"

The officer stood and grabbed the mic sitting on her shoulder.

"Sergeant Jones, this is Reid, and I have someone here the detectives will want to talk with."

"Come back, Reid?"

Matt contemplated throwing the car in reverse and taking off, but he knew whatever happened had nothing to do with him. The intrigue he held from Number Two calling him earlier in the day had gotten the best of his curiosity, and he now wished it hadn't. He was supposed to be home by six for a dinner date with Kate. He figured she would have a new dog, so the plans would change but that didn't matter. He told her six, and he hated being late. No outcome he processed in his head got him out of here quickly and home on time.

Matt listened to the law enforcement conversation crackling over the female officer's speaker.

"Send the individual down and have them park behind car twenty."

Matt looked through the windshield and saw what looked to be another cop, waving his hand toward female officer Reid and his Tesla. Matt looked left and saw Reid wave in acknowledgement. She bent down and spoke with a firmer voice. It was confident, and Matt picked up on the new tone that now held condescension.

"Drive down to the officer who just waved at us. Park behind the car he is standing next to, sir. Go straight there, park and stay in the car until directed. Do you understand?"

Matt, now pissed, managed to hold his cynical tongue out of fear. He replied, trying to be polite.

"Loud and clear, Officer Reid."

Feel the Care

Matt eased his Tesla behind car number twenty, opened the door and got out. He bumped his head on the door and let out a foul word, rubbed his head, and wondered if it would start bleeding. Two cops started walking around his car, ogling it. He assumed they were cops anyhow. A woman and man. Neither dressed professionally, though they looked like they had given it their best effort on throwing something together, department store worthy. The woman dressed better than the guy. Matt figured she must be in charge based on nothing more than she looked more professional. The guy looked like he rolled out of bed in his outfit.

"Nice car. What is your name, sir?"

The male reached out to shake his hand. At least Matt thought he reached out. Matt awkwardly started to extend his hand before he realized the bastard made a jerking motion to stretch his shirt sleeve out under the suit jacket. He flashed a badge he gathered from a pocket.

"Detective Cole, and this is my partner Detective Graley."

"Seriously," Matt spit out.

"Seriously, what?"

"Nothing, sorry, my name is Matt Walker. This used to be my house."

Detective Mara Graley jumped in and took the lead, wasting no time questioning Matt.

"Walker, huh? You used to be married to Betheny Millstone-Walker, then?"

"Yes, a long time ago. Actually, not that long ago, it just seems like a long time ago."

"Why do you say that?"

"Well, let's just say that the marriage was odd, and I got out of it as efficiently as possible."

The male detective, who quickly ignored Walker after the introduction and a flash of his badge, had finished his fascination with the Tesla and stood next to his partner now.

"How often did you beat your wife, Mr. Walker?"

Matt felt his head twist sideways. He couldn't imagine he heard the cop correctly. He relayed this fact without hesitation.

"Excuse me?"

"How often did you beat your wife, Mr. Walker? It's a straightforward question."

Matt, pissed, and a bit frightened, responded with what disdain.

"I never laid a violent hand on Betheny, asshole!"

"Someone did a number on her and tore the hell out of her place. All she keeps muttering is 'Matt, Matt, Matt.' So, two and two being four, last time I checked anyhow, makes you a damn good suspect."

Detective Cole was proud of his little comment. His stern face didn't show the smile he had inside.

"Well, two and two could be twenty-two if you think about it, and I haven't seen her in, well..."

Matt hadn't heard the name Betheny in over a year and a half near as he could figure. He couldn't even remember the last time he saw her. Must have been the night he went back to gather belongings after walking out on her. Lawyers handled everything from there on. He didn't even make a court appearance.

To Matt's relief, Detective Graley decided to speak again. Detective Cole, with calculated effect, had gotten under his skin.

"Please follow us, Mr. Walker. There is someone we'd like you to see."

Matt got in step behind Graley. Cole was close behind in single file. Matt turned to look over his shoulder and thought he caught Cole looking at his ass. Perhaps the Tesla wasn't the only thing of Matt's the detective liked.

Matt stepped around several uniformed officers through a wide open front door. His old home had been ransacked for sure. Looking around, he was more than a little surprised. Everything, at least items not scattered, looked to be the same as when he left almost two years ago. He figured Betheny would have been dating by now and changed out everything in the place. Perhaps she didn't despise him as much as he thought.

Cole led him into the Great room and Matt saw two paramedics surrounding Betheny. One on the couch next to her, and one kneeling in front of her taking her pulse. Her face looked unrecognizable. If it weren't for the fact they were in this house and the striking red hair, Matt could have walked right past her. Matt heard her mumbling his name as she rocked her head and shoulders back and forth in a slow motion.

Glancing up at Cole, then at Matt, she jumped to her feet almost knocking one of the paramedics over.

"Ma'am, please. You need to let me finish," the kneeling paramedic barked.

Ignoring the order, Betheny ran over and put her arms around Matt with endearing affection. She squeezed Matt like she never had before. Matt could feel her skin reverberate and shake, like someone had just pulled her out of a frozen lake. The care she held in the embrace rippled through is skin.

Cole and Graley both appeared puzzled as they looked at each other. Graley, surprised at the unexpected reaction from Betheny, had hoped this was going to be an easy case. Now, in the body language of the abused woman, she knew it would not.

Matt let Betheny hold tight for a minute or so. When the sobbing eased, he put his hands on her shoulders and backed away enough, so he could look her in the swollen, bruised, and blood-stained face.

"Betheny, who did this? Do you know?"

Betheny, sobbing again, worked at getting her breathing under control, so she could speak. Another minute or so passed, and the room was silent as everyone waited to hear a name.

"It's okay, Betheny, take your time. You are safe now."

Betheny reached out to Matt trying to wipe tears on his shirt sleeve. She tried to speak. Matt saw a twinkle in her eyes. An action no one else, save her parents, would probably recognize. She was getting ready to lie.

"I don't know who it was, Matt. It happened so fast. I think I passed out after he kept hitting me in the face. I was afraid to open my eyes."

Matt watched her eyes dart over to the detectives. He knew it was a lie. Matt, knowing Betheny better than anyone else in the room, felt a sense of loyalty and didn't want to call her on it. She had her reasons, and he was touched how glad she was to see him. He wasn't going to betray her. At least not yet. He decided he would give her time to come clean. It appeared she wanted to, from the look in her pleading eyes which were asking him to keep quiet.

Detective Graley moved toward them, taking Betheny carefully by the arm.

"Come on Miss, let the paramedics finish and get you down to the hospital. We'll need to talk more after you've been examined fully."

Chinese Food

Matt eased into the seat, shut the door, and guided his Tesla out from behind the police car. He didn't tap on the steering wheel, didn't click the key fob or anything. Smiling, he figured the break in behavior must have something to do with the stressful situation. Ironic, since he thought stress brought his OCD on.

Matt developed the frustrating behavior while married to Betheny. Stress brought it out, his therapist told him. She also said that the quirky behavior was there all along. If he thought about his past behavior and reactions enough, he'd be able to remember earlier tendencies. Matt thought the mental affliction was a weakness and should be overcome. His therapist differed with her so-called professional opinion. Regardless, Matt worked toward minimization of the disorder, so he didn't feel like a fool.

Not tapping on the damn steering wheel eleven times was a great start. He would be ready next week to discuss this occurrence with Dr. Farley. Matt reflected momentarily, realizing the tapping would not be the seminal moment of the night. He contemplated going to the hospital. His wristwatch said a quarter past six o'clock already.

He pressed the call button on the steering wheel and scanned for wife number three, Kate. She was number one on the speed dial.

Kate picked up on the second ring.

"Hey handsome, where are you? Going to be late yet again?"

She giggled, knowing Matt being late was a rare event indeed. She was perpetually late herself and was frustrated at times with Matt's ability to always be on time. This was a treat for her in a way. Might take pressure off her for a couple of days in terms of knowing Matt was not, in fact, perfect.

"Kate, I am hardly ever late. And I have a good reason."

"I know, you goofball, and I'm teasing... lighten up!"

Matt pushed the turn signal, accelerating onto the freeway.

"I am getting on the freeway now. I should be home in no more than fifteen minutes. We can still make our dinner reservation, so don't worry."

"I cancelled dinner, Matt, so don't rush. We have a new addition to the family and I didn't want to leave him alone so soon."

Kate waited for a negative response from Matt. She knew he wasn't crazy in love with the idea of getting a dog. She had always wanted one and now that she lived in a home with such a great yard, she had the perfect opportunity. Working from home doing medical billing and research, Kate knew the dog would have lots of company.

With Matt working so much during the week, and on occasional weekends, the furry company would be nice for her. Not having any kids of her own, nor the ability to produce a child herself, a pet made sense. She knew cats were cute, but so damn aloof and independent. She wanted a dog. Dogs were gregarious to a fault. Exactly what she wanted.

"What did you get, Kate? The black lab puppy we were looking at? He was sure a cute dog. I am certain you will love him," Matt said, feeling not nearly as positive as he tried to sound.

He cringed thinking about all the shit the dog was going to leave all over the house as Kate attempted to potty-train it. There would be yelping of loneliness and chewing of furniture, urination on every flower and shrub they owned, and he would most likely lose the normal use of his favorite chair in the living room. The damn dog would be in it constantly. And labs, they never seemed to get full.

"Nope! Went a completely different direction. I love the puppy as you know, but I decided to adopt at the shelter. I couldn't justify in my mind buying the lab when there are so many dogs in need. Not to mention the fact, since I volunteer there, the message it would send for me not to adopt. There is this Pittie-Lab mix I fell in love with the last couple of weeks. Someone left him at the shelter about three months ago, ragged and damn near hairless. He had been chained up and was covered in sores and hadn't eaten properly for who knows how long. The photos of what he looked like when he arrived were disgusting. One of the other women, Delores, had been helping him recover, and I always noticed how gentle and sweet he seemed when she walked him.

Broke my heart to think he had been so abused. I was impressed how he was healing, and how beautiful he was. Anyhow, I sat with him and we seemed to click right away. He laid his head in my lap. Delores said she had never seen him do that with anyone, including herself. She seemed jealous! So, I filled out paperwork and paid the adoption fee, which was half of what the lab would have cost, by the way."

Matt smiled thinking about Kate's ability to talk nonstop.

"Oh, I almost forgot, he is potty, and cage trained. Not that I would ever put him in one, but I thought you would like to know. He doesn't appear to be a chewer either, so it is a win-win-win! Me, you, and him."

Matt chuckled and pushed the turn signal up on the steering column. He eased his Tesla down the driveway to the garage. The quarter mile drive amongst the oak, fir, and pine trees was always calming for him. The refuge he had always wanted with a woman who, so far, seemed to be a like-minded spirit. He craved a healthy, lasting relationship. Regardless, if things did fall apart, this was one home and property the wife would not get. He saw to that in the prenup.

Matt reached up above the rearview mirror and pressed the button for the garage door.

"Hey, I hear the garage door, Matt. You home?"

"Yep, pulling in now, beautiful. Hold on to that dog so he doesn't come running out and jump into my car will you please?"

"He is checking out the backyard, Matt, and I am sitting on the patio watching him. Come out and meet him, okay? Oh, and Matt, on your way out, please bring me a glass of wine, the 2014 Weisinger Tempranillo, okay? Love you."

Matt chuckled at Kate's propensity to direct a conversation her way. She was skilled at it.

"Okay, give me five minutes. I need to use the restroom."

Matt hung up and proceeded to call information for Medford General Hospital's phone number. He pressed button one to be automatically connected. The hospital had no information on Betheny yet. Matt figured she probably was in the Emergency Room or being registered if they were keeping her overnight. He decided to call in another twenty minutes. Perhaps they would know something then. He looked at his watch, saw it was almost 6:30, and made a mental note to call just before seven.

Getting out of the car, Matt looked around the garage, and saw everything was in its place. He looked at his bicycles hanging from the ceiling and wished he could go out for a long ride, knowing it would clear his mind. He sighed. There wasn't time this evening. He needed to go meet this new dog and spend time with Kate.

"Shit," Matt blurted out. If they weren't going out to eat now, what would be for supper? He should have stopped for Chinese food and would have had he known they weren't going out. Matt knew Kate wouldn't be fixing anything. She was a disaster in the kitchen. She tried but didn't enjoy it and every bite of food she prepared reminded him of that fact.

Matt pressed the garage door button by the side door. His ears registered the sound of it closing as he entered his home heading straight for the bathroom.

Life's a Bitch, and Then...

Police Detectives Graley and Cole waited outside the Emergency Room entrance. Cole was chain smoking again, and Graley wanted to punch him in the face. The smoke made her sick, and Cole was weak for not being able to quit.

Graley herself had quit after getting out of the military. She woke up one morning, reached for the pack of cigs and slid one into her mouth. Looking around for a lighter, or matches, unable to find either, and without waking the woman in bed next to her, she dug through the visitor's handbag thrown hastily on the floor. Graley couldn't remember her guest's name, and didn't feel like waking her to ask, so she put the cigarette back in the box, threw the pack in the trash, went to the bathroom and brushed her teeth, and never smoked again. That was over twenty years ago. If she could quit, Cole could.

"Those things are going to kill you, ya know."

"We all have to go eventually, Graley. What do you care?"

"Because they smell disgusting and I have to ride around with you all day."

"The damn car of ours is loaded up with air fresheners Graley. I don't know how you can smell anything but perfumed vanilla and cherry. *They* make *me* sick."

"You are such an idiot, Cole. With all the scientific evidence we have, you know they are sending you to an early death."

Graley knew the words, and breath, were wasted. The two had this same damn conversation at least once a week. She kept on though, figuring she would eventually beat Cole down or get him to ask for a new partner. She wanted both, but one or the other would satisfy her, for now at least.

"Why don't you go to an E-Cig at least? Water vapor, and you can still get your nicotine fix. At least the smell won't bother me and we can eliminate half those damn air fresheners."

"Tried 'em, don't like 'em. Besides, it would make you happy. I can't have that."

"You're an asshole, Cole."

"Tell me something I don't know, douche-bag."

Kicking at the ground in abject frustration, Graley looked inside the Emergency Room door. Walking inside she went to the admitting desk.

"Excuse me. Any word on Betheny Millstone yet?"

The nurse looked down at the computer screen. Made a few clicks with the mouse and stared back at Graley.

"Nothing yet, Officer, and we have her registered as Betheny Millstone-Walker by the way. She was the redhead with the banged-up face, right?"

Graley nodded and the admittance clerk continued.

"Check back in another ten minutes or so. We might have pertinent information by then."

"Okay, thanks. And it's Detective."

Graley spun around and walked away. She wondered why she felt the need to correct the young man over the word officer. The kid was polite and meant nothing by it. Graley felt embarrassed, and disappointed in herself, for having said anything at all. She vowed not to make the correction next time.

As Graley stepped back outside, Cole lit up another cigarette. Nervous boredom, Graley thought, propelled the skinny asshole to smoke.

The cigarette dangled on the edge of Cole's lip as he spoke. Graley couldn't figure out how the tightrope act with was possible.

"Is she in a room yet or getting released?"

"The nurse doesn't have any information yet, Cole. Said to check back in ten minutes."

"What the hell, Gray? She didn't seem that bad. I mean yeah, she got the shit beat out of her, but looked like mostly bruising and a crushed spirit. No broken bones, so what the fuck?"

"God, you are a prick, Cole. Someone came in the woman's home, beat the hell out of her, sounds like he threatened her, and then apparently walked out without any fear of being caught. The woman is terrified and, I am certain, sore as hell. Not to mention she had her face rearranged and there will be temporary, if not permanent, damage to her body and psyche for that matter."

"Life's a bitch and then you die. Right, Gray? Isn't that what you always tell me your drill instructor told you?"

Graley took a seat on the bench in a position she hoped was upwind of Cole's smoke. The cool night air brought a chill to her. She wished she had a heavier jacket. Pausing in deliberate thought, Graley waited a couple of minutes before engaging Cole again in conversation.

"Cole, were you watching when she ran up and hugged her ex-husband at the house?"

"Yes, why?"

"Notice anything peculiar?"

"Not really."

Graley watched Cole pause in thought of the earlier encounter before he continued.

"Other than the fact the guy seemed surprised by her hugging him. Why, did you see something?"

"I had a better angle on her face than you did. I could have sworn I saw her wink at the guy while she was sobbing. I got the feeling she wanted to say something to him. Quietly, if you know what I mean."

"I admit I didn't trust the guy at first, but after I saw the victim run up and hug him, I changed my tune a bit. Seems unlikely the ex gave her the beating unless they are both into pretty kinky shit."

"I agree. She appeared genuine the way she hugged him and regained confidence when he arrived. She was talking with her ex though, with her eyes. I'm sure of it."

"Well I guess it's why we are the detectives, Gray. We will have to figure it all out.

Graley, not sure how to respond to Cole or if she should at all, felt a sense of relief when the Emergency Room door opened. Talking with Cole wore her out.

In a rush, the male attendant who moments earlier had told Graley to check back in ten minutes came outside in the cool autumn Southern Oregon air.

"Detectives. The doctor would like to speak with you right away."

Koda

(pronounced: koh – dah)
Short for Dakota

Means Ally or Friend in "Dakota" Sioux

After flushing the toilet, Matt washed his hands at the sink, then wiped them dry on the dark blue hand towel accented with small white flowers on each end. Betheny's favorite color was blue, and almost everything she owned had some semblance of a flower on it. Similar to Kate's tastes, Matt realized for the first time, wondering if it meant anything.

Staring at himself in the mirror, Matt paid close attention to his blue eyes. He felt as if staring at them would replay in his mind the look Betheny gave him less than an hour ago. He remembered the look, sure enough, but it didn't offer any clues as to what she was thinking. As much as he had avoided her since the divorce, he was now anxious to talk with her. He wanted to know what in the hell happened, why the deep embrace, and why she felt the need to lie to the police. It was rare for Matt to have his curiosity piqued to this level.

Matt wondered if Betheny knew the person that assaulted her. Since she didn't want the cops to know who the attacker was, it made sense that it was a recognizable face. He couldn't think of anyone who would do such a thing. He was not with her long enough to know her entire circle of friends. The burden of stress pushing on his shoulders, Matt's frustration hung around his neck like a noose not tied to anything.

"Dammit," he mumbled, realizing he didn't even know all of Betheny's family. The woman wasn't the type to have enemies and everyone Matt knew thought the world of her. Which brought him full circle to the question, how well did he really know her. He contemplated striking the mirror as he thought, how well does a person ever really know someone else?

Matt opened the door, then stopped and straightened the towel, evening up the ends before heading back to the kitchen. Once there, he knew he needed to tell Kate why he was late, not make up any bullshit but something pulled at him to lie. His head was churning with all the different possibilities. He stopped at the refrigerator and tapped the handle five times before quietly blurting an expletive.

"Shit!"

He opened the door, looking for a cold beer. Full Sail Pils or Deschutes Black Butte Porter? He grabbed a Pilsner then turned and set it on the counter. He moved over to the wine chiller checking the temperature out of habit. It showed a perfect fifty-five degrees. He grabbed a 2014 Weisinger Tempranillo and set it, with care, on the counter next to his beer. He pulled the cork and set the wine aside to let it breathe. Matt kept being told the breathing mattered, but he wondered.

Taking a bottle opener off the side of the refrigerator, Matt opened his beer. He tossed the cap in the trash then grabbed a Riedel Vinum wine glass, Kate's favorite, out of the cupboard, wondering how long until the new dog broke one of the expensive glasses. He contemplated putting the fermented Rogue Valley grape juice in a red solo cup, but decided against it, not wanting to ruin Kate's experience. Matt poured a healthy portion for Kate, so he wouldn't have to return inside too soon. He put the cork back on the Tempranillo and left it on the counter. Grabbing his beer, Matt took a nice long pull on his favorite Pilsner and headed outside.

Closing the sliding glass door behind him, Matt walked over and handed Kate her wine, kissed her on the cheek, pulled up a green Adirondack chair next to her, and sat. He was determined to enjoy the environment and company despite his evening so far.

"Hey, beautiful, how are you doing?"

Looking out over the backyard, Matt could see the newest addition to the family running around as if he had just been set free for the first time in his life. Matt contemplated life in a cage and concrete. What a miserable existence. Kate was sweet to rescue this dog from that punishing cold, sterile life.

Matt hadn't settled in his seat when Kate started asking questions.

"So, how was your day, babe? Anything unusual or exciting happen? Sounds like you were busy as always. At least according to Jane."

Matt wondered if Kate was going to take a breath. She was clearly excited about the dog. Tonight, unlike others, he hoped she kept right on asking questions. He would decide which ones to answer and which ones not to, so he wouldn't have to lie.

Taking a deep breath and settling back in the deck chair, Matt started to respond when Kate took the one-sided discussion a new direction.

"Come on, babe, walk with me down to the lake. I want you to meet Koda."

Shit, Matt thought to himself. The chair was comfortable. He could return in short order, though, thinking the dog could be a welcome distraction.

"Okay, I'll follow your lead, sweetie."

Kate stood and blushed. Matt knew she loved it when he called her sweetie. She had always wanted her father to call her sweetie, but when he made affectionate attempts, they were stilted and forced. Matt was the first male to come into her life where the use of the word didn't piss her off. A "good sign" her mother constantly told her, when a man calls you sweetie and you like it. She would tell her to be careful as the word could be quite condescending.

Matt reached out and took Kate's outstretched hand. She led him down the steps of the deck onto the lush grass of their home which led all the way to the bank of the lake. His name was the only one on the deed, and Kate said she was fine with it. Matt wondered at times though.

"I don't plan on going anywhere," she would say to Matt, "and if I do, I won't want anything that belongs to you. Trust me."

Matt had to be careful since he was the sole proprietor of his business and had already given up ownership of two homes with former wives. He couldn't afford to do it again. Hell, he couldn't afford to give up the last one either, he thought, as the edge of the lake, and the new dog, grew closer.

Before they reached the water's edge, a good fifty feet or so from the dog and the lake, Kate dropped Matt's hand and got down on her knees calling to Koda.

"Come here, Koda! Come on, boy!"

Nothing. Matt thought it was nothing more than the dog not yet knowing his name. Kate, however, appeared frustrated.

"I don't get it. He has hardly left my side all afternoon. Koda, come here, boy. Come on, dog. Here boy!"

"He probably isn't used to his name yet is all. Probably sees a fish or frog. Let's walk down to him. And why call him Koda?"

Matt thought whatever Koda saw must be interesting beyond the norm. The dog was not only barking at the water but wouldn't move. Kate didn't respond to his question about the name Koda, but Matt knew there would be plenty of time for explanations later.

Kate reached the dog and bent down to pet him. Matt, a few feet behind as they approached the bank, stared at the water. Kate was focused on Koda while he tried to see what their new canine family member zeroed in on. It didn't take him long to understand the dog's reaction.

"Kate, get the dog by the collar and follow me okay?"

"Why?" Kate asked, then returned her full attention to the dog.

"What's wrong, Koda? What's wrong? Good boy. You are such a good boy. Everything is safe now. This is your yard and home now, boy."

Matt didn't want to get between Koda and the water's edge. He didn't know the dog at all, and Koda might take it as an aggressive move. Frustrated, Matt got to the point without further hesitation.

"Kate, there is a dead body floating face down about fifteen feet out from the edge of the water. You need to get Koda up and into the house while I call the police."

Remembering the morning sunrise, the geese in the lake, and the thing, now he knew it was a body, floating in the water, Matt watched as Kate stiffened. Her face turned noticeably pale against the framing of her dark black hair. Matt wished he had covered his ears as Koda continued barking and Kate, now looking into the lake, screamed.

Unexpected Deaths

Graley rose from the bench and stretched to get her blood warmed up. She was tired—too many late nights caring for her father—and the cold steel bench hurt her ass. Moving her head left to right in a slow deliberate motion, she tried to pop her neck.

"Come on, Cole. Put out the damn cigarette and let's go see what the doctor has to say."

Cole obliged. His fingers felt the coarse material as he rubbed the cigarette into the sand-like substance atop the trash can. The nasty habit was reducing his life span, and he felt like crap, all the time. He vowed never to let Graley know. His inner voice, which he didn't trust, told him he should tell her, thinking she would help him. The fucking Girl Scout always wanted to help everyone.

"Right behind you, your highness."

Graley led Cole to the emergency room and the waiting doctor.

"Detectives, follow me, please."

The doctor led them through a door off the emergency room lobby. Graley figured he was leading them back to see their victim. Instead, both detectives were surprised to see nothing more than a room with a couch, two chairs and a window with a plant on the sill.

"I am afraid I have bad news. Betheny Millstone-Walker has died."

Graley, stunned, looked at Cole, then back at the doctor.

Cole wandered over to the window and stared out into the Pacific Northwest night sky bathed with stars.

Graley recovered from her surprise.

"What the hell, Doc? She didn't look that bad!"

"Near as I can tell, Detectives, she had a brain aneurism. We won't know with certainty until we run tests."

"A what?" Cole asked, still by the window, his back to the other two as he continued staring into the night. He was thinking the way his mouth always tasted disgusting from the cigarettes.

"A brain aneurism. It's essentially a little balloon-type pocket in the brain that fills up with blood. About four percent of people have them. One of you could have one."

Cole turned and looked at the doctor like he was the biggest asshole on the planet. Graley smiled noticing the doc had gotten under Cole's skin.

"Great, thanks for the positive information, Doc," Cole wasted no time replying.

Graley smiled again and made a mental note to use this aneurism news with Cole when the next opportunity presented itself.

Graley watched the doctor's face. The distinguished looking MD appeared unfazed by her or Cole's reaction as he continued.

"Most of us live normal lives without incident. Others are not so fortunate, as these aneurisms can be fatal, as we have seen tonight. Our guess right now is that Ms. Walker had one. The trauma she received to her head in the attack weakened the aneurism, causing it to rupture either in the ambulance ride over, or on arrival. We rushed her into surgery, but it was too late. There was nothing we could do. Perhaps if she had come in sooner..."

The doctor didn't finish his thought. Graley knew where he was going but didn't second guess herself. The paramedics were on sight and were the ones to make the call to get her here. Graley watched the doctor fold his arms, rotating his head back and forth in a motion she assumed was being done to relieve tension. His action made her want to pop her own neck.

"Do either of you know if she smoked?"

Graley looked at Cole, then back to the doctor.

"I don't think so, Doc. At least I didn't notice any sign of it in her home, but I wasn't looking for it either."

"She didn't smoke." Cole commented. "Why, doc?"

"Smoking increases the risk is all. Just curious. An autopsy will provide more information."

Graley looked at Cole, she rolled her eyes and shook her head.

"See, you dumb ass, you need to quit," she said.

Cole responded with anger. Fear, and the sudden thought of his mortality, had a hold of him for the moment.

"No shit, asshole. Now fucking drop it."

Graley addressed the doctor again.

"The autopsy, Doc, how long will it take and what do you expect to learn?"

"This is considered a murder, correct?"

Graley wasted no time in responding, the wheels turning in her head replaying the scene in the house, the way she hugged and looked at her ex-husband, and how someone beat her. Was death the intention, or was it a burglary gone bad?

"Yes, Doc. For now, at least.

Graley paused in thought before continuing.

"We won't know the specific charge until the autopsy is complete. Regardless, whether accidental or deliberate, someone committed a felony here."

The doctor appeared jumpy to Graley. She figured the stress from a failed surgery, and who knows what other kind of crap he had dealt with today, made him this way.

"Well, your involvement will speed up the process, but my guess is a good week. Perhaps sooner. Just depends on what the priorities are with the coroner. I am sure you two will have a say in the matter. Or at least the Police department."

Graley looked at Cole. "Call the coroner's office in the morning first thing, Cole, and get this fast-tracked."

Cole gave Graley a salute as he walked out the door. Graley sighed knowing her partner wanted nicotine to soothe his tweaked nerves and wondered if he had a blood-filled balloon in his own head. She turned her attention back to the doctor.

"Well, Doc, thanks for the information. I wish it were better news."

Graley reached out and shook the doctor's hand, who was already heading toward the door trying to get out of the room. She followed him into the emergency room lobby before heading out the big sliding doors on her own. She moved to the side as a patient in a wheelchair, looking like he was in a lot of pain, moved himself through the doors. Graley, curious about the person in the wheelchair, looked over her shoulder on the way out, then walked up to Cole. He was standing by the bench they had both been sitting on less than fifteen minutes ago. She expected to see a cigarette hanging from his mouth. Even though she wanted him to quit, part of her hoped he was smoking. She felt a tinge of guilt at her disappointment, noticing Cole was on his cell phone rather than warming his lungs.

Cole turned to Graley as she contemplated sitting down on the bench. Instead, she again attempted to pop her neck. Coming up empty she gave Cole her full attention.

"You aren't going to fucking believe this, Graley."

"What, Cole, your mom call and promise to tuck you into bed tonight?"

"Kiss my ass, biatch."

Cole kicked the ground. Graley wasn't sure if he was mad at her for the comment, or about the phone call.

"Leave my mom out of our banter, you jerk. Family is off limits. Remember?"

"Okay now, don't go crying on me Cole. Who were you on the phone with?"

Cole placed his cell phone in his back pants pocket, then reached into his jacket and grabbed his cigarettes. He took one out, lit it up, and took a deep long drag. Graley watched his demeanor change as she assumed the smoke soothed his lungs, calming his nerves.

Graley was incredulous with Cole considering what they both had just heard from the doctor, but she kept her mouth shut waiting for Cole's reply. Guilt surrounded her conscience over the fact that she wanted him to quit, but also to keep smoking. She couldn't believe she disliked him enough to want a blood bubble to burst in his head. Yet the dark thoughts were there, but she would keep them to herself.

"It was Dispatch. Matt Walker just put a call in to 911. He claims there is a dead body floating in Emigrant Lake near his yard."

Graley, lifted her eyebrows, wrinkled the skin on her forehead, and tilted her head to the right in a perplexing reflexive action. Thoughts of malice on her partner were eviscerated by the words flowing out of the cigarette-holding mouth. Words, which were pieced together in a mouth-dropping fashion that she did not expect to hear.

A Growing Mess

Kate struggled to get Koda back in the house. As strong as the dog was, his size was no match for her determination. Dragging him by the collar as carefully as she could for about five feet, Koda figured out he was in a no-win situation. Matt watched, glad to see Kate confident about handling her new dog. A damn shame the evening had to be ruined for her.

Dialing 911, Matt explained the situation giving detailed directions to the location of his home. He described where the body was and stated he would show the police when they arrive. Off the phone, impressed with the calm, fluid manner of speaking by the 911 agent, Matt turned back around to the lake and watched as the body, face down and fully clothed, move with the motion of the water. Tempted to wade out and drag it to shore, he passed knowing the police would be upset. At least he thought they would, believing the less he interfered the better. His nightmare of a day already involved the police with the incident at his former's place, so he left the body to the will of the lake.

The thought of Betheny prompted him to dial the hospital again.

The attendant at the hospital picked up on the first ring.

"Hello, Rogue River Medical Center, is this an emergency?"

"Hello, and no. I am checking on the condition of Betheny Millstone. Can you give me an update please? Millstone-Walker that is. Sorry."

Matt added the sorry remembering the last time he called.

"One moment, sir."

Waiting, Matt stared at the body, then across the lake wondering if this was an accident. Was he being watched? He didn't see any boats on the lake. Scanning the opposite shoreline, to his disappointment, revealed no onlookers.

"This is the E.R. nurse. May I help you?"

Shit, Matt thought to himself, *she is still in the E.R....*

"Yes, I am checking on a Betheny Millstone-Walker. I believe the ambulance brought her in about an hour ago."

"Are you family, sir?"

Matt had a puzzle look on his face as he contemplated how best to answer.

"Um, not any more. What does that matter?"

"Well, sir, we are only authorized to give information to family members."

"I am her former husband, that should still count as family, in a way," was all Matt could think of to say. He figured it wouldn't work but was worth a shot.

"I am sorry, sir, but no. Is there anything else I can do for you?"

Matt heard a noise from the house and watched as Kate let two uniformed officers—looked like state police by the color of the uniforms and hats—out through the sliding door. He hung up on the hospital and started walking toward the officers.

"Hello. This way officers."

"Who were you on the phone with, sir?" One of the police asked Matt as they walked up to him.

"The hospital. A friend of mine, a former wife, was taken there this afternoon, and I wanted to see how she was doing."

Matt stopped at the shore a few feet from the water's edge. He pointed toward the body, surprised it had hardly moved.

"Is this where you found the body, or has it moved?"

Responding with puzzlement, Matt shook his head realizing he was thinking the exact same thing. For a moment, he thought about saying he saw it floating at sunrise during his morning coffee, but quickly surmised that would bring more questions he didn't feel like answering. So, to keep a guilt free conscience, he told himself he wasn't sure what he saw bobbing by the geese this morning.

"Yes, it's right where we found it. It's strange to me it hasn't moved much. Usually sticks and such drift out, or in."

The officers looked at each other and one of them got on their mic attached to the shoulder strap. The second such one he had seen within hours.

The other officer spoke to Matt.

"Where is the best and closest place to get power to the lights when the investigators get here?"

Matt pointed to the lower deck a few feet away. He had power run out to it not long after he bought the place.

"There are a couple of 120 outlets on the deck. If they need more, I would have to run extension cords from the back of the house. Not sure if I have long enough ones though."

"Don't worry about that. Supplies won't be an issue. They will have a generator as well, among other things, if needed. It is nice to have the outlet option to get set up is all."

The other officer hung up his phone and wasted no time addressing his partner.

"Okay, investigators are on their way. It's the Old and Restless of course."

The two officers laughed. Matt thought of Graley and Cole, then wondered if all the detective pairs were assigned nicknames.

"Do you guys need me down here anymore, or can I go up to the house?"

"Not planning on making a getaway, are you?"

"No. Uh, you serious?" Matt, nervous at the question, answered a little too quick and too defensive, he thought.

"If you were thinking about it, your garage is blocked with our car and another car behind ours. The forensic team and detectives should be here in minutes."

Matt felt his body temperature rise as the incident at Betheny's place, along with this new find, had him fidgeting more than normal. He wondered if anyone else could tell. Thank heaven Betheny was okay and ran up to hug him. He didn't know who the current body in the lake was. He figured it ultimately didn't matter since it had nothing to do with him other than being closest to his property. Why the hell couldn't it have drifted over to the neighbors? Matt shook his head thinking of Hee Haw and the, *if it weren't for bad luck* saying so famous on the show.

Wandering toward the back of his house, Matt wanted to get inside and tell Kate, now more than ever, about Betheny. With everything going on, this wasn't the time to be holding on to information for ideal timing. Reaching the back deck, he felt the two state police trailing behind him, making him feel like he was a felon. On arrival, Matt watched as the sliding door opened. Out walked Graley and Cole.

One of the state police, with a raised voice, said, "If it isn't the Old and the Restless. You two girlfriends still fighting over smoking?"

The other state cop laughed.

Matt let his chin lower a second. He closed his eyelids before he regained his composure and brought his chin upward with feigned confidence. He stared at Graley who looked at him with sad eyes. Cole stared at him like he was going to shoot him. Neither one of them gave Matt any comfort in the growing mess.

The Edge of the Lake

Detective Graley looked at her watch. *Shit*, she thought to herself, realizing it was much later than she wanted. She was missing Wallander on TV. Still unable to grasp her DVR, she was relegated to watching her favorite police show in real-time. The DVR was set to record, that much she knew, but figuring out how to play the correct episode back had so far eluded her.

Matt broke the awkward silence.

"You two the only detectives in town? Or did you come here to arrest me for beating up my former wife?"

Cole gave him an up and down stare. Matt noticed tension and condescension in the expression. He didn't like Cole. From the way others reacted around Cole, Matt figured he wasn't alone in his distaste or assessment of the chain-smoking detective.

Graley appeared to be made of a different ilk. She had the good cop role down pat. She reached out and put a hand on Matt's shoulder. Matt wasn't expecting it and guessed the warm gesture was a precursor to bad news. He could feel sad energy flowing through Graley's touch.

"Mr. Walker, I'm afraid we have bad news. Ms. Millstone suffered a brain aneurism as a result of the beating and died this evening on the operating table."

Matt felt an energy pull down from the top of his head landing hard in his feet. It was a deep, sickening feeling stretching and pulling at his skin. A sensation that left him more exhausted and spent than the worst day he could remember. The one when his mother and father died in a car accident. He didn't think anything would ever top the sad blow that event had dealt to his psyche. This was close.

Matt lowered his eyelids and moved his head in a slow side-to-side motion. He responded in a low, sad, and cautious tone.

"What? Are you serious? She died?"

Matt could feel, and he looked to confirm, Cole staring at him trying to decide his innocence or guilt. The detective's eyes were intent on being judge, jury, and executioner, right here and now. And if the look were any serious sign to Matt, he was guilty in the eyes of the chain-smoking cop.

Graley removed her hand from Matt's shoulder.

"Why don't you pull up one of these chairs and take a moment to breathe. I am sure your body feels drained and perhaps even light-headed."

Matt turned and looked directly at one of the chairs on his deck. He stood, staring, deep in thought of Betheny. He felt his body should be moving forward to sit down, but he stood there wondering why the chair wasn't getting any closer.

Graley grabbed him by the arm and moved him toward the Adirondack. Sitting down, Matt focused on his breathing. He felt like tapping the arm chair a comforting eleven times. Right now, he knew it would look ridiculous, so he concentrated, flexed his shoulders backward, and then held any tapping action at bay.

"The doctor told us she probably had a weak vessel or pocket in her brain already. Apparently, a lot of us do, and the trauma she took to the head exacerbated it bringing on the aneurism. It was over before they could do anything. Quite sad, and I'll say unexpected," Graley said with empathy as she pulled another chair up and joined Matt in a sitting position.

Cole paced around the deck staring out at the activity going on near the water's edge.

Matt held back tears and responded.

"I can't believe this. I haven't seen Betheny in, heck, probably a year and a half. Then today at work she calls out of the blue."

Cole spun around with this news and walked back over, stopping and standing in front of the seated pair. He stared down at Walker.

Walker, feeling like the detective wanted a response, obliged.

"My administrative assistant took the call."

"What did Betheny say?"

"I don't know; I didn't talk to her. I was late for a meeting and had just gotten off the phone with my wife, Kate." Matt cut his eyes towards the sliding door, a few feet away, as if the gesture would explain to the dynamic duo who Kate was.

Graley spoke.

"So, you didn't talk to her?"

"No, like I said I was late for a meeting."

"Did your secretary talk with her?"

Matt couldn't hold back his smartass response. This was a fastball down the middle of the plate and it begged to be smacked.

"Like I said, she answered the phone, so of course she spoke with her, detective."

Matt held back a big smile, but he noticed Graley did not.

Cole looked so pissed, Matt wondered if he'd take a swing at him.

Detective Graley, still smiling, added her thoughts to the conversation.

"Please be more specific, Mr. Walker."

"Jane, my administrative assistant, spoke with her. I don't know how much though. I told her to put Betheny through to my voice mail. It's why I decided to drive over to her place this afternoon. To find out why she called."

Cole pounced. "You say it's been a year and a half since you've spoken with her, and today you just decide to drive over to her place? You couldn't just call her? Or was it you forgot something after beating her up, and you wanted to go back to get it? Or possibly finish her off?"

Matt stood. Looking down at the smaller, diminutive Cole who had a smirk on his face, he held back building rage. At six feet four inches tall, Matt found himself staring down at most people. He wanted to punch the piece of shit detective but went for the stare down and choice words instead.

"Listen, asshole. Why I went there is no one's business but my own. And if you want to arrest me, then do it."

Matt paused, expecting to be wrestled to the ground, or at the very least handcuffed. Since neither happened, he concluded.

"Then grow up and act like a professional."

Graley stood, pushing Cole back she got between the two.

"Go have a smoke, Cole. Then walk down to the lake and the body. Start getting a layout of what is going on down there." Cole didn't budge.

"Now, Detective!"

Cole turned. Smiling, he reached into his coat pocket and pulled out his cigarettes. Walker watched as the cop walked down the steps of the deck onto the grass. Matt noticed the damn ground needed to be raked as Cole dragged his feet through the autumn-colored leaves as he made his way toward the floating body. He wanted to chase after the asshole and give him a beating, hoping the release would somehow make him feel better.

Matt turned and looked through the sliding door into his home. Gazing inside and seeing nothing, he felt the resurrection of a sick feeling deep in the pit of his gut for Betheny. Wishing this were all a nightmare, Matt moved the tip of his right foot up, then down, then up, then back down. The soles of his rich brown leather shoes smacked the wooden deck eleven times.

Interesting Indeed

Matt stood next to Detective Graley on the deck. Kate joined them with Koda, on a leash who sat dutifully next to his new best friend without a command or even a hand gesture.

A nervous Matt, impressed with the dog's obedience, felt more guilt sweep through him like a southwestern flash flood. He felt as though he had done everything he was being questioned about. It was demoralizing how the mind worked and, in this case, clouded his judgment as if he were guilty. Matt watched enough Law and Order to know a murder was almost always the spouse or related to the spouse. Law and Order be damned, he had nothing to gain from Betheny's death, and he hoped the detectives would soon realize it.

Matt decided to quit stalling. He wanted to tell Kate about Betheny before Cole got back on the deck. Turning, he looked straight into her gorgeous blue eyes and the words stumbled out of his mouth with the grace of a lumberjack.

"Kate, I was late this afternoon because I swung by my former wife's place."

Kate's demeanor went from confused to upset. Matt recognized the change at once. He wondered if Graley noticed as well. He braced himself for heat.

"Number two, Betheny, to be specific, dear." Matt let the words fall out of his mouth in a slow and deliberate fashion. As if the way he announced it would have an effect on Kate's demeanor.

Graley, watched with purpose and intent focusing on both players' facial expressions and body language.

Kate, whispered "Namaste" and breathed. She gathered herself, looked down at Koda and patted him on the top of his head before speaking.

"I know who number two is, Matt. Why did you go over there? You haven't seen her in over a year or so, right?"

The way Kate emphasized the question, with possible doubt, made Matt feel even worse. If someone asked him the range of emotions he had gone through the last couple of hours, he had no words, other than gut-wrenching.

"She called out of the blue today, Kate."

Matt felt the guilt swirl and crash inside his chest. *Shit*, he thought to himself, *now my heart*. He felt as if the flu were coming on and his body was under mental assault. One that was having a negative impact on him more than just mentally. Physically, he was taking a pounding on a molecular level. He'd had enough depressing arguments over the years with a loved one to recognize the feeling. Often, he got physically sick as a result.

Kate looked dejected as he continued.

"Jane tried to get me to take the call, but I had just gotten off the phone with you and was late to my afternoon meeting. You know how I hate being late, so I told Jane to put her through to my voicemail. Anyway, after work my curiosity got the best of me, so I decided to swing by the old place and see what she wanted. I know I could have just called, but something pulled me there. I can't explain it."

Matt's insides relaxed as the words flowed out of his mouth. He realized Jane would be able to confirm this line of events since she did take the call from Betheny. Not only would she back up his story, she would most likely talk with Kate about it without him asking her to do so. Perhaps tomorrow night when the two went out as they did almost every Friday night.

Graley relaxed, realizing she didn't need to focus on the couple's conversation with the same intent. Body language had calmed in the two, and a gentle touch from Kate to Matt spoke volumes to Graley about the two's affection toward each other. She continued to listen closely, focused on trying to understand, and read between any lines. Many years of detective work told her she might be able to pick up the minutest, and critical detail. So, Graley stayed focused. Besides, Matt hadn't told his current wife the critical aspect of his visit yet.

"Well, why didn't you tell me when you got home, Matt?" Kate reached out and took hold of Matt's hand.

"I was going to."

Matt stammered. Only Kate noticed.

"I was waiting for the right moment. I didn't want to spoil your enthusiasm about your new friend and figured it could wait. You know how I am always looking for the perfect moment, which by now one would think I was wise enough to know doesn't exist. Lesson learned, sweetie."

"You've said that before, Matt."

Graley noted Kate's quick response.

Swallowing, Matt squeezed Kate's hand and tensed up again. He steadied himself mentally in anticipation of the next bit of information he would spout. But why? He didn't do anything wrong. Why did he feel like a damn teenager about to get caught doing something wrong by his father? He braced himself, waited for a hand drop, and an upset Kate.

"Hang on Kate, this gets worse."

"In what way?" Kate replied with clarity and poise.

Graley was impressed with the way this woman handled herself.

Pressing on, Matt regurgitated facts like a spigot that hadn't been turned on for months; now cleansing itself of all the grime built up in the pipes.

"Well, when I got there, cops were all over the place. They had the street blocked. I had to stop, was told to roll my window down, and they asked me if I lived on the street. I said no, but I used to. I told them where specifically, when asked, and realizing Betheny's house used to be mine, they had me go to the house to talk with the detectives. Graley, here, being one of them."

Matt nodded to Graley standing next to him. She scribbled on her notepad, which made Matt tense up again.

Graley looked up at the mention of her name, acknowledging Kate.

"God, Matt, that must have been scary," Kate replied.

Matt was appreciative and relieved in the way Kate was behaving so far. It helped him carry on.

"Scary isn't the right word, but definitely nervous. Anyhow, when I got there, Betheny looked like hell. It was as though she had been in a one-sided boxing match."

Kate dropped Matt's hand and put her hand to her mouth. Her eyes flashed fear and surprise.

"My God, Matt, what happened?"

"I don't think anyone knows yet, Kate. Isn't that right, detective?"

Graley, not wanting to tip her hand in any way, simply nodded. She didn't want Matt to know they had absolutely no idea what the hell happened.

Matt placed his attention back to Kate.

"There's worse news, Kate. After I left, the ambulance took Betheny to the hospital. I planned on calling to check up on her, but it doesn't matter anymore."

Graley made a note on her pad detailing Matt not telling Kate about Betheny running up to hug him when he arrived on scene. Not a crime, not even a blip, but an observation. She wondered if Matt would ever tell Kate. Graley knew Matt could be glossing over the fine details right now to speed up the outcome. Nonetheless, Graley found it an interesting piece of human behavior.

"Why doesn't it matter, Matt?"

Matt thought Kate let the question drag out almost as if she knew what was coming next. He reached out and put a gentle hand on Kate's shoulder.

"Because, Kate, when the detectives got here a few minutes ago, they told me Betheny had a brain aneurism and died."

Kate sat down in the chair. Koda put his front paws on her knees and tried to crawl into Kate's lap. Matt reached down to pull the dog off, but Koda wouldn't budge. He wanted to smack the darn dog out of reactive fear, but maintained his composure, choosing instead to admire the dog for wanting to comfort Kate.

"I know, Kate. Can you believe it? Anyhow I planned on telling you, then everything went to shit."

Kate, looking up at Matt, believed him. Wanted desperately to believe him. Matt had never given her any sign he was anything but honest.

"Can I get you a glass of water, Ma'am?" Graley blurted out and regretted her words the instant they left her mouth, knowing she shouldn't leave these two alone. She needed to hear what was being said.

"No. Thank you, though. I appreciate it. I'm fine, just startled. A lot to digest for sure. My God, Matt, this is so sad."

"Yes, it is. Thank you for being so supportive. I should have told you right away."

Graley wanted to break up the love fest, so she asked a quick question.

"Mr. Walker, I never asked you–what did the deceased say in the message she left on your office phone? Assuming she did leave one."

Matt, puzzled, responded right away.

"Damn, detective, I don't know! I forgot to check my messages. I was swamped at work today and don't typically get a lot of voicemail, so I never checked."

"Okay, well we are going to need to check, okay?"

Graley made a note in her pad to check the voicemail.

Cole returned to the base of the deck with two paramedics, or at least medical officials, interrupted.

Matt figured the two with Cole must not be paramedics since the body was clearly dead. They looked the part, though, in their outfits. He didn't know exactly who they were, but his curiosity had hold of him.

"Mr. Walker, could you please come over here? I would like to see if you can identify the body," Cole spoke with a commanding voice, not a requesting one, Matt noticed.

"Yes." Matt replied with trepidation.

Matt made his way across the deck moving forward on the stairs, landing on the bottom step of the deck. The gurney was close enough that he didn't need to go all the way to the ground. Cole pulled the sheet back over the body revealing a recognizable face beyond what he could fathom as possible. Matt could only imagine what he must have looked like. Cole had the facial visibility this time, not Graley. Graley stood next to Matt and focused on the body.

"Ah, you recognize her, then, Mr. Walker?"

Based on Walker's reaction, Cole figured he did know the woman. Further, Cole expected Walker to lie about it.

Graley noticed Mr. Walker's tapping while reaching into her jacket pocket and pulling her notebook back out. She clicked her stainless steel mechanical pencil. A gift from her mother and father the day she made detective, almost twenty years ago. The youngest woman detective in the history of the Medford police force. Her father was so proud, he couldn't stop smiling. He agreed to one photo after another for the only time Graley could remember.

Readying herself to write, Graley put the pencil to the pad letting the lead hover just off the paper, thinking the night was getting interesting indeed.

"Well, Walker, what is it? You recognize the body or not?" Cole interjected.

Graley watched Walker's face as he responded in a sad and quiet voice. Much softer and lower than before. Graley couldn't imagine his next words.

"Yes, I do."

Matt swallowed hard and tapped his left hand against his thigh eleven times before he spoke.

"It's my first wife, Sharon."

In the Name of Odin

Matt watched the two men cart his first wife away. He tried to stay attentive as Graley spoke to Cole. He couldn't remember when focusing was such a challenge.

"Any idea as to the cause of death yet, Cole?"

Cole shook his head. Grinning, he directed his attention toward Matt Walker.

"Nope, too early to tell, Graley. Perhaps drowning, maybe a small caliber bullet to the back of the head and the bullet rattled around turning her brain into scrambled eggs, or perhaps she was poisoned and dropped in the water."

Matt held back his anger. He had a good idea what Cole was up to and didn't want to give the arrogant cop the satisfaction by losing control. He wanted, and needed, to stay calm.

Stunned, Matt wasn't sure what to think. He had no ill-will for Sharon. Even though she was a former, he never would have wished an early death, let alone murder–assuming it was a murder. She had good friends on the opposite shore of the lake; perhaps it was an accident. He found the idea hard to believe as he knew Sharon was more than capable in the water.

Graley jotted down a few notes, including Walker's use of the term "former," which she found odd, and looked at Matt. With not a lot of homicide experience under her belt, she tried to figure out what direction to take the questioning.

She'd had a couple of nasty homicides early on in her career, but they were easy to solve. A homeless man killed by another vagrant, and a teenage girl who had overdosed on heroin. Charges were brought against a pimp in the teenage girl case. Both cases were cut and dry and solved within days. Graley still had the image in her head of the girl who she herself had found in a concrete overpass in the middle of Medford. She was close to the age of a friend's daughter. It affected her for months.

Cole, on the other hand, had never had a single case that Graley was aware of. She could see that her partner was almost giddy with the day's events. She felt sour bile trying to rise in the back of her throat and felt bad for Matt and Kate Walker. Keeping her composure was a must right now. As she learned with the teenage girl, she found almost a decade ago, feelings could come later.

The present situation, the death of two women, for all Graley knew, was the responsibility of Matt Walker. She didn't happen to think so, but she couldn't afford to make any assumptions. She certainly couldn't allow the asshole Cole to start making them.

Graley jumped in and took charge of the conversation's direction.

"Cole, go talk with the guys hauling her into the morgue. See if they found anything on the body. Take good notes because you don't know what matters and what doesn't at this point."

Cole looked at Graley like she was an alien. Graley noticed him looking down at her notepad.

"You don't have a notepad do you, Cole?"

Cole didn't want to admit this little fact in front of Walker, so he lied.

"It's in the car. I'll get it and then question the jerkoffs about the victim."

Cole looked Walker in the eye as he stressed the word "victim." The rookie detective was pissed when the intended dig didn't seem to have any adverse effect. Cole figured the S.O.B. had something to do with these deaths. He just didn't know what, exactly, but told himself he'd find out. With this, his first opportunity on a murder case, failure couldn't come. Solving cases like this were a great ticket for advancement in the police force, and he wanted out of his Podunk little fucking hometown. The quickest way out was solving a big case, getting the attention of those in the Eugene or Portland PD, and then watching the Rogue Valley disappear in the rearview mirror.

Cole spun around, then headed around the side of the house. He kicked at the dirt trying to figure out where the hell he would get paper or a notepad to write on.

"Ah, fuck it," he said out loud as he caught up with the body escorts. He had a great memory. He didn't need a notepad like the old bag Graley.

Back at the deck, Graley turned her attention to a visibly upset Matt Walker. His wife Kate was trying her best to console him. Graley felt there might be tension between the two. She chalked it up to a jealous wife trying to deal with an ex. Throw in an ex-wife's murder, and hell, there were bound to be raw nerves. She made a note in her notepad anyhow. *Leave nothing to chance*, she reminded herself.

"Listen, Matt, pay no attention to detective Cole. He is a definite work in progress," Graley said, biting her lip but unable to stop the harsh words from rolling out of her mouth.

"He is being a childish dick. Excuse me, Ma'am."

"No, I agree, he is being a dick." Kate responded.

Graley's calculated gamble paid off. Kate relaxed and consoled Matt. The detective had enough experience with body language through the years to recognize the difference. She needed these two to trust her, and the quickest way was through the wife. Graley knew the real power always lay in the hand of a woman.

"Thank you, Ma'am. Cole thinks the quickest way to get himself promoted is by solving a murder case. Problem is, he doesn't have the first clue how to go about it. I will keep him reined in."

Graley continued looking at the two.

"If he should get out of hand, let me know," she added as an afterthought, to continue working a bond development with the couple.

Graley noticed Mrs. Walker was listening, but she didn't think Matt Walker heard a single word. She didn't know what the relationship was between Walker and his exes, yet. She would, given enough time, figure out their strengths and weaknesses toward each other.

"Mr. Walker, we are going to have to take you into the station for questioning. Do you have a problem with this?"

Nothing. No visible reaction whatsoever. Not a head shake, flinch, or squirm was noticeable in the Adirondack chair Walker's butt had taken residence in again. A slumped-over Walker was either in shock, or a pro at ignoring people. Nothing he did tipped Graley off in any meaningful way.

"Matt, honey, Officer Graley is asking you a question."

Kate Walker patted Matt on the shoulder and then squeezed, trying to get him to acknowledge what was being said.

"It's Detective, Mrs. Walker, and thanks."

Graley noticed this interaction got Matt Walker's attention. Simple words between her and Mrs. Walker seemed a peculiar way to wake him up. Graley chalked his sudden attentiveness to loyalty toward Kate. Matt Walker had a propensity for occasional oddities about him for sure. Nervous tapping, what appeared to be talking under his breath, and odd ways of touching his leg or objects around him. If Graley didn't know any better, she thought the guy had OCD issues. Being loyal to a spouse, a note Graley jotted down, was a check mark in the positive column.

"I'm sorry, Detective. Please forgive me."

"It is quite all right, Mrs. Walker. It isn't easy to make detective, so we get a little fussy over the title is all."

Graley turned her attention back to the now attentive Matt Walker.

"We need to take you downtown for questioning, Mr. Walker. My recommendation is that Mrs. Walker stay here. The crime scene specialists at the lake may be a while longer. She can certainly come down to the station and wait if she chooses. We should have you out of there in an hour or so. How does that sound?"

Matt stood out of creaking deck chair and faced Graley. To his surprise, Koda stood steadfast next to him, as if man dog were in this together.

Matt didn't glare at Graley like he had Cole moments earlier. His voice was calm, controlled, and confident.

"It sounds like shit. That is what it sounds like."

Matt inched forward toward detective Graley expecting her to react.

"Arrest me if you want and take me in, because I am not voluntarily going anywhere tonight. I didn't do a damn thing. I am tired, pissed, scared, and need to think."

Matt held his hands out in front of him waiting for cuffs. He didn't care what happened at this point. He watched Graley lean back. She had a surprised look on her face as she got in a defensive position. When she didn't say anything, Matt responded.

"No? Okay, then. I will be down at the station in the morning after I have had a chance to call my lawyer."

Matt grabbed Kate's hand, took Koda's leash and pivoted away entering his home through the sliding patio door. Dog and wife number three were both in step. Graley dropped her chin, shook her head, thought she might have to rethink who held the power in this relationship, and wondered what in the name of Odin just happened.

"Two"

Graley stood outside a closed patio door holding her notepad in a clinched fist. She felt the paper crinkle under the pressure of her fingers. Noticing the cloudy glass door splattered with bugs, Graley contemplated Matt Walker's reaction. Part of her wanted to rush in after Walker, slap the cuffs on him, and take his ass down to the station. Thinking he was not himself, in shock about the losses, saved him from Graley's wrath. The fact that she thought he was innocent also helped his cause.

Matt Walker being the murderer didn't make sense, logistically. He had to be innocent; she thought again, as if trying to convince herself, so her mind and body would act. He seemed to be a stand-up guy and didn't appear like the murdering type, as if that meant anything at all. The whole "looks can be deceiving" was something Graley was aware of. Hell, she had nothing to arrest him on. Any attorney worth their salt would have him released in an hour. Watching Walker's former wife Betheny's reaction when he arrived at the crime scene, Detective Graley figured the guy had to be a decent man.

Decision made, releasing her fist from around the notepad, Graley slid the glass door open. Walker and Kate were standing in the kitchen. Mrs. Walker with a glass of wine, Mr. Walker with a beer. The dog, Koda, sat dutifully at Kate's feet. He started to move toward Graley until Kate told him to stay. An appreciative Graley stepped inside.

"Mr. Walker, please be at the station at 0900 tomorrow. With or without your lawyer. If you can't make it by then, we will be forced to come get you. Understood?"

Graley stood her ground, kept her head up projecting authority–something she did not lack while in uniform. Part of her expected Walker to ignore her altogether and then she would be faced with a new challenge. She was relieved when he responded right away.

"Understood, Detective, and thanks. I'm more than stunned and confused right now. I apologize for my reaction a few minutes ago."

"Well, I would like to say I understand, but I don't. Thanks for the apology. See you in the morning, 0900, and don't be late. Mrs. Walker, here is my business card. If either of you need anything before tomorrow morning, you can call me at any time, okay?"

Handing the card to Mrs. Walker, Detective Graley stepped back outside and slid the door closed. She felt better about the current situation, for the moment. The likelihood that Walker would run was slim in her mind, but Graley knew she was taking a risk not questioning him at the station tonight. Cole would, of course, disagree and want to sweat Walker all night. Graley knew the statistics didn't support sweating suspects. If anything, the act typically did nothing more than force false confessions. Besides, she knew Walker was far too smart to talk with them at all without an attorney present.

Walking down the steps of the deck, Graley peered across the lawn at the lights flooding the dimming bank of the lake. Investigators were still swarming but appeared to be winding down for the night. She figured they would be back in the morning scouring for any clues and potential evidence. The CSI were relentless in their dogged determination to find the smallest items which may prove fruitful in solving a case.

Around the side of the house approaching the front, Graley watched as the two body snatchers, paid by the county, climbed into their vehicle leaving Cole standing by himself. She approached Cole, who lit a cigarette.

"Well, what did they say, Cole? Anything?"

"Not shit. Other than the body being heavy. They thought it should have been lighter than it was. One of them said the other was full of shit, the body felt normal, and to stop dreaming of alien abduction or something. Hell, Gray, I couldn't follow what the hell they were saying."

Cole took a long drag on his cigarette and blew smoke high into the crisp air. Graley watched as it hung like warming smoke around

Rogue Valley pear trees. Then he dropped his cigarette on the pavement and smashed it with his left foot moving back and forth, smothering any potential threat.

"Not sure what women see in Mr. Matt-fucking-Walker, but all three of his wives are smoking hot. I bet you noticed that, Graley."

Graley cut her eyes at Cole who never missed a chance to rib her about her sexual preference. Neanderthals weren't on her list, and it pissed Cole off.

"Hard to miss Cole, especially for a freak like me. Get everything they said down in your notebook?"

Graley already knew her partner's answer but asked, anyway. She wanted to see what bullshit Cole would spin.

"Fuck you, Graley. I don't need a notebook."

"All right then, Sherlock. Let's go."

"What do you mean, go? Where's Walker? We are taking him in, right?"

"No, we are not. He will be down at the station at 0900 with or without his attorney. The poor bastard has had a rough enough night already. We don't need him down there tonight. Besides, there is a football game on. I figured you'd be pleased and heading to the bar."

"Fuck the game, the Rams will destroy the Seahawks anyway, let's sweat this guy. He knows more than he is telling us. I can sense it."

"Oh, you can, huh? Well I made the decision to let him get a good night's sleep. We will be better served if he is thinking clearly. He won't be tonight, I can tell you that. Get in the car, Cole, and drop it. My call."

Cole took a step toward the Walker's front door as if he were going to go in and make an arrest in spite of Graley's order. He shook his head, dropped his chin and spun back around to the car. He climbed into the passenger seat slamming the door. Graley walked over to a police car behind her car. Two cops were standing alongside.

"Gentleman. Not sure who is in charge here. You, Fontana?"

Graley hadn't recognized either of them. She picked out the one that looked to be the alpha. She was correct.

"As a matter of fact, Detective, I am. Why?"

Graley smiled and without hesitation replied, "Well, we need to leave a car here overnight. Mr. Walker is expected to be at the station at 0900 tomorrow. I want to make sure he gets a good night sleep and then has an escort in the morning, okay?"

"Understood. I will call it in and make the arrangements. Is that all, detective?"

"Yes, and thanks," Graley answered as she reached into her jacket pocket, pulled out a business card, and handed it to the officer. The card read Fratellis Restaurant, with her name written in precise block letters on the lower left. On the back was printed, dinner for two—Graley's tab.

"Here is an Italian dinner on me for the both of you at Fratellis."

"Shit, thanks, Detective Graley!"

Fontana looked at the card and then back at Graley.

"No worries. My friend's restaurant, and she will take good care of you. Only two though. If you want dates, they are on you. She is a stickler and the back of that business card says "two," so that is what she'll give you."

"Got it, Detective, and thanks again."

Officer Fontana touched the tip of his hat and nodded.

Graley spun around and headed for the squad car, bracing herself for an earful of pouty-shit from Cole.

Drifted Apart

"See, sweetie, that wasn't so bad."

Matt appreciated Kate's upbeat effort, but today had to be one of the worst days he had ever dealt with, and he did not want to be upbeat. Hell, he didn't even want to feel better right now. Not yet, at least. Depression and mourning were warranted. Weren't they?

"You don't want to piss off the police, Matt," Kate continued. "Anyone who watches any TV at all knows that."

Matt turned from Kate, setting his beer on the counter. He placed both hands on the sink, staring out the window toward the lake. The light shining off the water, where his first wife had been left floating like a rotting log, seemed more intense tonight. He couldn't imagine why anyone would do this to her. She was a fantastic person. A respected nurse, involved in the local community, plenty of good quality friends, and a nice home. In many ways, a pillar of the Rogue Valley professional community.

Koda walked over and sat down next to Matt's leg, pressing up against him. Never much of a pet person, he was touched. The energy transferred from the dog comforted him. He bent down to pet Koda on the back. Koda rewarded him with a big wet lick on the cheek. Matt, thankful he turned his face at the last second, gave the dog an extra rough rub on the neck.

"Wow, I can't believe what I just saw, Matt! I don't remember him kissing me yet! Should I be jealous?"

Matt shrugged, turned, and in a gruff voice replied, "Hardly."

"Look, Matt, I don't know what to say. All right. Is there anything I can do for you?"

A loud click came from the back yard. Matt stood and saw the crime scene lights turn off. Resting his hands on the counter again, he stared out the back window into the vast dark space over the lake, thinking about what Kate said.

"I don't know if I ever told you what happened between me and Sharon, Kate."

Matt picked his beer back up and turned facing Kate, now with large alert eyes. He pressed the warm, smooth edge of the bottle against his dry, chapped lips and took a long drink, draining the last of the local Pilsner.

"No, handsome, you didn't."

Waiting, thinking of the words to choose, Matt paused before continuing.

"Well, she was a good person. Probably too good for the likes of me. We met in college, fell in love–so we thought–and got married. Too fast. Things went well for a year or two. No major fights, just petty relationship crap we both let go of right away. She was getting her career going, and I was getting my business going, so we were both busy. This provided a great window shade on intimacy, unfortunately."

"What was her career?"

"She was an RN, and a damn good one. She won all kinds of awards and was on a fast track for promotion at the hospital."

Matt pictured Sharon in her uniform. She had them professionally cleaned. They were always perfectly pressed. If she got any stains on them at all, they were donated to the local Goodwill and she purchased new ones.

"She was great at her job. Earned second in charge within five years, and last I heard was in complete charge of the nursing staff at Medford General."

"Wow, she must have been good. Well, what did you guys in? Why did the marriage fail? Who left who?"

Matt walked over to the recycle bin, dropped the beer bottle inside, and returned to the refrigerator. This time he selected the porter from Deschutes Brewery. He returned to the sink and leaned against the counter facing Kate. Koda laid at her feet.

"He seems like he is going to be a sweet dog. I am glad you got him Kate."

Kate bent down and gave Koda a couple of gentle pats on his head. The dog's tail sped up its wagging.

"I'm not really sure what happened to us." Matt replied in a distant, monotone voice.

"Come on, Matt. Everyone knows. Most don't want to admit it, but everyone knows, and usually before it ends. I never have taken you for one of those "bury your head in the sand" type of people."

Matt took a long drink of his beer. He swirled the dark Porter around in his mouth feeling the richness as it warmed his skin and stuck to his teeth. He picked up the smokiness and his palate thought it could recognize coffee tones, perhaps subtle hints of chocolate. Swallowing, he directed his attention back to Kate as his mind contemplated how best to answer her question.

"I loved her, Kate. She was good to me. I was shaken-up when she left. Neither one of us cheated on the other person, we never fought, enjoyed spending time with each other, and the sex was good. Just too infrequent. But doesn't everyone complain about that?"

"Is that true, Matt? Are you saying you complain about not getting enough sex with me? I can remedy that right now if it is a problem."

Kate winked and smiled at Matt. He noticed her continuing effort at lightening his mood. He was still not ready to let go of the anger and his stress.

"Hell, no, Kate. If anything, with you, I need a break from time to time. But my male ego and fear of never having sex again keeps me coming back for more."

The two smiled at each other. Kate stood there, tense. Matt could see she was losing motivation at cheering him up. He wondered what she was really thinking. Did she now have doubts about him as a man and husband? Did she think he killed the two formers? Questions lingered and festered in the back of his mind as he continued discussing Sharon with her.

"In short, Kate, we were both young and busy, so wrapped up in our careers we didn't make time for each other and just drifted apart."

"Well, Matt, people do drift apart. I'm sorry. Not for the divorce, but for the death. This can't be easy for you, and clearly you still care for her."

Matt watched Kate set her wine glass down on the counter, kneel, and pet Koda again.

"Matt, do you mind if the dog sleeps in the house tonight? I want him to be an outside dog, but the first night would be better for him to be inside. I promise I won't make it a habit."

Tipping the Porter back, pressing it firmly against his mouth, Matt didn't remove the craft beer from his lips until the final drop trickled over his lip. Setting the bottle on the counter, he stared out the kitchen window one more time. A full rabbit moon, bright with intensity, ricocheted off the glass-surfaced lake. Contemplating how Sharon's body got in the lake and why in the world someone would want to kill her, Matt couldn't imagine a single soul that didn't like her. Pivoting, he watched as Kate gave her animal-loving affection to Koda.

Kate rose and walked the few steps over to Matt, taking him by the hand.

"Come with me, handsome. Time for bed. You are going to have another stressful day tomorrow, so let's see if I can't do something to bolster your fragile male ego."

A Hundred Different Things

Graley grabbed the grime-covered gear shift. Thinking about the level of germs on the grip, she put the police car in drive. The rear-view mirror showed two officers standing by their squad car outside the Walkers' home as she drove away. Grimacing, bracing for tension, Graley waited on Cole's whining, which she knew was coming. He started before she had a chance to leave the Walker driveway in the rear-view.

"Please explain to me the brilliance behind letting Matt Walker stay in his own home tonight after his ex-wives, or formers, were murdered. I don't fucking get it. And who the hell calls an ex a former? Something is off about that guy."

A strategically prepared Graley ignored the "former" comment for now. She didn't want to say a damn thing now, but since he was her partner, he had the right to know what she was thinking about the case. Despite his being such an asshole. Didn't he against her better judgement; Graley relented.

"First, his ex-wives are dead, but we don't yet know they were murdered, do we? One was attacked, it appears, but we don't know that definitively. Second, the woman in the lake may have drowned after slipping on the shore, a dock, off a boat, hell a hundred different things."

Graley didn't believe what she espoused, but was trying to bolster the decision to let Matt Walker sleep in his own bed tonight. A decision she hoped like hell wasn't going to be met with regret.

"Whatever you have to tell yourself, Graley. I am going to put it on the record that I disagree. We should be questioning him right now."

"Whatever you want to put in your report is your business. I don't give a shit, Cole. I am lead on this case and it's my call."

Cole pulled out a cigarette and lit it up. Graley, watching as Cole rolled down his window, hoped the smoke would get sucked outside. She knew better though. Most of it would linger inside the car, like always.

Graley smiled and let Cole have his little cigarette victory. The smell pissed her off, but she wasn't going to satisfy her partner's immature want for conflict by vocalizing her displeasure. There would be a better time to do battle.

"Listen, Cole, we don't know what happened. I don't think Walker had anything to do with either death. We could take him down and sweat him and piss him off, sure. But, he wouldn't answer a single question without an attorney present. I saw the look the wife who we think was attacked gave him when he arrived. She wasn't scared of Walker at all. And again, we don't know what happened with the second body in the lake. I want Walker on our side working *with* us, not keeping information from us. If for some outlandish reason he did do it, we will find out soon enough."

Cole fidgeted and threw his finished cigarette out the rolled-down window. Graley watched out of the corner of her eye as he blew his last puff of smoke forward. It slid off the windshield, then blew back from the vents. Graley could feel the anger and tension coming off Cole. She also knew he was smart enough not to push his displeasure too far with her.

Graley put the turn signal on, decelerating off the highway heading into the heart of the city.

"You want me to drop you off at the station, or your favorite watering hole, Cole?"

Cole couldn't believe how calm Graley could be. This pissed him off more than anything. The bitch had to get rattled sometimes, didn't she? Cole contemplated the question a second, already knowing what his answer was. *Fuck it*, he thought to himself. He was glad they weren't questioning Walker tonight. He wanted to unwind. Perhaps the hot little brunette would be at his favorite craft brew pub tonight.

"Drop me off at Outlaw River Craft Ales, please. I'll grab a cab home. I need to let off steam."

"IPA or Ale, Cole?"

Cole smiled and anticipated the beer smell and hoppy taste sliding down his throat, warming his belly.

"IPA, of course. The hoppier the better. Why? You know anything about beer?"

Graley laughed.

"I have been drinking beer longer than you've been a man, Cole. I prefer Ales. Don't like what the hoppy IPAs do to my sinuses. I get all stuffed up. Never could get past the bitter taste, either. I know they are all the rage right now, but not for me. I have tried plenty of them, but just don't like the lingering bitter taste."

Graley accelerated from the stopped position at the four-way stop. She turned left into the parking lot of Cole's favorite brew house.

"Well, I get it. Took me a while to develop a taste for them, I admit. Stouts and Porters are my bane. I can't stand them."

Bringing the car to a stop, Graley tried to see which Vendor truck was outside. It looked to be the cheese sandwich mobile. Probably good. She thought about joining Cole and grabbing dinner here, but tired and a little more than stressed, she decided to get over to her father's house sooner rather than later.

Cole opened the car door, paused for a second, then stood and slammed the door starting to walk away.

Graley watched Cole stop, turn and come back to the car. She knew the way he hesitated getting out of the car that he wanted to say something. Bending over, resting his hands on the door Cole put his head partway in and talked with a calm voice, for once.

"I get why you did what you did tonight by not bringing Walker in, Graley. I do. I don't agree with it, but I get it."

"Thanks, Cole, I appreciate you saying something. Enjoy your beer and call a damn taxi, okay?"

Cole, with his predictable smirk wasted no timing in replying.

"I am hoping to get a ride home from a lady-friend tonight. Something you would like, I am sure."

Graley took her foot off the brake easing the car forward. Cole held onto the door and wouldn't let go walking sideways with the slow moving car.

"Come on already, Cole. Go have a beer. I want to go home."

"One last thing."

Graley applied the brakes.

"What, Cole? I want to get home and get some sleep."

Cole looked down at the ground, kicked a pebble with his right foot, and then looked back up at Graley.

He wondered if he should say anything at all as he knew his efforts at frustrating and pissing off his partner today were more successful than usual. He pressed forward leaving any worry of a potential bad outcome to drift away in the fall air.

"Aren't you worried at all about Matt Walker's current wife, Kate?"

Short Notice, an Adirondack Chair, and a Falling Star

Matt rolled over to face the clock. 12:30 AM. His head hurt, his brain was racing, and he couldn't sleep. Kate did what she could for him in the way of relaxation. However, a relaxed body wasn't his problem now. A restless mind was.

Seeing Sharon's floating body in the lake tarnished his memories in unimaginable ways. He hadn't seen former number one in years. Seeing her body and discussing the past with her brought back a flood of emotions and recollections. He still cared for Sharon, knew he always would, and was overcome with sadness at the finality of her death.

Thoughts bouncing back and forth between finding Sharon in the lake and the eerie look in Betheny's eyes wouldn't allow Matt's brain to settle. He moved the sheet and blanket aside, sat up, pivoted, and then set his feet on the floor.

Looking back over his shoulder, Matt watched Kate, in a deep peaceful sleep, breathe. He couldn't fathom the idea of anything happening to her. Another thought which couldn't escape him now. What are the odds of two separate accidents happening, on the same day, to both former wives? He wasn't sure, but figured he had a better chance of winning Mega-Millions.

Rising from the edge of the bed, he snatched his cell phone from the nightstand and headed downstairs. He thought about a cup of coffee but knew the caffeine this late would guarantee he got no sleep. Walking into his office, he couldn't believe he forgot to call his attorney friend. Jim Davies had handled lots of business work for him over the years, but nothing criminal. Trusting Davies, Matt hoped he could handle the current situation. He didn't feel like shopping for someone new.

Swiping his way through contacts on the phone, not finding what he wanted, he gave up and typed in 'lawyer' in the search box.

There it is, Matt said to himself.

He dialed the number, preparing to leave a voice message.

"Hey Jim, Matt Walker here. This isn't work-related. I need to know if you can help me out with a personal matter. Both my former wives were found dead yesterday and suspicious activity lingers around both deaths. I am being questioned tomorrow morning at 9 AM in Medford at the police station."

Matt paused for a second wondering how much he should or shouldn't say.

"Oh, sorry for the late call and short notice. The police left here not too long ago."

The thought intrigued Matt's curiosity, so with the phone still against his cheek, he made his way over to the front door and peeked outside seeing a police car still parked in front. He stood looking out the window while finishing his message.

"One of my former wives, Sharon, was found floating in the lake at the edge of my yard. Anyhow, if you can please meet me in the morning. Thanks–and Jim, I appreciate anything you can do for me. Hope to see you in the morning."

Matt pressed the pound sign on the screen and waited for the phone's voice mail to confirm his message had been sent.

Koda, restless as well, or just curious, walked in the office. To his surprise Matt liked the company. Making his way into the kitchen, Matt set his cell phone down on the counter, then reached down patting the new family member on the head who was shadowing him.

"Want to go outside, boy?"

Koda recognized at least one of the words, and excitedly moved his body in a back and forth snakelike motion, his tail wagging with the steady rhythm of a helicopter rotor. Matt slid on his outdoor slippers, then pulled back the sliding door. Koda led the way.

The once warm night air had cooled with the moon's rising. Matt loved the crispness of the air in Southern Oregon. He had traveled the world and always took a deep breath heading off the airplane when landing at Medford's airport. The Pacific Northwest air was like no other to him. He wondered if Koda, sniffing the ground in a zig zag motion heading to the water's edge, smelled anything significant.

Matt stepped over an extension cord running to the police lights. Wanting to flip them on, more out of curiosity than anything, he wondered if he could turn them on. Keeping his curiosity at bay, Matt made his way over to the lower deck and stepped up the three steps to reach the main platform. Sitting down on one of the Adirondack chairs, he made himself comfortable. Staring up at the stars, he started to count them. Reaching a rhythm, he stopped at thirty-nine, knowing his effort was futile.

Finding a comfortable position at Matt's feet, Koda laid his head down. Reaching over, Matt grabbed a cushion off one of the other chairs and placed it behind his head. He appreciated the connection of another living being, and the warmth of Koda's skin against his ankle.

Matt tilted his head back, eyes intently scanning for the dippers until he found them. At least he thought he did. No matter how many times he stared at the night sky, he never fully understood what he saw.

A falling star raced against the dark, sparkling canvas, plunging downward toward the lake. As Matt's eyes closed with the heaviness of the day's events, he wondered for the shortest moment if the star fell into the lake.

The Fleeting Dream

Graley eased the police cruiser out of the parking lot, coming to a complete stop at a four-way intersection. She checked the rear-view mirror and saw that no one was behind her or heading toward her. Sitting there thinking, she weighed on what Cole had moments ago asked her.

"Aren't you worried at all about Walker's current wife?"

Contemplating driving back to the Walker residence, Graley thought again about bringing him in tonight for questioning. She knew she could permanently piss him off, all but guaranteeing no cooperation. Bringing him in would make sure Mrs. Walker would be safe. At least for a night. But there was a police cruiser outside Walker's home and if for some strange and unexpected reason Walker was the guy, he wouldn't do anything tonight. She hoped.

Decision made, the detective turned the car's turn signal on and headed for her father's place, leaving Matt Walker alone with his current wife. She reached over and turned on the radio, searching for the XM dial for the Billy Joel channel. Captain Jack was playing.

Nothing like a little downer to cap off a strange day, Graley chuckled to herself. She was just months short of retirement from the force, where she could draw a pension and get a job making real money, and now two suspicious deaths had happened. Well, at least she wouldn't be bored for a while.

Graley, tired of chasing down stolen car leads, missing bicycles, and domestic disputes where potheads were beating their wives or girlfriends sighed. She had hoped for a little excitement on the job, but unexplained deaths weren't on her exhilaration list. She reminded herself the deaths were unexplained. No murder had been confirmed yet, at least with the woman in the lake. The death of Walker's second wife was strange, and even though she died from the aneurism, the case could be made that the assailant exacerbated it, causing her death. Shady area, but it would have to be pursued as an unintentional manslaughter. For now, at least.

Graley caught herself singing along to Joel while wishing she could find a hole to crawl in. Her husband did the typical cop-wife thing fifteen years ago and left her. She couldn't blame him. She was never home and when he was; all she thought about was the damn job and being with someone else. Strange thing was she didn't even like men, or being a cop. For some inexplicable reason, all Graley could focus on was making it thirty years on the force come hell or high water so she could enjoy life. One that always seemed down the road. She contemplated realizing the need to focus on being in the present. Bullshit which always alluded her.

At the age of fifty-three, she was alone. Only her father, who struggled sometimes to remember who she was, would have anything to do with her. Her son and daughter were living in other states with their families, living their own lives. She talked to them at Christmas, sometimes on their birthdays if she remembered to call, and that was it. So, the goal of thirty thankless years had gotten her to this point and time. Living with her decaying father, no partner, and kids who couldn't care less if she was alive or not. A lonely existence.

Graley turned the vehicle left and watched as a deer walked across the road bouncing into one of Southern Oregon's hundred plus vineyards. The thought of getting home to her father, who would repeat over and over like a goddamned parrot, "It's never too late, it's never too late," depressed her. She hated when he said the phrase but knew it to be true. She needed to get her shit together and start getting out. Start living. She couldn't remember the last time she had been paddle-boarding or hiking. Growing up in Southern Oregon, her teen years were spent on the Rogue and Applegate rivers, and the High Lakes. Not spending time on them now was downright wrong. So many outdoor options, and yet she took part in none.

Graley sighed again as she eased the car into her parent's driveway, to a home that would be hers one day. Sitting in the driveway she contemplated falling asleep in the car. It wouldn't be the first time.

She wasn't sure she had the energy for her father tonight. She'd spend a few minutes reminding him who she was and, "Yes, I saw you this morning before I left for work." She knew she would have to put her father into a home soon or hire full-time home care. Neither of which she wanted to do.

With another sigh, Graley gripped the door handle with her left hand, pulled the dirty latch and placed her feet on the asphalt. It felt like her knees popped while she stood. She closed the door and pressed the key fob to lock it thinking about getting back to yoga. Her body was talking to her.

Heading to the side of the house, she moved the trash and recycle cans to the street's curb. Shoulders slouched, dragging a bit from the crazy day, she continued her slow pace. Today's deaths made her remember how life can end at a moment's notice in any number of ways.

Reaching the front porch, she thought about her paddleboard in the garage. It was probably filthy, sitting unused for years. As soon as she was done with this case, she was going to take two weeks off and head up to Lake of the Woods and spend time on the water. Perhaps she would even bust out one of her father's old fishing poles. Knowing damn good and well the pole would stay where it was, she enjoyed the dream.

Graley unlocked the door and entered the furnace atmosphere. Her father had turned the heat up again, thinking he had turned on the air conditioner. She walked over and switched the thermostat to the off position and started to open windows to cool it down. Graley could hear her dad moving around in the kitchen. She walked in to say hi and make dinner.

"Hi, Dad."

"It's never too late, it's never too late. Who are you?"

"It's your daughter, Dad, Mara, remember?"

Graley patted her father on the back. He looked down at his feet, shuffled them like he was Gene Kelly, and repeated the phrase she despised. Her stomach turned at the thought of putting her father in a retirement home.

In a Foul Mood

With the efficiency of a pro ball receiver, Cole headed for the counter where the craft brew staff were moving in a feverish pitch to serve the line of hop lovers. The wait wouldn't be too long tonight. Only a couple of minutes max. This gave Cole enough time to look at the chalkboard bragging about the week's beer lineup.

The menu was the same, save one new beer. A Mazama Imperial Stout, on nitro. Not one he would be trying. He considered telling Graley about it, got pissed about the suspect being allowed to stay home, and mumbled *fuck you* under his breath.

Cole stood in line wishing people would know what they wanted when they got to the counter. He couldn't help but notice Diane serving customers. She had on a tight black top and her standard Levi 501 jeans. All he could think about was getting her in bed. They had been out a couple of times in a group setting, and Cole knew she liked him. He wasn't confident how much though.

Tonight, he decided he was going to ask her out solo. After today's deaths, which were now an active part of his imagination, Cole realized life could be too short for certain people. He thought about regrets and how tiring they were. Glancing up at the one TV screen on the wall as he waited to be served, he saw the Rams were already up 14 in the first quarter. Figuring it may be time to switch allegiance from the silver and blue team, he finally heard, loud and clear, what had been alluding him.

"Next please," came the voice from the young guy behind the counter.

Shit, Cole mumbled under his breath. He wanted Diane to wait on him. He turned to the older couple behind him.

"Go ahead. I am not sure what I want yet."

A white lie as Cole knew exactly what he wanted. Beer was second on tonight's list of desires.

The couple said thanks and moved around him as he stepped back to clear a path. Once they reached the bar, Diane turned from the taps and called out next. She smiled when she recognized Cole.

Cole made his way over to the bar telling himself to relax and have fun.

"Hello, Officer. You on or off duty?"

"Hey, Diane. Off duty, thank the gods. I am tired and thirsty and need a good IPA. What do you recommend?"

Diane pushed her dark hair behind the ear on the right side of her porcelain face. She reached across the counter and lightly touched Cole on the wrist.

"You usually go with the Seven Oaks IPA, don't you?"

Cole smiled, pleased she remembered.

"Yes, I do. I will take one of those, please."

Diane spun around, grabbed a glass, found the IPA tap, tilted the glass slightly and started pouring. The distance wasn't too far to talk, so Cole continued.

"You closing tonight, Diane?"

Diane kept pouring and didn't respond.

Cole was wondering what the hell, but figured she didn't hear and asked again.

"Are you closing tonight, Diane?"

Diane, turned her head slightly, smiled but gave no response. She straightened the glass and topped off the beer with a nice minimal head. She glided back over to the bar and set the glass down talking with Cole in a lowered voice.

"I don't like shouting, Officer. People know my business when I shout, and I don't like people knowing my business."

"Please, Diane, call me Doug or Cole, but not Officer. I get that all day long, and I'm off duty now."

"Okay, Doug, you got it. And no, I don't close tonight. I am off at ten. Why?"

"I thought we could grab a bite to eat afterwards, get a coffee, and go somewhere else for a drink, perhaps. Just you and me, not the bar group."

"Sure, Doug. Sounds good. But my mom will want me home by eleven, so it will have to be quick. That all right?"

Cole must have looked like he was lost on a lonely dirt road. Diane started laughing and reached across the bar and gently slapped him on the shoulder.

"I'm kidding, Doug. Man, you need to relax. Cash or card?"

Cole laughed, trying to cover up his embarrassment. He wished he could slug her in the gut. He reached for his wallet and tossed a twenty on the counter.

"Keep the change."

Spinning away, avoiding her eye contact, Cole walked away without saying anything else. His childish reaction, based out of embarrassment and fear of rejection, left his intended target standing in disbelief. He wished he could take back his behavior just now. Another fucking regret as he halfheartedly looked around for someone to talk with.

Outside in the open air, Cole found an empty table near the vendor truck. Tonight's vendor was "Cheese Please." Cole had heard good things but them, but hadn't sampled their fare yet. He took a small drink of beer before setting it down on the table, along with napkins he didn't remember picking up. *This should let all the other assholes looking for a seat know to back off this area*, he thought.

Walking up to the vendor, Cole got in line and grabbed his cell phone out of his back pocket. He looked online at Facebook and Diane's profile, wondering why he got so mad. She was clearly joking with him, but he hated when people joked at him. He knew he was good at giving but horrible at receiving. Diane had great photos of herself on her Facebook page, but nothing too risqué and not too much personal information, which Cole liked. She seemed to be reserved in the right way. He had probably blown it.

"Next."

Cole hadn't even looked at the menu on the side of the truck. He glanced at it while stepping up to the window.

"I'll take a grilled cheese with pastrami and loaded fries please."

"Name please?"

"Huh?"

"Your name please, for the order, sir?"

Fuck, what was it tonight, Cole thought to himself? He wanted to reach through the small window on the side of the vendor truck and strangle the pimple-faced kid taking the order.

"Cole. Doug fucking Cole."

The young, startled kid turned to look over his shoulder at the man running the grill. The guy gave Cole a look letting him know he needed to get himself under control.

Cole didn't need a public incident tonight, so he backed off. Any more knocks against him and he could forget about any opportunity for advancement any time soon.

"Cole." He then turned his head, so the kid wouldn't hear, and whispered, "Asshole."

The kid smiled at the beast flipping cheese sandwiches and turned looking at Cole like he had just won a pissing contest.

"Eleven dollars, Cole. Cash or Card? If you use a card, we must charge seventy-five cents fee the first time. There won't be any other fees with additional purchases tonight though."

Cole grabbed his wallet and got his last twenty out. He handed the money to the kid without saying a word.

"Nine dollars is your change and we'll call your name out when it's ready."

Cole put the change in his wallet, except for a one which he dropped in the tip jar, then took it back out, sliding it into his front pocket unnoticed. He was in a foul mood and zit-face should have been nicer.

Cole returned to his tattered and scarred picnic table. Fortunately, no one had sat down in his spot. He wouldn't have been polite to anyone after the smack-down he got from the kid, and Diane's humiliating attack on him. Not to mention Graley's complete disregard for Cole's desire to sweat Walker. All this shit had him in a mood and he wanted, in a way, to strike back.

Sitting down, Cole took a drink of his IPA. Glancing down at the tabletop, wishing her weren't alone, he saw names of beers, a few women, and one guy, were etched into it. Moving his attention to his phone, he started to open the beer app, to log his location and drink, but looking up, and over his shoulder, he could see there was a clear viewing path to the bar. Diane was in eyesight. He stood and moved to the other side of the table. He wanted another beer but didn't want to stand in line. Perhaps the only knock on authentic warehouse-craft breweries, no waitresses.

Tonight's weather was nice for the fall. A slight chill in the air, but warm enough to be comfortable. Cole looked up at the heaters, standing static like long necked men with top hats on. He wondered if the staff would fire them up tonight.

Emotionally, Cole felt lousy and didn't know what to do about his attraction to Diane. He felt as though things could be different with her.

Hearing his name called in what sounded like a teenager dripping with condescension, Cole wished he hadn't ordered any food. He wanted to leave.

A Day Full of Surprises

Graley tugged at the bed sheet covering her dad's chin and then folded it back in a nice neat fashion. Just like he liked it.

"Don't do that. Why are you folding it back? I want it under my chin, you idiot. Why can't you be more helpful?"

"I'm sorry dad, my mistake. I will try to remember how to do it next time for you."

Fear of the obvious gripped Graley, then pulled at her yet again. She would have to make a phone call tomorrow and quit putting off her father's needs, not to mention her own.

"You only get one life," she whispered to herself.

Graley turned and walked away, stopping at the door in an exasperated fashion.

"Dad, you want the light off or on?"

"Off, stupid. How can a person sleep with the lights on?"

Her dad rolled to his side, appearing frustrated to Graley. She watched as the man who taught her so much about the world pulled the covers over his head like a four-year-old would in a fit of frustration.

Turning the light off, she left the door partially open. Her toes caught the edge of the rug on the hardwood floor. Stumbling, her hand reached out and braced against the wall. She stayed upright, this time. Not wanting her father tripping if he got up during the night, Graley bent and picked the rug up, nesting it under her left arm. Walking down the hallway, out through the kitchen, she opened the laundry room door and put the rug on top of the dryer. She figured she would wash it, eventually.

Closing the door behind her, Graley turned and walked the few short steps to the refrigerator, wishing she would see gin, but knowing there was none. She started for a beer, then changed her mind and grabbed for the flavored seltzer water with an orange on the label.

Setting the bottle on the counter, she opened the cabinet and got out a glass. Filling it with ice from the door of the freezer, Graley topped off her glass with the effervescent flavored water. She watched the bubbles as they hissed and popped, shooting upward off the ice. Her eyes focused in the center of the glass as the day's events replayed in her head. Lost in thought of a beaten body and a floating one, Graley noticing the water had settled. She added a bit more seltzer to the glass before returning the plastic bottle to the refrigerator.

She headed for the living room and plopped down at the end of the dark brown couch. The weight lifted off her lower body felt good. She set her glass down on the tattered and warped coaster sitting on the end table.

Adjusting the pillows to sit under her arm, she grabbed the remote off the coffee table and switched on the television. Graley wondered how many episodes of Wallander were left to watch. There were only three or four long episodes a year for the show.

As the Amazon video started up, she remembered she was in season two. Sighing, she tossed her head back in a slow and deliberate motion. The tired detective longed to fade into the Swedish detective's troubles and forget her own for the next ninety minutes.

Taking a swig of water, waiting for the internet to catch up and Wallander to start, Graley looked at her cell phone. It showed nine thirty. She wanted to be in bed by ten tonight so getting down to the station by eight and prep for the Walker interview wouldn't be an issue. What she wanted to do, other than transport herself to Sweden and work with Wallander, was to go sit outside Matt Walker's house and make sure he showed up to the station on time.

Knowing she couldn't leave the house at night leaving her father unattended, she tried to relax and focus on the TV. Graley knew she shouldn't even be leaving her dad home alone at all during the day, but she had limited options on a cop's salary. The nurse, partially paid by her cop's benefits, came at eight AM and left at four PM. Too many hours alone for her father. Her electric bills were proof.

Graley wanted to pound the sofa and cry. She would have to go to the bank tomorrow and move money over from her father's saving's account into her checking account and write a big fat check to the senior home. With the only other family being a sister who was three hundred miles away in Portland, and didn't care anyhow, Graley was out of options. Her father was not going to be happy, but at this point it didn't matter. Wanting a hug, she wished and dreamed of a loved one to talk and cuddle with right now.

Graley looked up at the screen in time to see Wallander yelling at the staff, frustrated over their lack of information about a suspect. Staring at the clock, realizing she was fifteen minutes into the show, Graley had no idea what had taken place so far. She was lost in a world of thought about her dad. Much like the way T.V. detective Wallander was with his father. The fictitious show had an eerie sense of realism to her.

Graley got to thinking about the show's writers and how they dealt with their parents. Someone on the writing staff had first-hand experience. The show spoke to the heart, Graley thought as she grabbed the remote and turned the TV off.

Standing, leaving her water on the table, she headed out to the back porch leaving the main door open behind her, Graley allowed the screen door to close, providing a welcomed blockade to any flying intruders. A slight breeze tingled against her cheek, warning of fall's imminent arrival.

Graley stopped at the railing and leaned forward against the fake wood, taking pressure off her legs and feet. The backyard she grew up in was dark and deep. The thick trees at the back of the property were silhouetted against the sky. The wind pushed its way through the branches as the leaves danced in unison, hanging on for another day as the moon smiled in a reassuring notion that all would be okay.

Staring at the horizon, over the statuesque trees, the night sky covered in stars, Graley searched for guidance about her father. As always, the stars floated in silence. Frustrated, Graley turned and went inside wandering through the kitchen before stopping at the front door.

Grabbing her cell phone, she dialed Cole, wondering how much he'd had to drink and if he was still at the craft pub.

Cole picked up on the first ring.

"What's up, biatch?"

"Lovely, Cole, as always. How much have you had to drink so far?" Graley asked as she heard her juvenile partner chuckle.

"I just finished one beer. Why? You going to rag on me about drinking beer now, too?"

Graley, in no mood to mess around with her understudy, cut Cole off and continued.

"No, Cole. Just shut up and listen. I was thinking about driving over to Walker's place and seeing what was going on, but I can't because I don't have anyone who can sit with my dad. Would you be up for going over there and checking in on the officer, or officers, watching the Walker's home?"

To Graley's surprise, Cole was more than eager.

"Seriously? Hell, yes. Not enjoying myself and could use a goddamned excuse to get out of here. Shit, I don't have my car, though. It's at the station."

Graley didn't hesitate at the opportunity for a once agreeable Cole.

"I'll put a call into the dispatcher and have them send over a patrol car that can either run you out there or take you back to the station and your car. "Hang on Cole. I'll call you right back."

Graley knew Cole well enough, realized he could change his mind as quick as he made it, and immediately dialed the police station dispatcher.

"Medford Police dispatch, may I help you?"

"This is Detective Graley. Do you have any cars near Outlaw River Craft Ales on Thorpe and Maple?"

"Hang on, Detective, let me check," came the matter-of-fact reply.

Graley tapped her left hand nervously on the kitchen counter staring out the front window as a raccoon ran down the driveway and headed for the garbage cans. She hoped she remembered to latch them shut.

"Yes, Detective, we do. Just a couple of minutes away. Why?"

"Please send them over there to pick up detective Cole and take him back to the station. He needs to run out to a crime scene and check on something. Okay?"

"I will put the call in now. The car should be out front of the pub in less than five minutes."

"Great, and thanks."

Graley pressed the end button and dialed Cole back. Cole picked up before the first ring finished.

"Cole here, Detective Biatch."

"Cole, a car is on its way. Dispatch said it was in the neighborhood and should be there in less than five minutes."

"Great. Once I get my car, I'll head straight over to the killer's place. Anything special I am supposed to do?"

"Just check on the officer and see if there has been any strange commotion going on at the house. People coming and going, lights going on and off with irregularity, Mrs. Walker driving out, or any car leaving the garage for that matter. Unusual shit, Cole."

"Got it." Cole responded enthusiastically.

"And Cole, don't go up to the house, ring the doorbell, and get cute with Walker. Let them sleep and have peace and quiet. Things are going to get crazy enough for them tomorrow."

No response didn't puzzle Graley at all. She could see Cole as if he were next to her. He had the phone in his hand, held away from his face, and was mocking her, silently talking into the phone like a child.

"Cole."

"Got it Graley. The car is here, gotta go."

Cole seemed a bit too eager to Graley, but she was tired and ignored signs she shouldn't have. Her phone still pressed to her ear, despite the now recognizable dead-air, she wondered if she had made a bad decision, in a day full of surprises.

Shadows in the Mist

Matt, bursting forward in his chair, woke, startling Koda. The dog yelped, then stared at Matt with bewildered eyes. Matt reached out and patted the dog's head in reassurance.

"Sorry, dog. Bad dream."

Koda licked his hand, in a forgiving gesture, and nuzzled up against Matt's leg. The temperature had dropped significantly, waking Matt to the realization he was cold and splayed across an Adirondack chair by the deck near the lake. Sliding out toward the edge of the chair he crossed his arms, squeezing them tight against his chest to warm himself. The effort helped, for a second.

"Come on, dog, let's go. It is getting too damn cold out here. Fall has arrived, little guy. We are going to have to get you a warm house out here, or let you sleep inside."

Matt reaching down, shook Koda back and forth in a vigorous show of affection, the dog's tail sped up its motion in approval.

"I suppose I could get a dog door installed in the garage as well, so you can come and go as you please. Come on, boy."

Stepping down off the deck, Matt watched as Koda stayed by his side. He thought about the damn dream he was having when he woke. He was in Betheny's home as a guest, near as he could tell. There were a lot of other people, none of them he recognized, and a man stood in the back, hiding his face and staring. Betheny walked up to Matt, her eyes fearful as she moved her face forward to whisper in Matt's ear. Right before she got a word out Matt was transported to the deck and Sharon leapt from the edge of the lake with her hands reaching out toward him as she pleaded for help.

"Shit, dog, am I glad I woke up! That was one weird dream."

The duo reached the sliding door. Matt slid it open, letting Koda in first. He followed and locked the door behind them. He stared out at the lake, wondering if Sharon was going to walk out of the lake and ask to be let in.

Matt slid off his slippers, then looking at his watch, which read about two-thirty, he turned toward the foyer. *Good,* he thought to himself, *I can get a few more hours of sleep in, this time in a warm bed, before facing the shit-storm at the police station.*

He hoped like hell his attorney would be there. If not, he decided, he wouldn't say a word until he showed up. Matt had watched enough crime television, and heard enough horror stories about people talking, confessing to shit they didn't do under the pressure of questioning. He didn't want to chance saying anything wrong.

Stopping at the front door, Matt looked out through the peephole to see if the cop car was still out front. Seeing the cruiser still in sight, Matt wondered if there were one or two cops sitting inside. Probably one under the circumstances, he thought. Not like the police force had a lot of resources and could afford to have two of them camped out in front of the house overnight.

If it was just one cop, Matt was curious if he was asleep or listening to the radio, and how hard it would be to stay awake. He knew he would not be any good at staking someone, or something, out. He'd fall asleep way too easily. Oh, how he longed for his usual quick sleep tonight.

Slogging up the stairs with tired and heavy feet, Koda following, Matt realized he left his cell phone in the kitchen. He headed back to pick it up while Koda waited at the top of the stairs. Matt smiled, thankful for Kate the dog fit in so quickly.

Matt grabbed the cell phone off the counter. While walking, he set the phone's alarm for seven. He normally got up at six, but he wanted extra sleep since he wouldn't be going to the office first. Matt stopped at the front door and this time peered out a window and saw the police car sitting, with its parking lights on. He thought about going out and seeing if the police person, not sure if it was a man or woman, wanted a hot cup of coffee.

"Nah that would be weird. At least at this time of the morning," Matt spoke, and then felt awkward wondering why he spoke his thought out loud. He made it up the stairs, not seeing Koda until he got into the room. The little shit had jumped up on the bed and was laying where Matt was supposed to be. Kate, still in a deep sleep, looked comfortable and lovely. Moving over to the side of the bed, Matt put a hand on Koda, and while pushing, whispered to him so as not to wake Kate.

"Okay, you little shit. Off the bed. I am not going to let you get in this habit."

Koda jumped down without coaxing. Matt set his cell phone on the nightstand and settled into bed next to Kate. Koda waited for Matt to get comfortable and then laid down in front of the nightstand.

Matt's thoughts drifted to the day's grisly events as he settled his head into the now cold pillow. Reaching over, with care, he touched Kate's warm and soft shoulder. The softness of her skin couldn't hide the sinewy strength of her toned muscles. He squeezed, trying to effuse love, willing it to move through his finger tips and reach her subconscious. He couldn't let anything happen to her, and for the first time all day he feared for her safety.

Closing his eyes, Matt's mind shifted to more of the dream he had recalled only moments ago. A vision of Sharon holding Betheny's hand. They walked near a cabin, among tall pines, as mist rolled through, setting a mood of doubt and fear. The former wives stopped and turned. Now facing Matt, Betheny's eyes pleaded for help. The same eyes he saw early this evening. Betheny turned to Sharon. Matt watched in horror as water gushed from Sharon's mouth, eyes, and ears. A creepy but familiar figure moved in the shadows of the mist and was gone.

Subject: Stop Talking

Matt, eyes wide open now, sat back up in bed. He looked down at Koda who had his head down and appeared to be asleep. He thought everyone could sleep but him. Kate rolled over and repositioned herself. Half asleep, she asked Matt if he was okay.

"Yes, just a bad dream. Go back to sleep."

Matt reached out and put his hand on Kate's hair, moving strands behind her ear. She moved her face in the pillow searching for the proper position as her eyes relaxed beneath the lids while her breathing settled back into sleep mode.

Matt sat looking out their second-story bedroom window, gazing at the lake. The full moon did her best to light up the lakeshore, and he could see the police equipment sitting static. The image of Betheny and Sharon replayed in his mind.

He closed his eyes and stared, hoping concentration would reveal more about the figure in the mist and shadow. Nothing but a shadowy presence. Though familiar, he realized it could be anyone.

Matt pulled the covers back and looked at his legs, moving them sideways in a slow and careful fashion so as not to disturb Kate. Placing his feet on the floor, he stood, turned, and pulled the covers back so Kate would not be exposed in any way.

Koda sat up, clearly frustrated over Matt's inability to settle and stay in one place. Matt placed his hand on the bed and whispered.

"Come on, boy, just this once."

Matt would later tell Kate he swore the dog smiled as it jumped hastily onto the bed, almost as if the dog knew he should take care not to disturb a sleeping Kate. Matt rubbed Koda's head as he got himself into a c-shape pattern and laid down close to Kate, closing his eyes.

Walking to the walk-in closet, Matt found a pair of grey sweat pants. He pulled them on. He then grabbed socks out of the drawer and put them on, left foot first, then right like always. Reaching up, he grabbed a black Oregon State Beavers sweatshirt and slid it on over his t-shirt. He knew he wasn't going to be sleeping anymore tonight, so he decided to head to his office and try to catch up on work.

Matt headed out of the closet, glanced over at Koda snuggled up next to Kate, and left the bedroom. He pushed the door almost closed, leaving it open a crack in case Koda wanted to push his way out. Matt wondered if the dog needed to go to the bathroom, if he'd try to wake Kate, come search for him, or just find a piece of nice warm carpet and do what he needed to do. Matt shook his head and hoped like hell the dog didn't crap or pee inside the house.

Now at the top of the staircase, he looked out the front window wondering what was visible. The cop car was still sitting out front. Parking lights were on, so the engine must have been running with the heater on, Matt assumed. Not cold, but chilly enough that sitting in a car for more than a few minutes would be unpleasant.

Taking one careful step after another, Matt made it down the stairs and swung left going down the hall to his study. He flipped the light switch upward upon entering. His desk lamp lit up and cast enough light so he could safely make his way in. He pulled the French doors closed behind him, glad the glass would allow him to see the new family member sitting outside if the mutt should need something.

Making his way over to the desk where he slouched into his chair, Matt flipped the lid of his laptop open and pressed the power button signaling the device to wake up. Entering his four-digit pass code, the PC whirred as it settled into the home screen.

Matt counted the eleven icons on the screen and then opened the chrome browser. He went to his favorite sports page and checked to see if there was any news on the Trailblazers' upcoming season. There was, which helped his mood for a few fleeting seconds as he transitioned back to Yahoo News.

Nothing else jumped out at him, so he went to the local Mail Tribune website with morbid curiosity. He saw nothing related to his day's events. Certain it would be all over the site and in the papers later in the day, Matt sighed wondering what in the hell would be said and whether he would be mentioned.

Matt opened his mind-mapping software and looked at his company plans for the next year, realizing he was behind in making the budget. He made a mental note to talk with Accounting later in the day and ask for the third quarter numbers. They should be ready to view now, and he wanted to see what recurring revenue looked like and whether they would be on track for another record year.

His marketing firm had a steady, increasing revenue for ten straight years now. Averaging seven percent growth over the same stretch, Matt built his firm into a twenty million dollar plus a year enterprise with no signs that growth would taper off. If he could somehow manage to stay out of jail, the ceiling appeared to have no limit.

Matt looked at his latest client to come on board, Jenson Sporting Goods. Matt Googled the store and owner, Jack Jenson, to get a better idea of what direction he would recommend taking the business in over the next six months. The owner, whose son was a pitcher for the Los Angeles Dodgers, and a bit of a local folk-hero, was the obvious choice to leverage to get people through the doors, but Matt and his firm were not known for doing the obvious.

Glancing down in the lower right corner of the monitor, Matt saw he had twenty message notifications. He clicked the notification icon and the action center flew in from the right side of the screen. Glancing over the messages, he saw several from Jane and one from the Medford Chamber of Commerce. The Chamber message he knew would be a request for him to speak again this year at their annual event. He had successfully turned them down for the last three years. There was a message from Kate, one from his attorney, and an email address he didn't recognize.

Matt opened the message from the attorney.

"*Matt, shit, life can suck sometimes. Sorry to hear about your day. Glad you called, and I'll see you down at the police station first thing in the morning. Jim.*"

Well, this was a bit of good news at least. Matt didn't like the idea of being down at the station in front of the detectives by himself. He could picture it now. He would get upset, mouth off, say something he shouldn't, and then get locked up as the chief suspect in something he had nothing to do with other than being a poor sap in the wrong place at the wrong time.

"Shit," Matt blurted out. He wondered about Betheny's little brother, who Matt always liked. This made him think of Kate's older brother, who was a prick. He wondered if he was still in prison. His minding racing all over the map, propelled him back to Betheny's little brother who Matt thought was living in Seattle. He was the only next of kin Matt was aware Betheny had. He wondered how he would get notified, and if he should call him. Could he call him, or would that look suspicious?

Matt thought the same thing about Sharon and her parents. He liked them, as well even though the former mother-in-law wasn't crazy about him, but the father-in-law liked him. Matt figured one out of two wasn't bad. Sharon didn't have any siblings, but there were several cousins and an aunt living in Jacksonville. If she was still alive, she'd see news plastered all over everywhere in the next day or two. Matt couldn't imagine finding out this way and wondered how the police contacted people about a death like this. It couldn't be the same, or as simple, as Law and Order showed on T.V., he thought as he opened Evernote and made a new notepad.

Questions to ask the attorney – Jim.

Can I, should I, notify family members of Betheny and Kate?

What do I have to allow the police access to?

Work files?

Voice mail?

My home?

My Office?

?

Should I hire a private investigator?

Do I need to hire security for Kate or can the police provide it considering what has happened? (My tax dollars do anything here?)

Should I represent myself since I didn't do anything?

Matt knew the answer to his final question already but hit the keys on the keypad anyway—stream of consciousness he figured couldn't hurt.

How much is this going to cost me?

I am seeing a therapist; do I need to share this?

Do I tell the cops what I think, or only what I know?

Clicking save, Matt minimized the software in case he thought of something else, which he was sure he would. He looked at his email again and started to drag the Russian Singles spam email to the junk folder. Changing his mind, he opened it. Matt couldn't tell who it was from as the return email address was gibberish. Matt had seen enough of the Russian spam messages begging him for a hook up over the years to realize this one looked different. The subject line simply read, "*Stop talking, K could be next!*"

Hesitating, Matt clicked the mouse not sure if he was scared or pissed as he opened the email.

Fast-Track

Wiping the corner of his mouth on his shirt sleeve, Cole glanced back over his shoulder to see what the line was like at the bar. He contemplated buying a Pilsner and chugging it, so he could loosen up a bit, but there were too many people in line.

He left his glass on the table, turning it upside down. He watched the remaining foam run down the side of the glass and float on the tabletop. It would leave a nice mark in the wood, he hoped. A woman at the table next to Cole noticed what he was doing. Cole gave her a "fuck-you" expression and turned to walk to the bar.

He pushed his way up to the front of the line as if he was in uniform, not his detective street clothes. One guy started to speak but Cole turned and looked at him with his *I will fucking destroy you* look. To Cole's disappointment, the guy kept his mouth shut.

Diane, standing at the counter, finished helping a patron. Cole stood directly in front of her and started talking before she looked up or acknowledged him.

"Diane, sorry, but duty calls. They are sending a police car over to pick me up. Emergency down at the station they need my help on. Rain-Check?"

Diane raised her head making her best effort to smile at Cole. He could tell it was forced, like she feared him. He was a bit turned on, wishing he could take her home, now that she understood her station in life.

"Um, okay, don't worry about it."

"Thanks, Diane. Sorry about earlier. Long, fucked up, day. Later."

He didn't mean it but forced out the comment figuring it was expected. He didn't wait for a response. Turning, he headed out the front of the warehouse bar where a police car waited.

Cole walked directly to the waiting police car. Opening the door, he climbed into the passenger side and slammed the door.

He was feeling much better about himself, and the night, now that Graley had come to her senses. *Stupid bitch,* he thought to himself. He extended his hand to the officer.

"Detective Cole. Thanks, Sergeant, for stopping. I need to get back to the station and get my car. I have to go over to the Walker home and the stakeout. You know, where the murder took place earlier today."

"No problem. Johnson, by the way."

The sergeant put the car in drive and eased out of the parking lot. Cole knew they should be at the station in less than five minutes, give or take.

"Murder, huh? The chatter is that a body was found, possible drowning, odd circumstances but no definitive murder yet."

Cole hated this guy already. *Fucking sergeant asshole,* he was thinking to himself.

"Well, that's the chatter, huh?"

He let the comment hang, his disdain drifting through the air. He wondered if the driver felt the familiar feel of heaviness he was so accustomed to himself.

"It's a murder. Too many coincidences. Graley thinks so, too."

Cole threw Graley's name out to lend credibility to the discussion. Her weight and reputation in the department was something Cole knew he would garner after a few more years on the job.

The sergeant chuckled.

"Well, then, if Graley says so."

Cole wanted to take a swing at this guy. He reminded him of his father.

"*Douglas, get your ass in here right now!*" He could hear his father's distinctive clarity. As if he were the sergeant sitting next to him at this moment.

"*Can't you do anything right, you little shit? How many times do I have to tell you how to put a trash bag in the can? Come here, Cole. Now! Just because you are nine precious years old doesn't mean you can't follow my instructions. Does it? Answer me!*"

"*No dad, it doesn't. I'm sorry. I tried to do it how you want. I did.*"

Cole continued reflecting on his father as the police car zigged and zagged its way toward the station. He remembered how his father would reach out and back-hand him across the face. Hard enough to sting but not leave a mark. Cole would cry and promise to do it better next time.

"I want right, not better," his father would say. "You are such a disappointment" or "You make me sick," depending on whether he was in a good or bad mood.

The damage done was internal. Cole wasn't smart or resourceful enough to understand one could change behaviors, so he continued with his father's legacy. He could hide it well enough to get on the force, but his actions from time to time betrayed him. He concentrated on his breathing right now to avoid saying or doing anything to Officer Dick-Face driving the car.

The cruiser eased up to the front of the station and came to a stop.

"This okay, Detective Cole?"

"Fine."

Cole opened the door and contemplated his next action. He thought about saying thanks to the sergeant, but figured it would just show his weakness, not emphasize his position on the scale of authority. Closing the door, he turned his back as he felt the car pull away. He smiled to himself over his little ego victory.

Cole stretched his arms upward, then reached into his pocket for his cigarettes. Not moving, he stood in the road as another police car pulled up to the curb, then headed behind the station. Pulling out his lighter, he lit a cigarette without acknowledging the car's presence. Taking a long drag, he returned his lighter to the front pocket of his pants and grabbed his car keys from a jacket pocket, then turned walking toward the back of the station and the policeman's parking lot. He liked being in charge and couldn't wait to get out from underneath Graley's grip.

The well-lit lot comforted Cole. He saw his Corvette toward the back of the lot where he always parked it, at an angle across two spaces. He had been warned by Graley more than once that parking across two spaces like a "prima-donna asshole" wouldn't go unnoticed, and one of these days his car would be towed. Another attempt by the bitch to control him. He decided he wouldn't cave to her recommendation. And of course, nothing happened.

Cole knew he could take a cruiser out, but didn't feel like going through the hassle of signing for one. Since he wouldn't be arresting anyone, he may as well drive his car. Graley, asked him to head out there, so, being official business and all, he could fill his gas tank, which just happened to be almost empty, on the city's dime. Perfect timing.

Cole smiled as he crawled into the driver's seat and fired the eight-cylinder beast up to its distinctive Vette growl. He eased the car out of the lot and onto the street. Feeling more confident than normal, he hammered the accelerator to the floor. The tires squealed against the cooling asphalt, then gripped hard propelling the car forward toward his destination.

Cole put thoughts into play revealing a pretty good idea that would speed this little investigation up and get him back on the fast-track for promotion. Slowing the Corvette, he eased the car into a gas station to fill up on the city's dime. Once full he guided his yellow chick-magnet on the highway toward Emigrant Lake and the soon to be exposed killer Matt Walker's home.

Reaching over, he turned on the radio to select his favorite satellite station, channel eighteen, the Taylor Swift channel. His own guilty pleasure no other cop would ever know if he could help it.

Singing along to Taylor's latest heartbreak, he made a mental note to remember to turn in the gas receipt.

Freak

Knowing what he should do with the email, Matt looked out his window toward the police car. He thought about circumstances for a moment and then did what he wanted, not what he thought he should. He forwarded to someone trustworthy, then deleted it from his inbox. The act of deletion, if nothing more than symbolic, felt as though he was eliminating the hint of a threat.

Matt's mind danced through a deluge of memories, scraping the recesses of his mind in search of someone capable of sending the email. How could they get his personal email address? He was careful who he shared it with and even though he had a public profile due to his marketing firm; he got little spam, save the Russians.

He opened the email trash bin and read the message again. Pressing Ctrl P, he made a print. Matt wished his printer were quieter but didn't think it would ultimately wake Kate up. He folded the fresh printed copy and placed it under his laptop. He thought perhaps he would take it with him to the interview—but he knew he wouldn't.

Digging into the company financials on his laptop, Matt hoped they would make him drowsy and enable him to sleep for at least a couple of hours. He figured he'd be in the shower by 7:30, perhaps a quick breakfast with Kate if she was up, and then he'd head to Medford. He'd be no later than 8:45 to the station. Plenty of time for his "mandatory" 9 AM appointment.

Hearing an unusual noise outside his door, Matt jumped. Not used to being so jumpy, he laughed at himself and settled back staring out the window. The blinds were open a touch, enough where he could see out, but not enough to make anything out with ease. He could see the police car, but nothing else moved, save a tree limb doused with color-changing leaves. Rustling leaves were not the sound he heard, though, as they scraped against the screens. He reminded himself he needed to make a call to his window guy and have them winterized. Stretched cellophane installed inside for added heat retention.

Looking left, Matt heard and saw the door creep inward. For a split second, he saw nothing and pushed his chair back in a defensive action, not sure if he was going to attack or retreat. Retreat where? Against a wall? Jump out the damn window? It didn't matter, his new best friend pushed his way in and started whining.

Relieved, Matt talked out loud to the canine.

"Well, dog, if that isn't a clear request to take a leak, I don't know what is," Matt said, patting the new friend on the head.

"Come on boy."

They headed to the kitchen, and in the moonlight bouncing off the cabinets, Matt found the leash Kate left on the built-in desk. Right next to cookbooks, the never-used phone with an answering machine, and a tablet which doubled as recipe finder and text message machine while Kate worked her magic in the kitchen.

"Let's go, dog. Get used to this leash, okay. At least until I know you aren't going to run."

Matt placed the leash on Koda's red and black Portland Trailblazers collar. He couldn't imagine where in the world Kate had found the thing. She was a basketball junkie and huge Trailblazers fan. Matt, a Blazer fan himself, was thrilled to have someone to share the games with. He bought Kate a Damian Lilliard jersey, her favorite player, which she wore with pride on game nights.

Koda whimpered again and started to head away from Matt, toward the back-patio door. The leash, taught now, allowed the eager canine to get no further than a couple of feet away. He started to lift his leg, at least Matt thought he did, and pee on the kitchen table so Matt hurried to put his slippers on and get Koda outside. The moonlight, wasn't bright enough inside to help Matt see as well as he would have liked. He bumped into the corner of the kitchen table, ramming his thigh and moving it a few inches across the mahogany hardwood floor.

"Shit, that better not leave a scratch, dog."

Rubbing his thigh with his free hand, Matt got Koda outside and down off the deck. Koda relieved himself, squatted and relieved himself further when Matt realized he needed a damn plastic bag or something.

"You little scoundrel. I better not be the one to have to do this on a regular basis. You are going to have to plan better, or you will not be staying in at night. Do you understand me?" Matt couldn't believe he was smiling as he talked to the dog.

Koda turned, pushing his back paws hard against the ground and scraping. He sent dirt and grass blades flying.

"What are you grinning at, dog? You're happy knowing I am going to have to clean it up, aren't you?"

Matt held onto the leash as Koda sat and looked up, waiting for acknowledgment. Matt rubbed the top of his head.

"Come on, boy, I need to get a shovel."

The duo headed down the back side of the house, around the end toward the garage and a shovel. Matt noticed the rhododendron grew a bit unruly the last months of summer and made a mental note to call the landscape guy. He wanted them trimmed back before the heavy rains started.

Matt contemplated leaving the steaming pile of Koda's masterpiece but knew he would forget and step in it if he didn't scoop. Or, he could leave it and hope one of the cops stepped in it.

"Nah that would be mean. Come on, dog."

He tugged at the leash with a gentle motion.

Koda followed dutifully. His behavior made Matt think he was a domesticated little guy and at one time or another had belonged to someone. He wanted to ask Kate exactly what the adoption shelter told her about him. There must be more of a back-story than what she already shared.

Matt reached the front of the garage and waived toward the police car. He had no idea if the cops saw him wave or not; the distance was a good fifty yards and the front of the garage wasn't lit well. The damn light was on the fritz again and the motion sensor didn't pick him up, so the floods stayed off. Normally he would be pissed, but tonight he had a lot more on his mind. He made yet another mental note. Ask

Kate to call the security company tomorrow and insist they fix the sensor again.

Matt waited for the garage door to open and passed the time by reaching down and petting Koda on top of the head. The dog seemed to like it, but Matt knew only time would tell. He didn't pull back a bloody hand, so the dog at least didn't hate it.

The garage door open, Matt walked alongside his wife's Jeep and stopped with Koda in front of the garden utensil rack. He grabbed a shovel, then looked around for a plastic bag or container. Not seeing anything, he headed back out the door.

Looking up the driveway yet again, Matt thought the police car seemed to move, rolling along at a slow pace. After staring at the green and white cop car for a good thirty seconds or so, he assumed he was seeing things; tired eyes in need of sleep but a brain that would not relinquish control.

"Come on, boy."

Matt looked down at his smiling buddy and decided he had himself a new best friend. Grinning at the thought, Matt decided he'd have to ask his attorney about writing this little guy into the prenup somehow.

Walking and talking, Matt took a big deep breath of the cool night air. He could smell the pine trees and a faint hint of fish smell coming off the lake.

"Dog, after I get your shit scooped up and thrown into the water, how about you and I take a cup of coffee out to the police? Since we can't sleep, may as well do something nice for them, huh?"

"Woof."

Matt laughed.

"Good boy."

He dropped the leash and scooped up the crap. "Stay next to me, dog, okay?"

Matt started walking down to the bank of the lake where he planned to chuck the crap into the water and let nature do her cleansing magic.

"Now let's get rid of the evidence, boy, and fast."

Matt tilted his head back and tried to shut down his nose.

"You need to drink more water, dog. This is horrific. Good God."

Right before he got close enough to the water to make his toss, Matt heard a familiar noise. His instincts turned him when a recognizable voice blurted out a clear, concise statement. He'd remember the words forever.

"Freeze. Don't you fucking move, freak."

Cole's Perspective

Cole sat in the cop car with a sergeant, a new guy who transferred from Seattle. He apparently moved back down to be near his girlfriend who had started teaching at Southern Oregon University in Ashland. He was about Cole's age, didn't mind if he smoked, and had a sense of humor.

Cole had arrived several hours earlier and decided to hang out with the guy. He parked his Vette down the road about a half mile or so and walked, not wanting to announce his presence in case Walker was up to more shit, which Cole fully expected him to be.

They talked about the outdoors, best places to fish, which was better–snowboarding or skiing, and cars.

"Only fags use skis," Cole told him.

Sergeant Gilliam told him he was full of shit and that the only reason anyone got on a fucking snowboard was, "they aren't athletic enough to ski, plain and simple. Don't worry, though, Cole, I won't tell anyone at the station you snowboard. We can keep it to ourselves."

"Fuck you, asshole."

Silence hung in the air for a short moment, then they both laughed out loud.

Cole grabbed his cigarettes and lit another one up. Rolling the window down most of the way, he concentrated on keeping as much of the smoke as possible outside of the car.

Sitting in silence for a couple of minutes, Cole pinched his finished cigarette butt, crushed the rest in his palm, and shook his hand outside the car.

"You haven't seen the prick do anything tonight, Gilliam?"

"Other than a few lights going on and off, no. All quiet on the front. I walked a few feet away from the car once to take a leak, but never turned my back on the place. I haven't seen anything. You really think he killed those women? He seemed pretty calm and upset that they were dead."

Cole turned and looked Gilliam directly in the eyes.

"He sure as hell did it. I can tell. Bastard was too cool and too arrogant. I wouldn't be surprised if he killed his current wife while we were sitting here and threw her in the lake as well."

"He would have to be an absolute idiot, Cole."

"Or very arrogant. And trust me Gilliam, this guy is about as arrogant as they come."

Gilliam reached over and slapped Cole on the shoulder and pointed toward the house.

"Look."

"What?"

Cole turned and looked toward the house. Standing in front of the garage door with his dog was Mr. Matt Walker himself. Cole watched as Walker swung his head back and forth as if he was on the lookout for something.

"He is probably trying to figure out how he can distract us long enough to make a run for it. Wife is probably bleeding-out right now."

"Well, what do we do then?"

"Nothing, Gilliam. Just sit here for now and watch while he makes a mistake. I don't know much about that dog, but I don't want to have to shoot the damn thing if it attacks, so we hold tight for now."

The two watched Walker pet the dog while the door was rising. There wasn't a lot of light in front of the house which Cole deduced was someone with a sneaky disposition. Fortunately, a near full moon allowed enough light for them to make him out. When the door reached the top, the opener cast enough light for better vision. Walker returned with a shovel, and the dog in tow.

"See, I fucking told you Gilliam! You stay here and call in for backup. I am going to go ninja and follow him. See what the hell he is doing with her body."

"You serious, Cole? What if he is just..."

Cole cut Gilliam off.

"Yes, I am fucking serious! Call this in, and now!"

Cole opened the door. Getting out of the car he held the door with two hands closing it with a slow, deliberate, quiet motion.

Gilliam reached for the mic on his shoulder and pressed the talk button.

"Dispatch, Sergeant Gilliam, car 91 at the residence of Matt Walker on guard duty, over..."

Cole jogged toward the garage, pulling his gun out of his shoulder holster. He made it to the edge of the house in seconds. He stopped and peered around the side in time to see Walker and the dog turn the corner. Pleased with himself for not being noticed, he worked his way down the side of the house. He saw the thick rhododendron plants and remembered how his mother used to love rhododendrons. He missed her.

A few moments later, he made it to the back of Walker's home and stopped, listening intently. Walker was going on with the dog in a pathetic fashion, like they were best damn friends. Cole thought the guy was not only arrogant, but soft. He knew if Graley had taken him in, like they should have, he could have broken him in less than an hour for sure.

Cole tensed as he heard Walker say, "Come on, boy, let's get rid of the evidence."

He pulled the hammer back on his gun and stepped out. Walker and the dog were heading toward the lake. Cole noticed Walker had dropped the leash and was carrying the shovel with two hands. This sick bastard was either feeding his wife to the dog or had chopped her up and was going to toss her in the lake.

As he walked forward, proud of his stealthy effort, Cole wondered how quick backup would arrive. If he was lucky, Walker would make a move for him and he would drop the bastard. Getting to shoot the dog as well would be a bonus. He got excited about the great story he'd have to tell his next ex-girlfriend.

Cole watched Walker twist from the waist up. He propelled his shoulder and arms forward as something flew off the shovel and landed in the water with a plunking noise.

A good thirty feet from Walker now, Cole placed himself into a trained firing position, took a breath, reminded himself not to jerk the gun and spoke loud and proud. Choice words he would remember but later on decided he would write down much differently in his report.

"Freeze. Don't you fucking move, freak."

A Real Piece of...

Laughing at the absurdity of what it must look like to Detective Cole, Matt couldn't believe what the universe threw at him. First, two former wives were dead within hours of each other. Both deaths involve him, albeit in indirect ways. Second, he makes an innocent trip to get a shovel and throw dog crap into the lake, whereupon his small world, already upside down, flips again in an instant. What the guiltless act looked like to the wannabe detective, Matt could only imagine. The gun pointing at him signified the detective's mind suspected the worst.

"It was only dog shit, Detective Cole. You don't need to shoot me."

"Dog shit. Sure. You must think I am an idiot, Walker."

Matt knew he shouldn't say what he wanted, but how much worse could things get? Counting to eleven, Matt shrugged his shoulders and plowed forward as detective Cole kept the gun leveled at him.

"Well, I didn't think you were an idiot, until now. Before this, I thought you were only an asshole. Now, well..."

"Shut up, you pretentious prick. Slowly place the shovel on the ground."

Koda growled. Matt gripped the leash a little firmer hoping like hell the thing held if the dog decided to make a break for the detective. He didn't want Kate's–hell who was he kidding, *his* new little buddy to get shot.

Matt placed the shovel on the ground and put a hand on Koda's head trying to calm him.

"Easy, dog. This detective here is likely to shoot the both of us if we make any movement at all. Just stay next to me and everything will be okay. Eventually."

Matt wasn't so sure, at-the-moment, that *any*thing would be okay. Saying the statement out loud was as much for him as for Koda.

Koda continued to growl. Matt couldn't calm him.

"Get that damn dog under control, Walker."

Surprised that Cole wouldn't lower his gun, Matt couldn't understand why he was a threat. Perhaps the cop was fearful of the dog? That was the only thing, at the moment that resonated in Matt's mind.

"My dog is under control, detective dick-head. Oops, did I say that out loud? I mean Detective Cole. From where I stand, my dog is being reasonable. He understands the situation and is protecting me. It would appear he doesn't like you, or the fact that you appear out-of-control to him. Just a guess, but I don't think he likes your gun."

"What the hell are you talking about?"

Matt's nerves continued to peak like a stretched rubber band about to snap.

"He doesn't like your gun, detective. Put it down or away."

Koda growled, as if on cue, when Matt said gun. He thought about Koda being left at the shelter, and his previous owners. What did they do? Why did they let this little dog go? And why the hell abuse him? More mystery for him to consider.

"Look, Detective," Matt barked. "Try putting the gun away, or this dog might not to stop."

Matt, impressed as hell, peered down at Koda. The dog was in a fight position, growling, and his short hair was standing. Matt gripped the leash with two hands and leaned back a bit, the position giving him additional leverage.

"Want me to put my hands up detective Cole? If I do, this dog goes free, and I wonder just how good a shot you are. A moving dog, coming right at you is a very small target. Mel Gibson's 'aim small, miss small' isn't going to help you much in this instance. Think about it."

Matt, pleased with himself at his use of the term from Mel Gibson's *The Patriot*, a favorite movie of his, smiled, though he was afraid the moment would be lost on Detective Cole. And he was right. The beautifully timed phrase fell flat, without any hint of recognition from the adrenaline junkie detective.

"What the fuck are you talking about, Walker?"

A new voice echoed from the back of the house. In seconds, Matt saw a uniformed police officer appear, his gun also drawn.

"Everything okay, Detective Cole?"

"Fine, Sergeant Gilliam. Just caught this perp throwing evidence into the lake."

"Evidence? It was dog shit, you idiot."

Matt couldn't hold his tongue as he watched the sergeant put his gun in his holster. Matt recognized this new cop as more rational, cool, and calm. He hoped to reason with his sensibility, so he addressed him.

"Sergeant Gilliam, is it? My dog apparently does not like guns. I am trying to explain to Detective Cole here, he needs to put his gun away. If he does, I can get the dog to calm down, and then you guys can cuff me, sodomize me, beat me senseless, and take me in, whatever Detective Cole here does. Okay?"

Matt watched Gilliam continue forward. Cole wasn't flinching, his arms appeared locked in position. Neither cop responded.

"You both can't be fucking clueless!"

Matt could see Cole tense even further with the last comment.

Sergeant Gilliam took a couple slower steps toward Cole's side so he could be seen, as well as heard.

"Detective Cole, perhaps he is right. Why not put the gun away? Let's see if we can't get the dog to calm down. I can cuff the "perp," as you call him, and we can get the dog inside the house. Sound good?"

Matt hoped like hell it sounded good. His forearms were getting tired, and he was afraid they would cramp soon.

Matt's tension started to ease watching Detective Cole lower his gun and put it into his shoulder holster. Koda started to relax as well, and Matt's arms eased at the decrease in pull on the leash.

"Good dog," Matt said. "Sit."

Koda sat without hesitation right next to him.

The uniformed police officer, to Matt's delight, took the lead.

"I am going to come get the dog, Mr. Walker, and take him into the house. Okay?"

Matt hesitated, then responded before the cop could move.

"I think the smarter thing to do would be for you both to let me take the dog into the garage, take his leash off, and leave him in there.

You can follow me so you don't have to fear I will make a run for them-there-hills."

Matt couldn't resist the opportunity to get in another smart-ass comment.

Sergeant Gilliam laughed, understanding the jab. Cole gave Gilliam a glare, and a look that Matt interpreted as pissed off.

Gilliam approached Matt and Koda with caution. "Go ahead, then. Take your dog to the garage and we'll follow."

Matt didn't say anything to the police. He addressed Koda with a calm voice.

"Come on, boy, let's go." He gave the leash a slight pull, Koda fell into step with him, and then led the way as if to say to Matt, I got this.

In the recesses of Matt's twisted humor of a brain, he thought about taking Koda for a short run, to mess with the cops. The smart part of Matt's brain kept him from doing it and probably kept him alive.

A minute later, they were at the garage and Matt entered the four-digit code into the keypad mounted on the side of the door frame. The door opened, and Matt led Koda over to the door leading inside the house.

"That is far enough, Walker." Cole barked. "No going inside. Take the leash off your dog, if you want, and then come with me."

"Can't I go in and tell Kate what is going on?"

"No, we will handle that. You are coming with me to the station."

Matt, not wanting to press his luck, obeyed. He took the leash off Koda and hung it on the coat rack.

"Sit, dog."

Koda dutifully obeyed and sat next to the door. Matt turned and started to head to the garage door where the two officers waited.

"You may want to wait to slap those cuffs on me until after the garage door goes down. If not, I have no guarantee my dog won't come to my aid. My bet, he will try to take one of your crotches out."

Matt smiled at the thought of Cole getting cute then getting a nice chunk taken out of his groin by Koda.

Cole who had started to reach for his cuffs, waited. Matt reached the policemen, stopped and turned, raised his right arm with the palm out.

"Stay, dog. Stay."

Koda obeyed, and Matt took another step or two over to the keypad and entered the code, watching as the door lowered. He tensed in preparation to react in case Koda came shooting out. Part of him was disappointed that the dog didn't. Matt did hear him bark loudly, then whimper, and he figured Kate would wake and come outside at any moment.

Cole grabbed Matt, spinning him around.

Two other police cars by now had driven up to the house. Matt watched as they blocked the driveway. Officers jumped out of both cars like they just found Bin Laden.

Cole spoke as he put the cuffs on Matt Walker. Matt grimaced as Cole forced his arms back. It hurt, but Matt didn't let the little wannabe detective know.

"Sergeant Gilliam, you go inside and see if Mrs. Walker is alive. If she is, get her up and let her know what is going on. You can tell her we are taking her husband down to the station for questioning and are charging him for suspected murder."

Matt chuckled in disbelief. "Suspected murder? Are you serious?"

Cole pushed Walker forward toward one of the police cars.

"You have the right to remain silent. Anything you say..."

By the time Cole and Walker reached the first police car, Cole had finished reading Matt his rights. The officer standing next to the car opened the door and Cole pushed Matt inside.

"Aren't you supposed to put your hand on the top of my head, so it doesn't bump into the doorjamb, Detective Cole?"

Walker was sure he had seen it done a thousand or more times on television. Continuing to try to irritate Cole, he wondered how successful he had been to this point. Cole slammed the door and turned to the cop.

"Take him right to the station. My car is a quarter a mile or so down the road. Drop me off there and I will follow you in."

The young cop replied dutifully.

"Sure thing, detective. Hop in."

Less than a minute later, the car was in front of Cole's Vette and came to a stop. Matt leaned over and squinted in the dim moonlight looking at Cole's car.

"Is that Vette a 1983, Cole?" Cole didn't respond as he got out of the car.

"You know, it is considered one of the worst Corvettes of all time. A real piece of…"

To Matt's pleasure, Cole slammed the car door before he finished his sentence.

This is Your Clue

Kate woke to a cop standing at the door of her bedroom talking to her in an odd, creepy voice.

"You okay, Ma'am? Are you awake?"

Sitting up, Kate rubbed her eyes, giving her brain a second to register the events laid in front of her. It was still dark. She looked left, reaching out to wake Matt. He wasn't there. Her mind spun up rewinding, then fast-forwarding, alert, ready for flight.

She thought about reaching underneath the bed. A thirty-two-inch Louisville Slugger sat on the carpet waiting for the right moment. It was a gift her father had given her years ago. Matt gave her a thirty-eight-caliber pistol, which she was amazing with, but it was locked in the closet safe. If the guy at the door was aggressive, and she ran for the pistol, he would be on her before she could reach it.

Her mind raced, thinking Matt had told her this very scenario could happen. He recommended the short barrel .38 be in her night-stand, saying, "We don't have kids. It's just you and me, babe. Safety shouldn't be an issue unless you happen to reach for the KY one night, grab the gun accidentally and put a bullet in my head. You won't do that, will you?"

Matt was good at making her laugh. She couldn't believe she was his third wife. He seemed like such a great guy. The events of yesterday, and the dreams of the night, planted a small seed in her mind. One of curiosity and potential doubt. Exactly why would two other women not last with her husband? A question she perhaps should have asked before saying, "I do."

"Ma'am, my name is Sergeant Gilliam of the Medford Police. There has been an incident, and it is best if you come downstairs with me."

"Where is Matt?"

Kate threw the covers back and started to walk to the closet. Kate noticed as Sergeant Gilliam blushed a bit and started to turn his head to avoid full out leering at her as she moved toward the closet in her tight-fitting underwear and revealing sleepshirt.

"Ma'am, where are you going?"

She stopped and faced him.

"Tell me where Matt is, please."

"He is being taken down to the station a little ahead of schedule. He's fine."

"Why ahead of schedule? What has he done? Or rather, what have *you* done, since the agreement was for him to be down at the station at nine this morning?"

"Detective Cole felt it best to take him in now. You are welcome to come down to the station if you want. We were concerned for your safety, and that is why I let myself in the house. My apologies if I startled you."

"Well then Sergeant, Gilliam is it? I am going to go into my walk-in closet and get dressed so I can go down to the station and be with my husband. Is that okay?"

Gilliam's first thought was she could go in there and get a gun, so many of the homeowners around here had guns. Most as hunters, but a few as home protection. He figured the Walkers were the later. He hastily decided Kate Walker wasn't likely to come out firing at him knowing he could drop her dead with a single shot.

"I'm going to go downstairs and wait while you get ready then, ma'am."

Kate spun around and headed into her closet, wondering where Koda was. *So much for a watchdog*, she thought before grabbing a pair of Levi's jeans, throwing off her sleepshirt, and sliding the worn denim pants on. Hopping a couple of times on the soft carpet, she pulled her jeans upward at the same time. Her morning Jeans workout, she would always tell Matt. She got the button fly closed and grabbed one of Matt's t-shirts. Her favorite one with a silhouette of a bicycle angled sideways across the front. It covered the entire face of the shirt. She bought it for him on their trip to Ireland only three months ago. She wore it more than he did though.

Pulling one of Matt's favorite hooded sweatshirts on over the bicycle shirt, she turned to the dresser and grabbed a pair of thick socks, sliding them on before heading out of the closet and turning the light off. She started to walk over to make the bed out of habit. Reluctantly she left it for later.

Kate headed downstairs to the kitchen calling for Koda.

"Koda, come here boy. Koda?"

She heard a noise, like a dog whimpering. It sounded like it came from the garage.

Officer Gilliam appeared from the edge of the kitchen. His right hand, Kate noticed, was always paused or hovering over his gun. Like he was about to draw and shoot her. In an odd fashion, the behavior made her feel both secure and threatened.

"We put him in the garage, Ma'am, for his own safety. He started to get protective of your husband. Fortunately, he was on a leash. You would have been proud of him. If I didn't know any better, I would have thought he had serious training."

Kate stopping at the bottom of the stairs, reached up and touched the side of her head feeling a migraine coming on. She pushed it back down, commanded it to back up. Now was not the time to be weak. Closing her eyes for several seconds she focused on her breathing.

"You okay, Ma'am?" Sergeant Gilliam wanted to move over and take care of the woman. He hadn't been around someone as beautiful as her. Not this close anyhow. His instinct was to rush to her side.

"I'm fine, sergeant. Just a minor headache. I'll deal with it."

She opened her eyes breathing in a smooth, deliberate fashion as she headed to the garage.

"Will you let me see the dog and bring him inside, sergeant?"

"Can you keep him under control?"

"I think so."

"You think so, Ma'am, or you know so? I don't feel like being attacked."

"Well, I just got him from the rescue yesterday, so I haven't had a lot of time with him. He'll be fine, though. I'll hold on tight."

"Go ahead, then."

Sergeant Gilliam took a couple of steps back and positioned himself behind the kitchen table as Kate made her way to the garage.

"Oh, Ma'am, I believe his leash is hanging on a hook by the coats in the garage."

Kate kept silent as the weight of the last few hours started to exert pressure on her shoulders. She reached the door, placed her left foot and leg outward making a barricade as she pushed the door outward. She half expected Koda to burst through, happy to see her or relieved to be let out of the garage. The other half had no idea what to expect.

Nothing happened. She reached out with her left hand, flipped the light switch on and grabbed the leash off the coatrack hook. Still no Koda, but she did hear a sad whining sound. Stepping into the garage she closed the door all but a crack so Koda wouldn't go charging inside and potentially get shot.

"Koda, come here, boy. Koda?"

Kate walked in front of both cars. The three-car garage was big. Plenty of space but little room to hide. Matt was meticulous and kept it cleaner than the inside of most homes Kate had seen. She liked it though. Felt good every time she pulled her car in. Something about the orderliness, knowing everything had a place.

She walked alongside Matt's car. Between the wall and the car sat Koda. He looked like he was frightened. Like he had failed somehow and was destined to be rejected yet again. Kate's heart felt a twinge of sadness.

"Oh, boy, it's okay. We're going to be okay."

Kate knelt and stroked Koda's head. He looked up at her with pleading eyes, begging for forgiveness. Kate leaning forward so she could get down to Koda's level. She hugged and talked to him.

"Come on, boy, this is your home. You're okay. Don't you fret Matt, he is a survivor. He'll be okay. He didn't do anything wrong, and you certainly didn't either."

Kate looked back at Koda's hind-end and noticed his tail perk up. It started to move back and forth in a slow but deliberate fashion. It looked to be gaining momentum as if the weight of it commanded a continuing motion.

Kate took the leash and clipped it on the black collar. Seeing the Trailblazer logo reminded her of five players working together. She knew she would need to work with Matt, as well as Koda now, to get through this in a healthy way.

"Let's go, boy. You and I are going to take a little ride down to see Matt, okay? He's waiting for us downtown."

Sergeant Gilliam's voice startled Kate. She stood, as did Koda, and turned back toward the door.

"I'm afraid your dog will not be able to come down to the station, Ma'am. You'll need to leave him here."

"Says who?" Kate questioned without hesitation as she and Koda made their way into the house.

Sergeant Gilliam stood aside seeing a restrained and under control dog. He didn't answer, so Kate continued.

"Whoever said he can't go, Sergeant Gilliam, get on your little mic there and tell them I am taking my dog with me to the station. If you won't let him come inside with me, then fine, but I am grabbing my jacket, the car keys, and driving down to the station. With my dog!"

Kate, moving past officer Gilliam and into the kitchen, grabbed her keys out of the basket and headed for the front closet to grab a jacket. She wouldn't need it in a couple of hours when the sun came up, but for right now the chill in the air was such that the added layer of warmth would be comforting. Koda followed dutifully, appearing grateful and relaxed.

"Uh, no one said he couldn't go, Ma'am. I just assumed you would want to ride down to the station with me, and I can't have the dog in the squad car."

"Why in the world would I ride down there with you? That would be stupid. Am I under arrest?"

"No, Ma'am, you are not."

"Well, then, I am riding down there in my Jeep with Koda. We will need a car to drive home when this is over."

Kate paused before continuing her train of thought.

"And I am assuming this will be over rather quickly. Matt's attorney is quite good. His reputation is stellar, I will say. I assume you all don't have anything serious in nature to charge Matt with, or you would have taken him in last night."

There was a pause. Kate slid her jacket on and closed the closet door. She looked directly at Sergeant Gilliam, who had followed her into the foyer. Koda sat next to her pushing his head up against her leg.

"I can't speak about the case, Ma'am."

"Of course, you can't. Come on Koda, let's take a ride and go get Matt."

Kate opened the front door and for the first time noticed, with a quick count, what looked to be five police cars.

"What the hell? You guys think you landed a serial killer or something, and he was going to make a run for it? Looks like you guys don't get to do this much, and you couldn't wait to bring out all your toys."

An embarrassed sergeant Gilliam knew she was right and was pissed at that asshole Detective Cole for what appeared to be a clear over-reaction.

"No need to get upset, Ma'am."

Kate tilted her head back and laughed out loud. A forced laugh. She knew it sounded fake, but the action of doing it gave her confidence and helped her focus. She didn't know why. She didn't care enough to make time to contemplate the reason.

"No need to get upset you say?"

Kate let the question hang hoping she wouldn't get a response. Sergeant Gilliam, realizing she was incredulous and getting more so by the minute, surprised himself by keeping his mouth shut.

"As I suspected, Sergeant Gilliam. You know I am right. I wake up to a policeman standing at the door of my bedroom with his hand on his gun. He is asking if I am okay. My husband is not in bed next to me. You tell me he has been taken to the station after we had already decided to be down at said place at nine this morning.

Said place? Kate thought to herself as she continued.

"My dog, that I just got yesterday, is nowhere to be seen. Then, as I dress, the policeman gawks at me like I'm a piece of prized meat and he hasn't eaten in weeks."

Kate stood looking at Sergeant Gilliam, with the front door still open and Koda dutifully by her side. Sergeant Gilliam, only three or four steps away, stared, unable to pick up Kate's clue. She waived her left, non-leash hand, in a sweeping motion across her waist toward outside. She waited, noticing Sergeant Gilliam's soft hands. There didn't appear to be any nicks or scrapes. A soft man with no evidence of any real physical labor. "*No character in a man's hands, Katie, tells you all you need to know*," her grandfather's words echoed in her head.

The impending migraine headache, now but a memory; had successfully been pushed aside.

Looking up, rolling her eyes, her hand still outstretched, Kate spoke in a calm and clear voice to Sergeant Gilliam.

"This is your clue to get out of my home, officer."

Leadership, Patience, And Lit-Up

Standing in the office with the door closed, Graley lowered her head. She had not yet heard the commanding officer yell. He'd been visibly upset more than a few times since his arrival, yes, but the yelling was new.

Her first reaction, which surprised her, was defensive, and then combative. Unsure feelings swirled; her brain worked on a plan of action, a calculated reaction of how she was supposed to react.

Coming up empty, she sat in silence, focused on keeping her body straight. A confident, no slouching look. Take the lashing like an outstanding cop and see where the wave of authoritative emotions ended.

She wasn't used to being defensive or combative, with a superior that is, and was grateful when the boss's voice softened, coming down to a normal discussion level.

"Okay, Graley, listen to me okay. You may sit down now, by the way."

Her commander stopped pacing and sat down behind his desk. He waived his hand in a casual gesture signaling Graley to take a seat which she did. The tension floated out of the room as quickly as it had stormed in. Graley took a seat, feeling the heaviness emanating outward, in a wave of energy as it escaped her body from both shoulders. Optimistic that the verbal beating was over, she turned to look out of the vinegar-cleaned, glass-covered office, to see several of her contemporaries gawking at the commander as he dressed down one of the most respected cops in the station.

The little wannabe partner of hers, Cole, was among those watching. They stared like someone would at an animal in a zoo. She didn't know whether to demand a new partner at this very moment or talk with Cole hoping to get something into the thick, stubborn, sexist head of his.

"As I was yelling, Graley—and my apologies, by the way—I am not used to getting a call from the mayor's office about how incompetent this office is. I've only been here a couple of months, as you know. I don't want to start my new position, one I have been working hard for twenty years to get, this way. Anyhow, I took it out on you."

Graley forced her lips upwards and smiled a nervous little smile, wondering why in the hell he wasn't, at this very moment, demanding Cole hand in his badge and gun. That's exactly what she thought should be done. She listened, with a genuine intent to understand.

Her boss swung around in his chair and started talking to the window before pivoting and looking Graley in the eyes.

"You are one of the best detectives we have at this station, and I hope you are aware of my feelings about your work ethic. I just laid it all out, blinds open, with the hope of getting the rest of the team's attention. This isn't about you, but if the department hears and sees me dressing you down the way I just did, it will hopefully get everyone to be more conscientious about doing their jobs the right way."

Graley swallowed, not sure this was the tactic she would choose, but he was in charge and clearly had his own method. She respected him for telling her straight out.

"Okay, Chief. Not sure I understand, but you're the boss," she responded.

Graley was regretful as soon as the words left her lips as her voice sounded weak and shaky. She hoped it only sounded this way to herself, not wanting commander number five in her career thinking she was weak.

"Listen, Graley, when I was in the military and going through basic training, I remember figuring out early on why the drill instructor yelled at me when I had done nothing wrong. It wasn't about me. It was intended for the guy standing next to me who the instructor didn't think had the mental fortitude to take a tongue lashing. Anyhow, he would pick a couple of us during training, me being one of them, and lay into us with everything he had with the hope of controlling the others. Fear-based management, I think they call it. Whoever the hell 'they' are."

Graley listened and waited patiently to chime in. She tried to think of a joke to say to lighten the mood.

"So, Chief, you sayin' I can take it like a man?" Graley, smiled, pleased with herself for coming back with what she thought was a well-placed, hopefully effective, smart-ass response.

"Partially correct, Graley. Leave out the man part though. Seems a bit sexist to me if you are asking."

Graley hung her chin a tad at the missed humor.

"What I am saying is that you are respected down here. I have confidence in your ability. You are aware enough of this situation to know you didn't do anything wrong. Perhaps a slight error in judgement in asking that little shit Cole to go stake out the Walker's place, but I get why you did it."

Graley recoiled internally, frustrated with herself over the "sexist" comment not accomplishing its intended effect, and a little embarrassed she made the damn statement to begin with. Rookie mistake. Graley paid close attention as the Chief continued.

"Here is how the next few minutes are going to go down, Graley. I am going to have Cole come in here and read him the riot act after he is afforded the opportunity to offer an explanation. I'm sure it's going to be a bunch of bullshit, which he won't get away with, so let me do my commander thing, okay?"

"Okay, Chief."

Graley liked what he was saying so far. She didn't know much about the new Chief. He was a transplant from back east, she had heard and read. Other than that, she made it a point to stay out of the department politics, and so knew little about him. When her father was consistently cogent enough to talk with her, he always said, "*Keep your head down and do your job. Let all the shit going on around you be outside your area of concern, and you will do all right in life.*"

Graley never claimed her father was perfect. She thought herself to be wiser and more polished than her paternal namesake, but she surprised herself with how often a statement would come out sounding like her father. The effect of the parental guidance, or lack thereof, always comes out, she determined.

Judging by a cop's standards, her judgement could be subject to normal interpretation, with so many of them having their own issues. What rattled or surprised her the most was when a glance or look in the mirror returned a reflection of her father. The older she got, the more frequent the reflective recognition took place.

The Chief stood and walked to the office door.

"Cole, come in here, please."

Graley wasn't sure if she was pissed at the Chief for having such a calm voice or impressed with his ability to be so matter-of-fact. She smiled thinking Cole was about to get lit up. The next few moments taught her a tremendous amount about leadership and patience. The disappointment would take her a while to understand.

A Pissed Off Chameleon?

"Come in, Detective. Good to see you. Please have a seat next to your partner."

Cole, feeling the bitter sting of disappointment and humiliation in what could only be described as inexperience, unprofessionalism, and a complete lack of sound police judgement on his part, focused on his newfound hatred of Matt Walker. He tried to pay attention to the Chief but struggled to take a seat in the chair next to Detective Graley, a partner who he knew didn't like him to begin with. Now, she probably wouldn't be able to stand him at all, and most likely would ask to be reassigned. He didn't give a fuck. He couldn't stand the self-righteous know-it-all bitch.

"Thanks, Chief," Cole responded in a lame-ass way, he thought to himself.

"So, let me recap a bit here, Detective Cole, so I can make absolutely certain I have all my facts right. So important in police work, wouldn't you say? Having all the facts, right? No need to answer, Detective Cole. A rhetorical question."

Graley couldn't help but notice the Chief's eyes as they bored into Cole. He was a tall man; Graley figured he had to be six feet five inches at least. Sitting in his chair, he almost appeared to be standing, he was so damn big. An intimidating man for sure. The eyes had a calm fury about them. They were directed at Cole with laser focus.

Graley held back her smile at the rhetorical question jab. She looked at Cole, who fidgeted in his chair. His pasty white skin, acne spot on his neck, and smoke-stained hands made her stomach turn. She never thought he was weak, just sloppy and undisciplined. That is, until she saw him sitting in the chair cowering at the Chief's every word.

Graley sat up straighter, wishing she had a video recorder, as the Chief continued.

"You, and the distinguished Detective Graley here, are called in to investigate a potential homicide at the residence of Matt Walker. From what I understand, and you can correct me at any time if I state something incorrectly, Detective Cole, Mr. Walker called in to the station and reported a body floating in the lake by his home. The body was face down and fully clothed, and once identified, was determined to be Matt Walker's first wife. Detective Graley appropriately takes the lead based on her many years of experience in police matters, then questions Mr. Walker and his wife. Detective Graley, as she has informed me, says the Walkers were both helpful and cordial at every step of the way."

Graley watched as the Chief paused. He reached over with his left hand covered in deep lines, beat up nails, and a strong weathered appearance, to grab a coffee cup on his desk. Taking a slow deliberate drink, the Chief set the cup down, turning his head back and forth popping his neck before resuming.

Cole sat not knowing if he should speak or stay silent during the long pause. He decided to stay silent. He was too scared to take any chances right now.

"Hmm, coffee is a bit cold. Now, where was I? Ah, yes, Detective Cole."

The Chief sat a little straighter in his chair, making himself even more imposing as he picked up the piece of paper, the report, off his desk and continued.

"While questioning the Walkers, the recovery team wheels the body up past Detective Graley and the Walkers, at which time Mr. Walker is asked if he can identify the body. He states it is his first wife right away. As I understand the situation from others, Detective Cole, the man didn't hesitate, hem or haw, kick the dirt with his feet, blink, bat an eye, look up at the stars, or anything of the sort. Simply said it was his first wife. Oh, and *he* called *us*, right?"

Cole, on cue now, at least he thought, started to respond until he saw the Chief's eyes, which were begging him to interrupt. Cole kept his mouth shut in a rage, feeling his partner smile next to him.

"Detective Graley here, who has had more commendations than any other police officer in Medford during her time on the force, decides it is in the best interest of everyone involved, based on the information at hand, to have Mr. Walker come in on his own this morning at 9 o'clock, correct?"

Graley watched as the chief paused, this time clearly soliciting a response from Cole, who sat in his chair getting smaller with every piercing word. Cole froze, stuck in silence.

"Are you going to answer me, Detective Cole?"

Cole flinched. Graley thought he was going to start crying.

"Yes, sir."

Graley watched as the Chief dropped the report, leaned forward and put his elbows on his desk, crossed his beautiful rough hands, and placed them under his chin. The Chief's words flowed with supreme confidence.

"Detective Cole, I work for a living. I am a Chief, a position I have worked hard to achieve. I am good at it. The job wasn't handed to me and I didn't learn it overnight. We can only hope you learn one day as a detective...but I digress."

"Yes, Chief," Cole whispered as he tried to imagine a shovel plowing into the side of Matt Walker's head.

"Good, then, we are all on the same page. Detective Graley, can I have my secretary get you a cup of coffee?"

Graley smiled.

"No thanks, Chief, I'm good."

"Fine then. Let me think a second."

The Chief leaned back in his chair, took his elbows off the table, and continued the grilling of the frail detective Cole.

"Detective Graley determines the best course of action is to question Mr. Walker at nine this morning. She, out of the kindness of her big and successful heart, drops you off at a craft brewery for a night cap or two, I can assume. She goes home to take care of her father, her second job at the moment, due to his advanced age and oncoming Alzheimer's. Is my assessment correct, Detective Graley?"

"Unfortunately, yes, Chief." Graley responded in a fluid, flawless motion.

"Damn shame, old age, Graley. My best in dealing with your dad, by the way."

The Chief talked calmly with Graley as if nothing was going on and Detective Cole wasn't in the room. She became more and more impressed with his every passing word.

"Thanks, Chief. He and I will get through it.

The Chief directed his eyes back to Cole and changed his facial expression like a pissed off chameleon.

"While contemplating the day's events and running everything back through her mental processor, Detective Graley thinks it best that either she or you go back on site at the Walkers to sit with, or at least check-up on, the police assigned to secure and monitor the crime scene. So, she calls you since she wasn't in a favorable position to leave her father alone for the rest of the night. She checks to see how much you've had to drink. You inform her one beer, so she asks you to check on the officer. She makes it very clear you are not to go up to the Walker's home. You are to monitor the situation only. Correct?"

Cole was either stupid, thick-headed, stubborn, or unable to think clearly when he was being challenged. Graley surmised it was a bit of all-of-the-above after Cole responded with disdain and an argumentative tone.

"But I had reason to suspect that Mr. Walker was burying a body with his shovel, sir, I mean Chief."

"Ah, the shovel, Detective Cole."

Graley watched as the Chief stood, went around the corner of his desk and stood at his window, which was now covered in a light rain. One raindrop after another, raced each other downward in a ballet like motion across their glass stage. The Chief talked into the window at Detective Cole.

"Sergeant Gilliam informs me that he saw Mr. Walker go into the garage with his dog, return with a shovel and head to the backyard. Which I assume you, based on your many months of detective work putting two and two together, figured Mr. Walker committed a murder and perhaps was going to bury the body of his third wife."

"Exactly, Chief." Graley noticed how eager and quick Cole's response was and recognized how out of his element her damn partner was.

The Chief turned and walked over in front of detective Cole, sitting down on the edge of his desk. He towered over the diminutive detective directing his questions at Cole while also speaking to Graley.

"Detective Graley. What do people who have dogs use shovels for?"

"To scoop their shit, Chief?"

Cole couldn't believe how timid he sounded. He couldn't stand the chief and it was all Walker's fault.

"Ah ha. Scoop dog poop. See how wise he is, Detective Cole? The shovel you wrapped up in plastic. By the way, nice work of wrapping, the CSI team tells me. Said the wrap job was top notch, top notch they said, Cole—their words, not mine. Apparently, their investigative efforts found the shovel covered in dog poop without a trace of blood. Preliminary reports say no evidence of blood at all on the shovel. Now we have a wronged citizen who may or may not have been involved in a murder locked up, a high-profile attorney calling the mayor direct, and me getting wakened by a phone call and chewed out because one of my detectives is an idiot!"

Graley watched the Chief stand in what appeared to be a well-choreographed thought when he said "idiot" to Cole. She thought the Chief might wring his neck. She didn't feel bad for her partner in the least. He earned it. She focused on not showing any glee.

The Chief sat stoic on the edge of his desk. He didn't say a word. It was as if his eyes were begging Cole to speak out of order again. Seconds passed. Must have seemed like hours to Cole, Graley surmised.

"Detective Cole. You are being placed on a ninety-day probation. If we weren't so short-handed, I would suspend you. You will follow Detective Graley's orders for the rest of this investigation. You will no longer smoke in the city of Medford's police cars, and if I see that piece of crap Vette of yours parked one inch over any parking line I will have it impounded and you will be forced to go through all the normal citizen channels to get it out."

With a lower and constrained voice, again, Graley listened as the Chief gave Cole one final order.

"Get out of my office, Cole. Don't give me a reason to suspend you and make Graley's day by giving her a new partner. Do I make myself clear?"

Waiting Dutifully

Finally, Matt's head hit a pillow and his brain quieted, albeit in a jail cell. His first, and hopefully only, experience inside the Ironbar Hotel wasn't bad. The cot provided a couple hours of rest, something he had been struggling with. Former wives, Sharon and Betheny, kept seeking him out in his dreams, but these were less scary than the first he had on the deck chair next to the lake with Koda. Either they were not as frightening, or he was so tired he kept on sleeping despite his formers' dream visits.

Kate arrived a while ago, he was told, but was not allowed to see him. The one phone call they allowed Matt to make went to Kate, but she didn't pick up. Matt could only assume she forgot her phone in the craziness that he was sure must have ensued at their home after the idiot Detective Cole jacked him up. Matt left her a message anyway, telling her not to worry. He would see her at nine, hopefully, when his attorney arrived.

Matt, prior to leaving Kate a message, had contemplated for an instant who to call, Kate or his attorney? He made the decision with little hesitation. Jim Davies, his attorney, would be here at nine anyway, so why not try to rest? He called Kate and left the message specifically telling her not to call Jim. He assured her he was okay; he was in the Ironbar suite, on his own with a toilet and cot, and was going to try to sleep. He finished his message to Kate while a policeman listened in.

"Kate, I love you. Everything is going to be okay. See you at nine, or thereabouts, with the attorney, okay?"

Matt looked at his wristwatch, which showed eight fifty-five. He wondered why they took his wallet but not his watch. Probably forgot. The belt he got. It could be a threat, a potential weapon, or suicide tool.

An oversight on the small-city police force leaving him his watch on his wrist. The damn thing could be a James Bond style toy for all they knew.

He pressed the dial on the side of the watch, reflexively, as if a laser was going to shoot out and help with his escape. He wondered why his brain would tell his finger to make the action knowing damn good and well there was no laser. He paced, moving his head side to side, trying to pop his tense neck.

Stressed and antsy, Matt knew he hadn't done anything wrong, but the felonious hotel had the ability to make him feel guilty despite his innocence. He couldn't see anything on the other side of the bars except a wall. He wished he had his cell phone for a selfie as he stopped pacing for a second, grabbed the bars with both hands and pushed his cheeks against the cold steel. He thought of Jack Nicholson in the Shining and thought about yelling out, *here's Johnny*—or was it something else? Not able to remember, and not wanting to get the line wrong he opted for, "WHERE IS MY LAWYER?"

Smiling, Matt released the bars and turned. He was pacing again when he heard a door open. Someone was walking toward his cell. This much he could tell. Absent was the sound of jingling keys the police were supposed to have in their hand. They had to have keys, right? Matt looked at the cell door and didn't see the big keyhole. Another disappointment he would share with Kate at when the time was right.

Matt, watched as a uniformed policeman stopped in front of the cell and grabbed a mic on his shoulder.

"Prisoner secure, open cell three please."

There was a click, and the officer pushed the door to the side.

"Well, what a major disappointment, officer. I thought for sure there would be key jingling and you would spend time searching for the right one."

"Come on, Walker. Your attorney is here."

"No cuffs, officer?"

The policeman stood at the open door and stuck his arm out. Matt got the officer's attention as he turned and looked around the cell before heading toward Suite Three's exit. He couldn't pass up the opportunity to make a wisecrack, hoping he wouldn't be back here again.

"Wait officer, I want to get one last look. I will never be in here again. I don't suppose you have your cell phone on you, do you? Would you mind taking a photo of me for my wife's Facebook page? It would be a hoot."

Matt smiled as the policeman stood there, stoic.

"No? Okay. I didn't think you would be up for it, but I had to ask."

"Come on Walker, will you? I have shit to do and standing here listening to you act like an asshole isn't one of them."

This guy hadn't done anything to Matt, so he decided to stop joking around.

"Understood. Just interesting is all. Can't believe I ended up in here."

Matt continued talking as the two left the cell.

"Your Detective Cole is a real piece of work, officer. You know him?"

No reply, so Matt let silence guide him the rest of the way down the hall and out the door which opened automatically. A left, then another short hall, and he found himself in a hall with several doors.

"Stop here," commanded the Policeman.

Matt obeyed and watched an older cop open a door. Inside the room was Matt's attorney, alone. Kate was absent. He was happy to see the attorney but did long to see his wife. He needed the face to reassure him she was okay.

"Jim, damn good to see you."

The door closed behind Matt.

"Is Kate okay?"

"She's fine, Matt. She's in the lobby waiting to see you. First, have a seat and let's chat. When we are done, the detectives will come in."

Matt grabbed a seat on the slick, dark green, perhaps black vinyl, showing signs of wear as he grabbed the edges of the metal chair. He wondered how many actual serious criminals had plopped their asses on this very chair, denying and lying, hoping to get away with their dirty deeds.

Jim remained standing. Matt watched as his attorney positioned himself on the opposite side of the table Matt now leaned on. Behind Jim was a mirror. Matt figured it to be a two-way. He guessed Graley and Cole were in a room opposite the reflective glass, watching right now.

"Are there detectives on the other side of that glass behind you, Jim?"

"Probably, Matt. Focus here, okay? I have stuff to do and the longer we bullshit, the more money this is going to cost you. Capisce?"

Matt smiled, liking Jim's lingo. He hadn't seen his old friend in a while. At least a couple of months.

"Good point, and thanks. I'm a bit frazzled, Jim. Not much sleep last night, the death of my two formers and all, not to mention ending up in jail, has me a bit edgy."

"Understood, Matt. Listen, they aren't placing any charges. At least not yet. This has turned into a massive fuck-up for Chief Barker. Good guy, who I have known for years. We went to college together at Portland State for a couple of years. Anyhow, when I got your message, I called the mayor who you know I have dinner with once a month, right?"

Matt listened. He had little other options as Jim didn't give him a chance to get a word in edge-wise.

"Anyhow, your shovel was covered in shit, nothing more, and detective Cole has been placed on probation for ninety days per my chat with Barker moments ago. No official word on Sharon yet. Could be nothing more than a drowning? I will admit, it is quite odd you found her floating in the lake by your house, but nonetheless, nothing official about a homicide yet. They won't know for a day or two. As for Betheny, it is much clearer. Definite manslaughter or homicide, but again with her death, nothing firm yet. You have an alibi for Betheny, so again they aren't pressing any charges for now. Detective Cole has put them in a very untenable position with his over-reaction this morning. Not that you didn't have good standing before his ill-advised arrest. The police are going to have to back off you now."

Matt listened, then watched for a second as Jim took a breath, before speaking.

"So now what? I get out of here, right?"

"Yep. I will signal the detectives to come in and they will ask a couple of questions, which you won't answer, I will press the urgency of an arrest or release, and we will be on our way. You got it, Matt? Keep your mouth shut. I do the talking. Three hundred bucks an hour adds up fast."

Matt watched, and understood, as Jim tapped his wrist watch then turned raising a hand toward the mirror. His attorney walked around the table and sat down in the chair next to Matt as the door opened. In walked detective Graley, by herself.

"Where is your dick-head partner, Detective Graley?" Matt couldn't help himself. Okay he could, but he didn't want to. He looked at Jim. "Okay, I am done now. Promise."

Graley smiled and stood opposite Mr. Walker and his attorney. She knew this charade was a formality only and they would be out of here in seconds, so no need to get positioned in a chair.

"He had paperwork to finish and is going to be busy with it for a while, Mr. Walker."

"Are you charging my client with anything, detective?" Matt listened, impressed with Jim's command of the room.

"No, not now. On behalf of the department, and my "dick-head" partner, Detective Cole..."

Matt smiled as detective Graley had a twinkle in her eye.

"...I would like to apologize for the way things were handled this morning at your residence."

Matt thought Detective Cole an even bigger coward for not being in here himself. Matt didn't know Cole at all, really, but what little he could surmise was the detective had an inability to control himself.

"I will need to speak with your client soon."

Graley directed the statement at Jim. Matt waited for a response, not knowing what direction this would go. Jim stood, put his hand on Matt's shoulder, then reached into his suit jacket's inner pocket and extracted a business card.

"Here, Detective. Call my office and my secretary will set a time up for all of us. I should be able to make the time when necessary."

Matt smiled, satisfied with Jim's confidence, pushing the questioning into the future, then regretted the thought as he realized this would drag out. He wanted it over with.

Graley shook her head, then dropped her eyes, pissed at Cole even more now for putting her in this submissive position. She didn't like it one bit. Taking the card, Graley glanced at the impressive silver embossed letters on a rich matte black backdrop. The Law Offices of Jim Davies. No number, email or anything else. She flipped it over and saw all the information she needed on the back.

"Thank you. I will call your office in a few minutes. Thanks again for your time."

Graley turned, and the door opened outward. Matt noticed for the first time that there wasn't a door handle on the inside of the door, just a ring-shaped device which was inset in stainless steel.

Is that even legal? He wondered.

"Come on, Matt, Kate is in the lobby and quite anxious, I am certain."

Matt remembered he had no belt. Standing, his jeans slipped a touch resting lower on his hips than normal.

"What about my wallet and belt, Detective Graley?"

"Just stop at the end of the hall. There is a processing officer at the window that will give you all your valuables. I am certain your lawyer must be familiar with the process."

Matt looked at Jim, who shrugged. Matt didn't think Jim had spent much time in here at all, since he was primarily a divorce attorney, but hell, who knew.

Heading for the end of the hall, Matt stopped at the thick glass as an officer slid an envelope through the slot. M. WALKER was written across the front in bold black ink. Picking the golden envelope up, he didn't like the way the person made the W. It was sloppy.

"Let's get out of here," he mouthed to Jim while checking the contents of the M. WALKER envelope.

All he cared about were his wallet and belt. The envelope felt heavier than what those two items would weigh. He peeked inside as Jim held the door open for him, and they walked out as if they were in a race.

Looking in the envelope he found his wallet, belt, loose change, and cellphone, which explained the weight.

Matt took the phone and started to dial Kate before remembering she was in the lobby. Walking out of the Ironbar Hotel forever, Matt entered the outer lobby and saw Kate sitting, gazing out the window. She had a hand on Koda's head; Koda was sitting dutifully next to her.

Walking toward Kate, Matt swore he saw a reflection of her in the rain-soaked glass. It looked like smoke billowed off her skin.

The Guilt Subsided

Cole picked up a pen from his desk drawer. He wanted to snap the damn thing in two and throw it, but slammed the drawer shut instead. The Chief was making him re-write his report on the Matt Walker case. He was told it was too short and lacked the necessary detail expected of a detective.

"Whatever the hell that means," Cole mumbled, which of course no one could hear.

The Chief also mentioned Cole wasn't to leave the building until he was satisfied the report was done properly. Cole knew it was absolute bullshit. The first report was adequate. Since when did the Chief give a damn about Cole's reports? Since he brought Walker in; the son-of-a-...

Across from Cole, Graley stood from her desk. Stretching, she grabbed her jacket off the back of her chair and talked to Cole. Pissed every time she had to look at him, she did her best to keep her cool.

"Cole, I have to run over to Westside Senior Home. I should be back in about two hours. If anyone important calls for me, send me a text. Also, let me know about any updates or reports from the forensic team."

Graley walked out of the office area, leaving Cole at his desk sulking like a scorned child.

Cole stared at Graley's back mouthing the words, *yes, sir, biatch.* He was furious she had the audacity to talk to him this way. She had a total disregard for his status as a detective. He may not be an equal in seniority, but he was a detective, like her. He fumed remembering that if Graley hadn't ordered him to go stakeout Walker's place, none of this would have happened. Then there is the pompous-ass Walker, who Cole knew was up to something. Cole swore to himself he would find out. He had to.

Graley headed out of the building amid a blowing mist in the damp morning air. Pulling her jacket's hood over her hair, she lowered her head a touch en route to the police cruiser. She made her mind up while the Chief yelled at her that her father needed to be in a senior home. He would not be happy about it, but Graley figured he wouldn't remember how he got there in the first place.

It was the safest thing to do. Anymore, her father could not be left alone for any extended time. It wasn't safe. Since this case would consume a lot of her time in the coming days, if not weeks, it made the most sense to relocate her dad. She needed all her focus on the job right now.

Shifting her thoughts from her father, Graley challenged herself to concentrate on the Walker deaths as she guided the cruiser through town toward the picturesque Southern Oregon University and Shakespearean theater town of Ashland. She had time to spare, so she kept the car on the back roads, off the interstate. More time to think.

The wine vineyards now consumed the landscapes, pushing out dairy farms and most of the fruit orchards. They were pretty, Graley thought, and there were worse things than grapes. Take the pot farms, with their ugly high fences and rancid smell come harvest time. She was grateful the vineyards had a couple of decade's head start on legalized marijuana.

As Graley looked out the window, she pictured driving through the Bordeaux region of France. She had read about the similarities and comparison in a Wine magazine the last time she was at her dentist's office.

Slowing for a stop sign, watching the car in front of her make a California stop, almost running over a pedestrian, Graley focused back on Betheny Millstone, "Former Number Two," Walker would have said. She was hiding something from the police. She was afraid, no doubt about that, but not in a being buried alive terror way. Graley thought it to be more like, scared as if you know there will be consequences if you are caught doing something wrong.

The woman had clearly given Walker a signal with her eyes. Was she pleading for help? Was she trying to tell Walker something that only he would know? Did Walker and Former Number Two have a secret?

That damn Cole. Questions she needed to ask Walker, would now be delayed for who knows how long. She made a note to talk with the Chief and see if he could help her get the questioning expedited since he knew Walker's attorney.

Now Graley switched her thoughts to Former Number One, found floating face down in the lake fully clothed. Much more of a mystery. She had never met the woman or seen her alive like Betheny. So much to be learned from a person watching them interact with others. Betheny, for example, liked to keep secrets. She was playful and a dreamer. She still had deep feelings for Matt Walker.

Graley had no trouble picking up on Betheny's feelings for her ex right away. The way she not only ran to Walker but held him. She didn't just lay her head in his chest, she nestled. She moved her chin ever so slightly back and forth. She breathed him in. That's what it was, Graley thought. She liked the way he smelled and missed it.

Graley picked up her mic.

"Dispatch, car six-seven, over."

"Go ahead six-seven," squawked the radio.

It sounded like Johnson, which was good for Graley. Johnson and she went way back.

"Johnson, that you?"

"Yep, what's up, you old lesbo? I heard you had a little run in with the Chief this morning. You okay?"

"Fine, you old prick, and yes I did. It was interesting."

Graley, smiling at the banter, put on the turn signal and made a left. She wished she wasn't getting to the senior home so quick. Driving through the country helped her think. When she was alone, that is. She smiled at the thought of Cole pushing papers.

"Well, the talk down here is you got lit up and he went soft on Cole."

"That's the talk, is it? Well, must be right then," Graley responded, not wanting to get into detail. Her mind was elsewhere.

"You going to let me talk, Johnson, or you going to just keep gossiping like an old hen?"

Johnson laughed. Graley's favorite thing about him. He had a fantastic deep laugh. He would always tilt his head back, open his mouth to let it out, and his eyes would squint so they were almost shut. Graley could always count on him for a smile.

"What do you need, Gray?"

"Can you put me through to the coroner's office? I want to see if they have any results back on one of the dead women that turned up yesterday. I need to get information if possible, but I am on my way to Ashland and can't run over there. I don't want it to wait."

"Oh, real quick Gray, not sure if you heard but someone called in a small fire on the bank of Emigrant. Said they thought it looked like a boat. An officer has been sent to check it out."

Graley didn't immediately make a connection, but a burnt boat did warrant an investigation.

"Damn, okay and thanks for the info, I hadn't heard."

"Okay Gray, hang on while I connect you and later you old battle-axe."

Graley laughed and a few seconds went by, perhaps thirty, in silence.

"Gray, got them on the phone. Go ahead, and I will talk at you later."

"Thanks, Johnson."

"Hello."

"Hi, hello. Is this the coroner's office?"

"This is Dr. Taylor. May I help you?"

Graley loved this guy's thick Australian accent. She found it to be quite alluring.

"This is Detective Graley. There was a body brought in last night. A brunette woman who was found face down in the water. I know it's soon, but have you had a chance to find anything yet? I need to get a jumpstart on this case."

Graley stopped talking and stayed hopeful, listening for the doc to call her "mate." She loved that.

"Well, mate, you are in luck. I just finished my preliminary. Looks like she was killed with a very sharp pointing object in the back of the skull. My guess is an ice pick. Her lungs were filled with water, so she drowned as well. Would have died from the pick, but not instantly. No sign of sexual assault, no defensive wounds of any kind, and no sign of any strike-back wounds. That is, no flesh or tearing of the nails. It would appear to me that this woman knew her attacker, or at the very least trusted the person."

Graley's heart sank, her stomach knotted, and she felt like vomiting at the thought of an ice pick being jammed into the back of her head. She didn't think Matt Walker the type to bury an ice pick in flesh, but one never knew.

"Geezus, Doc, thanks. When will you have the full done? You did say prelim, right?"

"Yes, I did, very good Detective. Well, mate, probably later today. I'll examine the other woman, who I am told could be related, about the same time. The second one appears to be more cut and dried. I don't expect to find anything sinister other than what the surgeons said. A burst blood vessel in the noggin."

Graley waited as the county's forensic pathologist paused. She was about to speak when he chimed back in.

"Anything else, Detective?"

"No and thank you very much. I'll stop by later this afternoon."

Listening as the coroner hung the phone up without a goodbye, Graley didn't know if she should be offended or not. Perhaps no goodbye was an Aussie thing.

Graley eased the police cruiser into the circular drive at the front of the Westside Senior Home. There was a heaviness on her shoulders. Pushing downward, the weight of guilt tried to creep its way into her psyche. She envisioned her father being here, being happy, and getting the proper care she wanted him to have. The guilt subsided. She knew bringing him here was the right thing to do.

Walking into the lobby, Graley thought about an ice pick to the skull. Would it be long enough to hit the brain? Did it need to hit the brain? She also wondered if it didn't puncture the brain, would it kill the victim on its own? The coroner said the lungs were full of water, so the woman had to have been sucking some in right, meaning the ice pick hadn't killed her? Did it even matter? Questions she hoped were intelligent enough to ask the coroner in another hour or so.

Cryptic Enough?

Matt hugged Kate, squeezing her firmly, as if the gesture alone would assuage her fears. Kate used her jacket sleeve, wiping her tears, as Matt looked on with a tender sadness.

"Are you okay, Kate? I'm so sorry about all this."

"Don't worry about the tears. They are more out of frustration than anything, Matt. I'll be fine. And for goodness' sake, it isn't your fault."

A seated Koda whimpered to get attention from Matt. Not wanting to let his new friend down, Matt obliged, patting the dog on the head, then rubbing one of his ears.

"How about you, Matt? Are you okay?"

Kate pushed herself back from Matt, still holding on to one of his hands.

"I'm fine. I was able to get a bit of sleep, so not all was lost."

"What happened? Why did you end up in here? The police wouldn't tell me anything."

Jim Davis, Matt's attorney stood nearby. He hung up his phone and turned toward the Walkers.

"Sorry to interrupt you two, but I have to go. Matt, we need to go over what's going on. Can you be at my office in, say, two hours? I have another meeting with the mayor that I can't delay."

Matt saw Jim look at his wrist watch, which made him instinctively look at his. It showed ten-thirty.

"Tell you what. Let's make it one. Will that work for you?"

Matt looked at Kate. So much was running through his head right now, he couldn't even remember what day of the week it was.

"Yeah, Jim. I'll make it work. See you at one."

Matt watched as Jim walked out of the police station with his cell phone planted firm against his ear.

"Did you drive down, Kate?"

"Yes."

"Okay, let's get out of here. We can talk on the drive home."

"Come on, Koda."

Kate gave a gentle tug to Koda's leash, and he was more than willing to follow.

"They let you in here with the dog?"

"I didn't ask, Matt. I just came in with him as if I owned the place. I figured if they said something I would lie and say he was my therapy dog."

"I bet it was nice having him with you, Kate."

"Oh, here Matt, I brought you a jacket. I wasn't sure how you would be dressed, and it's damp and chilly out right now."

Kate handed Matt a jacket, and he slipped it on.

"Thanks, babe. Glad, we're getting the rain, we need it."

Matt held the door open and they, along with Koda, made their way to the parking lot.

"The Jeep is right over here, Matt."

Kate and Koda led the way. Matt looked around noticing the grey skies and mountains shrouded in fog and clouds. The damp, cold air did its best to usher in winter, which Matt wasn't ready for.

"I need to get the windows done soon. Fall seems to be colder than normal this year."

Kate pressed the button on her key fob. The rear door of the Jeep responded, swinging open. She reached down and took off Koda's leash.

"Get in, boy."

Matt watched as Koda got a couple of steps head start then bounded upward into the Jeep. Koda laid down on a blanket Kate had laid out earlier. She pressed the fob button again, and the door closed.

"You want to drive, Matt?"

"Not really. Do you mind?"

"Not at all."

The two got into the Jeep and Kate started the vehicle. She turned to Matt before pulling out of the parking lot.

"I'm glad you are okay, but what are we going to do? Are we safe? And why in the hell did they bring you in? I thought we were all set up for nine this morning?"

Matt rolled his eyes, closed them, and moved his head back and forth in a slow motion as he responded.

"Remember Detective Cole, the young guy who was at the place yesterday with the female detective?"

"Yes, he was with Detective Graley, who I liked, by the way. I thought detective Cole was an asshole."

Kate eased the Jeep into reverse and pulled out of the parking lot.

"Well, you are spot on as always, beautiful."

Matt squeezed her leg and left his hand mid-thigh, in his typical way when she drove. He liked feeling connected to her and there was no better way while she drove. Holding hands was nice, but always a little awkward not to mention a tad dangerous.

"Apparently, Detective Cole saw me get a shovel out of the garage around four this morning and thought I was burying you, or something, in the backyard. He came out back and watched as I threw a pile of your boy's steaming crap into the lake. I heard "Freeze" and turned to find him standing there with his gun pointed at me like I just committed a murder."

"Oh my God, Matt, he could have shot you!"

"Yes, he could have. I'm lucky he didn't. The guy is twitchy, nervous as hell, and not very experienced. That much is clear."

"Why were you up so early?"

"I couldn't sleep. I fell asleep on the deck chair for a while. Your dog was by my side the whole time, by the way. We came in and I tried sleeping next to you and couldn't, so I got up to work in the office."

"It's so nice to see you and Koda taking to each other so quickly. I was a bit worried bringing him home. I know you weren't excited about the idea of a dog."

Matt squeezed her leg and turned looking over his shoulder toward the back of the Jeep, smiling approval at Koda.

"He is a good dog. You chose well, Kate."

Matt watched Kate take a turn at smiling before she asked him another question. "Did Koda go with you?"

"No, I let the little turd get up on the bed with you and he snuggled in. I must have been in the office a good forty-five minutes or so when he strolled in whimpering. I took him out back thinking he had to pee. He peed *and* crapped, so I went to the garage to get a shovel and get rid of the evidence when the damn rookie detective jacked us up."

"God, Matt, I'm so sorry."

Kate pulled off the road easing the Jeep into a Dutch Brothers coffee stand. Matt was glad. A hot coffee right now would be good.

"Usual, Matt?"

"Yes, please."

"Good morning, Ma'am, what can I get for you this morning?"

"A large soy chai, no foam, and one large black coffee."

The coffee attendant took Kate's card and rang up the order. A minute later Kate took both the drinks and handed Matt his rich, black Java.

Pulling away, Kate put the brakes on, looked down the street both ways, before easing the Jeep forward.

"So now what, Matt?"

"Well, for starters, I want to get home and shower... Shit!"

"What, Matt?"

Matt set his coffee in the console cup holder and grabbed his cell phone out of his pocket.

There was a moment or two of reflective silence between the two. Koda let out a quiet bark as he saw a man with his dog walking on the sidewalk.

Matt broke the human silence, talking to Kate, as he continued to move his way through his phone's screens.

"You will be glad to know your little dog is a badass."

"Really?" Kate questioned. "How so?"

"Well, when Cole leveled his gun at me, Koda stood right next to me. He had this menacing, nasty growl. It was as if he knew I was in trouble or being threatened on some level. The little stud didn't like it.

I had to forcibly restrain him, or he would have gone after Cole. It was a nice feeling."

Matt redirected his attention back to the phone.

Kate thought about everything the adoption shelter told her during the adoption process. What was necessary to qualify her as a dog partner and adopter? She couldn't remember anything about Koda having watch-dog tendencies, but then again, the shelters didn't know everything about the dogs they took in. They focused on who were aggressors, biters, good with kids, bad with cats, other dogs, etc. The basics which would allow them to give information necessary for an adopting family. She mentally left the shelter and got back in the conversation with Matt, who was still fiddling with his phone.

"I'm glad to hear that, Matt. Especially with certain events spiraling out of control. Nice to know someone besides you has my back."

"It does make me feel better."

"Funny, Matt, but now that you mention it, the little guy wouldn't leave my side this morning after you left, and I got him out of the garage. He insisted on being in the bedroom and the bathroom with me while I got ready to go to the police station."

Matt drifted in and out of listening.

"I completely forgot to call Jane. She needs to know what is going on. I finally found the number."

"Already done, babe." Kate took a long drink of her soy, enjoying the warm feeling she could feel hit the back of her throat and cruise toward her stomach. She loved the way Dutch Brothers made their chai.

"When, Kate, and what did you tell her?"

"When Koda and I were waiting in the station. I told her about yesterday, what happened with the two formers, and that you were one of the suspects, presumably."

"Okay, thanks. I better call her anyway."

Matt pressed the phone's screen, then placed it up against his ear. Jane picked up on the first ring.

"Walker and Associates Marketing, may I help you?"

"Jane, it's Matt."

"Oh, thank God, Matt. Are you okay?"

"Fine, Jane. Listen, please reschedule everything for me the rest of the week. Clear my schedule. Anything you can't move please give to Deb. Oh, and let everyone know I'm okay, my two formers are dead, both appeared to be murdered, and It Was Not Me. Okay?"

Matt couldn't believe the last statement was coming out of his mouth. Seemed surreal and not something he could ever imagine saying.

"Got it, Matt."

"I'll be checking in, and call me if you need anything, Jane. I'll pick up if I can. I must meet with my attorney in a few hours, and as for the rest of the week, I'll be trying to figure out what in the hell is happening. Anything else, Jane?"

"Don't worry about work, Matt. You know us. We'll take care of everything down here."

Matt thought Jane was finished and started to remove the phone from his ear and press the red button on the screen to end the call.

"Matt! Matt!"

"Um, yes Jane? Sorry, I'm still here. What is it?"

"I got this email today, forwarded from you as near as I can tell, and it looks like you and Kate are being threatened. What is going on, Matt?"

"Shit," Matt mumbled. He forgot he sent her a copy of the message.

Matt's mind danced trying to figure out what to say. He could hear the worry and fear in Jane's voice. He felt bad and wished there were a way he could comfort her, but right now the heaviness on his shoulders increased with the memory of the mysterious email he received sometime during the night. He could see the words on the monitor as clearly as if he were staring at the screen.

"Stop talking, K could be next."

"Just hold on to it, Jane, in case we need it, okay? Kate and I will be okay, and thanks for asking."

Matt hoped the reply was cryptic enough that Kate wouldn't ask about the message. If she did, he would have to tell her. He didn't want her to worry any more than she already was. He wanted the message in Jane's hands in case anything happened to him and/or Kate.

"Final thing, Jane. Kate and I will keep you updated, okay? If you must call me about work, go ahead. If you want to chat or get an update, then call Kate. Everything is going to be okay."

Matt hung the phone up, thinking about his final sentence to Jane. He wasn't confident his words were true.

Same Cole, Different Day

Cole sat at his desk plinking away on the computer keyboard, searching for anything and everything he could find on Matt Walker. They guy was a ghost for the most part, which only added fuel to Cole's already raging fire.

Outside of meaningless bullshit having to do with the guy's marketing business, Cole couldn't find anything. Walker didn't have a personal social media presence at all. No Facebook or Twitter. There was LinkedIn, but all again having to do with his business, nothing personal at all on the murderer. Cole didn't know it was possible these days to be so publicly hidden in plain sight.

He switched tactics and started searching for Betheny Millstone-Walker and Sharon Walker. Both ex-wives had social media presence. Betheny more than Sharon, but neither one had much going on. Nothing that jumped out at Cole and certainly nothing that pointed to anything related in any way to them being killed.

Standing, Cole walked over to the break room with his coffee cup. In a hasty manner, without thinking, he reached over and turned the faucet on rinsing out his cup. Standing at the sink he got lost in thought replaying the prior night's events over and over in his head. He wished he hadn't blown it at Walker's place and could let go of his bitterness. If Graley had done her job, and they had taken Walker in when they should have, he wouldn't be in the fucking doghouse right now.

"Hey, Detective, you going to stand there all day and run the water?"

Cole snapped his head around and came out of his daze. He reached over and turned the water off. Turning to the coffee pot, he grabbed it and filled his cup. He slammed the pot back onto its warming base causing liquid to splash out of the top. Normally he would consider wiping it up, but not today.

Walking out of the break room, Cole felt as though everyone was whispering about him. Returning to his desk, he kept his head down, avoiding eye contact.

Cole sat down and moved his mouse, so he could locate the pointer. He opened a browser and found the shortcut to the police station's name-searching software, where he typed in Betheny Walker, Medford, OR. He went through a couple of gyrations, verifying Walker's full name and age. A couple of minutes later, he got a return on possible family members. Nothing jumped out at Cole, but he wasn't necessarily expecting it.

He clicked on "Print," sending the information into the print and copy room. Next, he started picking out names under Matt Walker. The ex-wives showed up, but he stuck with Walker's immediate family figuring the wives were in no way related and someone wouldn't take them out unless there was a reason to get at Walker. Walker had to be the key. Cole's experience with his own messed up family prodded him to keep his focus on Walker.

Cole picked out what appeared to be Walker's sister and a brother and typed their names into the police criminal database. Neither returned any criminal hits. He did the same for a mother and father; both came back as deceased. Cole, frustrated, pushed his chair back and put his hands on top of his head.

Standing, he grabbed his cell phone off his desk and headed to the back of the building where he stood under the overhang. He lit up a cigarette and took a long drag, allowing his lungs to warm. He felt his nerves calm and hoped like hell he didn't have any blood blockage in his damn brain. What a way to go. Several officers came and went through the rear door of the police station. Cole paid no attention to them. He dialed Diane's cell number.

"Hello."

"Hey Diane, Cole. Hope I didn't call too soon."

Cole didn't wait for a response, diving into the deep end of the conversation.

"Hey, I was thinking we could go out this weekend. Which night are you free? I'll pick you up and we'll go to dinner or something."

"Cole, Geezus, you woke me up. What time is it?"

Cole didn't answer since he didn't wear a watch and he didn't want to take the phone off his ear to look. He looked around outside the building even though he knew there wasn't a clock outside.

"Listen Cole, you seem like an okay guy and all, but I'm really busy at work. When I get off from the pub, I usually come home and go to sleep so I can get up early enough for my day job at the craft store. I just don't have any free time. I don't think we would work out."

"All I wanted to do was take you out on a date, not get married. Fuck you then." Cole pressed the end button.

Looking around and seeing no one, he flicked his cigarette butt into the rain-soaked parking lot. He turned around and slammed his fist into the door, leaving a small dent in the metal frame. He looked at his knuckles on his right hand. Blood started to ooze around two knuckles. He didn't care as he rubbed the back of his hand against the side of his pants. In his head, he replayed the interaction with Diane last night at the craft brew pub. The bitch must have taken offense to his comments. *Fuck her*, he thought. There were plenty more women out there he could date. He didn't want to spend any time with someone who couldn't take a joke. He stormed back to his desk and slumped in his chair.

Picking up the phone, he dialed the coroner's office.

"This is Detective Cole. Can I speak with whoever is handling the two women's bodies that were brought in last night?"

"Hang on a moment, please, Detective."

Cole tapped his foot and stared outside the window covered in dancing water drops. The sun looked to be making its first appearance of the day as the clouds grew lighter and spread. The clean air made for a bright blue Oregon sky behind the clouds.

"Detective?"

Cole brought his attention back to the phone.

"Yes."

"The Chief Coroner said he doesn't have any new information since he talked to you a little while ago."

"What are you talking about?"

"Forgive me Detective, I'm not certain. Just that the coroner said he just talked to you and he doesn't have anything new. He said check back with him later today."

"But I didn't—" Cole pause mid-sentence. "Never mind."

Cole hung up, thinking Graley must have called. He felt worthless. Completely out of the loop.

He slammed his fist on the top of the desk and spoke out loud not caring who heard.

"Fuck, this is bullshit!"

Of the half dozen or so co-workers who were in the room with Cole, only one of them turned their head. "Same Cole, different day," Cole could have sworn he heard one of his so-called associates say.

Rising swiftly, almost knocking his chair over, Cole grabbed his jacket. Feeling the weight of his car keys, he headed to the requisition clerk to check out a camera. He decided to take a little drive.

Dreams Help Provide Clarity

The rain soaked the ground enough to wash the rubber and oil residue off the pavement. Kate could tell by simply looking at the road. A trick she learned from an uncle who taught her to drive in rain-soaked Portland.

Looking out the window, she took in the changing color of the vast variety of Southern Oregon trees, one of the many reasons she loved the place. Mt. Ashland already had a jump start to its foundation with early snow visible from the freeway. The talk was, Ski season was going to be fantastic again this winter. Kate could hardly wait to get back up there and take a long sweeping run down her favorite slope, Caliban.

She tensed at the thought of giving Circ Bowl a shot again. Regardless of the difficulty of run, she loved knowing Matt would be in the lodge. Usually sipping on coffee and Baileys, reading a book, waiting for her. She put the turn signal on the final time before arriving home.

"So, what's the plan, Matt?"

"I don't know, Kate. I suppose, take a shower, and perhaps do a few minutes of work if I can keep my mind on it, and then run down to Jim's law office. I need to get the interview over with him and figure out what I can and can't say to the cops."

"When the cops question you, Jim will be with you, right?"

"Yes, why?"

"Nothing really."

Kate paused, thinking how best to finish her thought without being condescending.

"Only thinking he'll be there to help you stay on point, so no need to worry about what you say."

Kate guided the Jeep into the garage.

"Good point."

Matt let Kate's last statement replay in his mind, wondering if he should say more.

Kate smiled at Matt and put the Jeep into Park.

"Why don't you go get in the shower? I'll get Koda and then make you breakfast. You must be hungry. They didn't feed you in there, did they?"

Matt got out of the Jeep and shut the door, waiting for it to close before answering Kate.

"No, they did not. I'm not sure if they have a kitchen at the Graybar Hotel. I think they are just holding cells."

"I guess it makes sense; not like it is a big jail. Cooking would be expensive," Kate replied, wondering if they did have food.

"Well, I wouldn't have been in the mood for eating, anyway. Stressful as hell being in there, locked away. What a cold, lonely, helpless feeling. Scary, Kate."

Kate closed her door and headed toward the back of the Jeep.

"I'm so sorry, Matt. I can only imagine what it must have felt like. That Detective Cole needs to be put on a leash."

Matt laughed.

"Koda is better behaved and more disciplined than Cole, babe. I'm going to get in the shower. I'll be down in twenty minutes or so."

Kate grabbed Koda out of the back and took him into the front yard where he wasted no time plastering his nose within an inch of the ground. The rescue dog moved his head back and forth in a sweeping motion. The thick grass, established bushes, plants, and trees, free from any known animal markings, were an empty canvas to the mutt.

Kate thought he was enjoying getting familiar with his new home. She watched, wondering what in the world was going on in their lives right now. Fear crept in more and more with every passing moment. She didn't feel safe, but wasn't sure how to broach the subject with Matt. He was under so much stress right now.

The two deaths couldn't be a coincidence. Both women were young and healthy. Someone wanted them dead, and she couldn't help but think she might be on the same list. She looked around, never letting her head and eyes stay still; half expecting to see something out of the corner of her eyes come for her at any moment. Koda would alert her, right? She hoped.

Kate thought about grabbing the dog and heading straight to the bedroom where she could listen to the calming effect of Matt showering. Being near him would be a salve of sort. It wasn't practical for her to shadow Matt everywhere though. Was it?

"Come on, Koda, finish up so we can go make Matt breakfast."

Kate bent over at the waist and patted both her legs with the palms of her hands to get Koda's attention. The dog responded before stopping, turning, and growling. Kate froze and tried to figure out where Koda was staring, and at what. Still as a stone, the dog looked toward the road.

A car appeared to pull away from a stopped position on the shoulder which meant they stopped for a reason. Was it to watch the house? Most likely, since there was nothing to view on the road except trees and their home. Perhaps someone pulled over to use a cell phone.

The car sped away. Kate heard the cracking sound of gravel rocketing out from behind the wheels. Koda, pleased with his ability to scare a car away, turned and ran over to Kate wagging his tail.

"Good boy, Koda, good boy."

Kate grabbed her canine buddy by the collar, looking around, half expecting to see a car come storming down their long gravel driveway, slam the brakes on, and throw her in the car never to see Matt again. A chill started at the small of her back and worked its way upward until it tickled the base of her skull at the hair line.

She stopped before reaching the garage door as her stomach sickened. Koda whimpered as Kate's body propelled her soy chai latte up and out spraying a boxwood shrub. He whimpered again as Kate stood, wiping her mouth on her jacket.

Koda took a whiff of the vomit on the shrub. Uninterested in Kate's creation, the dog headed into the garage.

"I guess I'm scared, Koda. You got my back though, don't you boy?"

Kate entered the garage, while Koda, now in the lead and already sitting on the step, waited to get into the kitchen. Kate took one last stare up the driveway toward the road as the garage door closed.

"Oh, Koda, I bet you're hungry. Let's get you something to eat, okay?"

Koda barked as Kate hung the dog's leash on the hook before opening the door to the kitchen. Inside the home, the warmth oozed over her body as the chill of fall remained outside.

Upstairs, Matt stood in the shower under the hot water. Not normally one to spend wasteful time in the shower—three minutes or fewer was all he needed—he put both palms on the wall under the showerhead and let the water pour down onto his scalp. He positioned himself as best he could to allow the water to make its way over his back and ass and down his legs for maximum coverage.

At a loss for what to do with Kate, Matt thought it foolish to leave her here alone. Even with their new canine family member proving to be a valuable protector, he couldn't think of a safe, productive solution. He knew she couldn't travel with him as he had very specific and distinct plans best handled alone. Family research and catching up with old acquaintances of former wives. His list of potential enemies was short, if any, outside his family. Inside his family there may be one just sick enough to pull off such heinous events. Someone he figured would do whatever was necessary to keep family secrets. But why the hell involve his former wives?

This is where his thoughts slammed up against a concrete wall, ricocheting back against his reasoning. He needed to be alone to figure any of this shit out.

Reaching down, Matt turned off the water. Standing for a couple of seconds, he lowered his eyes and watched the water drip off his body. He thought he looked decent for his age, but constantly worried about it, wondering if Kate felt the same way.

Grabbing the towel, he dried his graying hair. At first glance in the mirror, his head looked grayer than it was only a day ago. Matt thought about how presidents looked before and after their presidencies. He felt older today than he did yesterday. Only one day. He couldn't imagine what the stress of the presidency could do.

The weight of his own events, and the added stress, took its toll on him in short order. He wanted resolution, and fast. Shaving, Matt finished rinsing off his razor and placed it in the cup at the back of the sink. He walked to the walk-in closet, pulled on a pair of jeans and socks before sliding on a plain blue V-neck t-shirt.

Looking at his arms, he thought his pecs were starting to sag. He needed to work out more. Matt returned to the bathroom and grabbed the roll-on deodorant from the medicine cabinet, lifted his shirt, and stroked his left arm pit and then the right. He remembered, for once, to put the shirt on first so he wouldn't end up with white deodorant streaks on the fabric.

Closing the medicine cabinet, Matt stopped and stared at his reflection in the mirror. He closed his eyes, visualizing Sharon and Betheny in his dreams. They were warning him of something, but what was it? The shadow in the dream faded with time. As spooky as the damn dream was, Matt hoped his formers reappeared tonight to help offer clarity.

Opening his eyes, Matt knew what he wanted Kate to do and he didn't think she would like it.

Efforts So Far

Trepidation dragged Matt into the kitchen. His idea to help shelter and protect Kate would not go over well, but he didn't see any other way, short of her being with him all the time. Joined at the hip right now wouldn't work. He needed to be unfettered. The thought of bodyguards popped into his mind, but in a passing way.

Matt decided if Kate were dead set against his preferred choice, he would investigate and see what personal security solution he could come up with. It wasn't the money for the bodyguards, which he imagined would be pricey; it was the loss of privacy. He didn't want anyone given easy access to his and Kate's life.

Kate, standing over the oven making Matt his favorite breakfast of fried eggs, bacon, home-fries, and rye toast, felt a tear move down the side of her cheek as Matt walked up and kissed her on the back of her neck.

She rubbed the back of her free hand against the cheek not wanting Matt to see her tears. Her body tingled, as it always did, with Matt's gentle touch of the lips.

"Shower feel good?"

"Yes, it did, thanks. Hopefully, I can catch a second wind now."

Matt headed over to the patio door and looked out.

"Glad to see the rain has subsided. Looks like it's going to be a nice day. I hope winter doesn't hit too early. There's a lot I want to get done around the house before it gets too wet and cold."

Kate didn't reply. She knew Matt wasn't looking for a response. She turned the burners off on the stove, then grabbed a plate out of the cupboard. The rye bread popped out of the toaster. Grabbing it first, she buttered it, stacking the rigid bread on the plate. Dishing out a healthy portion of potatoes, she slapped a couple of strips of bacon on the plate before lifting the egg skillet and sliding three organic eggs, with their deep orange yolks, onto the plate.

Matt insisted on organic eggs. Kate always laughed at him because it had nothing to do with the chickens per se, but the fact the eggs tasted better. She would rib Matt about being a taste bud environmentalist.

"Here you go, babe. Coffee and juice this morning?"

Matt turned from the patio door and the disturbing view of police equipment in the backyard.

"Looks like Koda is having fun out there. You did a good job selecting him, Kate. I'm glad you brought him home."

"Me too, Matt. Coffee and juice?"

"I'm sorry Kate. Coffee is fine. I don't want the sugar from the juice this morning. I want to avoid any carb crash. I need to be on my toes. So much is happening."

Matt sat, took a healthy bite out of a piece of rye, and then reached for the salt and pepper. Once more, he contemplated telling Kate about the email, but his gut told him it would be a mistake. How much did she need to know? It wasn't like he was being dishonest with her. In his mind, it came down to protection from needless stress and worry. If she didn't agree to his plan, he would have to tell her.

"Matt, babe, I was thinking. Why don't I go stay with my parents for a while? With everything that's going on..."

Matt cut her off.

"Are you being serious?"

Matt couldn't believe she came up with this solution.

"You can't stand your parents, and you hate Bend!"

"Well, perhaps it is time to forgive and reconnect. And no, I am not fond of Bend, but I don't hate it, Matt."

Matt chopped up the over-easy eggs with his fork and spread them around with the potatoes. Kate, not the best of cooks, did make fantastic fried potatoes. One of his favorites.

"I racked my brain in the shower. The only thing I could think of, outside of bodyguards, was for you to go spend time with your parents. I thought you would object."

"I have to admit, Matt, I'm spooked. I can't help but feel like I am looking over my shoulder all the time. For me to even think of hanging out willingly with my parents, you know I must be on serious edge here."

"I can only imagine, sweetie. I am sorry. I wish like hell there was something I could do."

Kate pulled a chair out, opposite Matt, and sat down with a cup of tea. She leaned forward and directed all her attention to Matt.

"When you came in to shower, I took Koda out of the back of my Jeep. He strolled onto the front yard, so I let him explore, hoping he would pee. After a couple of minutes, he stopped in his tracks. He stared up the driveway toward the road and started growling. He was frozen stiff! His hair stood up on his back."

Matt, resting his fork on the edge of his plate, eyes focused and chin tensing, directed his attention toward Kate.

"Shit, babe!"

"Well, Matt, Koda's behavior made me feel protected and scared at the same time."

Matt let go of his fork, slid his hand across the table and grabbed for Kate's free hand. Squeezing, he tried to comfort her with affectionate warmth. He loved her. She was different from his formers. Either that, or *he* was much different now. Probably a bit of both, he surmised.

"Let's check. I am almost certain we can get you a flight out of Medford this afternoon."

Matt didn't wait for a response before continuing.

"You going to call your parents, then?"

Kate sighed, taking a drink of her tea.

"Yes, I'll call them. Mom will act excited. Dad won't give a shit. Probably make a comment about me getting divorced or needing something from him. As if..."

"Listen, Kate, I don't see any other way. I'm going to have to come and go. It isn't practical for you to be with me all the time, and I don't want you alone."

Matt paused in thought. He finished the food on his plate and used the last remaining bit of rye bread to wipe over his plate a couple of times to get all the seasoning and remaining egg-yolk.

Kate watched. Normally Matt's bread swiping action would elicit a comment from her, but she was so preoccupied she wasn't even aware he had done it, or simply had no energy for a response.

"Shit, Kate, you are scared. I just did a couple of extra swipes with my bread and you didn't say anything."

Kate stared directly at Matt. The stare, to Matt, felt as though she looked through him as if she were in a different place. Matt waited patiently for her to say something. Another minute passed before Kate spoke.

"I wish my dad was a normal father."

"Perhaps this will be a chance for him to pull his head out of his ass. Heaven knows you have done your part. He needs to stop acting so damn childish and realize how wonderful a daughter you are. Life's too damn short."

Matt, standing, let go of Kate's hand. He took his dishes to the sink.

"I'm sorry, babe. The last thing you need is me getting upset about your dad. I don't get the man. But hell, you already know it."

"It's okay and thank you for caring. It makes me feel good. I like you sticking up for me. So, don't stop, okay?"

Matt noticed Kate was almost pleading.

"I hate seeing you like this, Kate. I'm so sorry."

Matt walked over to Kate, who now paced in the kitchen, and stood behind her. He placed both hands on her shoulders and squeezed, rubbing gently, trying hard to exude warmth and love through his fingers.

"We'll figure this out, babe. I believe Graley to be confident and competent. Cole, not so much, but it sounds like he has been put on probation, so Graley should be handling everything from here on out."

Matt kissed Kate on top of her head.

"Don't buy a plane ticket. I'll drive, Matt, so I can take Koda with me. I like the idea of my new little canine bodyguard being with me. Plus, I will have my Jeep. If I need to get away for a time, it won't be as hard."

"Shit, you're right. I forgot about the little guy. I'm not crazy about you driving, but if that's what you want, I suppose it does make more sense."

"It does, Matt, and I want the ability to get away in a hurry should I need one. Having my own car makes it less challenging."

Matt grabbed Kate by the hand as they moved over to the sliding glass door. Kate giggled and Matt smiled as they watched Koda lift his leg on the police's light-trailer. The newest addition to the Walker family did his best to let the cops know what he thought of their efforts so far.

An Absolute Ghost

Cole set the camera down in the passenger's seat. Pressing the accelerator to the floor, the Vette responded with raw force moving forward on the asphalt. The tires slipped, spitting gravel backwards. He could hear and feel the rattling of the cinders on the wheel wells of the Vette. He didn't care. He was consumed with disdain and anger toward Matt Walker.

"Fuck!" he screamed out loud, pounding his right fist down on the center console.

Cole at once felt pain in the heal of his hand. He didn't think Walker's wife saw him. If she did, he was parked alongside the road, too far away for her to recognize the vehicle. It would be nothing more than a car speeding away was all. He hoped.

Looking through the camera lens did nothing more than reinforce to Cole how beautiful Mrs. Walker was. The type of woman Cole dreamed of, except for the confidence she exuded. He had no idea how to deal with a woman, who could say no and back it up, like her. Women were supposed to be meek, submissive characters like his mother had been, and like god had intended.

"*God took a rib out of a man and made a woman. So, she can be controlled and provide. Women don't have the ability to run things, or be in charge, Cole. God made them this way for a reason. So, they can do what a man wants and needs.*" Words from his father echoed in his head almost daily.

Cole accelerated onto the highway heading toward Betheny Millstone-Walker's home. He hoped to find something at crime scene number one that everyone on sight missed. He thought of the movie "Seven." Perhaps there was a secret message behind a picture on the wall, under a rug, behind a refrigerator or under a bed.

His mind wondered aimlessly trying to come up with the semblance of a plan on this bizarre case. Other than Walker, how were the women connected, if at all? Was this more about Walker's current wife, Kate, and not Matt Walker at all? He laughed at the absurdity of his latest thought as he reached over and turned the radio up. Pearl Jam sounded better loud, he thought.

Checking his speedometer, which read seventy-nine miles an hour, Cole slowed the car to sixty. He couldn't afford to attract more attention to himself. The Chief would suspend him for sure. The asshole was looking for an excuse to suspend him at this point.

Cole knew he did the right thing last night with Walker, or the Chief would have suspended him. The Southern Oregon transfer lit into Graley big-time, after all. All the cops could hear the yelling coming from the office. And when the Chief asked Cole into his office, it was civil. Perhaps the Chief was getting pissy with Cole in front of Graley to show that his partner messed up, and that Cole could handle the pressure? A test perhaps of Cole's competence?

Cole turned down the street to Betheny's place, stopping out front. The police tape, prohibiting entry, still hung across the garage and front door. Getting out of his car, he looked around the neighborhood. One red older model Ford F-150 pickup, a black Volkswagen Jetta, and a bluish colored Chevy Malibu were in the court.

Walking around to the passenger door, he opened it and grabbed the camera off the seat. He looked at the photo setting dial on the top of the camera and set it to full auto. Hoping for useful images, he snapped perimeter shots of the neighborhood court making sure to get license plates on the cars before heading to the back of the house. *Who needed a notepad? Graley and her high and mighty attitude.*

Entering an unlocked side gate, Cole walked around the back of the home. He reached into his jacket pocket and pulled out a pair of thin rubber gloves. Setting the camera down on the deck, he struggled with the sticky gloves a minute before the latex conformed to the fingers on his hands. Picking the camera back up, Cole thought he would have to break a window to enter the home. He hoped the damage would be chalked up to vandals.

Looking around to see if anyone was in sight, he picked up a rock, then dropped it deciding to test the patio door first. It was unlocked. A major oversight on someone's part. Smiling at the thought of a fellow cop being reprimanded, he decided to report the information as soon as he returned to the station.

Stepping inside, Cole noticed the large number of windows in the home which allowed more than enough daylight to make it easy to snoop. Walking around the entire home, noticing more than he did yesterday afternoon, the woman had a nice place. There were several photos of her with an older man. A father, Cole surmised. None with an older woman and none showing her with a man her age. A couple images of her as a youngster with a young boy. A brother?

The biggest surprise was the number of photos with her and Matt Walker. Wasn't the divorce less than amicable? She still had a thing for the guy Cole thought. Either that or she couldn't let go. Didn't matter now. Delighting in possible grief for Walker, Cole smiled. Then feeling bad about the dead woman lying in the coroner's office, he straightened his lips and moved his head side-to-side.

Snapping a couple of photos of the images with Walker and Betheny, his instincts kicked in. He lifted paintings and wall deco's away from their resting places but found no secret messages. He wished he had a black light. Perhaps they were written in secret ink, not seen by the naked eye. Nothing under the bed but a stray pair of socks and a baseball bat. He pulled the refrigerator forward, scratching the floor. More like a gouge in the hardwood; he hoped no one would notice.

Seeing nothing behind the refrigerator he slid it back in place, opened the door, saw minimal food, a pitcher with lemons floating in it, and a six pack of cold beer. Looked like foreign shit. German printing on the label, looked to be. Slamming the door, he peered around wishing something would jump out at him.

Cole, now in the living room where the victim had run straight into Walker's arms in a public display of sickening affection, plopped his ass down on the couch.

He stared around in a fleeting attempt to come up with the magic clue that would not only solve this incident, but the whole damn case. One where Walker would be convicted, locked up forever, Cole's reputation would be restored, and he'd console Kate Walker and show her how a real man treated a woman. He fantasized about slugging her in the gut, then shook his head thinking Kate Walker would hit him back and perhaps even work him over a bit. Wondering if his way of showing affection and authority to women wasn't all that good, Cole shrugged his shoulders, raised up off the couch, and headed for the kitchen.

Convinced there was nothing to find that would help him, Cole left the home through the sliding door and got back in his car. Taking the gloves off and putting them in the seat next to the camera, he grabbed his cigarettes and lit one up. Blowing smoke out of the window, he looked around at his car. He liked his car. Walker was an asshole. That "*one of the worst Vettes ever made*" crack stuck in his mind. What the hell did Walker know about cars?

Cole started the car, accelerating out of the court, and got back onto the highway. He decided the next stop would be the coroner's office. Something had to break in this damn case. No one could be an absolute ghost and get away with this shit.

Constance

Graley left the senior-home feeling better about her father's future. The research she had done made it look as though this place was on the up and up. The residents seemed happy. There was no one tucked away in the corner of a room that she could see, slobbering all over themselves. No screams in the distance or residents begging not to be beaten or begging to be fed.

She had read all the horror stories online the past several months. Like anything, she knew there were bad places out there, but they all couldn't be bad. With three days left with her father before he could check in, she made a phone call to the At-Home Nursing Company. They greeted her politely as always.

"At-Home Nursing, this is Melody, may I help you?"

"Hi Melody, Detective Graley here. How are you today?"

"Good, thanks. How is your father?"

"Oh, he gets a little worse every week. I am checking him into the Westside Rest Home in Ashland in three days. Can I make arrangements for a nurse to stay at my father's place all the time until then?"

Graley held her breath expecting a bad response.

"Sure. We can do that. You want me to see if Misty can stay the night? If she can't, do you have a problem with it being someone else?"

Graley, excited over the quick offer, didn't hesitate to respond.

"If Misty could stay, that would be fantastic. Father is used to her. Not sure if he always remembers her, but I certainly like Misty and trust her. I would be willing to pay extra if need be."

"No worries, Detective. Let me call Misty and get back with you. We'll figure this out. And I am sorry, by the way. I know how hard a decision it must have been for you to move your father to Westside. It's a good place. He will do fine there."

Graley appreciated Melody's kind words.

"Okay, thanks. I'll wait to hear back from you."

Graley pulled the car out of Westside's circular drive. As she headed for the freeway, she glanced at the half dozen or so elderly people sitting on benches near the fountains out front.

She wanted to head over to crime scene number one, thinking they had all overlooked evidence there. While Graley was reflecting on the evening and the way Walker's ex-wife ran to him, her phone rang. She reached over to her phone sitting in the windshield cradle and pressed the answer button.

"Hello, Detective Graley."

"Hi Detective, Melody from At-Home Nursing. Misty said no problem at all. She's clear the next three days and would be glad to stay. She'll need to run home this afternoon to get her things but shouldn't be gone more than an hour."

"Fantastic! Thank you so much, Melody."

"No problem, Detective. Have a great day. Oh, and Misty said to tell you that your dad is doing fine."

"Thanks, Melody. Good bye."

"Have a nice day, Detective."

Graley pressed the red "end call" button on the phone and gave her full attention back to the road in front of her. Getting the cruiser up to speed, she put her turn signal on, wiped a tear from under her left eye, and entered the freeway.

Several minutes of positive self-help talk later, Graley shifted her focus back to the recent deaths. Betheny wasn't yet classified a murder, but her death looked more like her attackers intended result. An ice pick? Graley shuddered at the thought of one being pressed against the base of her skull wondering if she could hear the penetration and feel the pointed object press through sinewy muscle. She shook her head and looked out the window willing herself to lose the though. Bringing her thought back to the pavement in front of her, and the sound of the car's engine, she wondered if she could find anything in the deceased's home.

Hesitating for a second, Graley reached for the turn signal. She re-engaged the cruise control and flew past the intended exit staying on the freeway. A trip to the coroner, not crime scene one, was the smartest thing right now. She considered heading back to the station to pick up Cole but laughed out loud at the foolishness of the thought. She had freedom right now and could legitimately leave his sorry butt out of things. She decided she'd do just that for as-long-as possible.

Graley eased the car off the freeway and pulled into The Human Bean for an iced coffee.

"Light on the sweetener, and extra cream please."

"You got it, and thanks again for stopping. Have a great day."

Never tired of how polite they were making coffee, Graley wished she'd had the brilliant business idea herself and opened a coffee hut years ago. She figured the small huts had to have low overhead, minimal building maintenance, no outdoor seating to maintain, and they could be run with one or two people at a time. She dreamed about simplicity of work and success. Retirement from the police force and a fresh start sounded appealing. She racked her brain the next several minutes dreaming of a golden idea. Nothing came to her; it never did.

Easing her car into the lot outside the city building which housed the coroner's office, among other things, Graley parked in one of the two slots reserved for police. Getting out, she stretched and looked skyward enjoying the brilliant blue Southern Oregon sky sprinkled with a few soft and fluffy white clouds. The giant pillow-looking kind that hung as if they were part of a massive child's mobile.

Heading into the building, Graley looked at her watch. She wondered if there would be anything new since she talked with the coroner almost two hours ago. She surmised he would have had a chance to start the exam on Betheny. If not, the trip would be wasted, and time she could have been doing research and investigation. Graley looked forward to the Aussie doctor and his accent. The guy was pretty much known as an egotistical asshole, but the darn voice would always add a little flare no matter who was in the conversation.

Entering the building, Graley visited the Ladies room. Looking in the mirror at her puffy, swollen eyes, she felt tears coming on again thinking about her father but held the sea of saline eye-flow back. The Aussie would have no patience for a detective with a penchant for emotion. She was sure of it.

The door opened and in walked the last person Graley wanted to see outside of Cole.

"Mara, my God, how are you? It is so good to see you! I thought you fell off the earth. I have been trying to get in touch with you forever, but then you already know that."

Graley waited for her old high school friend, and former lover, chuckling at the thought of the word former, to catch a breath.

"Hi, Constance. How are you?"

"Well, I am so glad you asked."

Graley leaned back as Constance stuck her right hand in her face; fingers outstretched and nails pointing down. Graley couldn't help but notice the rock, but decided she was not in the mood to be happy for her old flame.

"Just get your nails done, Con? Nice. Not the color I would pick for you, but not bad."

Graley turned and finished washing her hands, planning for a quick dry and escape. She didn't have the time nor the desire, to reminisce, and Constance could talk forever.

"Mara, you are incorrigible. My ring." Constance waived her hand in the mirror and Graley couldn't avoid the shiny rock any longer.

"One hell of a sugar momma, Mara. Congrats!"

Graley watched as Constance looked around as if others weren't supposed to hear what she was about to share.

"That's the thing, Mara, it's a man."

Graley, stopped drying her hands, tossed the paper towel into the trash, then looked in the mirror and laughed.

"Are you kidding me, Constance? You hate men! Always have!"

"I know, Mara, right? That's what I thought. James is my first, and he is so sweet. He really makes me feel special. Oh, and you will never believe it. My dad about had a heart attack, he's so happy!"

Graley turned toward her former, thinking of Matt Walker's phrase, and gave Constance a deep, firm, hug full of care.

"I'm happy for you, Constance. Congratulations. I take it I will be invited to the wedding?"

"That's why I've been trying to get in touch with you, silly. I want you to be my bridesmaid."

Graley turned as pale as the tile. She didn't see this coming. Constance was the eloping type to her. Not the nice dresses, pretty flowers, seating by the groom's or bride's side character. But this was a man she was marrying, which turned everything upside down, so why not a full out wedding as well?

"Will I have to wear a dress?"

Constance tilted her head back and laughed. Graley noticed the skin on her neck and marveled at the smoothness. She imagined how it smelled and felt.

"I knew that's what you would say. I told James those exact same words. He can't wait to meet you. How is your dad, by the way? I hope he comes."

Graley closed her eyes and dropped her chin, ever so slightly, at the thought of her father.

"What's wrong, Mara? Is your dad okay?"

Graley decided to lie.

"He's fine, thanks. Getting older, as you know. I'll try to bring him."

Constance reached out and squeezed Graley's shoulder. Graley knew that Constance was aware she was lying, but both women decided not to face the bull head-on, letting the white lie float away unanswered.

"Listen, Con, I came down to see the Coroner. Important case going on, and I must get details, okay?"

"Is it about the two dead women, Mara?"

Graley wasn't sure how in the hell Mara would know this. Her detective instincts, and a desire to end this conversation, told her not to ask. For a court reporter who was trained and paid to keep her mouth shut, Mara always seemed to know everything going on in town.

"Con, you know I can't talk about my cases. One of the reasons you dumped me years ago, remember?"

"Whatever, Mara. You know it wasn't just about cases, but we don't need to beat that old mule anymore."

"It's horse, Con."

"What?"

"Oh, never mind. Good seeing you, and yes I will be your bridesmaid, but I better not have to wear pink."

Constance reached out and gave her a big hug and a kiss on the lips.

Graley loved the way her lips felt. Just the right amount of pressure and, oh, she smelled so wonderful. Her breasts pushed against hers and Graley remembered how much she loved physical contact with Constance.

"Great. I'll be in touch with the details. Spring wedding, so we have time."

Constance, as quick as she blew in, turned and propelled herself out of the bathroom.

Graley laughed knowing her former would get half-way back to her office before she realized she had to go to the bathroom.

Something is Rotten

Graley finally made her way out of the bathroom expecting to see Constance coming back in. To her delight, there was nothing but an empty, well-lit hall, with cheap tile and scuff marks from less than eager city employees. She headed down the hall and back into the lobby before making her way down the stairs to the bowels of the building and the autopsy rooms. Dark, dreary, and no windows. *The perfect environment for the creepy, death-dissectors*, Graley thought.

Standing in the hallway, outside the main autopsy room where Graley's last visit was for a dead homeless woman, stood Cole.

Graley wasn't sure if she was pissed, irritated, or indifferent. She did know she was surprised.

"I thought you weren't supposed to leave the kennel, Cole?"

"Fuck that, Graley. I am no good sitting at my desk. I need to be out in the streets doing my thing."

Graley laughed.

"Your thing? What's your thing?"

Graley could see the laugh stung Cole, and the stings were adding up recently. She figured he didn't have much room left for any more stinging.

"Being a detective, Graley, come on, you knows me, I gots to be out here man, wit you."

Graley's furrowed her brows over Cole's newfound playful attitude. Cole took a small jab at her left shoulder in an effort to lighten the mood and diffuse any tongue-lashing. Graley liked the effort but not the bizarre Ebonics he spewed.

"Cole, since you're here, when we go in, I do the talking, not you. Unless I ask you a question, okay?"

Cole started to speak.

"You understand, Cole? If you can't keep your mouth shut, go back to the kennel and play crosswords or Sudoku."

"Understood, Gray. You in charge and I's just gonna shadow."

Graley tilted her head and scrunched her eyes. His speech pattern was weird to her, and she was sure her face must have shown it.

"And for God's sake and mine, Cole, if you talk, please like you and not some wannabe. Your new street slang is disturbing. As a matter of fact that crazy shit stays out here. You get it? And don't answer. Just stop it."

"Last thing Gray, before we go in. I got a call from sergeant Lamond, out at Emigrant Lake."

Graley paused, looking at Cole's small, pale hand resting on the door knob.

"Dive squad right?"

"Yep."

"Well what did he say?"

"They swept the lake around the body and finished up at the lake. They found nothing else."

"Okay thanks for letting me know Cole."

Cole held the door open, and the two entered. They were promptly greeted by the coroner's receptionist, probably more an intern than anything. Graley assumed there wasn't much need down here for a proper reception area. Most of the people that came down were other doctors, police, or family members escorted by police to view bodies.

"Detectives Graley and Cole here. We're stopping in to see Doctor Taylor about the two women who were brought in yesterday."

Graley watched the young female intern fumble with her hair, rub her eyes, and straighten her collar. She swore the woman picked up pheromones off Cole or was desperately trying to send her his way.

"Right, sorry. Bit messy down here. We're more busy than normal with the two women coming in yesterday. Of course, oh, God, I'm rambling. Sorry."

The woman came around the front of the desk, extended her hand, and then retracted it just as fast wiping it on her smock.

"I'm sorry. Just a minute."

Turning, the woman walked a couple of steps back to a cupboard behind the desk. Opening the door, she reached up and grabbed a container of what looked like sanitary wipes to Graley. They were. The woman extracted a couple, wiped her hands, and threw them in the trash. Returning, she extended her hand again.

"Sorry, one can never be safe enough with germs. I always want to err on the side of safety. I'm Dr. Daphne Rourke, Dr. Taylor's new assistant."

Graley reached out first. She could only imagine what her pig of a partner Cole was thinking.

"Detective Graley, and this is Detective Cole."

Graley liked the young woman's handshake. Confident without being obnoxious. Graley noticed how soft her skin appeared. She thought the job and the chemicals would make it rougher.

Daphne paid little attention to Graley and went on the prowl with her Cole handshake.

"Nice to meet you, Detective Cole. You have a first name, or is it Detective?"

Graley, smiling, shook her head and looked up at Cole. One couldn't fault this woman for making it clear what her interests were. Cole blushed, which surprised Graley. She had never seen him embarrassed by anything.

"Nice to meet you, Doc."

Graley watched Cole hold on to the handshake as long as he could. The doctor and Cole stood there looking at each other, shaking their hands in a fashion that seemed to Graley that momentum would never allow the shaking to stop.

"Okay, lovebirds, now that we have all met, how about we get in to see Dr. Taylor now? Can you do that for us, Daphne?"

Graley watched as Cole blushed again. She had to figure out a way to tell this young woman to stay as far away from Cole as possible. She didn't want to see her get hurt, and if she messed around with Cole at all, she was going to get hurt.

"I'm sorry, Detective. Follow me please."

Cole fell into step behind Daphne. Graley followed, noticing the angle of Cole's head was such that he wasn't looking ahead, but down. She knew why, and promised herself she would get Daphne aside, somehow, and explain to her just who Cole was.

Daphne stopped outside two big swinging doors. Pressing a button on an intercom, she spoke.

"Dr. Taylor, I am coming in with two detectives who wish to discuss the female victims brought in last night."

"Okay, we can go in now."

Graley chuckled at the thought of the doctor requiring notification before they entered. Her mind wandered as to why.

Cole jumped in before Graley could speak.

"He didn't respond; how do you know we can go in?"

"Oh, a little rule that Doctor Taylor has. Give him a heads up when coming in with guests. He never responds. Now, this way please."

Graley grabbed Cole's arm, holding him back. She put a finger to her mouth in a be-quiet fashion.

"Remember, Cole."

Cole shook his head reminding himself to keep his mouth shut. He knew he couldn't afford to push it with Graley. He was already relieved she was letting him come with her.

Daphne led the detectives over to the main autopsy table. At least Graley thought it was the main one. It was in the middle of the room and had more lights over it than the other two tables flanking it on each side.

"Doctor Taylor, I have detectives Graley and Cole here to see you."

The doctor revved the motor of his coroner's Dremel tool which Graley thought for sure was for effect before lifting a face-shield and smiling at them.

In a heavy Australian accent, he greeted them.

"Ah, nice of you to make your way down to the dungeon. Good to see you again, Detective Graley. I believe I spoke with you on the phone a few hours ago. Correct?"

"Yes, you did. Good to see you again, Doc. Thanks for letting us pop in, by the way."

Graley saw Cole look at her with a sad puppy dog left-out feeling. She didn't care, he dug his own hole.

"No worries, not much new since then. A bit of an oddity with the younger blonde woman who I have on the table now."

Graley perked up. Cole was staring at Daphne, wondering if she would go out with him.

"What did you find that was odd?"

"Well, she did die of an aneurism, no doubt about that. Sure, signs of bleeding and an increase in pressure. The woman didn't have a chance, really."

"Is that what is odd?" Graley asked.

"No. The beating she took," the doctor started, pointing at the body while talking. "The bruising around her arms, shoulders, hips, and back of the head are a clear sign she was in a struggle. She was a fighter. Look at the defensive bruises on her forearms."

Graley wondered why they didn't notice them at her home earlier.

"Did she get anything under her nails, Doctor?" Graley asked.

She noticed that Cole was about to speak. He acted antsy like a child raising his hand, knowing an answer to the teacher's question. He kept his mouth shut, for once.

"No. I know where you are going with the question detective, but no. I found nothing under her nails. Her nails were quite short anyhow so finding anything would have been a stretch. Body looks to be clean of any foreign materials. Just her own fluids, clothing fibers, hair, etc. Oh, and I found cat hair as well. Pretty common stuff."

"So, is that what is odd doctor, that you found nothing but normal?"

Graley felt she was going to have to slap the doctor on the back to get the oddity part out.

"Right. Right. No, the oddity is this."

Doctor Taylor rolled Betheny on her side. "Come around here, mates."

Graley and Cole crowded around toward the front of the table where the doctor held the head of the body up off the table. He pointed at the base of the skull.

"See this little mark here?"

"Yes," said Cole, and Graley gave him an elbow.

"Ah, good. I was beginning to think you didn't have a tongue, Detective."

"He is on strict orders to keep his mouth shut, Dr. Taylor. He has a bad habit of saying things he shouldn't."

Graley took the opportunity to get a point across to Cole and, hopefully at the same time, make Daphne question her interest in him.

"Isn't that right, Detective Cole?"

Graley addressed Cole directly. He raised his chin in defiance before shaking his head.

"Well that is interesting. Anyhow, detectives, this mark looks to me to be made by the same instrument that killed the other victim. My guess is an ice pick to the lower skull."

Graley looked at the doctor, then at Cole. This was a break. Didn't give them any specifics, but did make it look like Betheny's death was by the same person, or persons, that killed Sharon.

"I can't know for sure, of course, but based on where it's located, and from the dried blood spot, broken skin, etc., it looks to me like a high probability that the murder was interrupted. I'm guessing that the killer held the object against her skull but changed his mind. It didn't fully penetrate. Damn shitty luck for this woman. So young."

Graley watched as the doctor, now silent, contemplated his next words.

"The stress from the ordeal must have exacerbated the weak blood vessel in her head, killing her. Either way, this woman died because of the incident. I will say as much in my report."

Graley got her notepad out and jotted a few things down before talking to the doctor who lowered the head letting Betheny's body lie flat again.

"What about the other woman? Find anything more on her?"

"No nothing more. Died because of the puncture wound to the back of the head. She had water in her lungs for sure, so she was thrown in the water before she died. Must have been terrifying."

Graley walked over and took a walk around Sharon's body. Another beautiful woman for sure. Matt Walker had an eye for beauty, no doubt about it. She made a few other notes.

"Doctors, I want to thank you for your time."

Graley put her notepad away and grabbed a card out of her pocket.

"Here is my business card. If you come up with anything else, please call."

Daphne took the card. Doctor Taylor responded with a head shake and lowered the mask on his helmet. He looked like he was going to get back to work on Betheny.

Smiling, Cole reached into his pocket and grabbed one of his cards and handed it to Daphne as well.

Graley left the room with Cole close behind like a puppy trying to keep up with its mother. She didn't talk, nor stop walking until she reached the top of the stairs at the lobby. She turned to Cole.

"Okay, it is official. We have two homicides now. They are related, not that there was ever any doubt, really."

"May I speak?" Cole interjected.

"You may, Detective Cole."

"What now?"

Graley didn't hesitate. We look at Walker's, Betheny's, Sharon's, and Kate's families, along with Walker's marketing business. Something is rotten, and we must figure out what before there is another victim. I have a sickening feeling this isn't over."

Road Trip

"Kate, I want a check-in every hour. Okay? And no BS about no phone signal. Stop off, let Koda have a break, and text or call me."

"I will. I promise, Matt."

Kate leaned out the driver's window. Squeezing her shoulder, kissing her firmly on the lips, Matt willed she would be okay.

"Kate, be careful. I'll keep you updated."

Looking in the back seat, Matt smiled at Koda. The dog was sitting in the middle of the bench seat, tongue hanging out and grinning. He was trying to wag his tail, but the position of the seat kept it from a full motion. Matt laughed.

"You take care of Kate, dog, or I will have your ass. You hear me?"

"Woof Woof."

"You be careful yourself, Matt. I'll call or text in an hour."

Matt stood at the edge of the garage as Kate guided her Jeep, a piece of luggage on the passenger side floorboard and her new bud hopping around in the back seat, up the driveway en route to her parents' home in Bend. It was less than a four-hour drive straight up the heart of Central Oregon.

Matt had fond memories of Bend, playing high-school baseball there and taking ski trips in college. One of his best games ever was in Bend going five for five at the plate. Mt. Bachelor, part of the Cascade Mountain Range, was known for her fantastic skiing, and had become a hotbed for techie companies and naturalists. So much so that it repeatedly showed up on "Best Cities in America to Live" lists over the last decade. The popularity pissed Matt off, firmly believing in the motto of "Welcome to Oregon, Now Go Home" he had seen on so many bumper stickers.

Matt grabbed his cell phone out of his back pocket.

He searched through his contacts until he found his therapist and dialed her.

"Offices of Dr. Farley, may I help you?"

"Hi, Matt Walker. I need to see if I can come in right away and see Dr. Farley. I have a bit of an emergency."

"Dr. Farley isn't seeing patients today, I'm sorry."

"Listen, please, two of my ex-wives have been killed in the past day. If ever I had an emergency, this is it. I need to see Dr. Farley. Can you at least ask her?"

"One moment, please."

Matt stood around the front of the garage pacing, looking up the driveway toward the road seeing if anyone was visible and spying on him. The driveway needed raking, the damn gravel was pushing out toward the edges again. He would have to call his driveway guy soon.

"Dammit, what is taking so long?" Matt wondered out loud as if it would speed the process up.

Gazing upward, Matt watched as a cloud moved its way in front of the sun, casting its shadow on him. The towering pines, which surrounded his property like a castle wall, swayed in the gentle breeze rolling down off the Siskiyou Mountains. The temperature seemed to drop ten degrees. He shivered, and the hair stood on his arms.

"Hello, sir, you still there?"

"Yes, I'm here."

Matt pressed the garage door button, hearing it close as he headed inside the house, pressing the phone to his ear.

"Dr. Farley will see you. When can you come in?"

"I will be there in less than twenty-minutes. Thanks."

Matt took the phone away from his ear and felt the blood rush around its outer rim as circulation was restored. Moving with deft quickness, Matt headed upstairs to get out of his t-shirt and throw on a white tee and V-neck sweater. He didn't want to wear a jacket today, not quite cold enough yet, but he also knew he would regret a t-shirt only.

Back downstairs, he started to head into the garage, when his feet stopped, a surprise to his brain. Spinning, Matt walked to the patio door and locked it, wondering why the cops weren't out milling around his back-yard investigating. Wondering how long their equipment would stay in the yard, Matt was glad his feet sent him a message.

Heading next to the front door, he locked it as well and for the first time considered a security system. Until now he always told Kate they were a waste of money. *"Anyone, Kate, who wants to get into our home will do so whether we have an alarm or not."*

Now Matt felt less confident about his standard line to Kate. Another thing to consider. Windows, gutters, drag the driveway, fix the front floodlight, have a security system installed, and figure out who killed his wives. The list was getting longer.

Matt made it out of the kitchen, closing the door behind him, and headed to his car. He thought about Cole for a minute, and that piece of shit Vette he drove. The damn kid probably thinks it is a stunning piece of Americana. In name only, Matt thought as he opened the garage door and climbed into his Tesla.

Matt gripped the steering wheel with both hands. He realized he hadn't been doing any nervous tapping or counting for a while now. He couldn't remember the last time. Perhaps yesterday when the cops were questioning him after he and Kate found Sharon in the lake? He concentrated, trying to remember as he drove up the driveway, slowly so as not to throw gravel up and chip the car's paint.

He knew Dr. Farley would ask. She always asked about his tapping and counting. The damn OCD, for which she hadn't yet been able to pinpoint a trigger. Matt remained frustrated with the sessions' lack of clarity on the matter. He hoped to figure out the damn compulsion, thinking it would alleviate stress and justify all the money he spent on therapy.

At the top of the driveway, Matt brought the car to a stop looking right first, then left. He normally looked left, then right, then left again, while tapping on the steering wheel eleven times. He fought the urge. Something pulled at him. He felt a chill run up the back of his spine. Staring straight ahead, across the road, he looked deep into the evergreens. The trees, skirted with ferns and rhododendron, provided cover. For what, he didn't know and couldn't see, but he felt like something stared back at him.

Matt slid the Tesla into Park. Getting out of the car, he left the driver's door open. Walking in front of the vehicle he stopped, staring left down the street, then right. He saw nothing. Looking straight ahead, deep into the woods, he searched for the recognition of the scene painted before him. A thousand times or more he had driven out this driveway and never had he been more aware of what was across the street than now. His habit was a left, right viewing. Never directly in front of him.

The image laid out in front of him took his mind straight back to his recent dream. Tall towering pines with a light Oregon mist around their trunks, obscuring what looked to be a cabin. The wind eased its way around the tops of the evergreens making them creak like a worn rocking chair. A sound Matt had never paid attention to until now. Looking around, half expecting something to grab him or jump out from behind a bush, he was cold. The air had an unexpected chill and a bite to it. Matt, hairs raised on the back of his neck now, hurried back inside the Tesla and accelerated toward his appointment. He wished he'd grabbed a jacket on the way out this morning.

Doctor-Patient Privilege

Entering the parking lot of his therapist, Matt steered the Tesla into a spot far removed from any other cars. Getting out, he looked around, again expecting to see someone or something. His phone rang in his back pocket and he felt his body jump. Matt pulled the cell out of his jeans pocket and looked at the screen. Recognizing Kate's big smile, he answered.

"Hey, babe, okay so far?"

Matt pressed the lock button on the key FOB as he talked.

"Yes, almost at Prospect and saw I had a good signal, so I figured I would call. Koda is sniffing around the woods. What are you doing?"

"Walking in to Dr. Farley's office right now. I thought it would be good to talk this out with her."

"Oh, good, Matt. I think it is a great idea. Don't forget you need to be at the attorney's soon."

"Yep. No worries, plenty of time."

"Okay. Sorry Matt, Koda is straying a bit. I better go. I'll text or call in another hour. Love, you."

"Love you, too, Kate. Be safe. Bye."

Matt pressed the red button on the screen and slid the phone back into his pocket. The air was warming as the sun did her best to hold off winter. Matt noticed the trees were in all their colorful glory as he entered the office of Dr. Farley.

The lobby was empty. It never was completely full, but today there was no one, save the receptionist.

"Hello, Mr. Walker. You may go right in, and I am sorry."

"Thank you," was all Matt felt compelled to say.

He moved down the hall without waiting for a response. He was never good with small talk and wasn't in the mood right now to work on it.

Dr. Farley's door was open, which meant patients could walk right in. Entering, Matt stopped short of coming in all the way, as Dr. Farley unexpectedly stood, came around her desk and greeted him at the door. She took his hand and squeezed while she placed her other hand on his upper forearm. The first time Matt had seen her do anything but sit or stand by her chair. He liked seeing this new, human, less stoic side of her. She oozed a warm and confident energy. Matt felt better being in the room with her.

"Matt, oh my God, I am so sorry. You must be devastated! I heard about the women on the news this morning but with no names released yet, I never imagined..."

Matt interrupted. He was on the clock already, he figured, and wanted to get to work.

"Yes, devastated pretty much sums it up, Doc."

"Sit down, Matt, please."

Dr. Farley motioned Matt to his customary position on the couch. Making himself comfortable, he took the usual two pillows, propping them next to him so he was between the arm of the couch and the pillows. He had his typical resting place now for both arms.

"Matt, today is on me, okay? Let's take as long as you need. I can only imagine what must be going on in your head right now. I know how much you cared about both women."

Matt sat straighter, surprised and pleased with her generosity.

Over the next thirty minutes, Matt recapped everything that had happened after he left this very office only yesterday.

"So, Kate is on her way to Bend, her parents place, and I am going to see what I can do to stay out of harm's way, keep myself from looking guilty, and try to figure out who would want them dead."

Dr. Farley, listening intently up to now, took a drink of water out of her clean bottle, and jumped in.

"Matt, why do you say, *keep yourself from looking guilty*? I am curious why you would say that."

Dr. Farley had a good idea but felt it worth exploring. She was never one to make assumptions when it came to a patient's thoughts, or so Matt surmised.

"Because I *feel* guilty. Don't ask me why, but I feel like the cops are looking at me as if I am the master-mind behind the whole damn thing. Kate looks at me differently. Not like she is scared, but a look like, *Do I really know who this guy is?* So, that's why."

"Okay, I thought as much, but I wanted to hear it from you. This is typical, Matt. All of us feel guilty in circumstances when we know others are in a place of judgement. Those of us which have a moral compass that is."

Matt fidgeted a bit on the couch and adjusted the pillows under his left arm. He wanted to believe her, but the guilt didn't rush out of his body like he wanted.

"Thanks, Doc, I appreciate you saying something. God knows I didn't have a shred of hate or bitterness toward either woman. You would know better than anyone on the planet as much as we have talked about them."

"Tell me about the look Betheny gave you again, Matt. I'm intrigued by it."

"Well, the police were basically hammering away on her with questions, I assumed about suspects, with me as an ex-husband being high on the list. At least that is what I surmised from several years of Law and Order viewing. So, I walk in and her entire demeanor changes in seconds. I could see it in her body language and felt it as well. It was like this nervous, scared energy was released from the room. I never saw Betheny so happy, except on our wedding night, perhaps."

He looked for a smile of recognition from the doc but got nothing in return.

"But the eyes, Matt, what about the eyes?"

Matt watched as Dr. Farley leaned forward in her chair a touch. She focused and engaged in a way he had never experienced.

"I don't know how to explain it. The way she looked at me. It was as if she was pleading with me to help her. Like I knew something."

Matt grabbed his head and rubbed both of his eyes. He longed to recapture a fading memory.

"Wow, Matt, I wished I knew what to say."

"I wish you did, too, Doc."

Matt checked his watch, cognizant that he needed to get going soon to reach the attorney's office on time.

"You have to be somewhere?"

"Yes, my attorney's office."

"Okay, good, Matt. Focus on the dreams and Betheny's look. I imagine there are things there which will trigger a thought or memory. Once you recognize exactly what, it should help you."

Matt stood and straightened the pillows the way he had found them when he entered. Dr. Farley stood as well and went to her desk. She grabbed a notepad and wrote on it.

"Here, Matt, my private cell phone number. If you need to talk and can't get an appointment, or don't have time, call me direct, okay?"

Matt, surprised, reached his hand out, took the paper, glanced at the number and slid it into his front pants pocket.

"Thanks, Doc. I appreciate it, and you seeing me today."

Matt watched as the doctor seemed to return to her familiar stoicism as she responded.

"Matt, before you go, there is something I should tell you. I couldn't share with you up until now, due to doctor-patient privilege."

Matt watched as Dr. Farley struggled to spit out what she wanted to say. A first as far as Matt knew. He had never seen the Doc search for words.

"What is it, Doc?"

"Betheny was also seeing me, Matt."

Committed to Crossing

"Geezus, Doc. You drop a bombshell like that on me as I am walking out? What the hell?"

Matt's attitude toward seeing a new side of the doctor today changed with a few words. Anger crept in, then hung in limbo as he tried to reconcile what his feelings were.

"Matt, it isn't a big deal. Take a couple of deep breaths and think about it."

Matt heard her and obliged. He felt better instantly as the spiked stress ebbed its way downward. The anxiety and pressure on his body subsided as quickly as it had come.

"I told you because there may be things we can discuss further which may help you. I thought you should know. I wanted to hear your unsullied take on all the events before telling you. Had I told you right off the bat, you wouldn't have been thinking clearly."

Matt rolled her words around in his brain and closed his eyes searching for the proper way to respond. He tried not to focus on the word, "unsullied" and Game of Thrones.

"Okay, I suppose I see your point. Is that ethical for you to see both of us though?"

"Well, she came first Matt. You and I were three or four appointments in before I put the two of you together. I was fine with it and didn't waiver at all. Patient confidentiality and all. To be sure, though, I talked with a couple of associates, neither of which thought there were serious ethical concerns. They helped me make up my mind. I in no way ever let anything I heard from either of you affect my diagnosis or advice. As a matter of fact, I was quite proud of myself."

Matt thought this a strange thing to say, but let the phrase hang, unanswered.

"Okay, Doc. I gotta go or I am going to be late. Can I come in tomorrow to finish this discussion?"

"Sure, I believe I have a 9 a.m. open. Check with Ruby on the way out."

Matt turned and opened the door. Walking out, he left the door open and headed right for Ruby.

"Dr. Farley said to pencil me in for tomorrow morning at nine. Thanks."

Matt walked out of the lobby and headed toward his car without waiting for any acknowledgment from Ruby. He wasn't in the mood. He checked his phone, wondering if he missed a call from Kate. No, but he did have a text.

"*M, I'm in Chemult. Cell signal weak, so sending text. Hope u get it. All ok-Koda is badass. I'll try again in an hour. Luv K.*"

Matt sighed with relief and responded as he got in his car.

"*Got it babe, thx. Stay safe. M. :-)*"

Checking the clock on the dash, he saw he had plenty of time to get to the attorney. He started the Tesla and eased it out of the parking lot. He started to turn music on but stopped his hand at the button. He held it there a second before putting it back on the steering wheel.

Thinking about the fact that Betheny had been seeing Dr. Farley as well, Matt shifted his focus back to his dreams, as well as Betheny's eyes and hug. Dr. Farley seemed to concentrate heavily on this piece of information. Made sense, as the action was important. Matt couldn't figure out why though. Not yet.

"Dammit," Matt mouthed in a soft voice, feeling frustrated.

He wanted to close his eyes, but the Tesla wasn't self-drive. He wished now he had sprung the extra money for the SD model. With cruise control on, Matt looked straight ahead, pretending the front windshield was a movie screen. He could see Betheny and Sharon. The water gushing from Sharon's eyes and ears was easy; she was found in a lake and her lungs were filled with water. The drowning finished her off. The water gushing from her mouth though, as if it were directed at him, not so easy.

Betheny, on the other hand, and those darn eyes. Matt always loved her eyes. They were crystal clear and the color of green, or blue, or grey, whatever, only seen in water. At least in his mind. Crater Lake always came to mind when he saw Betheny and those eyes she walked around with.

There was a figure, looked to be a man from the size and movement, in both dreams. One in the background at Betheny's place, and the other in the mist with Betheny and Sharon. The figure's shape and size made Matt think the culprit had to be a man. Feeling a bit silly, he wanted to dissect the visions with Dr. Farley in the morning. He failed, so far, with the lack of a clear understanding of the dreams increasing his frustration.

Matt turned off I5 and in less than two minutes, pulled into the parking lot at the attorney's office. Being early, he parked and looked around for a Dutch Bros. In luck, per his phone mapping app, he walked the map's recommended three blocks in less than five minutes.

Iced coffee in hand, Matt left his customary tip and headed back to the attorney. While standing at the crosswalk in front of the office, Matt's phone rang. He didn't recognize the number, which normally meant it went straight into the blacklist bin. Today he felt like picking up.

"Hello."

Nothing but dead air.

"Hello."

Finally, in an odd and muffled voice, which sounded disguised or fake to Matt, there was a response.

"If you talk, she dies."

The line went dead. Stunned, Matt stepped into oncoming traffic to the sound of loud honking horns and screeching brakes. Matt, who had dropped his iced coffee, stared down at the rough pock-marked asphalt. He looked up at the car and the driver that almost ended his life.

Mouthing the words, "*I'm sorry,*" Matt stared at the elderly woman driving. She held her chest. Her face was as pale as the clouds hanging in the sky. Committed to crossing, Matt, picked up the now empty plastic coffee cup, and jogged across the road. He started dialing Kate.

Straight to voice mail. He hoped she was in a dead cell spot. Common through that part of Oregon. He left a short voice mail and concentrated on not sounding panicked.

"Hey babe, just checking in to see how you're doing. I'm about to go in and meet with Jim, but if you call or text while I'm in with him, I will answer. He won't mind. Love, you."

Matt hung the phone up and headed inside the offices of Jim Davies, Attorney-at-Law.

Vanilla All Over

Leaving the Coroner's office with few helpful questions answered, the short drive back to the station seemed long and stressful. Graley kept reminding herself about being present; in the moment. She figured once her father was in the senior center, she would have options. Then she'd get tears in her eyes and contemplate retiring early, at least until her father passed. Should she live with him during his remaining years? What were her obligations? What were her desires?

A new set of tears, born of frustration, followed each thought. She knew she wasn't equipped to take care of him all by herself. She simply didn't have the financial resources. Her father had quite a sum tucked away, but she felt as though she shouldn't touch it. Crazy, she knew, since he wasn't capable of going anywhere and doing anything significant. A new sickness swirled in her stomach at the thought of family members waiting for her dad to die so they could dip their palms into his fiscal trough.

Graley pulled into the station parking lot noticing Cole had beaten her there. Sitting in her car for a moment, she couldn't help but notice Cole had parked his car across two spaces as if the Vette was a prized show car or something. She couldn't help but think Cole was a lost cause. He didn't get it. Life is a game to be mastered with a little deft skill. He had neither the deft, nor the skill, and no desire to learn.

If the Chief took a stroll through the parking lot today, Cole's Vette would be impounded. Graley knew Cole was doing the only thing he understood well—being passive-aggressive. He stood to gain absolutely nothing by challenging the Chief. Getting out of the car, Graley contemplated whether she should say anything to Cole. Perhaps the

Chief? A quick decision was made–no. Cole was an adult and Graley was not responsible for him. Her father was quite enough. And she wasn't a snitch, so no going to the Chief.

Wiping the dried tears from her eyes, she massaged the skin under them with her fingers to get blood flowing and hopefully tighten the skin a bit. Turning, she stood at the top of the short staircase at the back of the building. Lifting her chin in the air, she closed her eyes. Graley took noticed of the cool but warming air, inhaling deep into her lungs three times. While exhaling, she focused on being in the present, in the now.

So many things were out of her control, true, but this case wasn't one of them. Opening her eyes, she saw a cloud shaped like a dog. Smiling, she wished someone else were with her to see it and confirm her artistic interpretation of the Cumulonimbus cloud floating inside the deep, rich, Oregon Blue, sky. Why a dog of all things? And why now? She shook her head, frustrated over her lack of decisiveness and the multitude of questions.

Graley spun around and headed toward the back door of the station. The cloud vision made her think of the Walkers and their dog–Koda, she thought they called it. Wondering what Koda meant, if anything, she opened the door and headed toward her desk deciding to focus on Kate's and Betheny's families. Cole would need to research Walker's and Sharon's.

She contemplated taking Walker for herself but putting Cole on Matt Walker's family would be good for him. He would either rise to the occasion or implode. Graley tried to let go of her judgement but couldn't escape her mind's hope for the latter. As she entered the station offices, Cole was leaving the break room.

"Nice you could make it, slow-poke. I thought you must have gotten lost."

Knowing Cole baited her, trying to draw her into a bitch session, Graley didn't respond. Maintaining composure right now needed to be a priority. She wanted her energy on the case. Work was the only respite she had at the moment, from her father's issues causing her guilt and stress.

"Cole, I want you to focus on the Walker family, Matt and Kate. I am going to focus on wives' number two and three. Let's dig up anything and everything we can. Statistically speaking, as I am sure you must know."

Graley had taken her first shot of the day at Cole. It wouldn't be her last.

"We are likely to find that our suspect is related."

"Why do I get Walker, Graley? Come on."

Cole protested, but he was glad he got Walker. He wanted to find dirt on this bastard and bury him.

"Because I have ideas about wives number one and two. Don't challenge me, Cole, just do it."

Graley sat down at her desk and reached under the cheap laminated wood top, pressing the power button on her computer. Looking across her desk at the neighboring cubicle, she saw Cole pretend to be upset. He was an easy tell. The man was vanilla all over and predictable.

Graley opened a browser and started digging.

"Shit," she said out loud, remembering she still hadn't questioned Walker.

She dug through the pockets in her jacket, hanging on the back of her chair, until she found what she was looking for. The business card of one Jim Davies, Attorney-at-Law.

She dialed her desk phone. The receptionist at Matt Walker's attorney picked up at once.

"This is Detective Graley of the Medford Police Department. I need to speak with Mr. Davies, please."

"I'm sorry. He is in with a client right now. May I take a message for you, or if prefer you can try to reach him in another hour or so."

Graley hated the 'or so' comment. What in the hell does it exactly mean other than the person saying they're too lazy to commit to anything?

"Tell him to call Detective Graley at the station as soon as he gets this message. It's urgent."

"Can you give me your number, please?" the voice on the other end of Graley's line responded.

"He has my number. I'll be waiting for his call. Thank you."

Graley slammed the phone down showing impatience.

Clicking the mouse, Graley did a search for Walker's first wife, Sharon. There was no shortage of information on the medical star. She was a regular fixture at all the hospital awards banquets, fundraisers, community grip and grins, and more. It appeared to Graley that Sharon started at Medford General right out of college. She had a quick rise through the nursing ranks and in only six years on the job she was made head nurse. The youngest ever at Medford General to hold the prestigious position.

A quick search of Medford's civil court records revealed no sign that she could find that Sharon re-married. Perplexed, she wondered what the women in Matt Walker's life were thinking. They didn't want to be married to him, but they also didn't want to get rid of his name.

Graley grabbed her spiral notepad and flipped over to a new page. She titled it "Questions for Walker's Attorney," then wrote the date. She wanted to know, from Walker himself, why neither of his ex-wives remarried.

"Hey, Graley. You going to notify Sharon's next of kin? Or did you do it already?"

"Shit," Graley said out loud.

How the hell could she have forgotten to do that? And why was Cole the one to point it out?

"Dammit," she mumbled to herself. Then speaking aloud, "Cole, you worry about your names, and I will worry about mine."

Graley watched as Cole, smug as ever, replied, "I didn't think so. Nice job, partner."

Sliding her jacket on, Graley headed back out to the cruiser for a trip to the hospital. Fifteen minutes later, she pulled into Medford General and parked in the police slot outside the Emergency Room.

Graley got out and stretched. Hungry, she decided she'd grab a sandwich on the way back to the station.

Heading directly to the EMG counter, Graley asked for directions to the Admin Office. Two minutes later, she spoke with the admin front desk attendant.

"Hi, I'm Detective Graley from the Medford Police Department. Can I please speak with the Human Resources manager?"

"One moment please, Detective."

Graley loved the effectiveness of mentioning "Detective" in getting people to cooperate. No arguing, hassling, stalling–get right to it.

She listened, watching the attendant dial the phone.

"Yes, a detective. No ma'am I don't know what it's about."

The secretary held the phone down against her chest and looked at Graley.

"May I ask what this is about, Detective?"

"It's about one of your employees. I don't have a lot of time. Take me in to see the manager now, please. I won't be long."

"You heard, Ma'am? Yes Ma'am."

The secretary stood and motioned to Graley.

"Follow me, please."

Graley entered the manager's office. She looked to be a professional woman, the way she carried herself, probably about fifty-five or so. They exchanged pleasantries before both sat down.

"What can you tell me about Sharon Walker?"

"In what way, Detective? One of the best employees we have. Why?"

"Haven't you heard?"

"What?" The manager's voice wavered with the loaded question.

Graley, in a hurry, didn't want to be flat-out cold to this woman. She might be close professionally and personally to the deceased.

"I am sorry to inform you Ma'am, Ms. Walker was found dead yesterday in Emigrant Lake."

"Oh my God! What happened?"

"We don't know yet, Ma'am, only that her body was found floating in the lake outside her ex-husband's home."

"She drowned? She was such a good swimmer though...how is that possible?"

"We are still investigating, ma'am. What can you tell me about her ex-husband, if anything?"

"Oh my God. Not much. I know Sharon talked highly of him when his name came up. His business donated money quite a few times to fundraisers we hold. I never heard her say a bad word about him. Not much else I can really tell you."

"Was Ms. Walker close with anyone here? Like a good friend or two?"

"No, not that I am aware of. She oversaw all the nurses and, being the consummate professional, she didn't like the idea of developing friendships with any of them."

"How about other staff or doctors?"

"I was probably the closest to her of anyone. And I wouldn't say we were close at all."

"Can you tell me if she had any family?" Graley asked, hoping for a little more than nothing at all.

"Wow. I don't know. Let me look in her file. I'll be right back."

Graley watched as the manager rose from behind her desk and left the room, leaving the door open.

Graley checked her watch. Moments later the woman returned holding a file folder.

"Sorry, couldn't find it right away. I thought for a minute it had been misplaced. Someone filed it under S for Sharon instead of the normal W for Walker."

"Does that happen often?"

Graley couldn't resist asking. She was forever a slave to an inquisitive mind. She never held onto a question she thought worth asking.

"Not to my knowledge, but it's a simple mistake."

Sitting back down, the woman started leafing through Sharon's paperwork. The last page was what the woman was looking for.

"Here it is. Single, filing head of household, no next of kin listed, and her emergency contact and beneficiary is Matt Walker."

"Are you serious?"

A surprised Graley sat forward in her chair. Her cotton dockets sliding forward on the fake leather, Graley stopped at the edge of the seat, perched.

"May I see the document, please?"

"I don't see why not, seeing how she is dead and all."

Graley glanced over the document. She got her notepad out, jotting down the following on a fresh page she titled "Sharon Walker":

No next of kin listed on the form at Medford General.

W4 / Single with two exemptions
Emergency contact – Matt Walker, 503-555-5555
Beneficiary, Matt Walker / 75%
M.G.H. - Those in Need Foundation / 25%

Her address was listed among a few other innocuous things just about everyone working in America had on their employment form. Nothing Graley felt worth writing down.

"I could make a copy of that for you, Detective, if you'd like."

The woman spoke after Graley finished writing, to her chagrin.

"A bit late now, thanks. I have written down what I need."

Graley stood, extending her hand.

"Thank you for your help. I'm done for now. I may have more questions later."

Graley handed her one of her business cards.

"If you think of anything else you feel may be important to my investigation, please contact me."

The woman looked around as if the wall had ears, Graley thought, then asked a quiet question.

"Was she murdered? Is that why you want to know so much? Do you think Matt Walker did it?"

Graley jumped at the opportunity. "Why? Do you think Matt Walker would kill her?"

The woman looked startled, then stammered, surprised at Graley's question or the possibility she hadn't thought through her prying words.

"Um, no. No. The few times I met him, he seemed nice, and Sharon never said anything bad about him that I am aware of. Like I said earlier."

Graley, pleased with herself she startled the woman, who she quickly surmised would never make her friend list, responded; in a cold and direct cop-fashion.

"Okay, thanks again. Please do call if you can think of anything else."

Reaching into her pocket for her cell phone, Graley picked her pace up as she left the building. Smiling, she shook her head in anticipation of the upcoming meeting with a certain suspect it was her duty to inform about a recent death. A suspect who it just so happened was listed as Sharon's emergency contact and primary beneficiary. A Mr. Matt Walker.

We Only Get One Life

Kate couldn't help but smile at Koda sitting on a blanket she had strategically placed on the back seat of the Jeep. He seemed so far away in the rear, so after the last pee stop, she moved him to the back seat. Koda was close enough now where she could reach back and touch him if she liked.

Occasionally, she would get lost in thought reflecting on the NPR discussion going on about immigration and what exactly "illegal" means. A warm nose on her shoulder, or a lick to her cheek always brought her back to the present. She wanted to have Koda up front with her in the passenger seat but was conflicted about his safety. It wasn't like she could strap him into the seat-belt. She wondered if they made seatbelt harnesses for the front seat for dogs and was determined to check once she arrived at her parents' place.

A couple of hours into the drive, with another two hours left, Kate reached over and turned the radio, and its noise, off. She reached back with her right arm and gave Koda, who now rested comfortably, a pat. Reflecting on the past twenty-four hours, Kate displayed a full range of emotions, from crying, to fear, laughter, and finally more doubt.

She didn't know how much of the last twenty-four hours she'd share with her parents. One detail, telling her parents everything, she did not discuss with Matt before leaving. Perhaps on purpose. She glanced at her cell phone in the holder attached to the front windshield, seeing the phone had no signal. She planned on stopping in LaPine, which was about the three fourths mark, and chat with Matt for a while, if he answered the phone. She hoped he would. If not, she determined to try again once she reached Bend. One last try before reaching her parents where privacy and an open conversation would be a different challenge.

In the quiet solitude of the highway, surrounded on both sides by towering fir and pines hiding all but a sliver of rich blue sky, Kate reflected on the last time she had seen her parents. It wasn't a fond memory.

Her and Matt's wedding had taken place at her childhood home on the Deschutes River. The picturesque amalgamation of breathtaking beauty, so often seen in Outdoor magazines all too eager to feature a trip to Oregon's central corridor, was a perfect backdrop to Kate's first and hopefully only wedding. She married late, much to the vexation of her father.

Kate spent several years in college at Portland State, following her father's dream of obtaining a law degree. She hated it from the beginning. Countless years of trying to please her father culminated in the realization that she had only one life to live. She was living hers for her father. So, she dropped out during her junior year and got approval, with much cajoling, for a degree-waiver and joined the Peace Corps. What was supposed to be a two-year stint in Africa, turned into twelve years of rewarding solitude away from her father.

When Kate returned, she enrolled at Southern Oregon University, in the quaint Shakespearean town of Ashland where she finished her business degree. She met Matt by chance at a symposium for local Southern Oregon businesses in search of summer interns. Matt interviewed Kate, and they hit it off.

Kate slowed the Jeep, watching several deer with a couple of yearlings close to their mommas cross the road. Accelerating back to speed in seconds, after checking her rear-view mirror, Kate laughed. She was deep in thought about Matt not selecting her to be an intern at his marketing firm. His voice, from the meeting, still rang clear.

"If I had hired you Kate, we might never have gotten married. You know I won't date people I work with. How would it have looked for the both of us if I brought you in as an intern and then immediately started dating you?"

Talking about the symposium and the meeting was a wonderful source of enjoyment for both Kate and Matt. Now, both their worlds had been turned on edge by a freak situation.

Kate knew Matt well, but she was beginning to wonder how well. There was so much, to her displeasure, that he wouldn't talk about. She knew hardly anything about his first two wives. She knew Sharon was his first, and Matt genuinely loved her, but both were so wrapped up in their work lives, they didn't make the time for each other necessary for a marriage to survive and thrive.

Matt would go on about no regrets, how life has its way of charting a course for each of us. No more than we can handle. The path is set. What would have been mumbo jumbo to Kate years ago, now resonated. She thought being an attorney was in her life-map, set in stone. Until one professor, in a business law class of all things, made a statement one day about how *we all only get one life so don't mess it up*, stuck in her mind.

The phrase bored deep into her conscience and wouldn't let go. When she found out about the Peace Corps, she begged and pleaded her way in, dropped out of class and never looked back, the phrase lost its allure.

Koda, stirring in the back, helped Kate focus back on the present.

"Hey boy, you have a good nap? I wish I could curl up with you. How about you drive, and I get to rest a while?"

Koda yawned, then yipped a little half bark, putting his head on Kate's shoulder. Kate, seeing the sign for LaPine ahead, decided to pull over at the Fuel Commander Market to walk Koda and call Matt. She wished he was with her.

Another Iced Coffee

Entering the attorney's office, Matt exchanged pleasantries with the receptionist. Never one for pointless banter, especially with someone he hardly knew, he walked the half-dozen or so steps to the coffee. He grabbed a cup, filling it half full knowing he wouldn't drink it all, then sat down on the expensive leather sofa he helped pay for.

Matt wondered how many cows were killed to make this abomination of a piece of furniture. He decided he would ask Jim and give him shit about it. Not too much, though, since he was a hypocrite and liked a good steak as much as the next person.

Matt rifled through the neat pile of magazines, settling on a copy of Outdoor. Inspired by the backpacker on the cover, he contemplated the idea of a big hike down the Rogue River next spring with Kate. They could start at Grave Creek and do the forty-mile hike to Gold Beach. He had done it once before, years ago with Sharon, one of his fondest memories. He wanted a new one to focus on, especially now that every memory of Sharon, good and bad, had turned into the nightmare he was living. Kate loved the outdoors and had never...

"Matt, come on in."

Matt dropped the magazine on the table, standing, he reached for Jim's outstretched hand.

"Thanks, Jim. I appreciate it."

"You haven't seen my bill yet, you son of a bitch. Don't start throwing pleasantries out until then, okay?"

Jim laughed his big jovial laugh and smacked Matt on his back. Hard enough for Matt to thrust his coffee hand forward to stabilize the black liquid surrounded by white Styrofoam. Successful on eliminating spillage, he shook his head at Jim, who smiled acknowledging his feat.

The two walked into Jim's office, adorned with more bold, thick, dark leather and heavy wood furniture. There were plaques all over the walls as well as key photos with local and state politicians. Matt had been here a couple of times prior, having to do with work issues, but each visit brought a new perspective.

"I felt better until you started talking bill already, Jim. You really know how to crush a guy's spirit. You know that?"

"Take a seat, Matt. Ah, don't worry, I'll be gentle. I have never screwed you too hard before, now have I?"

Matt didn't know if he should laugh or cringe. He chose somewhere in the middle.

"Ah, I suppose not," Matt responded, knowing he sounded about as unsure as a child's first visit to the dentist.

Jim sat as his desk flipping through papers as if talking to Matt but was only rambling. It frustrated Matt that his three hundred fifty dollar an hour attorney always seemed distracted. The guy didn't stop flipping, looking, hunting, and gathering information, occasionally busting out an over-sized magnifying glass. Matt assumed Jim's eyes must be near shot if he needed them to read. Feeling different about things in-light of the unnatural situation he found himself in, Matt spoke up for the first time.

"Jim, no disrespect, but do you think since you are charging me so damn much money each hour, you could stop flipping and talk to me? Seems like if I am going to get "screwed," as you put it, to the tune of three fifty an hour, I shouldn't be paying you to look at someone else's paperwork."

"To the point, today, huh Matt?" Jim laughed. Matt thought it was a nervous, busted laugh, but he didn't know Jim well enough to be sure.

"I'm sorry, Jim, a bit on edge."

Matt looked away, out the window, and tapped his right foot. He started counting and stopped at nine. *Shit*, he said to himself, he didn't need to get to eleven.

"Don't worry about it, Matt. I would say I understand, but I have never been in your situation. I have had several clients that have, but not myself."

Matt sat in silence. He didn't know what to say. He was waiting for Jim to take the lead. Watching, Matt noticed as Jim shuffled a few more papers, straightened a few stacks on the corner of his desk, and then pushed his chair back and placed his feet up on the desk. Matt noticed one shoe sole was scuffed up more than the other and had a piece of dried gum on it. He wanted to scrape it off.

"Matt, the floor is yours. Let's start by bringing me up to speed on all the pertinent information, leading up to yesterday's events on up through your incarceration. Don't worry about leaving anything out, or rambling on too much. We won't be relegated to one discussion. If I have questions, I'll interrupt."

Matt sat straighter in his chair and pushed both palms downwards against his jeans, cleansing any residual sweat his hands may have been holding. His palms felt uncharacteristically clammy, and it irritated the hell out of him.

"Leslie," Jim yelled to Matt's surprise.

The door opened, and the receptionist popped her head in.

"No interruptions at all for the next sixty minutes. Matt here will hold me to it, so I am serious, okay?"

"Understood, Mr. Davies. Anything else?"

"No, that will be all. Thank you, Leslie."

The door closed. Matt watched as Jim nodded his head.

"Go ahead, Matt. Let's get this train rolling."

For the next forty-five minutes, Matt told Jim everything he could remember. Almost everything, that is. He held back the email threatening him. He didn't know why, yet, but somewhere in the recesses of his mind, there was a tug. A gentle pull to keep this bit of information to himself. He was innocent. He didn't need to give all the info up. Not yet, at least.

"Well, shit, Matt. This is something you see on T.V. or read in a book. If you hadn't been arrested, I wouldn't believe most of it."

Matt tilted the Styrofoam cup back, emptying the last bit of lukewarm coffee into his mouth. He looked around for a trash can, then settled for setting it on the table to his right.

"It feels made up. Not sure it has settled in yet. And on the drive over here, I got even more down knowing I have a record now, right?"

"Hell no, Matt. You haven't been charged with anything yet. They have no evidence, no serious theory as to why you would try to kill one woman, let alone two–then on top of it, be stupid enough to call and report one of them and show up at the scene of the other one. You would have to be psychotic."

Jim stared at Matt. Matt could sense the sudden reluctance in his attorney's words and now piercing look. Drifting, as if pulled reluctantly by his mind, Matt stared at the art on Jim's wall. The eclectic mix of modern nouveau and cheap classic knock-offs had him wondering who decorated the office. It couldn't have been Jim.

"You aren't psychotic, are you Matt?"

Matt responded in a low, methodical, almost mechanical voice as he fought off daydreaming about a better place, and time.

"Shit, Jim. I don't think so, but do any of us really know what we are capable of?"

There was a long pause between the two before Matt finished his thought.

"How come you haven't asked me if I did it?"

"Well, whether you did or didn't doesn't matter to the law. Only if someone can prove you did it. My job is to prove your innocence if it comes down to formal charges. Frankly, I don't think it will. They have nothing at all. Again, if they did, you would be locked up."

Matt swallowed, not feeling any better about the events. He watched as Jim glanced at the watch on his fat lawyer wrist. Fighting the continual battle of thinking of something other than the present moment and time, Matt did not have a problem with focusing, until today. Perhaps the sleep deprivation and stress? He wasn't sure, but he did not like the lack of control.

"What is Kate up to, by the way Matt? I am surprised she isn't in the lobby waiting on you. She must be scared, huh?"

"She is headed up to her parents in Bend, Jim. We thought it best if she weren't around and thought being with them made the most sense. Why?"

"Ah, just curious. Good decision. You will need to be mobile for a while and don't need to be worrying about her."

Matt thought it sounded as if Kate were a burden. He took a couple of deep breaths and focused on relinquishing his defensiveness toward his lawyer and hell, friend, when it came right down to it.

"Listen, Matt, one last thing. Do you want me to pursue any legal action on your behalf against the MPD?"

This surprised Matt. His mind pulled out of the cold water, leaving him standing on the edge of a cliff, senses heightened and total focus on the question.

"A lawsuit?"

"Well, false arrest for starters. The police had a specific agreement with you to come in at nine this morning. That was interrupted by a zealous, inexperienced detective who should be punished."

"How so?"

"Ever heard of someone being arrested for scooping dog shit in their own yard and tossing it into a lake? I can only imagine what the judge would say to the detective in a case like this."

Jim laughed. Matt tried to force a smile himself.

"No Jim, I don't think it's necessary. Makes for a good story when this is all over with if nothing else." Matt's weak reply frustrated him. Why the hell was he lingering in this funk? He wanted to snap out of his doldrums and stop feeling like a little pansy-ass.

Jim let out another large belly laugh, deep and heartfelt, as he stood from his chair. He walked around the side of the desk. Matt stood and met his outstretched hand.

"Look, Matt ole boy. You are going to be fine. Normal to be stressed and flustered with what you have been through the last twenty-four hours. Be easy on yourself."

Matt listened but didn't reply as the two walked to the office door.

"Try to get back to your normal routine. Go into the office even if for only an hour or two and let your employees see you are alive and doing okay. Keep in touch with Kate and tell her to keep that new dog of hers next to her at all times."

The two stopped at the door, and Matt reached down and grabbed the door handle to let himself out. He turned and looked at Jim, who took a step back to avoid being too close to each other.

"Shit. I forgot to ask. What about my interview with the police, Jim?"

"I'll handle that, Matt. I am certain they'll be calling me today to set it up. We will meet here on our turf. They had their chance with you at the station. When I arrange it, I'll let you know."

Most of the stress and worry that Matt took with him into the office, left with Jim's confidence and reassurance on full display. Something Matt hoped for when he entered.

"Okay, Jim, and thanks."

The two shook hands again, an awkward should-we-do-this-again-so-soon shake. As Matt walked out of Jim's office, Leslie, sitting at her desk, turned to acknowledge the two men. Jim nodded. Matt took the gesture to mean Jim wanted his secretary to pay attention to what he was going to say. Jim then directed a final question to Matt, with Leslie listening in.

"Your cell number hasn't changed, Matt, has it?"

"Nope, same number I have had for the last decade."

"Good. Leslie will get in touch with you when the police call. If not, I will."

"Like you know how to dial a phone, Jim." Matt sarcastically replied.

Jim let out a big laugh again, slapped Matt on the back, and responded.

"There's the smart-ass I expect."

Jim turned, lumbering past the receptionist's desk, heading back inside his office.

Matt, shoulder stinging a bit from Jim's big hand, left without saying anything further. He chuckled at Jim's affable attitude, trying to remember how and when they met. Taking two steps at a time down the stairs, Matt decided it was time to try to hold on to another iced coffee.

Regretful Words

Detective Graley sat in her car, thankful for the beckoning of autumn and all the beauty Southern Oregon had to offer. The trees hung on to their leaves, now making their chameleon like change. Deep colors across the spectrum; Walt Disney would be proud. She smiled thinking about the times her father would say something about, "looks like Walt Disney threw up," any time a reference called for a lot of color.

Graley thought about running by the house to see how her father was doing but decided against it. She couldn't face him right now.

Instead, she rummaged through her coat pocket and pulled out Matt Walker's business card. She dialed the number.

"Hello," the voice said on the other end after only one ring.

"Mr. Walker?" Graley replied.

"Yes, who is this?"

"This is Detective Graley, Mr. Walker. Do you have a minute?"

There was a long pause.

"Mr. Walker?"

Graley questioned his presence on the other end of the line.

"I'm here. I thought you were supposed to call my lawyer?"

"Well, I am when it's in direct relation to the case, but this isn't about the case per se."

Graley could sense Walker smiling on the other end of the line.

"That sure sounds like a detective splitting hair, Detective Graley. But I like you, so go ahead. What is important enough for you to call me, not related to the case?"

Graley regretted the words that came out of her mouth while the syllables rolled over her tongue and filled the air with noise. The mind is funny, Graley thought. The words had to be formulated ahead of time, so why no regret as the formulation process is taking place?

Instead, the mind, hers at least, deciphered the difference between a wise choice of words and regretful ones while speaking them.

"I'm calling to inform you of a death, Mr. Walker."

The cell line was silent again. Cars whooshed by her police cruiser, spraying a fine mist of water up from rain-soaked asphalt.

Pausing in disbelief, the dead silence on the other end of the phone gave her a short time to try an apologetic recovery. She hustled in the effort.

"Oh my God, Mr. Walker, I am sorry—it isn't Kate! It isn't Kate. Shit, that was stupid of me. I'm sorry. Are you still there?"

Graley could only imagine the emotion ripping through Walker's mind, considering the last twenty-four hours. The poor guy had been hammered from all ends, including the police. She had now, unwittingly, done her part to make his day worse.

"You realize, Detective, I just dropped my second iced coffee of the day. Would have been nice had you started out with, 'This has nothing to do with Kate,' before your statement. Don't you think?"

Graley hammered herself mentally for the clumsy, rookie-like mistake she made. The poor guy didn't deserve it.

"Matt, I am so sorry. You're right. I didn't think before opening my damn mouth, and I should have. Please forgive me."

"If I didn't know any better, Detective, I'd think you and your partner were harassing me."

"Fucking Cole," Graley mumbled under her breath while making a half-ass effort to cover the voice speaker on her cell phone.

"For what it's worth, Matt, I don't think you had anything to do with it. I shouldn't be telling you this, but you are more help to us, potentially, if you know where I am coming from."

Graley felt the energy flow through the phone, releasing the conversation's tension. Next, she heard it in Walker's voice.

"Good to know. What is it you called about now, Detective?"

"Oh, right. A cheesy way to get you on the line, really, so we can set up a time to talk. I have to ask you a few questions and get this case on track."

Graley waited for a response realizing that since she didn't ask a question, one might not come. Plowing on, she laid out specifics.

"I was at Sharon's place of employment, Medford General, to inform their H.R. department of her death, and to question them about her. They informed me that you were listed as her primary beneficiary and point of contact."

No question again, but this was a statement Graley knew would elicit a response. Unless Walker already knew he was the beneficiary.

"Are you being serious, Detective?"

"Yes, Mr. Walker." Graley dropped calling him Matt now that the mea culpa was done, and she needed to be more professional. Put the small wall back up between them.

"I am surprised, to say the least. I don't know what to say, Detective."

"Well, I thought you should know. Sorry again about the way this conversation started. How is Kate, by the way?"

"Fine, as far as I know. With everything going on, she took off to stay with her parents for a while in Bend."

Cringing, Graley kept silent. She wasn't sure her leaving was a good idea. The police didn't lay out any ground rules for the Walkers staying present, and they probably should have now that she thought about it. Since they didn't, the Walkers could do as they pleased. She would talk about it more in front of the attorney. She thought about asking Walker for a phone number but figured she could search Kate's parents in Bend easily enough to come up with a number.

"Anything else, Detective? I need to order a new iced coffee for the third time today."

"Um, no. Uh, wait. Mr. Walker, could I have Kate's cell number? I would like to give her a call."

Graley listened as Matt Walker let out a laugh. It was a genuine back of the throat funny laugh. She liked this guy and was attracted to him. She couldn't figure out why she was unable to remember the last man she'd been attracted to. Attracted wasn't the right word. Appealing. That was it. Matt Walker had an appealing way about him.

"I can assure you, I have not killed her, Detective. You can give her a try. Cell range is spotty between here and Bend.

Graley grabbed her notepad and wrote down the number, wondering why at the last second, she decided to ask him for it.

"Thanks again, Mr. Walker. I'll give your attorney a call as well and set something up. Are you available later today? I'd really like to get this behind us."

"Me, too, Detective–and yes."

"Okay, I'll talk with you later."

Graley hung up the phone and looked at Kate Walker's phone number on the notepad. She entered the digits on her cell phone, reminding herself not to say anything Cole-like to her, and listened as the phone rang.

Overwhelmed

Matt couldn't believe his coffee luck for the day. The number of spilled iced coffees equaled the number of dead former wives. At this rate, Dutch Brothers were going to think him a caffeine junkie.

After his latest spill, a large dog ran over. Looked to be a mutt, with no collar or tag. Looking around, Matt scanned for a possible owner, then reached down and patted the dog behind the neck. Matted fur and dirt caked the canine which tried to lick the coffee and soy from the ground.

Thinking of Koda, Matt looked around the immediate area for a store and saw a mini-market behind the coffee stand. As he headed toward the store, the dog, done with the spilled coffee, followed, to Matt's pleasure. He wasn't sure what had come over him in his concern for the dog. He saw strays often and never seriously thought about doing anything with them. He figured, giving it careful consideration while walking to the store, the reason was his newfound appreciation for life and how everything now seemed connected. Matt spoke to the mutt as he entered the market

"Stay outside, dog. I'll be right back."

Matt wondered if the dog would be there when he returned. His head turned back and forth with the deftness of a gymnast as he surveyed the store and its surroundings. His eyes settled on the front counter and its occupant.

"Where is the dog food? Do you have any?"

The register attendant lifted his smoke-stained face up from what looked to be a graphic novel, long enough to grunt and point. Heading in the direction of the point, Matt found a few cans of food and a small bag of dry food. With no can opener, Matt opted for the dry food. He saw a small plastic bowl next to the food, so he grabbed a blue one and headed to the counter.

Setting the items down, he waited several seconds before the attendant looked up, rolled his eyes, and set down the novel. Matt glanced at the cover. Red, black, and white graphics of a sultry looking man, or woman, on the cover. The large title across the front read, Alyxandria. In lowercase print at the bottom was A Modern-Day LGBT Warrior. Matt tried to see who wrote it, fully intrigued now in light of his recent appreciation for life in general, but the kid grunted.

"Seven ninety-nine, please."

Matt handed the kid a ten-dollar bill.

"Is that good?"

"Is what good? Your money, old man?" the smart-ass kid replied.

Matt chuckled, happy with himself for not taking the bait and engaging the kid with a battle of smart-alecky wit.

"No, the graphic novel."

The kid perked up. He straightened, held his head a little higher, and his eyes brightened. Matt couldn't help but notice the change in demeanor. He found it fascinating. All from one simple question.

"Yeah, it's great. A young guy from Southern California wrote it about his take on sexuality, how it affected and affects his life, and how all of us are searching for a way to feel normalcy. Trying to connect with something, someone, everyone, and everything. It is hard for me to explain, but it makes me feel like there's hope in humanity when I read it. I have read it five times already."

Beaming with effusive energy, the kid reached out with Matt's change. Matt wanted to experience the high the novel brought to the kid.

"Keep the change, kid. Tell me, where did you get the novel?"

"Mystify Comics, two blocks down on Fourth and Stewart. Why?" the kid asked with trepidation.

The door to the market opened and Matt watched as a mother and small child walked in together holding hands. The mother smiled as the two headed toward the back of the store. Matt could see the dog standing outside waiting, which pleased him.

"Because if it makes you feel this good about things, I want to read it."

The kid beamed and responded right away.

"Well, they're open now. Head over there. Last time I was there they had several copies left. I don't think many people know about it. Plus, throw in the fact that it has a rainbow with LGBT across the front cover and most people think freak and fringe, so they don't have the courage to check it out."

"Thanks, I might head down there now. Have a good day, kid."

"You, too, Mister, and thanks for the change."

Matt grabbed the small bag of dog food and the plastic bowl off the counter and headed outside.

"Hey, mister."

Matt stopped and turned back to the kid. "What's up?"

"You have a cell phone?"

Matt felt in his back pocket making sure it was there.

"Sure, why?"

The kid laid the novel flat on the countertop and spun it around to face Matt.

"Take a picture of it so you can show them at the book store. They'll find it quicker for you since it's tucked away."

Matt smiled, set the recent purchases down, grabbed his phone and snapped a quick shot. The whole time the young kid was beaming. Matt liked the feeling of connection between two seemingly disparate human beings. Both wanted to belong. The kid called it normalcy. Matt wondered if the planet could ever achieve such wonderful simplicity. He hoped so, but the cynic in him doubted.

"Listen, thanks kid. Enjoy the novel and have a great day. Life isn't so bad when we all work together, is it?"

The kid picked the book up and smiled as Matt gathered up the bowl and dog food and headed outside, successfully this time. His new buddy waited patiently as if he knew Matt had gone into the market for him.

"Okay, dog, here you go."

Matt set the bowl down and tore open the bag, pouring the food out until the blue plastic bowl couldn't take anymore. The dog sat and waited patiently, which Matt thought odd for a stray. His condition smacked of an abandoned loner. No collar, matted fur, ragged look, and it smelled. Not in bad shape overall, though, so it must be good at scavenging at least.

"Go ahead, dog, eat." Matt pushed the bowl toward the dog and it began to eat in gulps.

Standing, Matt looked around wondering what to do with the food remaining in the bag. Watching as cars drove by the mother and daughter walked out of the store.

"Cute dog, Mister. What's its name?" the little girl asked.

"I call him 'dog.' He is cute, isn't he?"

"May I pet him?" she asked.

The mother looked at Matt, sizing him up. He figured she wondered if he and the dog could be trusted. Matt wasn't sure, since he never had kids, but he figured he would react the same way if he were the parent.

"May my daughter pet the dog? Will he bite?"

"Well, he isn't my dog, Ma'am. I saw him across the street and thought he looked hungry, so I brought him over here and bought him food."

"Lucy, let's let the dog eat, okay? Dogs don't like to be bothered while they are eating."

The mother gave the child the command. Matt, never having had kids, found himself bewildered as the child obeyed dutifully.

"Are you aware of the Jackson County animal shelter over on Maple?" the lady asked.

"No, why?" Matt replied.

"Well, I volunteer there on the weekends and they take strays like this in. They clean them up and work toward getting them adopted out to the public. If you feel like it, you could take the dog over and drop it off. Tell the front desk that Belinda Waters told you to stop by. I know they have extra capacity now and they should take the dog in. It looks to be one they should have no problem adopting out."

"Why is that?" Matt asked, curious.

"Well, it's a good size, doesn't seemed phased by children, no aggression while it is eating, and the fact it followed you across the street and waited makes me think it has belonged to someone before. All conjecture, of course. But I have a keen sense about animals, particularly dogs."

Matt stared at the woman, looked down at the dog eating away and then back at the woman. He was fixated on what truth lay behind her dark brown eyes. He was never one to trust easily, but this woman seemed genuinely concerned.

"Okay, thanks. You said on Maple?"

"Yes, less than ten minutes from here. So, are you going to take him over?"

"I guess. Why?"

"Well if you aren't, then I will. This dog shouldn't be on the street. It needs a chance for a good life."

"Okay, I'll take it." Matt replied a little irritated, feeling as though the woman was questioning his intentions and care for the animal.

Reaching out, the woman put a hand on Matt's arm.

"Thank you, sir. It's so thoughtful of you. Good things happen to people who have a heart for animals. I wish there were more people around like you."

She gently tugged on her daughter's hand.

"Come on, Lucy. Let the dog finish eating."

As the mother and daughter walked away, Matt could hear the mother talking.

"That nice man is going to take the dog to the shelter where mommy volunteers, so they can find a home for it."

"Really? He is a nice man, mommy, isn't he?"

"Yes, he is Lucy."

Matt sat down next to the dog. The coolness of the concrete permeated through his jeans. In no time, a chill forced its way past his jeans through his skin and muscle, pushing up against his bones. He reached over and touched the dog, feeling an immense amount of love and care. Suddenly overwrought with a sense of dread for the animal, Matt looked around to see if anyone watched, wondering if they could see the sadness he felt.

"Why would anyone want to kill Sharon and Betheny?" Matt said out loud as he kept his hand on the matted, musty back of the dog.

Overwhelmed with grief, Matt lowered his head and started sobbing as his phone rang.

The Proper Way

Graley listened as the phone on the other end of the line rang, one annoying burst after another.

"Hi, Kate here. I can't take your call right now. Leave a message and I'll get back with you. Bye-bye."

The woman sounded way too perky for Graley. It had to be fake, right? No one could be so happy. Could they?

"Mrs. Walker, Detective Graley from the Medford Police Department. I need to ask you a few questions. Please call me when you have a minute. I promise it won't take long."

Graley left her number, with a few other pleasantries, then hung up.

Looking skyward, the tired detective leaned against her car noticing the massive white clouds. They seemed to float with joy in the rich blueness of their sky. Not a care in the world, except to dance with the wind.

Graley fetched Matt Walker's attorney's card out of her pants pocket, finding the number nestled in the card stock with its tiny font. Dialing, she wondered how far from Bend Mrs. Walker was. She decided to try calling her again in fifteen minutes.

"Law offices of Jim Davies, may I help you?"

Good Lord, perky number two. Seriously? Graley wondered if she was too sullen and these people were normal. Nah, no one should be this damn bubbly.

"Detective Graley, Medford P.D. I need to speak with Mr. Davies, please."

Graley looked at her watch. One o'clock. Plenty of time to get something set up for this afternoon as far as she was concerned. She would insist.

"Mr. Davies is in a meeting ma'am. May I take a message?"

"Son-of-a-bitch," Graley blurted out. "I'm sorry, didn't mean to say that out loud. Long day and I am not making the progress I want on my case."

"Would you like to leave a message, Detective?"

Graley's father's voice echoed in her head. "Sweetie, always use 'honey,' even for the most mundane things."

Scraping the gravel-laden ground under tired feet she responded in a professional manner with a smattering of language syrup.

"I would like to leave a message, honey, thanks. I love your voice, by the way. It sounds so pleasant."

Graley pulled the phone away from her head, rolling her eyes at the unnatural words flowing out of her mouth. She felt embarrassed and guilty.

"Thank you, Detective. A lot of people tell me that."

Graley continued, "Please tell Mr. Davies I need to speak with him right away. It is urgent, honey. It must be today. Do you understand?"

"Absolutely, Detective, and don't you worry. I will have him call you as soon as he is available. I promise."

Graley smiled. *Damn, the honey shit works*, she thought mumbling to herself, "thanks, dad."

"Excuse me Detective, did you say 'dad'?"

Oops too loud, Graley thought.

"Um, no. Thank you very much. Have a great day, and I'll expect to hear from Mr. Davies soon. Bye."

"Sure thing, Detective. Have a nice day."

Graley hung the phone up.

Climbing into her car, she put the keys in the ignition and turned the key. The engine revved to life as the Wallander ring-tone on her cell blared. Glancing down, she didn't recognize the number. Reluctant to pick up, she hesitated, then answered.

"Detective Graley."

"Hi, Detective."

For a Dr. Seuss slice in time, the slimmest of slim, Graley thought Ms. Bubbly from the law office was calling her back already.

"Detective? Kate Walker, you asked me to call you."

"Oh, hi Mrs. Walker. Thank you."

Recovering her focus Graley engaged Kate right away, ignoring the high-pitched voice as best she could.

"I spoke with your husband a little while ago and he said you were on your way to your parents in Bend, correct?"

Graley let the question hang, hoping she wasn't being too obvious, but realizing there was no avoiding it. As a detective, almost every time without any effort on her part, people were on edge when she spoke to them.

"Um, yes, I am. Why?"

"Well, Ma'am, I hope you can understand, and don't hold it against us," Graley said, using 'us' as in police, wondering if Mrs. Walker would even notice. "I just want to make sure you are okay."

"Fine, Detective. I should be at my parents in another hour or so. Koda and I are just outside of LaPine getting gas. Matt and I figured it would be better if I got out of town."

Kate paused. Graley wasn't sure if she should respond or wait for her to continue. She found it best over the years not to interrupt someone willing to talk. Give them plenty of rope. Diarrhea mouth has a way of revealing much. Kate continued without prompting.

"My parents were really the only place within driving distance I felt safe, so I am on my way. Is this a problem? Should I have stayed in Medford with Matt?"

The woman could certainly talk fast. Throw in the high-pitched carnival bubble aspect of her voice and it was like watching a bad skit on SNL. She didn't remember Mrs. Walker's voice being so obnoxious in person. Perhaps there was a change due to her stress level.

"No, it isn't a problem. I would rather you stayed home, but under the circumstances, I understand. May I check in with you from time to time? I would feel better knowing you are okay. I may have a question or two as well."

"Please do, Detective. No problem at all. Do you have any leads? You know my Matt didn't do this, don't you? You shouldn't waste your time even looking at him. Someone wants to hurt him. I don't know who, but someone clearly does."

Graley massaged the words in her head trying to pick up on anything that may trigger a thought, or a direction to go she hadn't already thought of. Nothing revelatory oozed forward. Biting the inside of her lower lip, she knew not to say what she was thinking, as it could negatively impact the case, but she plowed ahead anyway, to her surprise and confusion.

"Well, Mrs. Walker, for what it is worth, I don't think your husband killed his ex-wives. Please understand, though, we must look at everything and everyone involved. Both directly and indirectly. It's the proper way to solve a case."

Ever Ridden in a Tesla?

Seeing the phone call was from Kate, Matt focused on getting his breathing under control. Still sobbing, he concentrated on deep, slow breaths to control the frantic shortness of sucking in air. He couldn't remember ever feeling so distraught. The weight of the formers' deaths had come crashing down on him in a sudden and unexpected manner.

This abandoned dog, who he scratched behind the ear, pulled, or rather, forced the reality of his current situation out in an unexpected way. The loss of control made him feel pathetic. Kate's phone call was well-timed. He needed a familiar and caring voice. Matt wiped his eyes with the back of his hand and pressed the answer icon on his phone.

"Hello."

"Hey, babe, you okay?"

"Hanging in there, beautiful. How about you?"

"The drive is beautiful as always. Big fluffy clouds against the blue sky. Just as I like."

"Good."

"What's wrong, Matt? You sound like you are breathing funny."

"Oh, nothing. I'm outside a mini-market near Jim Davies' office. I found a stray dog who looked like it was starving and needed help. So, I bought food for the damn thing and now I can't get rid of him. Seemed like a good idea at the time; now I'm not so sure."

"How sweet, Matt. Animals are cheering in heaven."

The feminine flint and wistful youthfulness of Kate's voice reassured Matt. His breathing felt normal again, and his hand no longer shook against the coffee-loving canine.

"Hah. Well I am not so sure about cheering, but they are probably clapping a little."

Kate laughed.

"So, what did Jim say?"

"Oh, not a lot. Keep my mouth shut, stay out of trouble, make sure you are okay, and not to talk with the cops unless he is present. He said they don't have anything on me, and no real reason to suspect me with the way everything has played out. Hopefully, I am going to meet with the detective at Jim's office soon."

"I got off the phone not too long ago with her, Matt."

"Detective Graley?"

"Yes. She called me and asked a few questions. Mainly wanted to see if I was okay."

"Well, that makes sense under the circumstances. I am worried about you as well. I am doubting our decision and wondering if you should have stayed here."

Matt let the statement hang, not sure he really felt this way but the words fell out of his mouth, regardless.

"Detective Graley ended the conversation, Matt, saying she didn't think you killed your formers, by the way. Sounds like she is frustrated about not knowing more."

"She said she didn't think I did it?"

"Yes, Matt. So, relax and help her in any way you can so we can get our lives back."

Matt, with a few words from Kate, felt much better. The simple fact that Detective Graley had told Kate he wasn't a suspect helped his demeanor push a soft-flowing surge of adrenaline through his body.

"What a relief. Now I'm not dreading the interview as much. How is Koda doing?"

"Great, Matt. He rides well in the car. Surprisingly well. I am so glad we decided to get him. He's on the leash right now, pacing back and forth in front of me while I stroll in the woods."

"In the woods? Where are you Kate?"

"Behind the Fuel Commander gas station in LaPine. You know, where we always stop to stretch our legs, wondering if we should turn around and go home instead of visiting my parents. Why?"

"I just want to make sure you are okay is all. If something happened to you, I don't know what I would do. Please stay in sight of people."

"Okay, Matt. I understand. Koda has my back though, trust me."

Impatient and angry, Matt lost his calm.

"Kate, people know how to take out dogs. Don't be foolish!" Showing no regret for the tone he took, Matt wanted Kate to understand the seriousness of the situation. *Shit!*, he thought to himself, *I should not have let her leave.*

The silence hung so long, Matt thought the signal was lost. He needed her to respond first, so he waited.

In her sweet voice, all wistful banter and intonation gone, Matt could tell Kate understood.

"You don't have to talk with me this way, Matt. I will let the tone slide because I can only imagine what you are going through right now. But let's be clear. I get it. I don't trust anyone right now outside of you and my family, okay?"

"Good, Kate."

"What are you going to do with the stray, Matt?"

Looking down at the dog sitting next to him, Matt saw a sadness in his eyes. Another creature who simply wanted to belong. He thought of the clerk in store, wondering if he would like a dog before drifting back to the conversation with Kate.

"A lady stopped by with her daughter and told me about a shelter not far from here that I should take him. I'll go over there when we get off the phone. We have Koda now, and as much as I am smitten by this little guy..."

Matt rubbed the dog's head playfully, which elicited a groan from the canine, before he continued.

"I don't have the time to spend with him right now. Hell, for all I know, he belongs to someone and they are looking for him. The shelter should be able to help with that. Right?"

Kate sensed a wavering hesitation in Matt's voice. She was not used to him wavering–at all. Her empathy flexed as she chose her next words with care.

"It's doubtful he belongs to anyone, Matt, since he's sticking so close to you, but it is possible. Listen, why don't I turn around and come home? You sound like you could use the support."

"Aren't your parents expecting you?"

Matt stood and started walking back and forth in front of the market. The street dog stayed glued to his side.

"I haven't even been able to get ahold of them yet, Matt. I left a message on mom's voice mail, so no, not really."

Matt thought it would be nice to have her around, but still thought it too risky.

"Kate, I would love to have you here with me, but it isn't smart. We don't know enough of what is going on. Let's see what the detectives find out in the next day or two, and what Detective Graley can tell me in the interview coming up. Then we can talk about it, okay?"

"Well, one thing I am glad about–you sound like the man I fell in love with again. Confident and sure. The beginning of the call, not so much. Glad you're feeling better, Matt. Let me get going. Koda and I have about another hour or so of driving left. Good luck in the interview and let me know what you find out."

Matt started to respond but Kate cut him off.

"Oh, and good luck with the dog. It is sweet, what you are doing, honey."

"Thanks, Kate. Love you and drive safe."

Matt pressed the red phone button on the screen, placed the cell in his back pocket, and turned to his new canine friend.

"Okay, dog, you ever ridden in a Tesla?"

Just a Distraction

Graley pecked away at the computer keyboard looking for anything she could find on Kate Walker. She was surprised, in this day of social media gluttony, how little there was about Walker's number three. Deep digging didn't expose anything relative. It looked as though Kate liked to volunteer at a dog rescue. There were various photos of her walking dogs, kneeling with dogs, static photos of her with dogs and people. The only thing in common in all the photos was the fact that the dogs had Adopt-Me vests on them. Bright yellow Adopt Me vests. *Well, good for Kate Walker*, Graley thought to herself.

A little more Google searching, pages deep, she came across a wedding announcement which read:

Local Medford businessman and Kiwanis board member, Matthew A. Walker, to wed former Ms. Bend, Katherine M. Campbell.

Further searching around this announcement revealed nothing. Kate Walker, former Ms. Bend, was private indeed. Graley hadn't run into any issues the past several years when searching for information online. Except for homeless people.

Graley printed out a few pages of everything she could find on Kate Walker. Standing from her desk chair, she felt a tightness in the small of her lower back. She bent over at the waist and let her arms hang. She could still touch her toes with minimal effort, which always made her feel good about herself. Especially now, since she hadn't been to yoga in almost three months. Her flexibility wasn't what it should be, so she made a mental note to go in the next couple of days, no excuses.

Standing upright, Graley knew Cole was not in the detective room since no comments were shouted about her ass. Her partner-child never missed an opportunity to make a comment when she stretched.

As Graley walked to the printer room, she saw Cole walking down the hall toward her. The partner-relationship swirled in her head, unable to clear her mind about Cole's unprofessionalism. She had a few good partners over the years, Cole was not one of them. Nothing, up to now, could be said synonymous with the Cole name fitting into the 'good' mold. He was negative—hell; he was just an ass, her thoughts on point as he spewed crap following her into the copy room.

"What are you up to, Graley? Printing out recipes for your LGBT club?"

"And there he is. The child is back," Graley mumbled under her breath in disbelief at what continued to come out of the man's, no child's mouth.

Cole had all but been suspended by the new Chief, and he still had the audacity to come on heavy with her. She stopped short of the printer and started to spin. She caught herself in time, her brain channeling LeBron in a state of mental athleticism, and realized a goading Cole wanted her to respond. Perhaps he was looking to entice her into a confrontation and risk getting herself reprimanded. He didn't have much more to lose.

"What are you printing, Graley?"

Graley grabbed her prints and walked past Cole looking him square in the eyes. She focused, with the best pissed off don't-mess-with-me look she could muster.

Cole backed up a bit and kept his mouth shut. A first, that Graley could remember.

After leaving the copy room, Graley heard Cole say, "Fuck," followed by a sharp thud. She imagined him kicking the bottom of the printer stand. Next came a loud crashing noise. Graley surmised Cole had either fallen in a futile effort to kick something, as she hoped, or that he had knocked the printer off the stand. Either option gave her satisfaction. Her partner was losing it. She knew he wouldn't be able to stand being shunned and completely shut out of this case.

Graley, back at her desk, leaned back in her chair to gaze down the hallway. She saw Cole leave the room with shoulders slouched and head down. Her partner headed back the same direction he had come in.

"What's wrong with your partner, Graley?" one of the detectives in the room asked.

Graley laughed before responding.

"Chief got pissed, reprimanded him, and now he's grounded. I think our little child is cracking up."

Graley chuckled again. The other three detectives in the room were saying something, probably to her directly, but she didn't listen, choosing to focus on the information recently printed on Kate Walker. She grabbed the manual three-hole punch out of her top right desk drawer and, smacking the paper on her desk to get the edges in line, she inserted them before pressing the lever down making nice clean holes. Looking around for a new binder in a large left-hand drawer, she saw none. She could get back up and go to the copy room and grab one but didn't want to be the last one seen coming out of there after Cole's loud exit.

Graley looked at a pile of paper on the left side of her desk and saw a binder labeled Senior Living Homes. Thinking of her dad and feeling guilty, she tore the label off knowing she would no longer need it since her choice, of residence for her father, had been made.

"Her choice," she mumbled to herself, guilt tearing at her heart like a narrow, stinging, paper cut.

Ripping the pages out of the binder, she threw them in the trash, pulled both tabs back, and watched as the three rings folded open like the claws of an upside-down backhoe.

"Graley."

Graley did not hear her name.

"Graley?"

Still oblivious to her name being called, she inserted the case pages into the binder and closed the claws.

"Jesus, Graley!"

Graley looked up to see someone standing next to her desk peering down at her. Her mind had been stuck between the Walker murders, her shit-brain partner, and her father.

"Yeah, Murdock, what is it?"

"You have a phone call. Line 1. And I ain't your personal secretary. When your phone rings next time, do us all a favor and pick it up."

"Thanks, and sorry Murdock."

Graley watched Murdock, the only detective in Medford with more seniority than she had, move with the athletic grace of a lumberjack back to his desk. She reached for the phone.

"Hello. Detective Graley."

"Detective Graley! This is Kate Walker. Someone slashed my tires! All of them! They are all flat! I was out walking the dog and talking with Matt on the phone. When I got back to my car, all the tires were flat. It looks like there are stab marks in them. What do I do? I can't drive it!"

In an instant, several thoughts flashed through Graley's mind. The one that surprised her the most, and it shouldn't have; perhaps Kate Walker was the target and Matt Walker merely a distraction.

A Different Conversation

Graley focused on the ideas and questions swirling through her brain.

"Kate, are you alone or in public?"

"I am standing at a gas station market outside of LaPine. Matt and I always stop here when we drive to my parents' house. There are a few people around, going in and out of the store or filling their cars up with gas."

"LaPine, you said?"

"Yes. At the Fuel Commander gas station."

"Okay, don't hang up. I am going to call the police in LaPine and get someone over there. Stay on the phone, okay?"

Graley could hear Kate telling the dog to sit. She reached across to Cole's desk and grabbed his phone. She pressed zero for the switchboard.

"This is detective Graley. Get me someone in LaPine, Oregon at the police station and now, please! This is an emergency."

"Hang on, Detective, one moment." The voice sounded confident on the other end of the line. Graley picked up her own phone again.

"Kate, you still there?"

"Yes, Detective Graley."

"Okay, I am getting someone from LaPine on the phone. Your dog is with you, right?"

"Yes."

"Okay, good. Keep him close to you. Hang on."

"Detective, I have the Deschutes County Sheriff's Department on the phone. You can go ahead."

"Hello, Detective Mara Graley of the Medford PD. I have a potential witness to a homicide in possible trouble at the Fuel Commander gas station outside LaPine. All her tires have been slashed. Can you please get a car over there right away?"

"Hang on, Detective."

Graley listened to the confident female voice on the other end of the line.

"Justin, Dispatch. You done with lunch yet, over?"

What seemed like an eternity to Graley was no more than seven or eight seconds before she heard another voice come over the phone.

"Good God, Dispatch, what is it now? And yes, I'm just finishing up."

"Head over to the Fuel Commander gas station in LaPine. The one on 97 near 31. There is a woman there, a possible witness to a recent murder in Medford and all her tires have been slashed. Medford P.D. is on the phone with me now asking for assistance."

Dispatch barked the command. Graley loved the matter-of-fact attitudes of police dispatchers. No tone, no agenda, just the facts. No more, no less.

"Shit, Barb. Okay, on my way. I can be there in ten minutes. What is she driving?"

"Detective Graley, what is the woman driving?"

Graley started to say she shouldn't be hard to find, but being a smart-ass right now wasn't going to help matters.

"Hang on let me check," she replied instead.

"Kate." Graley realized she was calling her by her first name, which wasn't how she normally operated. She wasn't sure what this meant if anything.

"Yes."

"What are you driving?"

"It is a red Jeep Trailhawk. There are only three or four cars in the station, I shouldn't be too hard to find."

Graley put Cole's phone back up to her face.

"A red Jeep Trailhawk."

"Justin, the woman is driving a red Jeep Trailhawk."

"Okay, Barb. I'm on my way. Whoever is talking with her, tell them to have her get inside the station's store and stay there. Tell her not to stand outside. If she feels she must, stay in the Jeep, lock all the doors, and be prepared to honk the horn like crazy if necessary. Okay?"

Graley heard the officer through the phone and started relaying the message to Kate Walker.

"Kate, get inside the gas station and stay around people okay? Staying in the Jeep and locking the doors is another choice, but you should go inside the store."

"What about Koda?"

"Leave him the car; he can take care of himself. Or if you would rather take him with you, it's a small town—I am sure they would let you take him inside if you ask."

"Okay, and thanks, Detective Graley."

"Sure thing. Oh, and Kate, don't call your husband. I am due to meet with him in about twenty minutes. Let me tell him. Otherwise he would probably drop whatever he's doing and race up there."

"Are you sure, Detective? I was going to call him next."

Graley grabbed the back of her neck with her free hand and twisted her head around hoping for a pop. Nothing but the sound of tendons and muscle grinding against each other.

"Yes, I'm sure. I'm heading out now for the meeting with him and his attorney. I will tell him. You get inside and stay safe. I'll be in touch."

"Okay. Thanks."

Graley heard the disconnect sound on the phone, then remembered she had the other phone still active.

"Hi, Detective Graley here again. You still there?"

"Yes, Detective."

"Thank you for the quick assistance. Much appreciated. We will get someone up there to take a report and help with our witness. Can I get a number to call for information?"

Graley grabbed a pen and wrote the number down, expressed her gratitude, then stood and looked around.

"Dammit, Cole," she mumbled. She thought having a normal partner right now would be helpful.

Graley put the piece of paper with the phone number in her pocket and grabbed the jacket off the back of her chair. She slid her cell phone into her back pants pocket and put the jacket on. She felt her neck pop and was satisfied with the release of tension it provided even if small.

Walking down the hall, still pouting but head up high again, was Cole.

Graley met him halfway.

"Come with me, Cole."

Cole didn't say a word, for once, and dutifully followed Graley into the Chief's office, whose door was open. She figured she would test out this open-door policy he always preached. She walked in and could feel Cole's meek, submissive presence behind her. He oozed defeat.

"Chief, got a quick minute?"

The Chief, writing something, looked up from his desk. Graley liked the color of his hands. They were dark rich chocolate on the outside and a creamy milky white-chocolate on the inside. She glanced at her hands and saw, with disappointment, one pale shade of white inside and out.

"Sure, Detective Graley, what is it?"

"Kate Walker, Matt Walker's wife."

The Chief interrupted, "From the double murder, yesterday? Those Walkers?"

"Exactly, Chief. Anyhow, Kate Walker was driving up to Bend, Oregon, to stay with her parents while all this was going on. I just got off the phone with her. She stopped outside of LaPine at a gas station to stretch her legs and walk her dog. When she got back to her car, someone had slashed all the tires."

"Fuck me!" Graley heard Cole blurt out behind her.

"Is she okay?" the Chief responded with a more attentive and slightly higher pitched voice.

"She called me, and our dispatch patched me through to their Sheriff's Department. They have a car on the way to her now. Should be there any minute."

"Okay, good. What do you need me for?"

"Well, we should go up there, but I have an interview in about fifteen minutes with her husband, Matt Walker. I don't want to postpone it. And..." The Chief cut Graley off again—not in a rude way, Graley noticed, but in an efficient let's get-to-the-point way that she found reassuring. What she had heard and seen from the Chief so far; a confident pro. His demeanor made her feel better.

"You want Cole to go up to LaPine, don't you?"

Now Graley was even more impressed. She felt a tingling sensation in her thighs and then felt a little flush. She couldn't believe it and hoped like hell the Chief couldn't tell.

"Well, I know you have him on a short-leash, but he already knows her, he's familiar with the case, and perhaps he deserves a chance to make good on his recent screw-up."

Graley cut her eyes over to Cole.

The Chief stood and walked around the edge of his desk. Graley felt physically small next to this man. He was at least six feet four and powerful. Impressed by his perfectly pressed uniform, she knew there was no softness about this man.

"Cole."

Graley grimaced a bit, expecting Cole to interrupt the Chief instead of letting him talk. To her surprise, and relief, he did not.

"Get a car from the pool. Get all the pertinent information from Graley and head up there. I think we should bring her back here where we can keep an eye on her. I can understand her wanting to be with her parents, but these tire-slashings have changed things. That can't be a random occurrence. Get her back here at once. Do you understand?"

Graley watched as Cole worked at projecting confidence in a meaningful and professional way.

"Yes, Chief, understood, and thanks. I do appreciate it, and I won't let you or Graley down."

"Good. Now the two of you get out of here and get to work."

The Chief returned to his desk.

"Oh, Cole, one more thing."

Cole, about to cross the door threshold, stopped. He did it so quickly Graley bumped into him.

"Sorry, Graley."

Graley was impressed with the last couple of minutes from Cole. She had never seen him like this before. Perhaps he was savable after all.

"Yes, Chief?"

"When you have the Walker woman in your car, call Graley. And you check in with her every sixty minutes until you're back here. Make it thirty minutes."

"Got it, Chief."

"And Graley, keep me up to date with everything going on."

"Understood, Chief," Graley replied, pushing Cole out of the office. Following him down the hall, she started talking.

"Cole, nice performance in there for once. I hope like hell you were sincere."

"Look, Graley, don't give me any shit, okay? I'm trying here. This place is all I have."

Graley watched as Cole veered off into the copy room. She stopped at the door and watched Cole pick up the printer and put it back on the table. She wondered what he had going on in his life that made him the way he is. She knew he had family baggage like everyone else, and that his dad wasn't much of a father, but she didn't know much more. She hadn't made the time to get to know him on a personal level because she disliked him so much. For the first time, she felt a twinge of sadness for Cole.

Cole returned from the printer room and stood next to Graley.

"Graley, do you know if Ms. Walker has their dog with her?"

"Yes, she does. Why?"

"Oh, I was thinking I should take one of the SUVs then, and not a squad car. More room in the back so the little guy isn't sliding around on a car seat."

"Good thinking, Cole. I'll walk with you to the car pool clerk. I am on my way to interview Matt Walker at his attorney's."

Cole headed back down the hall toward the back of the building and the car pool parking lot.

"The incident took place at a gas station, this side of LaPine on highway 97 at the route 31 intersection. It's called Fuel Commander."

Cole laughed. "I know right where that is. I stop there on the way up to Mt. Bachelor when I go skiing."

"I didn't know you ski, Cole," Graley said, working at sounding caring.

"Love it. Mt. Ashland usually, but occasionally I like to go up to Bachelor for longer runs and more variety. Snow is different as well. More powder."

Graley reached into her pocket and grabbed the piece of paper with the phone number she had written down a few minutes ago.

"Cole, take a picture of this number. This is the dispatcher at the Deschutes County Sheriff's Office. A direct line. You can give a call on the way up and see where they have her, okay?"

Graley watched Cole as he dutifully grabbed his cell phone out of his pocket, started the camera app, and took a photo. His hands were frail and soft looking. The skin was pale and smooth. The inside of his hands had a pinkish, very childlike, hue to them. She felt more sadness for him looking at his hands.

"Got it, Graley. Let me get the SUV and get going. I should be able to be there in less than two-and-a-half hours."

"You sure you took a photo, Cole?"

Graley took a shot at Cole and his less than average photo ability. Cole rolled his eyes and looked downward. Graley felt like a heel.

Patting Cole on the shoulder, she said, "Keep me posted, okay?"

"Will do, boss, and thanks. I know you could have figured something else out. I mean it, Gray."

Graley smiled, wanting to believe Cole's new attitude. She turned, heading out the door to the parking lot and her car. Checking her watch, she realized she would be a couple minutes late. She dialed operator's assistance and asked for the law office of Jim Davies.

Driving out of the parking lot with the lawyer notified, she looked at the piece of paper for the number to dial the Deschutes County Sheriff's Office when her phone rang. The number was the same number she was about to dial.

"Hello."

"Is this Detective Graley?"

"Yes, it is. Is this Deschutes County?"

"Yes, this is Barb, the dispatcher. We talked a few minutes ago."

"Yes Barb, what's up? You guys get Kate, the woman at the Fuel Commander gas station, picked up okay?"

"Well, Detective, there's a problem."

Graley grimaced in anticipation for what she would hear next.

"She isn't there. The Deputy is on site and can't find her. The dog is in the Jeep, but she is nowhere to be found. We were wondering if she called you."

Graley turned into the law office parking lot and pulled into the first spot she could find. It felt as though someone had reached up inside her chest and squeezed her heart. The pressure was immense as if she were having a heart attack.

With sagging shoulders and a heaviness of regret flooding her body, Graley slumped in the cruiser's bench seat, reached for the key, and turned off the car. She contemplated a completely different conversation with Matt Walker now.

A Deep Stinging Pain

Matt dropped his new buddy off at the shelter and in a matter of minutes felt comfortable about the decision. An energetic young woman, almost too perky, scanned the dog for a microchip and found he already had a home. She told Matt the dog was probably just lost. The shelter said the dog didn't appear to be homeless. He was "too well-behaved and appeared healthy," but it was good that Matt brought him in.

With assurances of the shelter tracking down the owners, Matt left. He did leave his name and number in case the owners didn't show. He was thinking in the deep, empathetic, recesses of his mind that perhaps he and Kate could keep two dogs. The young lady asked Matt if he was related to Kate Walker. She attempted to draw Matt into a conversation, but he didn't have time. He needed to get over to Jim Davies and face questioning from Detective Graley.

"Thanks," he said hurriedly. "Sorry I can't talk more, but I'm late for an appointment. The dog put me behind schedule. Thanks again."

Matt walked out, the door clanging shut behind him. Sliding into his car, he thought he could smell a faint odor of wet dog. He lowered the windows a crack and turned up the fresh air vents. He decided to take the car over to the detailing shop for a good cleaning after his appointment. As much as he loved dogs, he couldn't stand their smell when wet.

In less than ten minutes, Matt sat in Jim's office in a small conference room. Jim, standing at the door to the room, asked his assistant, Leslie, to get two water bottles and a cup of coffee for his friend Matt.

"So, Matt, we just got a call from Detective Graley that she will be a few minutes late but is on her way. It will give us a chance to talk strategy, okay?"

"Strategy?" Matt responded with skepticism. "Why do we need strategy if I am innocent and have nothing to hide?"

Jim smiled.

"Okay, perhaps strategy is a poor choice of words, Matt."

"For what I am paying you Jim, I expect you to have the right choice of words."

Laughing, out loud, Jim rocked back in his chair, caught his breath and shook his head back and forth.

"Touché, my friend, touché."

"Just messing with you, Jim."

Matt smiled as Leslie walked into the conference room through the glass door. Matt liked the room, which was evidence that Jim was doing quite well for himself or was in serious debt. There was a very expensive oak table with a glass inset. The chairs were leather, and comfortable wasn't an apt description. There were six of them, and they had to be five-hundred dollars each. One end of the room had a two-foot-high bonsai tree. Matt had no idea how much it cost, but it couldn't be cheap. The southern facing wall was nothing but glass panes from ceiling to floor and had a picturesque view of the Siskiyou Mountains. Mt. Ashland already had snow on her and the deep, rich Southern Oregon blue sky made her stand out today with a pompous display of pride.

"Here you are, Jim. Mr. Walker, water and coffee. You like your coffee black, right?"

"Yes, thank you very much."

"Anything else, Jim?"

"No, Leslie. Thanks. Please send Detective Graley right in when she arrives. We'll be ready for her straight-away, since we have nothing to hide."

Jim smiled. Matt took a turn at a small laugh as Leslie nodded and left.

"Okay, Matt, here's the deal. I lead. I tell you what you can and cannot answer. I don't care if you have nothing to hide or not. My job is to see that you..."

Matt reached over and picked up the cup of coffee, listening as Jim continued to speak. The mug, heavy and black with the words Rogue

Roasters etched in white on the side, felt substantial. Sipping the rich hot java, the flavor held up its part of the sturdy black mug.

"...stay out of trouble. Understand?"

"Got it, Jim. I won't say a word unless you direct me."

"Another thing. If you start to get to chatty, I will put my hand on your arm, meaning to end the answer quickly, or flat out tell you 'enough' if I want you to stop right away."

"Got it, Jim. This is good coffee by the way. What is it?"

"I don't know. Leslie picks it up for me. She lives in Grants Pass and is always going on and on about this place that roasts their own."

Matt pointed to the side of his cup, "Rogue Roasters" by chance?"

"Probably," Jim chuckled. "I think most coffee tastes the same, like crap, and don't drink much. Anyhow, as I was saying, I have been involved in enough cases over the years where everything seems to be cut and dry and my client should be in and out of here in thirty minutes, only to have the questioning take an unexpected turn. I leave nothing to chance. If something like that happens today, I will most likely end the questioning, ask if they are charging you, and if so, make the charge now or leave."

"Damn. Seriously?" Matt sat a little straighter in his chair.

"Yes, Matt. The law can be a fickle thing. Medford's police, for the most part, are inexperienced with murder. We have a lot of drug crimes, petty larceny, standard B and E's, that type of thing, but not much murder. Anyhow, they may be looking for a quick close to this and try their damnedest to convict you so they look good to the public. So, I am prepared for anything today.

I did some quick research on our Detective Graley. She is seasoned and professional. She handled a couple of murder cases years back with a couple of druggies. We will know right away on her approach. I suspect she is not seriously looking at you, based on the facts."

"Well she seems to have been very fair to me and Kate so far. Her partner, detective Cole, on the other hand, has been a total ass. Is he going to be here today?"

"No. Graley only, which I insisted on. Her partner, Detective Cole, has been reprimanded, apparently. Not sure to what degree, but his arresting you put a serious detour in his career path. The whole thing was handled poorly. We have that in our favor."

The door to the conference room opened, startling Matt for a second. Leslie walked in and then stood holding the door.

"Jim, Detective Graley is here."

Jim stood.

"Detective Graley, please come in and have a seat. Would you like water or coffee?"

Matt watched as the detective sauntered in. Something seemed different about her. His mind tried registering the difference in the normally confident and professional demeanor he had seen in her to up to this point.

"No, thank you," Graley replied.

"Okay, well, please take a seat."

Jim pointed to a chair opposite he and Matt at the conference table.

"I have something I need to tell the both of you, and you aren't going to like it," Graley said.

Jim looked at Matt and nodded as if this were something not to worry about. All part of the game, or what not, is how Matt interpreted Jim's look.

"Well, what is it, Detective Graley?"

"Mr. Walker, sometime within the last thirty minutes, your wife has disappeared."

With this news, Matt started to slump. He felt the immediacy of defeat and depression, and in an instant decided he was not going to let the feeling consume him. Raising up, his chair fell backward hitting the floor with a thud. He wished the detective had uttered the words, "You are under arrest," rather than telling him Kate has disappeared. A deep, stinging pain reverberated through Matt Walker's chest.

I Will Be in Touch

"What the hell do you mean, disappeared?" Matt took a step toward Detective Graley as if closing the distance between the two would lead to clarity.

Graley put herself in a defensive position out of instinct, but realized Matt wasn't being aggressive toward her, just the news. She relaxed.

"Mrs. Walker called me from a gas station outside of LaPine. She was upset saying the tires on her Jeep had been slashed."

"Slashed? What the hell? I talked to her as well while she was at that station. She was out walking the dog. She hung up with me and said she was heading the final hour to her parents."

Matt paused but didn't leave enough time for a response before finishing with. "Why did she call you?"

Jim Davies, jumped in. He walked over and picked up Matt's chair.

"Matt, please sit down and let the detective finish, so we can figure out what to do."

"I am leaving and heading up there, that's what I am going to do. You two can sit here and chat all you want."

Matt started to head for the door and Detective Graley reached up and firmly grabbed him by the arm.

"Matt...Mr. Walker, please sit down. Your attorney is correct. Give me a couple of minutes to talk with you about this and then let me do my job. I am good at it."

Matt did not want to stop, but he sensed a genuine care and concern emanating off Graley. Frustrated, scared, and not knowing what exactly he could do driving up to the station, he turned, adjusted his chair, and plopped his ass in the chair, the weight of the news pushing down lower than normal.

Jim Davies sat as well, so Graley pulled a chair out for herself and joined them at the table.

"Mrs. Walker calling me was the smartest thing she could have done. Now, we can react much quicker. Had she called you, Mr. Walker, it would have still happened, but we wouldn't have found out about it until possibly hours later."

Matt jumped in.

"Well what did she say, exactly?"

"She said she took the dog for a walk and when she got back to the car all the tires were slashed. I stayed on the phone with her and immediately called the Deschutes County Sheriff's Office. While we were on the line, they dispatched a patrol car to her. The policeman that was on his way, only ten minutes away from her by the way, told the dispatcher to have her go inside the gas station and stay around people. She could leave the dog in the car or take him with her, didn't matter, but regardless of the dog, she was to go inside. She agreed, said she wanted to call you and I told her no. I said I was due to see you here at your attorney's office in about twenty minutes. I didn't want you getting startled and worried for nothing."

"Well, how do you know she has disappeared, then, detective?" Jim piped in.

"Because the dispatcher from the Sheriff's office called me right before I got here. The patrol officer showed up and Mrs. Walker was nowhere to be found. The Jeep was locked, and the dog was inside."

"Is the dog okay?" Matt didn't know what else to say.

"I wasn't told specifically, but if there were harm to the dog, I am certain they would have told me as much."

"Good God! Do you think she is dead? What do we do now? I can't just sit here."

Matt stood. He started pacing back and forth along the glass windows staring out at the green rolling scenery of the Rogue Valley.

"I need a few more minutes to think, Mr. Walker." She started to tell him that Detective Cole was on his way up to meet Kate but decided against it. Now she wasn't sure sending Cole was such a good idea. Hopefully his ass was no longer a storage site for his head and he would help the situation rather than hinder it. She could mention this to Walker later; now was not the time.

"Have you noticed anything unusual in the last few hours, Mr. Walker?"

"Like what, Detective?" Jim piped in.

"Anything directly or indirectly odd. Anyone strange approach you? Did you receive any phone calls? Anything odd going on at the house?"

Detective Graley knew the questions were weak. She was buying time in an effort to process which direction to take.

"Other than me finding a stray dog and buying him food, then dropping him off at the shelter, no. Nothing."

All three sat in silence for what to Matt seemed like far too much time.

"Okay, here is what we are going to do. You are going to go home and stay there. I need you by the phone in case Kate tries to call, or in case she ends up there somehow. I am going to head up to LaPine myself, right now, and look at the scene and talk with the Sheriff's department."

"No way!" Matt blurted. "I am not going to sit on my ass while my wife is missing. We don't have a damn phone at the house, anyway. We use our cell phones. Shit, have you tried calling her cell phone?"

"No, I didn't," Graley responded while Matt pulled his phone out and already had it pressed to his ear.

"Dammit! Straight to voice mail." Matt started pressing the screen of the phone, and Detective Graley surmised he was sending her a text. She stood and walked to the opposite end of the room, with her cell phone now pressed to her ear.

"Dispatch, Detective Graley here. I need you to call whoever it is you call and put a trace on a cell number. This is possibly a matter of life or death."

Matt put his phone down. He stepped toward Detective Graley, wanting somehow to help. Graley put her left hand over the bottom of the phone and whispered to Matt.

"When I ask, give me her phone number, okay?"

"Yes."

"Hang on. Okay, what is it, Matt?"

Matt recited the number as if Graley were in remedial studies and couldn't absorb information quick.

"Yes, that is correct," Graley replied into the phone, looking at Matt.

"This won't take long if she has it on and with her," she told Matt.

"Okay. Thanks," Graley said as she disconnected the call.

"What is it?" Matt asked, not liking the way she was looking.

"Her phones at the location of the Fuel

Commander gas station. My guess is it's in the Jeep or near it. Let me call the Sheriff's Department."

Matt sat back down at the table next to Jim, who leafed through papers. Matt felt as though he was already moving on to something else and didn't give a shit about Kate.

Graley reached into her pocket, withdrew the piece paper put there less than an hour ago, then dialed her cell.

"Hey Barb, Detective Graley here in Medford. We spoke a little while ago about our witness's tires being slashed...Yes, that's right. Can you call the Deputy on scene and see if there has been a cell phone found? I did a trace on it. Looks like it may be at the scene."

Graley listened briefly.

"Oh, I see...Uh huh...Yes. Thank you. I'll be in touch soon."

Graley ended the call turning toward Matt. She wondered if her voice had any hint of the worry she held in her mind. She hoped not, for Matt's sake.

"The phone was in the front seat of the Jeep, apparently."

Matt pounded his fist down on the table.

"Unbelievable."

Darkness Followed

Contemplating the instructions given to her, Kate looked down at Koda who was pacing behind the Jeep next to her. She slapped her hand on the rear deck where she wanted the dog to go.

"Get in the back, boy. Go on. Good boy."

Looking around, fearful of what lay behind the trees at the edge of the parking lot, Kate reached up and closed the rear hatch. On the one hand, she reasoned, if she sat in the Jeep with the doors locked, she felt secure with Koda by her side. And surely no one would think of doing anything to her in a public parking lot even though it was somewhat isolated. Would they? On the other hand, staying inside the Jeep put her in a trapped box. She wasn't sure she wanted to go inside the store. Perhaps the tire-slashing culprit was in there. At least in the Jeep, she could start it up and get away or drive closer to the store even if the tires were flat.

Kate gripped the door handle of the Jeep. *That's it*, she thought to herself. *I'll drive the Jeep over to the front of the store next to the entrance and wait for the police there.* She didn't want to take Koda into the market, and for all she knew the person who slit her tires was in there right now.

Hearing gravel crunching, Kate tensed while looking down at her shaking hand gripping the door handle. Her knuckles were white around the joints. The bones in her frail hands felt as if they would snap should she exert anymore pressure. The gravel noise stopped, but she was afraid to turn. She began a course of self-talk. Putting off the avoidance and telling herself, "*Come on Kate, you can do this*," she turned.

Kate's hand relaxed and a warm flow of relief eased through her body. She recognized her brother sitting in the pickup that pulled up next to her. Not the closest of relationships–twisted; he was a bastard for sure, but at least he was family. Talking with Koda, she glanced at her cell phone on the Jeep's front seat.

"Good boy, Koda. You are going to meet my brother, Dennis. Stay alert, buddy, someone could still be out there."

Koda barked, then started a menacing growl.

Dennis parked his Ford F-150 next to Kate and the Jeep. He jumped out and ran around to Kate's door.

"Long time, sis. I thought it was you in the parking lot when I drove by. I can't believe it has been, what, ten months since we've seen each other?"

The two hugged as if they had never hugged before. Kate felt a distance that was more of a gap than ten months would create. There was a childhood history with Dennis. One successfully buried, with no care to dredge it back up. She knew, though, if she didn't talk about it, dormancy would rue the day.

"At least you jerk. Not my fault we haven't seen each other. Every time I visit mom and dad, you mysteriously disappear."

Dennis opened the passenger door to his pickup.

"Jump in, sis. I'll get the dog. What's its name?"

"Koda. Matt and I just adopted him. He's a sweetheart. I'm not sure why he's barking and growling so much. He must know I'm upset."

Kate stood outside the Jeep and started to talk to Koda, trying to get him to settle down. Dennis responded quickly.

"Go ahead and get in the pickup, Kate. He's probably spooked because of the tires being slashed. Dogs are smart. He knows something is up."

Smiling, and relieved her brother had arrived, Kate agreed. She thought something was off with him, but it had been so long she'd seen him, she pushed the feeling aside and climbed into the pickup.

Dennis shoved the door shut and ran around to the driver's side. He climbed in and slammed his door beside him.

Kate, confused, addressed her brother. "Hey, Dennis, what's up? What about Koda?"

She held a slight pause, skirting the edge of fear before adding, "and how did you know the tires were slashed?"

"Just a second, sis."

Dennis looked around, sure no one was watching them. There was a pretentious couple laughing outside their Mercedes. They appeared to be having fun washing their windows while the attendant gassed up their car. The spectacle made Dennis want to smash something. He pointed to the couple, a good hundred feet away, and addressed Kate.

"Look at them. They are pathetic. No one can be that happy."

"What are you talking about, Dennis? You're making me nervous."

Reflexively, Kate reached for the door handle to jump out and get Koda. Her dog was going berserk in the back seat of her crippled Jeep. Kate watched as he jumped from the back of the Jeep to the driver's seat. He was scratching and clawing at the door window in an effort that Kate could only assume was to get out and help her.

She heard a click and recognized the sound of a car door locking. Her immediate reaction was to look at the door button. It was in the down position. She started to reach for it and manually pull it up, but instead she pulled at the door handle. Feeling no response from the latch, she turned to look at her brother. She didn't recognize him. Oh, she knew it was Dennis, but the hollow darkness in his hazel eyes terrified her. She saw a similar look once before, years ago, from her father. A look that flooded her mind with memories of guilt, anger, and fear.

Smelling a soft lovely hint of lemongrass, Kate pressed the door button in a frantic effort to escape her brother's scented trap. She screamed, hoping someone, anyone, would hear. A tear pushed its way from the corner of one eye as her stomach sank, the recesses of her brain elicited the smell of burning flesh, flooding her mind with painful memories.

Kate watched, in a stationary, helpless, horror as Dennis's hand raised up and smashed across her temple. Her head crashed against the door window. Darkness followed.

Kid Gloves

Pressing her cell phone against her ear, a familiar and indifferent voice on the other end picked up after a single ring.

"It's Graley. Is the Chief available?"

"One moment, please. I'll put you through," the chief's secretary responded.

Graley started to say thank you but changed her mind.

"Graley, what update do you have?"

"It isn't good, Chief. Mrs. Walker wasn't at the scene when the Sheriff arrived. Her dog was in the Jeep, along with her phone and purse. Looks as though she has been snatched."

Graley forgot she wasn't alone in the room. Staring at Matt Walker she wished she hadn't said snatched. She thought about stepping out for privacy but changed her mind. On further reflection, she wanted Walker and his attorney to hear. She needed them on her side, not second-guessing her honesty.

The Chief responded in a firm voice.

"The fact that her purse and phone were in the car with the dog. I could see a reason for leaving the dog behind, but not her wallet and phone as well."

"Right. Good point."

Graley appreciated the comment but didn't have the time to get caught up in the need for a self-esteem boost from the Chief.

"Well, Graley, now what?"

Graley expected the question, but still wasn't prepared to respond. She let silence hang in the air.

"Graley? You there?"

"Sorry, Chief. I'm thinking. Tough call to make right now. As you know, Cole is on the way there. I suppose I will call him and see where he is, then decide what to do. Might make the most sense for me to get up there as well and take Matt Walker with me. You have a problem with that, Chief?"

"Graley, do what you have to do. Trust your instincts and stop sounding so hesitant. You are a good cop. Now figure it out and keep me posted. I need to go."

Her phone beeped, and she looked at the screen as it changed from a conversation to a keypad waiting for her to end the call.

She spun around to a stunned looking Walker and his attorney, quiet and attentive, listening to every word.

Matt Walker spoke at once.

"Well, what did your Chief say?"

"To trust my instincts."

Graley walked closer to the two, focusing her thoughts.

"Did I also hear you say Cole was on his way up there?" Walker asked.

Walker paused as worry reflected in his eyes. If Graley had known him better, she might have thought he was on the precipice of collapsing. It only took a moment, though, before he continued with new found fight in his voice.

"Why in the hell would that little shit be going up there? I thought he was suspended?"

Graley delayed responding on Cole for the moment.

"Look, Mr. Walker..."

Graley paused as she made her way near the door. She stopped next to the table to speak to Walker, who was at the window staring toward the Siskiyous.

"Here's the thing. I think you and I should leave right now and go up there. Cole and the Sheriff's Department can investigate the scene around the Jeep while we are on the way. Once we get there, you can help with your dog and get the tires fixed on the Jeep."

"Son of a bitch!" Matt said furiously.

Graley listened to Walker respond as he spun toward her taking a couple of aggressive steps.

"I can't believe this is happening!"

"Look Matt," the attorney injected the voice of reason. "I can only imagine what you must be feeling. Detective Graley is making sense. I have to think though, you will be way too uptight if you stick around here and wait for news."

Graley watched Walker's face as his attorney talked. She thought he looked angry and perhaps scared. Both of which were understandable. Her detective instincts were overriding her own fear as she watched Walker's behavior, seeing if she could glean anything from it. The attorney continued.

"Go with her and help find Kate."

Graley liked Walker's attorney's response. It was confident and direct, not to mention he backed her up.

Walker walked back to the window and stared out. He didn't say a word. Graley wondered what the hell was going through his mind.

"Mr. Walker..."

Graley addressed him again, this time in a colder, more distant way. Her patience was starting to wane. She knew precious moments were being lost.

"Are you going to come with me or not? Time is a wasting, and I want to get on the road."

Staring through the glass at the snow on Mt. Ashland, Walker tapped eleven times on the window sill. Graley wondered why he tapped, then wondered why she counted. She watched as Walker spun from the window, then headed toward the door.

"Let's go, then, Detective Graley. Jim, thanks for everything. I'll give you an update once I know what is going on."

Graley and attorney Jim Davies stared at each other over Walker's abrupt exit.

Davies spoke first. "Take care of him, Detective. I have never seen him this quiet and upset."

Graley spun around, saying as she walked out, "Not to worry, I have my kid gloves in the car."

An Unexpected Moses

Cole pressed the accelerator as he made his way past the Diamond Lake exit. The 370 Horsepower V8 under the hood of the Charger was awesome. The Dodge handled fabulously, for a muscle car, and had plenty of power. He couldn't help but think of Matt Walker's disdain for his Vette as the police car moved through the corners better than his Chevy, which he hated to admit was getting tired. The police car lights remained on, so everyone got out of the way without issue.

The current rate of speed, he figured, would have him on site in less than an hour. He had asked for an SUV at the station, but there were none available for another hour. An hour he didn't have. If he did need to transport the Walker's dog, the backseat would have to do. He visualized the dog during his arrest of Walker. The damn thing would have liked to take his head off, given the chance.

Cole, swallowed hard and fidgeted in his seat, figuring he could worry about the dog if and when the time came. He looked at his phone on the dash and saw no bars for signal reception, so he picked up the mic for the two-way and called the dispatcher.

"Detective Cole here, over."

A slight crackle of noise came from the radio before a voice responded.

"Go ahead, Detective Cole."

"Patch me through to Detective Graley, please. My cell phone has no reception."

"One moment, please."

A minute later, two more cars hurriedly pulled to the side of the road, and detective Graley came on the phone.

"Hey Cole, where are you?"

"About forty-five minutes from the scene, give or take. Any news, Graley?"

Cole kept his eyes peeled on the road. Now that he was on highway 97, he knew he could press the accelerator down even further. Cole loved the frantic drive as the Dodge hummed along.

"Yes, Cole. You will be arriving to a crime scene that now goes beyond slashed tires. It appears to be an abduction. Kate Walker is missing."

"Are you fucking kidding me, Gray?" Cole instinctively glanced down at the two-way radio as if it would somehow reveal honesty.

"No, Cole, I am not. Kate Walker is gone."

Graley walked out of the building with Matt Walker next to her. She nodded to him in a follow me motion.

"What in the fuck is going on, Graley?"

"Look Cole, all I know at this point is that the Jeep is in the same place. The dog is inside, and Kate Walker's cell phone and purse are apparently inside the Jeep as well. Has the feel of an abduction. I need you to get up there and start asking as many questions as possible."

"You got it, Gray."

Matt Walker shot Graley a pleading look. No words were exchanged. They weren't needed. Graley had a damn good idea what Walker was thinking. She responded to Cole accordingly.

"And Cole, don't you dare act like a know-it-all up there, do you understand? Act like you did with the Chief earlier today, and you will get their full cooperation. You go in there with an attitude, and they are going to be far less likely to help us in any meaningful way."

Matt Walker whispered to Graley as they approached her police car.

"You may want to warn him to stay away from Koda. That dog doesn't like him and probably likes him even less after he arrested me."

Cole heard a voice talking in the background. He thought it sounded like Walker, but couldn't make out what the person was saying, and exactly who it was.

"Oh, and Cole, keep your distance from that dog, Koda. Hopefully they can get a K9 Sheriff on scene to assist."

Cole knew from his partner's response that Graley was with Walker. No one else would have asked Graley to mention the dog. He wondered why they were together, then remembered Graley was questioning him at the attorney's office.

"Understood on all counts, Graley. I will be on my best behavior. I know I dug a hole with you and the Chief, but tell Walker I won't dick with his dog, and that I will find his wife."

Cole struggled with his sincerity. He knew he meant it—well, thought he meant it, but wasn't sure if the effort came across as genuine. He was torn between being himself and trying to be what he knew he needed to be to keep this job. He shrugged his shoulders as if someone, in his presence, watched his every move.

Cole didn't like playing kiss-ass, but he knew he needed to. And was he being a kiss-ass, or just a normal professional? This new ground for him would take work. He had a flash of hitting his girlfriend in the gut. Ex-girlfriend. Why did he feel the need to hit women?

The sound of Graley's voice brought him back to the two-way.

"Good, Cole. I'm on my way up there as well. Just talked to the Chief, and he agrees I should head up there. I'm bringing Matt Walker with me. He can help with the dog and the Jeep, not to mention ideas on finding Mrs. Walker."

Graley pressed the unlock button on the car's key fob and entered, sitting down behind the steering wheel. She glanced over and watched as Matt Walker got in the passenger's side and buckled up.

"Got it, Graley. I will get as much information as I can. I'll keep you posted on the way."

Cole put the mic back in its cradle ending the call by not talking anymore. Looking forward, the towering pines were majestic lining the highway almost leading the police car toward its destination by itself.

Cole applied more pressure to the accelerator as the car moved past the one-hundred mph mark. He couldn't believe Kate Walker was missing. He wondered who in the hell could be doing this. Matt Walker hadn't taken Kate, so who? Was Walker working with someone? Was Kate Walker a target completely independent of Matt Walker's first two wives? Questions flooded Cole's mind. Cars, one by one, peeled off the side of the road and let him through as if he were Moses himself.

Old-Fashioned Childhood Fun

Kate woke with a throbbing headache. She grabbed toward the source of the pain but didn't reach the target. Looking down seeing that her hands were bound behind her, her mind registered discomfort and fear. She felt the tape sticking to her skin, tearing the flesh, she thought. Both wrists were bound tight. She could feel her pulse trying to move from her arms to her hands, and back again under the gray tape.

Unclear about what was going on under the pressure of the throbbing in her head, she strained to focus her eyes. Making a futile effort to free her feet and hands, familiar smells creeped into her psyche. Confused, in trouble, and anxious, Kate slumped on her four-legged prison.

Focusing to regain control of her breathing, she took slow and methodical breaths. Her nose burned with familiar smells of pipe tobacco and hints of what she thought were honeysuckle and lavender. Memories, both pleasant and vile, rushed through her brain with the realization that she was in her parents' cabin. A family-built structure nestled in the towering Douglas Fir and Ponderosa Pines which guarded the shores at the Lake of the Woods.

Fighting back tears, Kate started to remember what put her in the old cabin her father loved more than anything. She shook her head as if the very action would wipe the events clean like the shaking of an etch-a-sketch. She did not want to believe her brother had smashed her face in his pickup. She tried to think of an Oregon spring run-off, its water flowing swiftly from the melting snow as it bathed and smoothed the ground below. She longed for the cleansing waters of a creek, wiping away today's excruciating events, cleaning her.

Instead of a purging, her mind raced to the last thing she saw. The jagged memory, only a flash, after her brother's hand violently forced her head against the pickup window, was that of a snarling Koda. Tears started to stream, first in fear, then in anger, as she longed for Koda and Matt. She willed her eyes to dry as she looked around the cabin wondering what she could do. Dennis had to be around, but there was no clear sign of where. Contemplating her escape she figured she could get out of the cabin and make her way around to the lodge where there was sure to be help, but getting out of the chair seemed hopeless.

Staring, she began to remember the cabin's ample size. She was in a large room with a fireplace below. Above, a loft for sleeping, and it covered most of the main floor along with the stone mantle surrounding the fireplace which held a plethora of family photos. A few of the photos normally made her feel welcome. Right now, not so much. Years of pain had been cleansed with her union to Matt. Years of struggle, regret, anger, and humiliation had all but faded from her memory, until now. She had become adept at compartmentalizing, blocking out the pain, pushing it deep inside of her mind. Recesses she didn't think would ever be unlocked until now.

Kate wasn't sure if it was the fear or pain driving her thoughts. Remembering the last time her father had caught her brother beating her and burning her with his wood burning tool flashed like a bad dream. Dennis's tool of choice, a damn craft tool. A gift her parents had given to him on his twelfth birthday. The day after his birthday, while their parents were out on a lake houseboat with friends, her brother decided to tie her up and proceeded to torture her for an hour or more, burning her feet and behind the knees. Only the sound of inebriated parents relinquished her brother's hold on her ten-year-old mind and body.

Fear of a replay the next time they were alone kept her from saying anything to her mom and dad. Her mother's questions about her walking funny for days following the burning brought tears to her eyes. Lying, she told her mom it was from walking barefoot around the lake. Why couldn't her mom figure out her pain and secret? Why didn't she hold her and ask her what was wrong? Only now did she feel there was the courage within her to speak up. If only her parents were here.

The door creaked open, then slammed. Startled, the chair propelled upwards, if only a fraction as Kate's body reflexively lurched. Her heart sank at the thought of her brother.

"So, what has little Kate been up to lately?"

Kate kept her mouth closed as her brother walked past with a brown paper bag. He set it down on the counter and started to put something from the bag in the refrigerator. Kate's stomach gagged toward vomit.

The energy that came into the cabin with her brother carried a darkness with it. She couldn't help but reflect on an awful childhood until Dennis was hauled off to a detention home for teens. She didn't understand why her mom cried so much when it happened. How could she not see the things that Dennis did and what he had become? She was only fourteen, and she knew what he was. Several times she tried to tell her dad. He would shrug her off and tell her to mind her own business.

"One shouldn't cast stones," he would say.

Kate had a canned response built over many hours of teen angst, "Well, one shouldn't burn sisters with a wood burning tool either," but she never used it. Fear of worse reprisals from her big brother always won out, and she kept her mouth shut.

"So, I see you and your new husband have been busy."

Dennis slammed the refrigerator door and turned to face Kate. Wondering if the tape would break if she could twist it a certain way, she wrestled with her wrists. The tape held fast. Matt explained to her once how to raise taped hands high above the head, then bring them crashing down toward the hips causing the tape to break. She didn't believe him until he taped her up and she tried it successfully. It didn't matter now though; her hands were bound behind her. She would not be lifting them above her head.

Kate wondered if her hands were wrapped in a rope as well but didn't think so as her mind only registered sticky tape. Wanting to question her brother she gagged as the rag in her mouth prevented her from talking. Kate focused on breathing through her nose. The damn rag tasted of staleness like it had been sitting in a musty cupboard for years without ever moving, somehow absorbing every particle of the mold and stale air in the room.

Kate watched, then tensed, as Dennis walked over to a shelf, moved a couple of boxes and brought down a thin narrow one.

Returning, he stopped in front of her and took a faded, creased, lid off the box revealing what she already knew was inside. Her brother pulled out his childhood weapon, whistled while plugging it in, and set it on the table to heat up.

The captor put a hand on her shoulder and squeezed.

"Now, let's have a bit of old-fashioned childhood fun Kate!"

One of Those, Huh?

Detective Cole slowed the police car easing his way into the parking lot. Next to Kate Walker's Jeep, Cole noticed a large flatbed tow-truck. The police were prepping the Jeep for its removal but waited as Cole had asked so he could take photos and give it a look-see. Crime scene images could come in handy.

Looking at the camera in the seat next to him, he wondered if the flash batteries would last long enough for more than a few shots. He hated taking pictures, and his photos were a mixture of crap and more crap. He was supposed to take a camera instruction briefing and photo scene class, but he intentionally never made the time.

Picking the Nikon DSLR up, he looked out the car window scanning the crime scene, then promptly dropped the black camera back down. Getting out of the car, Cole walked the fifty or so feet over to the Jeep, extended his hand, and introduced himself to the Sheriff.

"Hi, Sheriff. Detective Cole, Medford P.D."

"Nice to meet you, Detective. I'm Sheriff Bill Davis. This here is Deputy Constance. Becky Constance. She's our K9 handler."

Cole extended his hand to the Deputy who smiled and shook back with extreme enthusiasm, to Cole's liking.

"She took the dog out of the Jeep and has him in a container right now in the back of the SUV over there."

The Sheriff pointed toward the tow-truck.

"Hope you don't mind. We know you wanted to see the scene as it was, but the dog was under a lot of stress. Deputy Constance was afraid he would harm himself, so we took the liberty of getting him out of there. Wasn't easy. That dang mutt has fight in him. He is looking to tear someone's face off."

Cole grimaced thinking of the dog's snarling appearance when he arrested Matt Walker.

"No, I understand, and thanks. That dog and I don't get along so well. We had a run in before, so I am glad as hell you have him locked up."

The Sheriff smiled as Cole walked over to the Jeep.

"I don't suppose anyone got photos, Sheriff?"

"I did." K9 handler Constance replied to Cole before the Sheriff could answer.

"A full crime scene series of stills. I am quite good at it."

Cole smiled, relieved he wouldn't have to take photos. He had never heard the term "stills" before, but realized she meant photos. At least he thought she did. He focused on the scene, not wanting to ask about the unknown term and potentially facing ridicule.

"Would you mind if I get a copy of all of them?" Cole asked.

The Deputy looked to the Sheriff who nodded.

"No problem at all. I'll go to my car, use the laptop, and put them on a flash drive for you." She smiled and walked away. Cole became aware of her femininity for the first time. She looked to be attractive. The uniforms did a good job of hiding most women's physical attributes for the most part, so it could be hard to tell how they looked. This one was different somehow. The way she moved or carried herself seemed odd. Perhaps the eyes? Cole couldn't quite put his finger on why, nor did he have the time right now. He needed to stay on point, lest he jeopardize his career further.

"So, Sheriff," Cole walked around the car projecting and lowering his voice as the Sheriff stayed put. "If I understand everything correctly, the victim, also the owner of this Jeep, put in a call to your department. She was told to stay in the vehicle or go into the store, correct?"

"That would be correct, Detective Cole."

Cole noticed the Sheriff standing with his hands behind his back carrying the look of an irritated or pissed-off cop. Probably missing Wheel of Fortune and Jeopardy and didn't want to be out here. Cole thought of his Chief and partner.

"*What would Graley do*," he mouthed to himself before speaking out loud.

"We appreciate your help and cooperation in this, Sheriff. We don't want to step on any toes here at all. We're certainly not looking to take over this event in any way shape or form, but since it is tied to our murder in Medford, we need complete access."

Cole watched as the Sheriff dropped his arms to his side, appearing to relax. The man's shoulders slumped, and his body lost an inch in height. The once perfect, erect, upright stance wavered ever so slightly. Encouraged by the Sheriff's change in body language, Cole continued.

"The woman who was driving this Jeep..."

Cole hesitated, trying to figure out how best to word the situation. Coming up with nothing specific, Cole, like a tractor-drawn disc harrowing through dark, rich, Rogue Valley soil, plowed forward.

"Well, her husband's first two wives have been killed. One, for a fact, we know deliberately. The other, we think an attempt was made but went bad. The perp attacked but fled for an unknown reason before his actions unwittingly finished her off."

Cole kicked the soil around the Jeep, his mind flooded with everything transpiring since the case started. Uncertain of what to do, he wished Graley were here to take the lead. Cole saw the Sheriff and Deputy hanging in attentive balance waiting for his next words. He continued with his false bravado trying desperately to sound not only authoritative, but knowledgeable.

"Anyhow, the perp fled, but as a direct result of the trauma the woman went through, she died within hours of a brain aneurism. So, we're treating it as a potential homicide. As you can imagine."

Fearing the last comment, a bit repetitive, he lowered his head peering at the Jeep as if he were in deep detective mode. Now on the opposite side of the Jeep, Cole reached down and slipped on a pair of rubber gloves he pulled from his jacket pocket. He opened the passenger side door and peered in. The Sheriff came over. Using his shirtsleeve to open the driver's side door himself, he glared at Cole.

"I appreciate you being forthright. We couldn't get much out of your office. We were told the two detectives handling the case were unavailable. My office got a call from your Chief, who asked us for help, so here we are waiting on you. Where is your partner, by the way?"

Cole snooped around in the car and didn't see anything other than Kate's handbag on the passenger's seat, along with a cell phone. He picked the cell phone up pressing the power button and the screen came to life.

"She's on the way here as we speak. About an hour or so out, I'm guessing. She has the husband of the victim with her."

Cole looked up watching the Sheriff's reaction, which he figured would be one of bewilderment and surprise. The Sheriff didn't disappoint.

"The husband?"

"Yes. Seems strange, I know. He was our lead suspect, but it isn't him. The guy is clearly a victim of sorts in all this."

Cole laughed at Kate's Blackberry. He didn't think they still made them. Surprised Kate didn't have a password, fingerprint scan, or swipe pattern, the screen granted full access. *Doesn't everyone these days use a password,* he thought to himself before responding to the Sheriff's question.

"Long story, but he was being questioned by my partner at his attorneys when we found out about this. She felt it was best to bring him. If nothing else, to help with the dog."

Cole couldn't find anything in the phone but a bunch of missed calls, all from the same number and a dozen or so text messages. Matt Walker's photo was next to the name and number. Cole pressed dial. He figured he could tell Walker, and subsequently Graley, about his being on site and that he held Kate Walker's phone. As quick as he pressed send, he pressed end, thinking Mr. Walker would think it was Kate calling. This was too cruel even for him. He hung his head a bit knowing the mess he created with Walker was no one's fault but his own.

"What's wrong, Detective Cole?" the Sheriff asked.

Cole brought his attention back around to the scene, letting go of childhood baggage for the moment.

"Oh, nothing. Nothing at all. Just thinking about the events of the last day or so. Been a bit crazy for us in Medford. Not like we aren't used to shit happening, but these murders are out of the norm. First case of this magnitude I've worked on. The husband is a respected businessman in the community and connected to the mayor in a roundabout way. So, I have to make sure I'm squeaky clean."

Cole did a quick look through the purse. It looked normal as far as he could tell. Hair brush, lip gloss, notepad, hair twist, or whatever the hell they are called, and other odds and ends. As far as he was concerned, a woman's handbag was a stressful thing to start poking around in. They were as mysterious as Pumapunku.

Not sure if he should bag the purse or leave it on the seat as he found it, Cole turned to the Sheriff.

"Hey, Sheriff, you think we should leave this purse here, or bag it?"

The Sheriff, looking down at the ground, perked up, to Cole's relief, and answered right away.

"We could certainly bag it. If it were me, I would leave it on the seat as you found it. Let your partner look. See what he thinks. I feel it is better for a couple sets of eyes to dig into an investigation."

Cole, relieved at the suggestion, agreed. He didn't want to, or couldn't afford to, mess up again so soon. Perhaps even with the new dickhead Chief who had it out for him.

"It's a she, and thanks. I agree."

Cole waited for the Sheriff's response. He thought the old guy look bewildered or confused.

"A she? What the hell you talkin' about, boy?"

"My partner."

"Your partner what?"

Cole smiled, relishing in the confusion. The backwoods Sheriff had no idea what he was talking about.

"My partner is a she." Cole replied.

"Oh hell, why didn't you say that to begin with?"

Out of reflex, Cole started to regurgitate a smart-ass response, frustrated by the Sheriff's tone, but once again he channeled Graley.

"Sorry, Sheriff. I thought I mentioned it already, or perhaps I didn't think it needed to be stated."

Cole, confused thinking he had already told the sheriff Graley was a woman, backed up. The Sheriff's Deputy arrived with the flash drive and handed it to Cole while the Sheriff replied, slamming the driver's side door of the Jeep.

"Oh, one of those, huh?"

Cole smiled, for the first time he could remember, feeling protective of Graley and wanting to let the Sheriff know his opinion. He again managed to hold his tongue, wondering if this was what it was like for successful people. A constant state of biting the lip, holding the tongue, putting a cap on what was really rolling through their minds. He didn't like it, but figured he could get used to it if it meant keeping his job.

The Deputy, a good foot shorter than Cole and with amazing dark eyes, talked in a confident, take-charge voice that impressed Cole.

"You can keep it."

Cole, still thinking about the "one of those" remark, stuttered a second looking for a response.

"Keep it?"

"Yes, the flash drive. We have fifty or so of them at the station. They're cheap. Anyhow, I have all the images of the crime scene on there. If you need prints, let me know. I can help with that as well."

Cole, losing track of the new forced demeanor he worked so damn hard to project, replied, "Don't suppose there are any photos of you on here as well, are there?"

The Deputy blushed and looked down at the ground.

Cole thought to himself, *shit, here I go again.* He looked over to see if the Sheriff heard his comment, sighing with relief upon seeing the salty old badge-man walking away from the Jeep toward the tow-truck. He either hadn't heard Cole or didn't give a shit.

"I'm sorry, Deputy, I shouldn't have said that."

"Why, I thought it was funny." The Deputy smiled, looked around to see if the Sheriff was watching, and then proceeded to blush again. Cole, sure she blushed, tightened his fist. His stomach retched at the thought of slugging her. He lowered his chin in disappointment over his lack of control around a woman he found appealing. He always wanted, hell dreamt of and desired, to make them small. Cole wanted help, but who? He closed the passenger door of the Jeep and wondered whether this little woman could take a punch.

Alone

Wishing he were driving, Matt did think Graley capable behind the wheel. She was going quite fast, but he thought he could do better. He'd take the corners differently. Enter them tighter, closer, and come out smoother. A confident Matt figured he'd get them to Kate's Jeep quicker and speed could mean life and death right now. He did not want to lose Kate.

The deaths of Sharon and Betheny were starting to sink in. Until now, with Kate's abduction, the deaths of his formers didn't seem real. Even seeing Sharon floating face down in the lake wasn't enough to bring the reality into focus. *More shit for counseling*, he thought. Just when he figured he was getting ready to end the weekly sessions with Doctor Johnson.

"How much longer do you think until we get there, Detective Graley?"

Matt knew the answer already, but asked out of boredom, nervousness, or a passive attempt at coaxing her to speed up. He watched Detective Graley look at the clock on the dash, then glance between the steering wheel. Matt presumed she eyed her speed and distance traveled before she responded.

"Within forty-five minutes."

Looking out the window at the passing thick Oregon Evergreens, Matt thought about Highway 97 etching its way through the central part of the state. The views from the asphalt provided a glimpse of Oregon's most beautiful mountainous scenery. The Cascade mountain range, which was Oregon's most impressive running from Northern California to British Columbia, didn't have the prestige of the Rockies, but too many it carried its own magnificent and majestic beauty.

During a sleepless night of Google boredom, Matt had learned another name for the mountains–the Pacific Ocean's Ring of Fire range.

It was sprinkled with majestic mountain peaks. Matt knew it wasn't uncommon for many of the mountains to have over five-hundred inches of snowfall annually. He loved this part of the state and was always amazed how when one mountain would fade from view, a new one would spring up and give another reason to keep looking forward.

The mountains rose from valley floors etched in picturesque styles as if they longed to mimic a Tolkien peak. His favorite, Mt. McLoughlin, lay to the south now, but he could still see Mt. Bachelor, despite the sun's retreat. The snow at the peak appeared to glow.

Matt looked around searching for the moon. From the shimmering of the treetops and the light bouncing off the mountain, he figured it had to be full. His ears picked up familiar asphalt road noise as he continued thinking about Kate.

Something else sounded in his ears but he couldn't make out what it was. Wanting to tap his hand against the door handle eleven times, he refused.

"Matt. Matt."

Matt felt a slap against his left shoulder.

"Walker! Jesus, you with me here?"

Matt turned his head toward Detective Graley, realizing she was part of the noise he had tuned out.

"Sorry, Detective. Thinking about Kate. What if she's dead?"

Watching Graley's face as closely as he could, Matt hoped to pick up truth from the side view he had sitting next to her.

"Well, I won't sugarcoat it, Walker. You and I both know it is possible. We will just have to deal with it one step at a time. The best thing both of us can do right now is presume she is alive. Okay?"

Matt lifted his chin. He struggled to keep his fear pressed down.

"What can you tell me about Kate's family?" Graley knew little about Kate, and even less about her family. They were Cole's part of this fiasco.

"Not much really, other than they weren't great parents. Who is these days, though, right? Both are retired and living in Redmond. I have been at their home only two or three times. Kate doesn't get on with them particularly well. Not sure why? She doesn't like to talk about it."

"Why is that?"

"Don't know, really. She has told me she doesn't hate them, but she'd rather surround herself with more supportive people."

"What the hell does that mean?" Graley replied inquisitively.

"I don't know. I am not the best when it comes to talking about personal shit. It isn't that I don't care, but I suppose..."

Matt lost himself for a moment, searching for the right words, as if they hung waiting to be plucked from a tree for this conversation.

"Suppose what, Walker?"

"Suppose I get more worried and won't have answers, or be able to help her, so I avoid the personal shit altogether."

Matt watched Graley roll her eyes. He wondered what her personal life was like and if she had demons and struggles, like everyone else.

"I hear you, Walker. I do. I have issues with my father right now, and I work as often and as long as I possibly can, as if that will somehow make everything better."

Matt stared back out his window as the dense woods zoomed by.

"Remember Walker, most women want a partner to listen, not fix."

Silence, let Graley's last statement go unanswered for a moment or two before she continued.

"She has a brother, right?"

"Yes. I don't know much about him. Last we talked about him, I believe Kate said he was in Portland somewhere. Not sure what he does," Walker lied.

"Shit, Matt, you are as bad as me and my father. No wonder you are on your third wife. You should try to ask a few more questions and perhaps your marriages would last a bit longer."

"Kiss my ass, Graley. None of your business. I was crazy about both my formers and they were both very loving wives in their own way. Just wasn't meant to be. So again, kiss my ass."

"Sorry, Matt. I deserved that."

Silence hung for a moment before Graley asked Matt another question.

"How long have you had OCD? I can't help but notice your tapping sometimes. Looks to be eleven, near as I can figure."

Matt hung his head a bit, embarrassed, and exhausted. He didn't feel like answering and was saved by the squawking of Graley's mic.

"Graley, come in. This is Cole, over."

Matt watched Graley grip the steering wheel, firm with her left hand, then grab for the mic off the dash with her right.

"Go ahead, Cole."

"Hey, Gray, I'm here with the Jeep. They are going to put it up on the tow truck and take it to the police station yard."

"Did you get photos, Cole? Find anything out of the ordinary?"

"They have a photo specialist on site, one of their deputies, who gave me a flash drive of all the photos she shot. So, we are good on that front. You know how lousy I am with a camera, so hers are going to be much better. I'm sure of it. No, nothing out of the ordinary. Mrs. Walker's phone and handbag were on the passenger's seat. Nothing strange I could see. A lot of calls to her husband, and a few other numbers I have no idea who they belong to."

Matt straightened hearing his name come out of Cole's voice. He still wanted to smack the little shit around, but he was picking up a different attitude right now. The detective's voice was different, mellow. He seemed less condescending and more empathetic if that were possible.

"The dog has been put in a cage and they're taking it down to the police station as well. They have a kennel down there. I figure that's best until you get Walker up here."

"I think you're right, Cole. Good call. Listen, we should be there in about thirty minutes. You going to hang out or get over to the parents? You and I haven't even had a chance to talk about Kate's family at all."

Matt wondered if Cole had found out about Kate's brother. It was only a matter of time. Basic internet searching and looking at police records would provide many answers.

"Shit, Graley, no. Nothing. I haven't really had the chance. So much has happened so fast, I didn't get to it. I was in the process of backgrounds on Mr. Walker's first two wives. I know quite a bit about them, but nothing at all about Kate's family yet. Sorry, Graley."

"Not to worry, Cole. You can only do so much at a time."

Matt watched as Graley glanced over at him. Her eyes were either hoping he wouldn't get mad, or that she knew he was holding back on her. Matt thought about coming clean on Kate's fucked up brother, but no, he decided he wanted the information for himself. Even though he couldn't justify withholding.

"Hey, Cole, does the gas station have any video?"

Walker heard Cole yelling over the mic.

"Hey, Sheriff, the station have any video?"

"Apparently, they do, Gray. I'm going to go inside and start looking at it. See you when you get here."

"We should be there soon, Cole."

Matt thought about justice and what it meant as he plotted getting away from the detectives to head south on his own. With a sudden surge of clarity, as the trees continued their blurry existence floating by outside the water-passenger's window, Walker had a damn good idea of where Kate either was or was en route to. He struggled internally on whether he should tell Graley. He looked down at his foot bouncing up and down, eleven times, against the floorboard carpet as he decided to keep his mouth shut. He wanted to find Kate, alone.

Two Down, One to Go

Outside the cabin, an owl screeched deep in the woods signaling that the sun had left for a time. Kate hoped she would feel the glowing warmth on her skin again. She longed for it almost as much as she longed for Matt.

Recognizing the smell of her burning flesh, Kate grabbed at a memory, fighting to hold back stomach convulsions. As a child, she could see the evil inside her brother's eyes. Now, the wickedness no longer resided in just his eyes, it permeated his entire being, surrounding him like moss on an Oregon tree.

Sitting in the chair facing him, he was a brother in appearance only. Kate's bound feet lay in Dennis's lap. He removed her shoes and socks as well as her hands from behind the chair. Quickly re-taping them with duct tape, by the wrists, he then placed them in her lap. Kate wasn't sure why yet; it would come to her in a moment, but for now she was grateful. Kate stared at Dennis as the decade's old wood-burning tool fit in his large, powerful hand better now. Fumbling, shaking, childhood fingers were gone.

There was something about the way he wielded the device that made her think that if they'd had a different environment, different parents, could her brother have been an artist? She envisioned a brush in his hand, specking and splattering paint against a canvas, instead of a tool used to burn her.

Kate held back her screams, not wanting to give her brother the satisfaction he craved as she felt a pattern of sorts, a figure eight perhaps, being seared into the bottom of her left foot. Her brother always started with the left. She had no idea why, or why she cared. By now, she knew the bottom of her feet was his area of choice because the feet were usually covered. Harder for parents to see his soft fleshy canvas.

Wondering what species of owl was floating around outside the cabin now, Kate wished it could sense trouble and bring a rescuer. Matt preferably. Thinking of his first wife floating in the lake, she wondered where Matt was right now. Was he searching for her? Did he even know she had been taken? Would her brother go so far as to make her next? Closing her eyes, Kate envisioned the swooping of wings, eyes darting back and forth searching the ground. She could almost feel the breeze against the feathers she now felt, floating, swooping, and owning the space between the pines.

The owl whispered to her, *Take charge.*

Kate opened her eyes. She summoned all the emotional courage she could muster, pushing the pain and smells to a part of her mind she would lock away. Now, more than ever, she needed full control of her pain-center allowing her to develop a logical plan of action.

The pain gone, she spoke.

"So, Dennis," biting the inside of her lip helped her sound calm. At least she thought she sounded calm as she felt blood start to ooze, then cauterize in an awful smell. Burning flesh was horrific enough, but when it is your own, Kate thought, the mind is challenged in a different way.

"Why do you always start with the left foot? Don't you ever think of mixing things up a bit?"

Kate felt a tear hanging on the lid of her right eye. She tilted her head back slowly, so the moisture would circle the eye and not fall. She did not want her brother to see tears, not this time.

Kate watched Dennis pause, lift his head, slide her pant leg up slightly exposing skin, then pressed the tool onto her right shin. Kate watched as the tip pierced the flesh. She clenched her teeth and looked directly into Dennis's eyes, challenging him as best she could.

"How was prison Dennis? Did you get raped a lot, or were you the one doing the raping?"

Kate thought she felt a tooth crack as she clenched her teeth between her questions. She probed, pricked, and prodded with Dennis, searching for an advantage. If nothing more than time for someone to arrive. Someone would arrive, wouldn't they?

She stared at her big brother—no an evil Dennis was who sat in front of her. This monster was no longer a brother. Not one she would claim ever again. He needed death to calm him.

"Why are you so scared of me, Dennis?"

Kate watched as Dennis's hand gripped the tool harder, his knuckles turning white under the strain. His eyes flickered back ever so slightly showing a glimmer of white.

"Do you remember when mom and dad used to talk about sending you to a psychiatric ward when you were eleven? Mom would always say how sick you were, and she didn't think you could be helped. Dad would make excuses and say that God made you the way he did for a reason and that prayer would be enough. As if you would be cleansed and delivered for a certain level of good."

Kate's anger grew at the thought of her parents not doing something with this walking horror story. She wondered how many animals he had tortured and killed over his lifetime. Was it just animals, or had the sick freak moved up the food chain? Did he kill Matt's wives? She wanted to know, feeling it would give her a better chance of getting through this ordeal.

"I think you're a child, Dennis, and don't have the intellectual ability to function in a normal society. I think you fear me because when I set my mind to a goal, I would go out and do it regardless of what path Dad wanted me to take."

The whites of her captor's eyes noticeable again, Kate watched as Dennis lost control. If but for a fraction of a second. The wood burning tool slid across the duct tape that bound her ankles. It wasn't long, but Kate thought the motion long enough to sear the edge. Watching her captor's eyes for recognition of the burnt defect in the tape, she didn't see them change. If he stayed on her feet and shin for a while, she could outlast him.

Her adrenaline was sky-high; the pain, though not subsiding, had tempered. Kate's mind reached a sufficient level of pain-blockage. *It is what it is*, she thought. A saying she hated. For once, though, it seemed proper.

"What the hell would you know about normal, you whore."

Kate smiled, knowing she had landed her first solid punch.

"Whore? Really? Is that the best you got, big broth... Dennis?"

Kate's body shook at the thought that she was family with this monster.

"Well, if the shoe fits, right? Wait, after I am done with you, your shoes won't fit for a while, will they? And who defines normal, you piece of trash?"

It was Dennis who smiled now, and Kate knowing the game was now on, couldn't help but be disturbed at her anticipation of a showdown. Letting the feeling slide for now, she wondered how could she get him away long enough to try tearing the tape from her ankles? Any attempt with him holding her feet would be obvious and the advantage lost.

"So, sleeping with my high school boyfriend, and then not again until I married Matt, makes me a whore? Is that what defines whore in your little mind?"

Dennis went back to burning. Kate looked at the tape. She was sure there was a slight tear. There had to be.

"I need water. Please?"

Dennis didn't look up but responded.

"Nice try."

"Come on. Please. I won't pass out as quick, and you know I'm right."

Kate knew she was close to passing out. The familiar feeling, not experienced for more than two decades, came back to her in an instant. Adrenaline and stubbornness kept her upright, for now. If she were going to try to get her feet and hands free, it would have to be soon. Once he moved on to her right foot, she wasn't sure of her ability to stay conscious. As a little girl, she would have passed out long ago. She would have woken up when Dennis would start burning behind her ears. That was not going to happen this time.

Kate screamed as loud as she could, "Get me a glass of fucking water Dennis, now!"

Dennis, startled, eyes cowering a bit, set down the hobby-tool torture device on the tabletop and stood. Kate felt guilt creep into her conscious, and disappointment, wondering what would have happened if, as a little girl, she had screamed.

Watching Dennis stand, a tear fell from the corner of her eye. He reached into his back pocket and pulled out a phone. Pacing, he dialed. Putting the phone up to his ear, Kate couldn't imagine who he would be calling. She figured it out soon enough.

"Ah, I had a strange feeling you might pick up. I'm glad you did."

Kate listened with curiosity, which turned to deep fear, as Dennis turned around and walked toward the cupboard.

"Two down and one to go, you woman stealing piece of shit!"

Piece of Shit

Matt's impatience reached its crescendo as Graley eased the police car next to the tow truck and Kate's red Jeep. The car had not come to a complete stop yet, and Matt was unbuckling the seat belt as if he were on an airline. His pushed the door open and jumped out, heading straight for the Jeep. He had no idea what he would find, but a part of him felt, hoped, Kate would be in there waiting for him with tears in her eyes and shoulder-slouching relief seeing that he had arrived.

There was no Koda, and more importantly no Kate. He reached for the Jeep's door.

"Hey there!" a stern voice that Matt didn't recognize called out. "Don't touch that handle and get away from the vehicle. Now!"

Matt spun and saw a uniformed police officer walking toward him. Within seconds, Detective Graley was at his side.

"Matt, this is evidence. We can't have you touching it, okay?"

Matt appreciated Graley's empathetic attitude and demeanor. He was feeling aggressive and willing to ruffle a few feathers. He pulled away from the door and took a step further away, alleviating any immediate temptation to get inside Kate's vehicle.

"Hi, Sheriff, Detective Graley, Medford P.D., and this is Matt Walker, the husband of the missing driver. Forgive us; we are both a bit anxious to find his wife, Mrs. Walker."

Matt watched as Detective Graley, exuding confidence and a smooth grace, took control of the scene. The Sheriff she was talking to was older and much bigger, but Graley made it perfectly clear that this was her show and she wasn't going to be challenged. Matt, impressed, wondered if Graley ever thought about entering the business world. He could use someone with her attitude and people skills.

"Hi, Detective. Sheriff Miller. Taylor Miller. We'd like to get this thing up on the tow truck now that you are here. Everyone and their mother, including your partner has gone over this damn thing with everything *but* a fine-tooth comb. I have decided to have it taken to the State Police's lab in Bend, if you are good with that. The boys over there can give a look-see in the morning and see what's what."

Matt watched the Sheriff cross his arms, leaning back with a bit of disgust on his face. He didn't appear to like being challenged by a woman. Matt smiled, watching Graley as she bobbed and weaved, ducked, danced and sparred with the Sheriff. She owned the ring, and Matt loved it.

"Well, Sheriff Miller. So very nice to meet you. The Medford P.D. is very appreciative of you and your office's support in this and we know that we owe you one. I'm going to spend a few minutes and give the Jeep a glance myself; I have gloves, not to worry."

Matt watched as Graley reached into her coat pocket and pulled a pair of latex gloves out, snapped them as he expected, and slowly slid them first on her left, then right hand. She turned and walked away from the Sheriff, toward Kate's Jeep in a controlled and orderly fashion leaving no doubt in anyone's mind who owned the space. She continued talking as she approached the vehicle.

"I imagine the tow truck driver knows where to go, correct?"

"Yes, Detective, Charlie has been there a few times."

"Good, then if you want to leave, by all means go ahead. I'll let Charlie know as soon as I am done, and he can get this over to the State Police lab and let those "boys" give it a look-see."

Matt chuckled as Graley reiterated the Sheriff's own words and teased him with a bit of condescending banter, stressing the "boys" part which clearly had pissed her off.

Graley opened the driver's side door and climbed in, sitting behind the wheel. Matt watched, wanting to ask her questions but giving her the space she needed, and demanded. He noticed the Sheriff walk over to the tow truck driver, made gestures, and then walked over to a female Deputy. He appeared to be giving her instructions as well, pointing to Graley and the Jeep. The Sheriff then climbed into his own car and sped away in an aggressive bit of quiet pettiness. Walker thought of Detective Cole.

"Sometimes, Matt," Graley caught him off guard by talking to him while he focused on the tow truck and the Sheriff's Deputy, "as a detective, one has to make it perfectly clear who the scene belongs to. There is nothing more useless and debilitating than joint jurisdiction and arguing over the same scene. Had the Sheriff wanted to play tough with me, it's his county and technically his scene, but it won't do us any good with them leading. I know what is going on, I don't want to fill him in right now and wait for him to make decisions. So, I took the bull by the horns, so to speak."

"I was amused and impressed, Graley. If you ever want to come to work for me down at the marketing firm, I could use someone like you."

Matt watched Graley's face, bathed by the dim light of the overhead lamps in the Jeep's cabin. Her eyes fluttered, and Matt figured she contemplated the idea of being something other than a detective if only for a moment.

"Why are you sitting inside there? See anything?" Matt asked.

"Trying to decide what Kate saw as she stopped here. What could she see, what couldn't she see? That sort of thing."

Matt watched as Graley looked in the rear view, turned and looked in the back seat, and moved the purse in the driver's seat.

"You are pretty good at what you do, Graley. Why are you in Medford and not up in Portland or any other large city putting your talent to real use?"

Matt waited for a response. He didn't get one, so he let the question hang unanswered. Graley looked intense and the last thing he needed to do was distract her. Kate's life hung in the balance.

Walking around the Jeep, Matt stared inside through the passenger door, then took a step back and wandered back to the front. Other than four very expensive destroyed tires, the Jeep looked normal. The tires were going to set him back $500 for the insurance deductible. Thinking of insurance costs at the moment made him feel a little guilty. Matt shook his head and flushed the thoughts, getting back to what was important. He contemplated whether the person who took Kate was the same person that killed Betheny and Sharon.

Matt watched Graley get out of the Jeep, closing the door behind her. She held Kate's purse in her hand as she walked over to him at the front of the Jeep. Kate liked to call her Jeep the "Red Sled." It was the first new car she had ever owned. Matt bought it for her their first Christmas together as a married couple. She cried tears of joy, Matt liked to point out to people. He had to make this clear while telling the story if for nothing else but to assuage his doubts.

The cold air floating off the Cascade mountain range, dancing its way around and through the evergreens, hung around Matt's ears and cheeks. The gentle sting warned of a cold night. As Graley approached, Matt wondered if Kate was warm.

"Matt, take Kate's purse and hang onto it."

Matt extended his hand. He held the purse, gently, as if it were an extension of Kate and needed to be cherished.

"And here, I want you to have the phone. Not as if anyone will call since whoever took Kate doesn't need to get in touch with her."

Graley handed Kate's phone to Matt.

"Okay," Matt said, nodding at the logic.

"One thing, though, Matt. Go through the phone and see if you see anything odd with text messages or a voice mail. You can get into voice mail, right?"

Matt tilted his head sideways in thought.

"Hell, I don't know. We never look at each other's phones. Never had a need to."

Looking at the Blackberry, Kate loved the tactile keyboard, Matt wondered about a password.

"Well, give it a go and tell me if there is anything I should know. And don't you dare hold out on me, or I will have your ass. And you know I mean it."

Graley stared directly into Matt's eyes and he smiled a nervous smile. He believed her, but he didn't agree with her order.

Matt straightened up, clicked his heels together and saluted.

"Aye captain, and yes I know you mean it."

"I'm going to go inside and talk with Cole. See if he found anything on the video tapes and touch base with him. Once you've looked at the phone, join me inside or wait by the car, okay?"

Matt watched Graley walk away. She stopped at the tow truck driver and had a brief conversation, which Matt assumed was about loading Kate's Jeep up and hauling it away. He strolled over to Graley's car and set the purse down on the hood. Leaning against the hood he put the weight of his butt and lower back against it. He touched the power button on the phone. It came alive. Matt looked for the messages app and opened it. There were a bunch of messages from him, a few messages from friends of Kate's and several from Jane, his secretary.

"Shit," Matt said out loud.

He needed to call Jane and let her know what was going on. He went to put Kate's phone in her purse when it started vibrating in his hand. Relieved the ringer wasn't on, which might attract attention, Matt looked around first to see if anyone was in earshot. The tow-truck driver had the Jeep halfway up the ramp, and the Sheriff's Deputy watched the loading process with curiosity or boredom, Matt wasn't sure which.

Looking back at Kate's phone, the incoming number was listed on the screen but there was no name associated with it. Kate didn't have the number registered as one of her friends. Matt, never one to answer an unknown number, felt different under the circumstances at hand. Curiosity, tainted with trepidation, propelled him to answer.

"Hello."

The words Matt heard on the other end of the phone introduced a new level of fear as his stomach retched with despair.

"Two down, one to go, you woman-stealing piece of shit!"

Joy and Sorrow

Waiting patiently, dodging the pain-drenched fear as best she could, the opportunity that Kate needed presented itself. Taking a deep, controlled breath, she twisted her ankles fast and hard. The duct tape stretched, tore, then gave. The tape stuck to the back of her legs keeping her ankles fastened in a haphazard way. She glanced up. Dennis stood at the sink, water running full blast, staring at his cell phone oblivious to her actions.

Reaching down with her bound hands, in a painstaking slow effort, she undid the tape from the back of one ankle as quietly as possible. Grimacing at the pain from the bottom of her foot, she glanced at the fireplace where her goal, her life-saving opportunity, waited.

Making her way, Kate dragged her foot, creating a noise like nails across a chalkboard. The cold and rustic hardwood floors, ripe with tattered imperfections splintered, piercing Kate's burnt foot. Blocking the pain, she made her way to the hearth. The short distance seemed to take longer than a snail moving across a morning dew sidewalk.

Still unnoticed and now at her destination, Kate reached toward the cast iron fire poker her dad had used so many times over the years. She loved watching her father build a fire and loved even more watching him magically rekindle a dying fire simply by using the poker to strategically move the logs.

Glancing over her shoulder toward the sink, Kate watched as Dennis turned his head at the same time. Keeping her mental wits, to her surprise, she stayed focused on the oncoming attack. Kate looked at the tray with the three fire tools on the hearth just before turning. Her mind, laser focused, measured the distance and proximity with near perfection. Keeping her eyes zeroed in on a charging Dennis, her hands found the tool; she hoped it was the poker and not the brush. Fingers finding a handle, she held tight and swung with as much force as she could muster.

Her timing was near-perfect. The side of the iron caught a ducking Dennis on the side of the head. The blow sent him reeling backward. Dazed, falling to one knee, he struggled to gain his balance. Kate, dragging her left foot, took an awkward step forward, cocked her arms again, and landed another blow to the side of his head. The half of a fleur-de-lis point had turned sideways, keeping her blows from killing her brother as his knees buckled, eyes glossed over, and blood trickled down the side of his cheek.

Kate felt acid race up the back of her throat, burning its way toward her mouth. Watching the stunned fear in her Dennis's eyes, she contemplated another blow, looking to see which way the point faced on the blood-stained tool. Hate and rage welled within her. She wanted to finish him off.

Thinking nothing of consequences, only about retribution and years of torment, pain, humiliation, and suffering, Kate twisted the fire-poker a quarter turn. With what she thought would be a lined-up point at the end of her weapon, she cocked her arms yet again.

Before she could swing and bring a final blow to the side of his head, like a storm swept tree in the woods, her brother fell to the floor with a muffled, heavy thud. His face hit last making a sickening cracking sound against the wood floor. A sound she would later tell Matt brought both joy and sorrow. A sound she would never forget.

Straight Highway

Recognizing the voice on the other end of the line, his thoughts racing, Matt listened as the phone went silent. The recognition wasn't instant but like a memory stuck in the recesses of the mind begging for recognition, the familiar intonation came to him. The voice caused anger to well up. Now, more than ever, he needed a vehicle. But how? He wanted a head start. One that provided significant time. Hell, what he really wanted was a clean getaway, without being noticed at all. He wanted hours, not minutes.

Looking up, Matt watched as the tow truck pulled away with Kate's Jeep secured on back. Scenarios raced in his head over how he could get a car and get away unnoticed. No scenario he could muster had an easy, unrecognized ending. Contemplation, of a slow nature–not something Matt was accustomed to–rolled around in his head. Perhaps he should tell Graley, see how she reacted. She seemed to be by the book, though, and Matt didn't want the damn book right now. He felt the only way Kate could survive this ordeal was if sanity and deliberation got thrown aside.

The empty parking lot loomed large in Matt's mind as the last vestige of Kate's existence left on the back of a truck. The Jeep would have been perfect, but he couldn't head south on wheels with punctured tires. The unmarked squad car could work, but that would be theft, and he wasn't sure his attorney could rescue him from grand theft auto. The only people he knew in the vicinity were Kate's parents. How could he get to them without drawing attention to himself? More importantly, how could he get keys to one of their cars, unnoticed?

Staring into the night sky, Matt's acid stomach rose again as he looked at the moonlight bathing a majestic Mt. Bachelor. The snowcapped mountain stood with unwavering steadfastness. The significance of its strength and stoic power sat in Matt's mind as he decided.

Gravel crunching under his feet reminded him of his grade school parking lot. The crunch, crunch, crunch under his canvas Converse as he walked to the bus. As quick as the memory came, it faded as he entered the gas station's market. Matt didn't see Graley.

"Excuse me," he asked the attendant, "Where are the police officers?"

A young man with a dirty baseball cap and scruffy beard needing a few more years to gain a respectable appearance, wore a t-shirt that begged to be read, but Matt refused to give it the attention, and instead waited for a response. He gazed at the dirty cap.

"In back, sir. You with them?"

"Thanks."

Matt made his way down the aisle filled with preservative-laden crap, reaching the back in seconds. He knocked on the door not labeled *Restroom*.

Hearing no response, Matt entered to find the Sheriff's Deputy and Detectives Cole and Graley huddled around a monitor.

"Ah, Mr. Walker, come on in," Detective Graley said, acknowledging his entrance into the room fit for a hoarder. Entering the less than small room, Matt figured it was one over its maximum human capacity as he looked around.

"You okay, Walker? Detective Cole has been going through the video for a while now and thinks he may have found something. Take a look."

Cole nodded. Matt could tell there was something different about the rookie detective. A subtle change only age and experience would notice. A less aggressive and more willing to reason demeanor, perhaps?

"Do you recognize this vehicle, Mr. Walker?" Detective Graley asked, pointing to the paused screen.

Matt bent over, looking at the monitor.

"No, I don't." he said without hesitation.

"That was quick," Detective Graley responded.

"Sorry, but I don't. Why? What's special about it?"

Detective Cole jumped in.

"Don't know...just the way it slows down and appears to be headed toward your wife's Jeep. Please watch again as we let it run."

The Sheriff's Deputy took the cue and let the video roll. Matt watched as the truck appeared to slow, angling its way toward the direction of the Jeep. He didn't see anything significant, but knew the police perhaps saw something he didn't. Or else why ask?

"So?" Matt replied.

Detective Graley jumped in before Cole lost his new professional attitude.

"It's all we have, Walker. I was hoping you might recognize the pickup. We can't make the plate out."

Matt stared at Detective Graley and tapped the side of his leg. He stopped at seven. He wanted to say something derogatory, but opted instead for, "So, you have squat!"

"If we can't make out the plate, we can't run it, Matt. We can send out an all points on the make of the truck, but the color and model is going to be tough around here. There are probably hundreds of them at the very least."

Blurting out expletives, Matt turned and walked out, slamming the door behind him. He left the market, walked over to the Deputy's car, and looking through the back window saw Koda stuffed in a canine crate. The dog was pissed and growling but calmed as soon as he saw Matt and recognized his voice.

Matt opened the car door, then the crate door. He grabbed onto Koda's collar. There was a leash laying by the crate which he promptly put on his new buddy. Koda, half out of the crate, still in the back of the SUV was at the same height as Matt. He wagged his tail licking Matt repeatedly. Matt stroked, then hugged the dog as he put the leash on.

"Come on boy, you and I are going to find Kate."

Koda jumped down and looked up at Matt. It made Matt think the dog understood him and was pleading with him to hurry up.

Turning away from the police cruiser, Matt looked at Graley's car. It was a good seventy feet or so away on the other side of the parking lot. Looking around, he headed straight for Graley's car. He hoped like hell she left the keys inside. Reaching the vehicle, he tensed hearing Graley's familiar voice call out to him.

"Walker?"

He didn't turn. Looking in the car it appeared the keys were in the ignition. He opened the rear door.

"Get in boy."

Koda obeyed, dragging the leash with him. Matt closed the door when he heard Graley's voice again.

"Matt Walker! What are you doing?"

Matt opened the driver's door. He turned facing Graley. She broke into a light jog toward him. Matt jumped in the car and slammed the door. He turned the key and brought the Medford P.D. vehicle to life. He was torn, he wanted to flee, but knew he shouldn't. At the same time, he knew precious moments were wasting.

Graley reached the driver's door and pounded on it. Matt started to pull away but instead put his foot on the brake.

"Walker, what the hell aren't you telling me? Get out of the car now!"

Matt stared out at the moon, noticing the tops of the tall fir trees. They gently swayed in the breeze. He wondered how tall they were. They had to be a hundred feet, he figured. The pounding continued. Graley made several attempts to open the locked door to no avail.

"Matt Walker, if you drive out of here, you will be in serious trouble. This is the last thing Kate needs."

Matt held his silence, thinking about the color of Kate's hair and the way her neck always smelled like vanilla. Her skin was soft and always warm. Kate broke the mold.

Turning from staring out the windshield, Matt looked at Graley and rolled down the window. Just an inch. Enough so he wouldn't have to scream to be heard.

Koda growled a low-pitch, don't-mess-with-my-master growl in the backseat.

"I know where Kate is, and I'm heading there. Now. You can either get in and join me, or watch me as I drive away, Graley. Your choice."

Matt, in a bit of disbelief, watched as Detective Graley walked around the front of her police car, never taking her eyes off Matt. He was perched with Jeff Gordon-like intentions behind the steering wheel. She stopped at the passenger's door and tried to get in.

"Unlock the damn door, Walker, now."

Matt obliged, despite Koda's growl, as Graley jumped in. He pressed the lock again instantly, in case someone, like Cole, lurked in the shadows waiting to pounce and drag him from the driver's seat. He let off the brake and pressed the accelerator hard, fish tailing the vehicle slightly before lurching the tires onto Highway 97 heading south.

Graley buckled up and in a reactionary moment threw her right hand onto the dash to balance herself in Matt's haste.

"What the hell is going on, Walker? No more withholding. Do you hear me!"

Matt smiled. A tension-filled smile born from an unsure feeling of how to respond. He really liked Graley. She was tough as nails and confident, he thought, as he responded, not wanting to disappoint her.

"I am pretty sure that Kate's brother, Dennis, is behind this. I think he took her."

Matt watched the speedometer climb to one hundred miles an hour.

"Where, Matt, and it won't do her any good if we don't get there in one piece. Take it easy on the speed. And turn the damn lights on."

Graley reached across her body and flipped a switch turning on the flashing police lights. Matt's adrenaline found a new level as he wasted no time in responding.

"Kate's brother is a felon; recently got out of prison, I believe. He is into torturing animals, people, and who knows what else. All in all, a real piece of shit."

"And why are you only telling me now?"

"I really don't know, Graley."

Matt paused deep in thought, trying to put reason behind her question.

"I don't know. Fear that it was him. I guess I hoped he had nothing to do with it. Still might not be him, but something in my gut is eating at me."

Matt paused, staring at the headlight-illuminated highway. Easily visible thanks to the full moon. It looked to be a rabbit moon to boot, Matt thought.

"Geezus, Walker. Quit playing games with me. What the hell is eating at you?"

"Sorry, Graley. Not trying to be a prick, just mulling all this in my head. I'm worried. I have been thinking about the way Betheny looked at me. It was as if she recognized the person who attacked her, and she wanted to warn me. The only person I know that could fit into that little slot of peculiarity is Kate's brother."

"Why is that?"

Matt heard the curiosity and care in Graley's voice. He was relieved that she was letting him continue his journey.

"At Kate and my wedding, Betheny attended and Dennis hit on her, hard. He was belligerent and very aggressive. Kate pulled me aside and told me I needed to keep an eye on her brother. I did, and he wouldn't back off. So, I approached him, pulled him aside where I thought no one could see and dressed him down. I told him to back off Betheny or I would throw him out of the reception. Kate's father saw, didn't like it, and then proceeded to tell Kate's mother, yada, yada, yada."

Matt looked in his rear view, then dimmed the headlights as a recognizable glow crested over a rise in the blacktop highway in front of him.

"What did Kate do?"

"Oh, in typical Kate fashion, she came to my defense and put her mom and dad in their place. It was a tenuous night from there on out. Dennis ended up in prison weeks later for beating a girlfriend of his."

"Holy hell, Walker."

Matt noticed that Graley tended to call him by his last name when she was trying to be more serious, frustrated or mad. It reminded him of his mother.

Starting to respond, Matt watched as Graley held her hand up to him.

"Hang on Walker."

She dug her cell phone out of her pocket, dialed and talked at once.

"Cole, Graley. Matt Walker and I are on the way to..."

Matt saw Graley lower the phone slightly from her mouth and cover the microphone with the opposite hand.

"Where the hell, are we going, Matt?"

"Lake of the Woods, off highway 140. Kate's parents own a cabin down there."

"I know where it is, Walker."

Matt listened to Graley continue with Cole, "We're heading to the Lake of the Woods. Matt thinks Kate's brother Dennis, might be behind this. Apparently, he has a violent streak, and he's a felon. Matt thinks he just got out of prison and as soon as he remembered, he told me."

Matt heard Graley pause and could tell she was listening to Cole.

"No, Cole. I think you should go to Kate's parents' house. Maybe he, or they, are there. We don't both need to head down to the lake."

Matt felt a twinge of doubt creep into his mind at the thought of Kate being at her parents and not the lake. The Lake of the Woods was a couple hours away, and if he made a mistake, it could be fatal. He calmed listening to Graley talk to Cole.

"First Cole, have ask the sheriff's department to do a search around the fuel station outside, with dogs preferably, while you get over to her parents and question them. Find out where her brother has been, the last time they saw him, have they talked to Kate..."

Cole must have cut Graley off, Matt thought, as she suddenly stopped speaking.

"Well, good, Cole. Yes, please call for backup and an ambulance from Medford. Have them meet us at the lodge. You work with the Sheriff's Department and call me if you find out anything."

Another pause as Graley listened to Cole.

"Yes, if you find something, we'll turn around and head back. I'll keep you posted, Cole. Oh wait, we have the Walker's dog with us."

"Koda," Matt said the dog's name, reflexively interrupting Graley.

"What, Walker?"

"Koda. The dog's name is Koda."

Matt watched Graley roll her eyes and end the call with Cole.

Both sat in silence for a moment as the police car glided down the two-lane highway. Matt held the speed at one hundred.

"Why did you cover for me with Cole, Graley?"

"What are you talking about, Walker?"

Matt looked left out the window as an eighteen-wheeler roared by toward Bend.

"You told Cole I told you as soon as I remembered Dennis."

Matt saw Graley cock her head sideways, then tighten her eyes inquisitively.

"You told me as soon as you remembered, right? That isn't covering for you."

Matt thought for a second before responding. "Yeah, I guess I did," he replied as he thought about whether to tell Graley about the phone call he had moments ago that propelled him into action.

Opting for no again, he pressed the accelerator down harder, knowing the next forty miles, or so, was nothing but a straight moonlit highway surrounded by Oregon pines.

I Won't Take Too Long

Kate dropped the fire poker and headed straight for the kitchen counter where Dennis left the roll of tape. Her mind begged to ascertain the damage to her foot, but her heart propelled her forward. Giving Dennis added time to recover could not happen. Kate knew Dennis's strength could overpower her with ease if she didn't have the element of surprise, and a weapon. Determined to win the war, she would not allow him the opportunity to regain any strategic opportunity.

Dragging her foot, hopping on occasion, Kate retrieved the tape and made her way back to the captor's body. Her hands still bound she lowered the tape to the floor, stood, then took a deep breath.

Raising her hands as high as possible, Kate forcefully lowered them, with as much speed as she could muster, toward her waist with the last vestiges of strength she had left. The duct tape split, just as Matt had shown her online. Surprised, but smiling at the thought of Matt, she wasted no time relishing in the small victory.

Kate sensed Dennis recovering, so she peeled the torn tape from her wrists, then moved to wrap his ankles with the roll of tape she recovered from the kitchen. Removing his shoes and socks, she thought about checking for a pulse but didn't want to risk him regaining consciousness before he was immobile. Kate did a quick wrap of tape around his ankles deciding to forgo a thorough job for the moment.

Concerned about subduing his hands as well, she moved on and upward putting Dennis's arms behind his back. The effort took less energy than she anticipated. The fact he lay face down, head cocked to the side, helped. Kate watched her brother's face to see if his un-battered eye showed any sign of recovery.

Finishing taping the wrists tight, she moved back down to the ankles and wrapped them with more tape, pulling with more intent this go-round. She inspected the tape, making sure it wasn't torn or had any weak spots.

Sighing, Kate turned and moved to a padded Adirondack chair, painted a bright Boston Green by her mother, where she planted herself feeling a heaviness descend from her lower back toward the hardwood floor. Taking a moment to feel the bottom of her badly torn up foot, she looked at her hands and realized she shook with disturbing force. Kate wanted to cry but held back the tears. Dennis would not see any fear in her, ever again.

Deciding it was her time to be the aggressor, Kate hobbled upstairs, and found a pair of socks in a dresser. She sat down on the bed and slid them on. Standing, the tenderness of her foot reverberated through her body and made her lower jawbone ache. Shaking aside the pain, Kate dug through her mother's dresser again, searching with nervous energy until she located another pair of socks made of a thick wool. Socks in hand, she turned and sat back down on the bed. Contemplating taking the first pair off, she opted for both sets and slid the wool socks over the top of the thin cotton socks, wondering if her mother had ever worn them.

Standing, the pain still almost unbearable, she noticed a slight difference. Kate hobbled into the bathroom looking through the cupboard for hydrogen peroxide, which her mother always had. A quick search found an unopened full bottle. Grabbing the dark brown plastic container, she set it on the sink and sat down on the toilet.

"Why did I put the socks on? Stupid Kate," she whispered to herself.

Bam! Thud!

Kate, hearing a loud noise from downstairs, used the edge of the sink to hoist herself up from the toilet and make her way downstairs. She took her time, afraid of what waited for her at the bottom of the creaking staircase. Halfway down the steps she could start to see Dennis. It looked as though he tried to stand and fell back down, knocking over the fire utensil stand in the process.

Kate watched his face and when he recognized her coming down the stairs, he started yelling with a different level of rage. One that frightened her worse than anything he had ever done to her.

"You fucking bitch! You god-damned fucking whore of a sister! I was going to introduce you to a little pain. Now I am going to kill you."

Kate reached the bottom of the staircase. She must have had a puzzled look on her face from watching Dennis, who grunted and groaned in apoplectic anger. He exuded the confidence of someone who wasn't subdued and she found his tone and reaction fascinating.

Walking over to the duct tape on the table, Kate ripped off a long piece, and walked back placing it over a howling Dennis's mouth.

Pleased with her efforts, she returned to the table and tested the wood burning tool on the old oak leg. Smoke circled from the tip as it seared the oak. She thought the smoked looked different, more enticing, as it ebbed its way toward the ceiling.

"Ah, good Dennis, it's still working. Be a shame not to test it out on something a little softer."

Kate noticed Dennis's eyes gain a new level of awareness. Smiling, she set the tool down on the table, and walked over to the sink. Dennis had left his cell phone on the counter. Feeling more secure, she contemplated calling Matt, but wasn't sure where he was, and how quick he could get here. She wanted a little time for herself before alerting anyone.

No one needed to know. At least not everything. Feeling the smooth handles of a cabinet, she pulled open the door. A large plastic bottle of Tylenol sat where she expected it. Her mother constantly went for the cupboard and the small white plastic bottle she called her "*coping medicine.*"

Unscrewing the cap, Kate tilted the canister, shook it on the palm of her hand and counted out four pills. Placing them in her mouth, she placed the cap back on and put it back where it belonged. She chewed the tablets, hoping the medicine would get into her bloodstream quicker. The pain pounded through her veins.

Kate grabbed a glass from another cupboard. Glasses her mother had ever since she could remember. They

weren't anything special, she didn't think, but they were solid. Not like anything one could find today. Wondering if they were worth anything, she thought about what her mother and father would do with this cabin as they aged. Sell it or give it to her and Dennis. Kate shuddered at the thought of sharing anything with the vile piece of shit on the floor behind her.

Moving to her left, now in front of the sink, Kate reached over and turned on the cold water. The tarnished faucet knob felt cold and dirty. She shuddered in disgust. The whole cabin felt dirty and vile as decades of painful emotions crept to the surface of her psyche. Placing the glass in the path of the stream, Kate watched with curiosity as the water swirled, diving downward, before splashing up and over the edge. She turned the flow down with her opposite hand, allowing the glass to fill.

Turning the water off, she took a big gulp, swirled it around in her mouth as if it were mouthwash, and then swallowed. She took several more drinks before the bitter taste of the medicine diminished.

Setting the empty glass in the sink, Kate turned toward Dennis. He struggled trying to break free. Kate relished in the fact that he might be afraid. Making her way back upstairs she went to her parents' closet and found two belts dangling on a hanger. Tattered and frayed leather; one black, one brown. Both appeared to be her father's.

"These should do nicely, Dennis," Kate yelled downstairs, knowing full good and well he could hear her.

Less than a minute later, at her brother's feet, Kate started to wrap his feet. Kicking and twisting, he tried with groaning desperation to break free. Kate grabbed the evening's weapon of choice, for her at least, showing Dennis the poker, he had become intimately familiar with only minutes ago.

"Stop kicking, Dennis," Kate said in a calm, indifferent, customer service voice, "or I will take this poker to your head again. I don't think you can take many more shots like the first one. Do you?"

Kate smiled. Her brother's eyes flickered. The questioning look of doubt and fear one gets when faced with a desperate situation. Kate turned her head sideways and relished the look in the familiar eyes. She couldn't remember ever seeing them this way. She wanted to see full-on fear in Dennis's hazel-brown eyes before the night gave way to the morning sun.

Kate set the poker down, picked up her father's black belt and wrapped it around the duct tape covering her brother's ankles. Next, she took the brown belt, and moving Dennis back on his stomach, wrapped the belt around his entire body, to include his bound wrists. It was tight, but there was enough length to clasp the buckle.

"Glad daddy has a gut, Dennis. The belt is just the right length."

Kate started whistling as she picked up the duct tape and wrapped more around the belt at the ankles, covering it. She thought about wrapping the belt around the waist as well, but figured he was secure. When the time came, she didn't want to make it too tough to release him.

"Okay, Dennis, you worthless piece of human debris, let's have a little fun now, shall we?"

Kate walked over and turned on her father's radio. It was set to his favorite country station. One of the few stations one could tune in at the lake, nestled at the edge of the famous Pacific Crest Trail. A trail Matt and she had hiked several times. Kate was always amazed to think people could walk the entire PCT length from Canada to Mexico. She wondered what kind of dedication and determination it must take to carry out such a task.

Listening to an artist on the radio croon about "loving her one more time," Kate returned to Dennis's feet. Grabbing them, she dragged him over near the table. She judged the distance of the cord and figuring his feet and head were within reach she dropped them. The heels hit with a thud and Kate, quite pleased, could see it caused him pain.

Kate grabbed the wood-burning tool off the table and kneeled at Dennis's feet. Putting the tool to his skin, Dennis started kicking violently. Kate couldn't figure out how to keep his feet still. She didn't have the strength to hold him with one hand while using the other hand for the tool. Looking around, she saw the tape. She got up, grabbed the silver duct tape, and returned to Dennis's feet. She thought about what the tape was really supposed to be used for. Not knowing, Kate released the fleeting thought and turned her back to Dennis, moving his feet close to a support beam for the cabin's second floor. Taking a long strip of the tape, she wrapped it around the beam and then his ankles. Repeatedly, she continued the effort until she didn't think he could move. Grabbing the smoldering tool, she pulled at it, in the hope it would still reach her big brother's precious feet. It did.

"See, Dennis, things just seem to work out right for good people sometimes. I was afraid it wasn't going to reach, but alas, luck is with me. You ready for a little fun?"

Dennis twisted and turned, but his feet barely moved as Kate moved toward him with the simmering tool.

Tilting her head back, she cackled a deep twisted laugh before she spoke again.

"Now don't you worry, Dennis. I won't take too long."

Kate smiled, joining the radio's Taylor Swift in song before placing the smoldering tool deep into Dennis' flesh. The ghost-white skin seared. Kate heard the sound for the first time. Something she hadn't noticed all those times her own feet were being burnt. Perhaps her brain, dealing with the pain, didn't afford her the ability to hear as well. Fascinated, she paused in thought before looking at a now crying Dennis.

"I won't take too long. On your feet, that is, big brother."

Any Sign of Kate?

"Not bad, Matt. If driving alone was a career on the police force, Medford should hire you."

Turning off Highway 140 onto the Lake of the Woods exit, Matt grinned a smile he thought should impossible right now. Acknowledging they had made good time, he looked skyward. He bent forward near the steering wheel gazing into the dark, clear Pacific Northwest sky. The rabbit moon showed herself in a bright and decadent way across the silver grass of Great Meadow.

Amazed at how the meadow had such a natural propensity to be like a chameleon, Matt daydreamed of better times where snowmobiles danced across its deep snow in the winter. In the spring, goslings hatched and swam in her clear shallow waters, and during an Indian Summer the grass of the meadow billowed back and forth with a mesmerizing flow from the breeze dancing off the Cascade Range. All this, of course, surrounded by majestic fir and pines.

No other place in the states that Matt had ever visited encompassed the variety of outdoors the way Southern Oregon did. Childhood camping entrenched his soul in so many of the trails, streams, and mountains, he felt as though he were part of the very soil that made Oregon his home.

"Matt. Earth to Matt."

Matt realized Graley was talking to him.

"Sorry, lost in thought."

"About Kate?"

"No, about Oregon. It's so damn beautiful. I can't imagine ever living anywhere else. This little section of the state is one of my favorites. A few miles in either direction has so much to offer. The perfect Mordor-like peak of Mt. McLoughlin behind us, the Pacific Crest trail a mile to the west, bald eagles at Upper Klamath lake just down the highway, Mt.

Shasta and her awesome snowcapped beauty to the south, Great Meadow that we're driving through, Fish Lake, Howard Prairie, Hyatt Lake, Willow Lake, Four-Mile Lake, Pelican Butte, and on and on. I love this place."

Matt put the turn signal on, then turned the car westward taking the drive into the lodge. His heart developed a new ache.

"Graley, I just realized I have no idea where Kate's parents' house or cabin is."

Matt eased the cruiser into the parking lot in front of the lodge.

Graley, frustrated yet again, addressed him as Walker, not Matt.

"Shut the front door, Walker! Are you kidding me? Please tell me you are just f'ing with me."

Matt, nervous at his failure to remember this important little fact, laughed a strained nervous laugh.

"Nope. No clue, Graley. Sorry."

"Sorry! Geezus. You are too much, Walker."

"Well, I know it's on the west side of the lake," Matt said opening his car door and stepping on the gravel packed parking lot and into the moonlight peaking her way through the massive evergreen trees that surrounded the high mountain lake.

Graley got out as well and walked around the front of the car. She now stood next to Walker and Matt noticed what a nice jawline she had. Then he wondered why in the hell he was noticing it now.

"Can we drive slowly and look for a name on the mailboxes, Walker?"

"No, too many homes, and most just have numbers with few names," Matt replied. He was ready to ask Graley to call Cole and ask Kate's parents the address when Graley's phone buzzed.

Matt thought Graley looked startled as she grabbed for the phone as if she had forgotten she had one in her pocket.

"Cole, Graley here. Glad you called. We just got to Lake of the Woods and have cell reception again."

Matt watched Graley closely, hoping for good news. He would remind her to see if Cole could get the exact address from Kate's parents. Otherwise, he would be relegated to hunting on Google, which could take time.

"Shit! Oh my God, Cole."

Matt watched Graley's face go expressionless. Any hint of humanity drained from her face, leaving it pale and still in the moonlight.

"Any sign of Kate? No, okay, that's good at least."

Matt forgot Koda was in the back seat until he woke from his slumber and barked. Opening the door, Matt let the dog out to stretch his legs and probably pee.

"Stay, boy, okay? Stay by me."

Matt watched Koda lift his rear leg and promptly relieve himself on the wheel of the police car. Smiling, Matt turned his attention back to Graley, wondering what the hell was going on in Bend.

"Okay, Cole. Well, we're at the lake now. I was hoping to ask you for an address to their lake home down here, but that's out of the question now."

Matt walked to the front of the car with Koda right next to him and stood within two feet of Graley. He waited patiently for her to finish.

"Okay, Cole, give me a few minutes to think and I'll call you right back. Yes...uh huh...sure, and thanks."

Matt watched Graley lower the phone and put it in her pocket. She hesitated for a split second and then dove in.

"Matt."

Okay, she said Matt, not Walker, so this is not going to be good, he thought to himself.

"How much did you like your in-laws? Hell, that isn't the right way to put it. How close were you to them, I suppose? Probably not very if you don't even know where their cabin is."

"Sheesh, Graley, what are they—dead or something? Spit it out!"

Matt was only half-joking, although he thought it could be exactly what she might tell him.

"Yes, Matt. Cole found them both tied up with plastic bags over their heads."

Hidden Beneath the Pines

Staring at a passed-out attacker-turned-captor, Kate lost zest for what seemed like delicious retribution. She seared his left foot superficially, not having the will or the stomach to damage her brother's foot the way he had done to her. She couldn't fathom what he got out of his torture of others.

Tears cooled the warm flesh of her cheeks as she set down the tool and pounded both her fists against his leg. She placed her hands on one of his legs, then rested her heavy head on her hands, repeating the words "Neti neti" out loud. Sitting up, Kate took deep, slow, breaths as she repeated the Sanskrit mantra.

After several minutes her stress level retreated, so she stood up. Staring down at her brother she realized how small he was for the first time.

"You are such a coward, Dennis." Kate spoke out loud to the unconscious Dennis as she went to the sink for a drink of water. Her foot throbbed with sharp sensations of pain each time she moved. She thought of Matt and how being wrapped in each other's arms would help.

Physically and emotionally drained, she wondered how far she should take this. The back of her mind told her something dark and sinister, but emotionally the mantra permeated the inner resources of her soul. She thought about calling Matt again when a new idea occurred to her.

Picking Dennis's phone up off the table, Kate searched through the screens until she found a recording app. Returning to her now rousing brother, she dragged him a little closer to the burning tool.

"I am yanking this tape off your mouth now, Dennis, because you are going to talk with me. Scream all you want, but you know it's wasted effort. Especially tonight. Hear the deep Cascade winds high atop the pines? Sounds like an ocean up there. Just like daddy used to say. Remember that, brother?"

Kate grabbed an edge of the tape across Dennis's mouth and pulled. She wanted to yank but creating extended pain and agony for him no longer interested her. Only the pain necessary to get what she wanted. Before the tape was all the way off, Dennis yelled.

"Fuck! I am going to kill you!"

A smiling Kate looked down at the phone and pressed the button starting the recorder. She hoped it saved like she wanted, and clearly enough to understand on playback.

"Okay, Dennis, where was I. Oh, that's right, time for a little work behind the ears."

Kate reached up with her left hand and felt the scars behind her hair and ear where Dennis had burned her so many times. More memories and emotions flooded back. Why in the world didn't she tell her parents?

As clear as if it were yesterday, she could see her mother standing on the front porch of this very cabin. The sun was out, and its rays penetrated alleyways between thick fir and pine trees, warming whatever they could kiss. The yellow sundress her mother wore flittered in the breeze. If the sun hit it just right, she could see through the fabric and see her mother's gorgeous legs. She hoped when she got older, she looked as beautiful as her mother. She so wanted to run to her and tell her everything Dennis was doing, but always stopped for fear of more rejection.

Kate had made several efforts to tell her mom before, but in between mother's drunkenness, it was a roll of the dice which woman she would get. The loving, caring, doting mom, or the angry, quick-to-judge, overreacting drunk. Better just to avoid her completely than risk the latter. Her father, a man's man, would sit stoic on the porch. A Neanderthal, at best, that thought a woman was on earth to cook, clean, and satisfy a man whenever he felt the need.

Returning to the present, Kate stared down at a sad, diminutive man.

"You know, I once told Dad you burned me. You know what he said, Dennis?"

Dennis lay motionless, seething in what Kate knew was pain, anger, and hatred.

"Uh, cat got your tongue big brother?"

Kate twirled the burning tool in her right hand and stared at the blackened tip.

"He told me to 'Grow up and listen to what your big brother says. He is a man and if he is telling you to do something, then you should do it and not whine'."

Kate chuckled, rolled her eyes and let out a nervous laugh before continuing.

"He said that, "Only little whiny girls were tattle-tales.""

Kate tilted Dennis's head to the side and put the tip of the tool just behind his ear, so he could feel the heat.

"Don't you dare fucking burn me, you little bitch. Dad was right, listen to me and don't be a whiny little girl."

"Ah, Dennis are you whining? I wouldn't move much if I were you. It'll only make the pain worse. Right?"

Kate touched the tip behind his ear, trying to press with care, not wanting to go to deep. Repeating the mantra to herself, she tried to stay calm and under control, but she couldn't hold the tip back. It went deeper than she intended. The singeing sound was different this time, she noticed. As if the blood percolated. Dennis screamed in pain, his head lurching violently, trying to bite Kate.

"Oh man, that has to hurt; bet that never happened to you in prison did it big brother?"

Kate taunted him. She looked at the phone, it appeared to be recording. Not wanting to stop and confirm that it was, she decided to trust technology. Tilting her head back she tried to relieve the tension in her neck before continuing.

"Here's the deal, Dennis. I am going to ask you questions. For everyone you answer correctly, we will move on to the next question. If you don't answer at all, or lie to me, you get to feel the tool behind an ear. Okay? Sounds like fun, huh?"

Smiling, Kate listened as Dennis tried a new approach. An approach she couldn't remember ever seeing from him. She struggled emotionally on whether to continue, but her base nature won the battle with her empathy. For the moment.

"Look, Kate, I shouldn't have been so mean. Let's just stop and call it a draw. I'll get out of here and take off, okay?"

Kate, startled at the pathetic response, laughed loud, forcing her head back. Forgetting the tool was in her hand, it caught Dennis on the cheek.

"God damn it, you bitch!"

Kate recovered.

"Oops, sorry about that, big brother. I didn't mean to get you on the face. Don't make me laugh anymore and that won't happen."

Dennis tried to spit on her; a weak effort of spray left his mouth. Kate felt it like the softest breeze blowing across the hair on one's arms. Barely noticeable, but enough to feel her skin react.

"So, let's get this right, Dennis. You say you shouldn't have been 'so mean', right? And that we will call this a draw. You don't say you're sorry, or that you shouldn't have been mean at all, just not 'so' mean. Are you kidding me?"

Kate laughed as she felt uncontrollable anger welling up inside again. The 'so mean' response elicited more anger, so she burnt Dennis behind the ear again. A quick shallow hit this time. He jerked in pain.

"Question one, Dennis. Why did you kill Matt's ex-wives?"

Kate focused her grip on the tool, readying herself.

There was silence. Defiance returned to Dennis's eyes. Long gone was his condescending attempt at empathy. Kate knew it was a show for him. Her brother didn't have the ability for empathy.

"Silence is the same as a lie, Dennis, so time to burn."

Kate moved the tool closer toward his head, a hair or two singed; the smell of burning hair was disgusting.

"Why do you think I killed them?" Dennis coughed out the words.

Kate pressed the tool into his skin watching his eyes flutter upwards. She retracted the tool in haste not wanting him to pass out.

"A question is not an answer, Dennis. Do I need to go through the rules again with you?"

Dennis took a deep breath.

"Because I wanted to make Matt pay for taking you away from me."

Kate watched as a tear trickled from the corner of one of Dennis's eyes. Thinking he had more fight in him, she expected a different answer than what she received.

"What are you talking about, Dennis?"

"You are fucking mine. Always were, always will be. Don't you get it, you little bitch?"

"Now, why all the name calling?"

Kate's fleeting moment of empathy left; as quickly as it came. She pressed the tool against his flesh again and another scream followed.

His head slammed against the hardwood floor leaving a blood stain. Kate wondered how difficult the blood would be to clean up.

"So, you admit you killed both women because I married Matt? You've been planning this for a while, then?"

Kate waited for a response, but not long.

"Yes, while you were dating him."

"So, in your sick, demented head, you thought I was your property?"

Kate turned his head and burnt behind the other ear. She dragged the tool down toward his neck leaving a long searing path of pain. Her mind, barraged with memories, fluttered on the edge of depression as the tool dragged downward leaving a foul stench hanging in the air.

The demented shit of a big brother she was torturing was nothing more than a product of her father. Dennis took it to a different level was all. At least she thought he did. What had her father really done? What were his demented fetishes? What was he capable of? Death? Kate began to wonder, for the first time, what her mother's life was really like. Beatings that no one saw? Verbal humiliations in public? Sexual deviance, or rape possibly? Her mind continued to race with little control.

Kate tried to wrestle it back from the brink loss. Instead, flashes of pictures recaptured from her youth, so many clues in front of her for so long—she had all but blocked them out until now.

A recess of her mind felt guilt, remorse, and even empathy for her brother. For a second, a trace of a second to be truthful, Kate thought of burying the wood-burning tool deep into one of Dennis's eye sockets. She always thought he was sick, now she was sure. She started to cry, wondering if she was no better than her brother or father.

Grabbing the phone off the worn-out wood floor, Kate stood and pressed the red button on the screen to stop recording. She walked over and unplugged the tool with the smoldering blackened tip saturated with burnt flesh and blood. Her damaged brother lay in pain on the floor, his eyes full of hate and rage. A hate and rage she shared, on some level, at this very moment.

Kate walked over to an oak-framed mirror. One her mother had hung, placing it on one of the walls she had told a young Kate would help make the room look bigger. Staring into the dusty reflective surface, she realized that the room had seemed much bigger to her as a child. Kate held back tears, gulping for deep breaths as her chest heaved.

Breathing now stabilizing, she looked closer, focusing on herself and not the room or dust. She noticed her clothes. A yellow sundress. She didn't own a yellow sundress; it occurred to her it was her mothers. The very dress she visualized earlier. Running her hands over the soft cotton blend, Kate couldn't remember putting it on. The flat stitching and soothing fabric, part of her mother's summer cabin wardrobe, felt reassuring against her skin.

Heading upstairs, favoring her burnt foot, Kate reached the top and entered the bedroom. She saw her clothes lying neatly on the bed. Her pants looked perfect the way they were folded and positioned on the heavy hand-stitched bedspread. Same for the sweatshirt she had on before changing.

Kate slid out of the dress, hung it back up in her mother's closet, making sure the hanger faced in the proper direction, and then put her jeans and sweatshirt back on. Moving into the bathroom she washed her hands and face and pulled her hair back into a ponytail before returning downstairs.

Dennis had not moved. Struggling to break free, his eyes followed her every move. Kate walked out the front door and onto the porch. She eased her way down the stairs, gingerly feeling dirt and the rough sting of cool pine needles on the bottoms of her feet.

Looking skyward, Kate noticed tears falling from her eyes, leaving a trail of coolness on her cheeks. She viewed a patch of night sky high among the trees, revealing a portion of a full moon. The night was so beautiful, she thought. Listening to the wind in the trees, she grabbed her brother's phone out of her back pocket, hoping the signal was strong enough to get through and dialed Matt.

Listening to the phone make noises as it dialed out, she stayed still, hoping her lack of movement would allow the phone signal to stay constant.

A hesitant voice, she recognized as Matt's, immediately answered.

"Hello?"

"Matt, this is Kate. I am so tired and hurt. I..." her voice trailed off abruptly, ending.

"Kate! Oh my God, Kate! Where are you, sweetie?"

Kate gasped for breath, looked upward, searching for the moon as if it would hold answers. As the clouds whisked to the north, revealing a deep white circular-beauty lighting up the woods, she thought of being in Matt's arms.

"Matt, I am Hidden Beneath the Pines."

I Didn't Know

Matt got enough, out of the broken, almost incoherent information from Kate to make it to Kate. He and Graley, along with Koda, made it around the lake drive in about fifteen minutes to find Kate wandering around in front of her parents' cabin, dragging a leg and looking like she wandered off the set of the latest zombie film. Koda reached her first, staying by her side. Kate showered affection on the dog before Matt reached her. Exhausted and emotionally spent, she fell into his arms.

"I love you, Matt. I'm so sorry."

Matt, tears welling up in his eyes, looked at Kate's disheveled appearance. A new round of anger surged inside him. The tears of sorrow for his wife faded, replaced with a furious desire on revenge.

Graley, a few steps behind Matt, spoke to Kate.

"Ma'am, are you okay?"

Kate lifted her head off Matt's shoulder and spoke.

"I'll be fine, detective, thanks."

"Who did this to you, Ma'am? Your husband thinks it may have been your brother."

Kate lifted her head toward the cabin and spoke in a soft, dejected, sad voice.

"Yes, it was Dennis."

Detective Graley directed her next statement toward Matt.

"The ambulance should be here soon. Go wait with Kate in the car until they get here. I'm going to go assess things inside."

Graley walked away. Matt squeezed Kate with a desperate sadness he had never felt. Intense love welled up inside him. Matt felt himself shaking. Scared, not sure what to make of the feelings, he held Kate as close as he could. He willed the strength of his arms, tightly wrapped around her, to somehow heal, making her whole again. Matt could feel desperate anger wash over him. Consumed by anger toward Kate's brother, he stumbled for soothing, empathetic words for Kate.

"I'm glad you are okay, babe. What a day, huh? Can I do anything for you? How badly are you hurt?"

Matt, pausing, took a breath and realized he was rambling, not giving Kate a chance to respond.

"Mostly my foot," Kate said in a sad, quiet voice that tore at Matt's heart. "My brother burned the bottom of it with a wood-burning tool."

"He what?" Matt nearly shouted, thinking he must have misheard her. "A wood-burning tool?"

"Yeah, long story. I have a splitting headache. My body feels like I was pressed through a meat grinder. I'll survive. Not my first rodeo with Dennis, but it will be my last."

Koda whimpered. Matt, glad Kate adopted the little guy, wondered about the dog he dropped off at the shelter. It seemed like a month ago now, not hours.

"Let's get to the police car and sit down. Can you walk, or would you rather I carry you?"

"I can walk. Just let me put my arm around your shoulder so I can take the pressure off my left foot."

Matt lowered himself as Kate put her arm around him. In no time, he was lowering her into the back seat of the police car. Koda sat down and turned around facing away from the car as if he was now officially on guard duty.

"I'm going to stand up and watch the road in case the ambulance misses the driveway. Okay, Kate?"

"Okay, babe, thanks. I can't wait for this to all be over."

Koda growled, a low cautious growl that Matt guessed was the dog's own form of disapproving anger. Matt smiled thinking about how much of a find this little guy had turned out to be. He couldn't believe he had been abandoned.

"It's okay, boy. Detective Graley is okay," Matt told the dog as Detective Graley walked toward them.

Koda stopped growling as Graley approached. Matt stepped to the side, giving Graley room to talk with Kate.

"Ms. Walker, your brother seems to be in quite a bit of pain, and perhaps even to have been tortured. Can you tell me anything about this?"

Matt's gut dropped in anguish, wondering what the hell went on inside the cabin.

Kate, without hesitation replied. "I tied him up after escaping. He burned the bottom of my foot," Kate lifted her foot up slightly making it clear to the detective which one, "and was going on to burn the other one as well. He then would have moved on to the skin behind my ears. Like he did when we were kids. This time, though, he said he was going to kill me. Like the rest."

Matt contemplated running inside the cabin as Kate spoke. He relished at the thought of finishing the cruel freak off himself. He looked back at the cabin wondering if there were a shovel to be found. He faded from the conversation dreaming of plowing the shovel against the side of Dennis's head. Kate's words brought him back.

"I managed to get free, hit him in the head a couple of times with the fire poker, and while he was unconscious, I tied him up."

Matt watched Kate take a deep breath, and a wave of what looked like sadness, and possibly remorse, washed over her.

"Anything else, Ms. Walker?"

"I'm sorry, Detective. I was so scared and afraid for my life. I felt like I had to fight back. I realize now I should have just called, but I was so angry, I wasn't thinking clearly. I wanted to kill him."

Matt started to say something, but Graley gave him an eye warning. He stopped.

"I'm sure you did, Ms. Walker, and that is completely understandable. I'm glad you didn't, though. That would have made it more difficult to convince a jury of your innocence. This situation though, considering everything else going on, will be easier to explain.

Kate reached into her back pocket and pulled out the cell phone, handing it to Graley.

"This is my brother's phone. There should be a recording on it of things my brother said about the deaths of Matt's ex-wives. Perhaps it will help."

Matt watched as Graley took the phone and placed it in her jacket pocket.

"Matt, you stay with Kate. I'm going to go up on the road and flag down the ambulance and additional police. They should be here soon."

"Ms. Walker, you are going to have to ride back with me. Your brother is in pretty bad shape and he'll need the ambulance more than you, okay?"

"Just make sure you cuff that piece of filth to the gurney, Graley, okay?" Matt added angrily.

Graley nodded, then turned and walked toward the road.

Turning back toward Kate, Matt noticed for the first time a placard nailed to a massive tree that read, "Hidden Beneath the Pines Cabin." He slid in next to Kate and held her. Koda sat rigid, poised for any necessary action. Matt knew of the cabin; Kate had shared the details many times. She always talked about how pretty it was and how much she hated it. Matt had never been here. Kate had never wanted to take him. Now he understood exactly why.

It was hard to tell in the dark, but the cabin looked to be in a fantastic location on the banks of the Lake of the Woods. This was Matt's favorite lake in Southern Oregon. He dreamed of a home on this lake. One where he could walk the bank and stare up at Mt. McLoughlin. Focusing, Matt swallowed.

"Honey, I have to tell you something about your parents."

"They're dead, aren't they..."

Matt turned his head sideways a touch, felt his brow furrow, and looked directly into Kate's eyes.

"My God, Kate, how did you know?"

Matt watched as Kate lowered her chin. He was now staring at the top of her head.

"I saw my mom on the deck of the cabin a little while ago. She had tears in her eyes. It was as if she was saying goodbye."

"You did?"

Matt felt his eyes puff up, his cheeks warmed, then moistened. A new level of anger and regret swept over him.

"She wasn't bad, Matt, she was just in a horrible situation. I feel so bad for her now. I wish I could have helped her somehow. I didn't know."

Matt bent down and pulled her against his chest. He squeezed tight and listened as Kate started to sob.

Epilogue

Matt flipped burgers on the grill and rolled the franks around, so they'd blacken evenly. Concentrating on the meat preparation, he smiled thinking this was a time when he would normally be tapping his foot. He couldn't remember the last time he tapped. The therapist told him the dramatic events that ensued had something to do with it, plus the work he had put in. Whatever it was, he didn't care. He relished the fact his OCD had stopped.

Twisting the cap off the barbecue sauce, Matt brushed it on the burgers as if he had an endless supply. Looking up through the smoke, he smiled watching everyone chat in their lawn chairs as they gazed out over the Lake of the Woods. The half dozen or so adults, friends of Matt and Kate, were having a good time, basking in the late summer heat. Paddleboards and Kayaks laid on the shore near the Walkers' lake deck, already well used for the day, now static.

Matt hoped the afternoon winds would die down as usual, so he and Kate could take a short trip down the shoreline together under a full moon. Perhaps if everyone left early enough, they would take the motorboat over to the lodge and grab a drink and visit with other lake friends. Kate loved hanging out at the lodge and liked the little general store even better. Not all her memories growing up at the lake were bad, and now, thanks to Matt she would say, there were even more reasons to love the place.

To Kate, the General Store was like stepping back in time. Matt smiled thinking about her love of the Smores Pop Tarts they sold. It made her seem sweet and innocent. He wanted to protect her. No, he thought, she proved she could protect herself. What he wanted was to love her, be closer to her, hold her, cherish her, and make her understand how special she was.

For today's shindig, Matt invited his secretarial assistant Jane, and the new boyfriend she met on an online dating site. Matt and Kate crossed their fingers for Jane, hoping this guy wasn't a bust like so many others. Matt had no desire to see her spreadsheet again, with all the guys and all the reasons they were a bust.

Detective Graley, and her almost senile father, were present along with a female friend of Graley's. Matt surmised she was a new significant other. After the case and court was all wrapped up, Matt and Kate became good friends with Detective Mara Graley. They had her over for dinner occasionally when she could break away from the job and check-in visits with her father. Matt looked forward to getting to know Graley's new friend.

Detective Cole, a lady on his arm, was also at Kate's cabin. The woman happened to be the Deschutes County Sheriff's Deputy, adept at taking photos. Cole, who recently moved, now worked at the police department in Bend, Oregon, as a detective. Matt, not one to hold a grudge, was glad Cole seemed to have turned a serious page in his life, according to Graley.

What impressed Matt, considering everything that had transpired, was the way Cole went out of his way to help and support him and Kate during the last year, which included a trial and the conviction of Kate's brother. Considering their rough start, and how much Matt and Cole initially despised each other, Matt realized tragedy has a way of bringing enemies together. "Keep your friends close, and your enemies closer" now had a whole new meaning to him.

Attorney Jim Davies, and his lovely wife of thirty-plus years, Marie, were entertaining the entire group, as they liked to do. Neighbors from a couple of cabins down, who had befriended Matt while he was remodeling, were on site as well, with their two youngsters. The two little ones were throwing a Frisbee around with Kate's "little guard," as Matt referred to Koda. Koda would stop occasionally, look for Kate, run to wherever she was, get a head pat, and return to playing with the kids. The dog lived up to its nickname and hardly, if ever, let Kate out of his sight.

On more than one occasion, Matt told the story of Koda and how he stayed outside the police car, sitting, basically daring anyone to come near while Kate sat in shock. A night Matt would never forget.

Kate's parents left everything to her demented brother in their will, to Matt's dismay and anger, though it came as no surprise of Kate.

Jim Davies got involved and through efforts of friends in the State offices, had the will rescinded somehow, giving full ownership of the entire will, save a few trivial donations to a Rotary club, to Kate. Matt didn't press the matter with Jim after making certain it was all legal. The whole thing had something to do with her brother being convicted and Kate the only sole relative surviving. Jim argued the will was done under duress of the abuse the parents had suffered at Dennis's hands. Kate wasn't sure, but Matt convinced her to let Jim press forward.

Jim did all the work for Kate pro bono, which touched Kate deeply, not to mention Matt. Not long after everything was handled with the will, Kate sold her parents' home in Bend and donated all the money, close to a million and a half dollars, to an abuse organization for women and children. She did it in her mother's name. Kate was presented with an award but refused a public ceremony. She said it wasn't about her and she didn't feel she deserved it. Matt teared up every time he thought about her and what she did, considering all she went through at the hands of her family.

The cabin you ask? Well, Kate decided to keep it after Matt took to his sledgehammer and saw. He did a bunch of work to the place on weekends and hired a reputable contractor from Klamath Falls, who promptly spent a bunch of their money to give it a new facelift. She also gave it a new name after her mother.

Matt took down the Hidden Beneath the Pines placard and had a new custom one made from Oregon Madrone. It read, "Patricia's Cabin." Kate cried when she finally saw it. Matt didn't present it formally, but rather hung it up one day when she was sun-bathing. He didn't say anything and waited for almost a month before she looked up one day, as they were driving in for the weekend, and saw it.

Turning the heat down on the grill, Matt watched as Kate came out the front door of the cabin wearing her favorite yellow sun dress. It was a soft buttery yellow Michael Kors, covered in small white and sky-blue flowers. Kate said it reminded her of one that belonged to her mother long ago. They noticed it on a weekend trip in Vegas to see Cirque du Soleil's water show. The dress hung at one of the exorbitant casino shops. The price was ridiculous, they both agreed, but Kate loved it. Matt thought she looked stunning in it and, well, they could afford it, so...

Out of twisted curiosity, Matt spent fifteen minutes on Amazon when they got back to Ashland from Vegas and found the exact same dress for half the amount. He never said anything to Kate. She smiled so happily when she slipped it on why burst her bubble?

At the grill, Matt swallowed, thinking how lucky he was to be her partner.

"Hey beautiful, the burgers and dogs are done. How is that potato salad coming?" he said to Kate out loud, so all could hear.

Kate, carrying a large blue bowl, winked at Matt, then glided down the steps.

Matt yelled out to Graley.

"Gray, come give me a hand with these burgers and dogs, will you?"

Graley made it over in no time.

"Dad doing any better, Gray?"

"Comes and goes, Matt. Today is a good day, so I'm glad I brought him. Thanks for the invite, by the way."

"You're welcome anytime, Graley. You should know that by now. And as a matter of fact, hold out your hand."

Matt reached into his pocket and pulled out a key, dropping it into Graley's outstretched hand.

"Kate and I want you to have this key. It's to Patricia's Cabin. You're welcome to use it anytime you want. Might want to check with us before heading up, but more likely than not, we won't be here."

Graley got a little teary-eyed and looked away. Matt, seeing she was touched, didn't know how to react.

"Wow, Matt, I don't know what to say."

"Don't say a thing, you goofball. Just help me out with these burgers and then introduce me to that vixen you brought with you."

Graley slugged Matt on the shoulder.

"Ouch. Well, are you going to tell me she isn't hot?"

Graley smiled but stayed silent. Matt swore she blushed before taking the plate he had piled high with burgers and dogs. Together, they turned and walked toward the table where Kate was getting everyone situated for an amazing meal on the beautiful shore of his favorite lake. His new window pane to stunning views of Mt. McLoughlin and Pelican Butte.

Kate stopped for a moment amidst the chatter of hungry adults, a couple of kids, and her "Little Guard." Looking skyward, through the massive trees, she watched as the sun bowed with the grace of the finest stage actor doing a curtain call. The sun started her bow behind the tall firs and pines standing shoulder to shoulder in the Cascade Mountains. She loved it when the final minutes of the sun's last act for the day occurred.

The sunsets never got old. She knew they were unique to everyone. The nuance of each one captured an individual vision and essence seen differently by all eyes. This was going to be a good night with friends and loved ones.

Kate sidled up to her Matt. She picked up her wine glass, tapped the side with her fingernail until everyone was paying attention, save the kids, and started to speak. Getting a little choked up, feeling the love and joy they were all sharing, Kate gathered her composure. Raising her glass high, scanning the table, she tried to make eye contact with everyone.

"Okay, folks, thanks for being here with me and Matt. We are so glad you could make it."

"Here, Here!"

"Thanks, Kate."

"Roof Roof."

"You want to say anything, Matt?"

Kate nudged Matt. He raised his beer and nodded to the entire group.

"Kate and I thank you all for coming. We're so glad you're with us."

Feeling his eyes starting to swell, thinking of tapping his foot, but abstaining, Matt raised his free hand and pretended to cough before finishing with, "Kate and I are happy you all joined us. We are grateful for our time with you here at Patricia's Cabin, Hidden Beneath the Pines."

Author's Notes

Thank you for reading Hidden Beneath the Pines. Please take a few moments, if you enjoyed the novel, and leave a review on the platform from which you purchased it. If you are interested in reading some of my advance copies of future works sign up for my email list on my website.

To join, go to mikewaltersnovels.com and you should be prompted to sign up. You will get sneak peaks at new work, deleted scenes and chapters from previous novels, chances to win signed products, and more. You can opt out at any time and I will not be sending a barrage of emails or creating any spam.

Thanks again, and until next time,

Mike

Website: https://mikewaltersnovels.com/
Twitter: @MikeAWalters
Facebook: facebook.com/MikeAWalters/
Instagram: mikewaltersnovelist/
Pinterest: mikeawalters24

Manufactured by Amazon.ca
Acheson, AB